Amy Myers was born [illegible] in English literature, she was director of a [illegible]ish-ing company, and is now a freelance editor and writer. She is married to an American and they live in a Kentish village on the North Downs. She also writes under the name of Laura Daniels.

Praise for Amy Myers' previous books featuring Auguste Didier, also available from Headline:

'Wittily written and intricately plotted with some fine characterisation. Perfection' *Best*

'Reading like a cross between Hercule Poirot and Mrs Beeton . . . this feast of entertainment is packed with splendid late-Victorian detail' *Evening Standard*

'What a marvellous tale of Victorian mores and murders this is – an entertaining whodunnit that whets the appetite of mystery lovers and foodies alike' *Kent Today*

'Delightfully written, light, amusing and witty. I look forward to Auguste Didier's next banquet of delights'
Eastern Daily Press

'Plenty of fun, along with murder and mystery . . . as brilliantly coloured as a picture postcard'
Dartmouth Chronicle

'Classically murderous' *Woman's Own*

'An amusing Victorian whodunnit' Netta Martin, *Annabel*

'An intriguing Victorian whodunnit' *Daily Examiner*

'Impossible to put down' *Kent Messenger*

Also by Amy Myers from Headline

Murder at the Music Hall
Murder in the Smokehouse
Murder at Plums
Murder Under the Kissing Bough
Murder Makes an Entree
Murder at the Masque
Murder in the Limelight
Murder in Pug's Parlour

Murder in the Motor Stable

Amy Myers

HEADLINE

First published in 1996
by HEADLINE BOOK PUBLISHING

First published in paperback in 1997
by HEADLINE BOOK PUBLISHING

10 9 8 7 6 5 4 3 2 1

ISBN 0 7472 4844 3

Printed and bound in Great Britain by
Cox & Wyman Ltd, Reading, Berks

HEADLINE BOOK PUBLISHING
A division of Hodder Headline PLC
338 Euston Road
London NW1 3BH

For James
car buff extraordinaire
with love

Author's Note

Murder in the Motor Stable would never have chugged out on to the road without the support of my publishers, especially Jane Morpeth and Andi Blackwell of Headline, and my agent Dorothy Lumley of the Dorian Literary Agency, and to them my great thanks.

I am also very grateful to Fred Ferrier and my husband James Myers, car buffs both, for their help and suggestions, and to Bernard Pfrunder.

Lastly, I owe an apology to His Late Majesty King Edward VII for having forced him to accept an engagement in Kent on a day when in fact he was beginning a three-day tour of Liverpool, Swansea and Birmingham.

Prologue

Hester Hart hailed the White Cliffs of Dover from the top deck of the Belgian mail steamer with an enthusiasm worthy of William the Conqueror leaping on to Pevensey Beach. A new kingdom lay before her, the land of her birth. The newly dubbed Queen of the Desert, daughter of Sir Herbert Hart, button manufacturer to royalty, was about to begin her next and most important conquest.

Below, on Admiralty Pier, as the ship docked, she could see porters and seamen swarming like ants, with several English policemen stolidly in their midst. You could find ants the world over, dragomen, muleteers, labourers of all sorts; a few shekels and they were happy. If only English society conformed to such simple standards, she would never have embarked on her travels; services rendered were repaid by disservices, unless you were among the élite. She smouldered as memories flooded back. Settlement of old scores required planning and thought, and she had had a long time to devote to them. Fifteen years ago, in 1889 she had set out to march in the steps of Jane Digby and Hester Stanhope. Now it was 1904, a new century, and unlike her predecessors she was coming back to force society to clasp her to its so tightly corseted bosom.

As the gangplank went down and porters swarmed up on to

the decks, she indicated her small baggage to a rough-looking Dovorian, comparing him unfavourably with the Arab dragomen who had enlivened her travels. Her corded trunks had been despatched in advance with the precious burdens on which her entire plan was based, and this fellow could wreak little harm on the possessions she had with her.

'London,' she told him curtly.

'First class, madam?'

Hester was annoyed. Couldn't the fellow tell? Naturally she was travelling first class. This was England, not Syria.

Inferior to dragomen the Dovorian might appear, but he knew when his 3d charge was at risk, and once past His Majesty's Customs led the way straight to a Ladies Only carriage.

The keen April wind strained at the hatpin moorings of her peacock-feathered large-brimmed hat as Hester paid the fellow off, now well pleased. *Ladies* Only. Yes, at last she would be awarded her rightful place in society, after all the snubs and rejections. She would storm its portals; not only would she ruffle the pretty feathers of those who had once barred her way, she would pick those pretty chickens off one by one.

And she had decided just where to start: the newly formed Ladies' Motoring Club, run by some tinpot Russian princess . . .

Chapter One

'I would rather die, son of a goat.'

Auguste Didier, distracted from the *filets de sôle à la Tatiana* by his chef's passionate cry, hurried to intervene. Common sense told him that this incident was one more round in the feud between his chef Pierre Calille and Luigi Peroni, the club restaurant's maître d', and if it were not resolved, dinner would be the principal victim. Grimly, he took control.

'What is so important as to interrupt the making of a mayonnaise?'

'Mint, Monsieur Didier.' Luigi was only too happy to impart the bad tidings to Pierre's superior who was, moreover, the husband of the Madam President of the Ladies' Motoring Club. 'There have been complaints.'

'But English ladies like mint.' Auguste was puzzled. 'Indeed, some recognise no other herb.'

'*Not* in rissoles.' Luigi oozed smugness.

'*Rissoles?*' Pierre shrieked. 'They were *croquettes* of the finest quality. Monsieur Escoffier himself encourages novelty.'

'Unfortunately, Pierre, ladies like Lady Bullinger do not always appreciate novelty,' Auguste said gently.

'And I do not appreciate being told how to cook by a mere waiter,' howled Pierre. 'How can I be a slave to English taste when I have come to reform it?'

Auguste had some sympathy with this viewpoint, but in the interests of his wife's club, compromise was obviously called for. 'Perhaps a little less mint—'

'It is unsubtle, like your cooking,' Luigi cut in, seeing the tide flowing in his favour. 'Not like basil.'

'Basil subtle?' Pierre's dark eyes flashed. 'I have read Mr Keats' poem "Isabella". Italians used pots of basil for burying heads in.'

'I will bury yours, dog.' Luigi was thrown from his usual poise by an unfair dig at his national honour. 'I am responsible for—'

'I,' Auguste informed them loudly, 'am responsible for dinner tonight. Shall we proceed?' He mentally thanked his father for choosing an English wife whose genes usually predominated in time of trouble, a useful gift for a Provençal stuck between the Milanese maître d' and the Marseille-born Pierre, he reflected. He liked both men though his preference was for the stalwart, philosophical Pierre. To look at they were not dissimilar; both were in their early thirties, of roughly the same height as himself, 5 feet 10 inches, both dark-haired, of medium build, with the liquid dark eyes and complexion of the Latin. Where Pierre's held passionate concern for his calling, Luigi's were amused and detached. The one, Auguste guessed, had a strict moral code; the other, he suspected, lacked it. However, all that concerned him was that when they were quarrelling the club failed to run smoothly. Like now.

'What is *that*?' He suddenly awoke to the fact that the far distant rumble of voices to which he had hitherto paid little heed was becoming not only louder but ominously so. Moreover the clang of the iron gates of Milton House in London's Petty France suggested the noise might have something to do with his wife's motoring club.

'Dolly Dobbs,' shouted Luigi excitedly.

'A new member, like Miss Hester Hart?' Auguste asked. He could not remember his wife Tatiana mentioning her.

'*Not* like Miss Hart.' Luigi laughed. 'Unless Miss Hart has changed into a motorcar.'

'No,' Pierre retorted. 'Miss Hart is a splendid lady, dog.'

This was not what Auguste had heard, and from Luigi's snort of derision not his experience.

'Where have *you* met her, peasant?'

'I have seen in the newspapers that she has accomplished great things. It is an honour to cook for her.'

The noise outside was growing even louder and the rest of the kitchen staff were edging towards the door, Auguste noticed.

'But what is this Dolly Dobbs?' he asked. He dimly remembered Tatiana saying something at breakfast about the arrival of a new experimental motorcar but as he had been meditating at the time on an exciting new recipe for a sauce for roast woodcock, he had forgotten the details. *His* duty, however, was to dinner, which Tatiana had maintained should be an extra special one tonight, and he was a little hurt to find that no one shared his concern. He cast an anxious and loving eye at the purée for the sole, then curiosity overtaking even him as to the reason for the hullabaloo, he followed Luigi and Pierre, mint forgotten, to the area steps. The racket outside did not suggest joyful welcome.

He was correct. As he emerged into the courtyard the whole of Petty France was seething with something akin to a French Revolutionary mob on its way to the guillotine with a few hundred prize aristos. In this case, their fury appeared to be directed against a large object swathed in canvas on a wagon drawn by two stalwart horses and at present wedged just inside the gates of Milton House, unable to proceed for the numbers of both male and female angry demonstrators surrounding it.

'Down with cars!' The shrill voice of the leader of the mob, a wirily-built lady of middle years with a determined chin and a huge placard bearing the legend 'The Car Is the Beast of Doom', brought more supporters pushing their way into the courtyard. 'Uphold the rights of the horse,' she shrieked, whipping her flock into renewed frenzy.

Those rights did not appear to include free passage to plod on their way, Auguste was amused to notice, as a forest of gloved hands clutched at their four-footed friends' reins. Their leader pulled off the canvas covering with a victorious cry of 'Hams!'

The mob pressed eagerly forward but the noise abruptly ceased, followed by a murmur of what might have been surprise, disappointment or merely regrouping for the final assault.

What had been revealed was, to Auguste's eye at least, merely another motorcar, its only striking characteristic the bright red paint. It was a landaulet, with an open top, a rear seat for extra passengers, four wheels and a steering pillar. There was nothing in front of the steering pillar to hold an engine, but even he was aware that in some motorcars that was not unusual.

What then was so exciting about the Dolly Dobbs? The expert eye, Auguste concluded, might be interested in the fact that the running boards curved up to extra wide and flat-topped mudguards, but to him (and he suspected to the mob, some of whom were looking as if they had been baulked of their prey) it was just an ordinary motorcar.

The brief flicker of his own professional interest aroused by the cry of 'Hams' also died, as his wife hurtled past him towards the fracas, hatless, gloveless and pausing only to command his instant assistance. '*Aux armes, mon ami*, it's the Horse Against Motor Car Society. That is the Dolly Dobbs, and *that* is Mrs Hortensia Millward.'

Auguste's view was that a motorcar should have the decency to arrive under its own steam – or petrol if it preferred – but he knew better than to voice it, much as he would have loved to call out like small boys everywhere at a car in trouble: 'Get a horse!'

Tatiana, her usual calm face alive with excitement, and regardless of her delicate cream linen summer gown, threw herself into the mob, now regaining its enthusiasm and to Auguste's added horror, this just as Hortensia Millward seemed bent on dragging the driver of the wagon, Mr Frederick Gale, the stalwart club engineer, down from his seat. As Mrs Millward hopped up and down, with the help of wheel and running board, impatiently hitching her brown skirt up to knee height in the interests of the Hams, Fred jumped up and flung his arms round the Dolly Dobbs's steering pillar in a loving embrace.

'*Now!*'

A small party of die-hards, who had obviously learned their tactics at the Khyber Pass, rushed forward at their leader's shout, to make a combined assault on Fred and his passenger, a mild-looking young man with spectacles who sat hypnotised with fright.

Appalled, Auguste dragged Tatiana back as she was about to launch herself at Mrs Millward in Fred's defence and nobly inserted his own body between Fred, half a dozen angular corseted bodies armed with stout wood placard supports, and a middle-aged man with the air of one finding himself in the midst of the Eton Wall Game by mistake.

'Mrs Millward, don't you dare touch him!' Tatiana shouted.

Hortensia, her purple silk hat knocked askew through hatpins insufficient to withstand the ferocity of her assault, was momentarily deflected from her purpose.

'Why not?'

'He's a living creature, just like a horse.'

'Then he should not work with contraptions of the Devil.'

Auguste, a placard jammed at his neck and restrained by three pairs of feminine arms, decided not to join the debate. He loathed motorcars.

'Motorcars are the future.' Tatiana finally forced her way though to Hortensia and faced her grimly, arms akimbo.

'Horses are friend to rich and poor.'

'And did not the poor benefit equally from the invention of the wheel?'

'How many more faithful friends are to be terrified or cast aside unwanted? How many more frail women tumbled off bicycles from fear of your monsters? They should never have repealed the Red Flag Act!' Hortensia, bored with rational argument, made a renewed assault on Fred – he was attempting to follow his passenger, who had now been released from his trance, had leapt from his seat and had sprung to the defence of the Dolly Dobbs. It was clear from the passionate way he spread-eagled himself against it that he was intimately involved with the lady; he gazed into a future of untold magnificence.

'My invention will revolutionise all your lives, ladies.' He opened his arms towards them in fervent appeal. 'Last year the Wright Brothers conquered the air. This year I, Harold Dobbs of Upper Norwood, will conquer earth.'

Hortensia was not impressed. 'What's this contraption going to do? Fly out of its stable?'

Harold Dobbs was saved from the crowd's apparent plan of

guillotining him forthwith by the arrival of the full majesty of the law in the form of two police constables who persuaded the crowd to retreat from the courtyard back into Petty France. Faces remained glued to the railings nevertheless, as the horses plodded round to the motor stable with their presumably precious burden.

'Do you think Hortensia won that round?' Tatiana asked glumly. The lace at her neck had been torn by over-eager Hams, and her green sash had disappeared.

Auguste had almost been garrotted by his apron strings, his white hat was jammed over one eye, and his eye would undoubtedly shortly be black. Nevertheless, he had a vague memory of having once promised he would care for and support this woman for the rest of his life. 'If so, she will not win the war, *chérie*.' Unfortunately, in his view.

'Hortensia has influence. Her husband is a well-known archaeologist. He was here today. They say he'll be knighted soon.'

'It is not like you to admit that this is a factor to be considered.'

'It is the way of the world and, more important, it is the way of London. I hope she does not deter ladies from joining my club. The whole point of my horse-training programme is that horses and motorcars can live together.' Tatiana was perturbed. Auguste had a faint recollection of her telling him recently of her rota to send members with their cars to horse owners' homes for training sessions to accustom horses to motorcars. It was Auguste's treacherous view, shared by most horse owners, that motorcars should accustom themselves to horses rather than the other way round.

'How could anyone not admire it?' Tatiana's dark eyes were fixed lovingly on the Dolly Dobbs as they followed the wagon round to the motor stable at the rear of the club's headquarters. 'But it is terrible that Hortensia got wind of its arrival – the car is supposed to be a secret.'

'What is so secret about it? It is painted bright red.'

'It is not a partridge, *chéri*; it does not need camouflage against its enemies. And it is *very* secret indeed. Its official Motor Club of Great Britain trials are on the twenty-first of July, next Thursday, and no one must even see it before its first public appearance this Saturday.'

'But now they have.'

'Aha.' Tatiana paused mysteriously, as lifting gear was lovingly placed by its inventor round his beloved's bodywork, once Fred had manoeuvred the wagon into the entrance of one of the motor houses.

The old carriage house had now been converted into a motor stable with ten motor houses, a repair and washing house and separate benzine house a short distance away. With all the motor house doors open this hot Tuesday afternoon, the motorcars looked uncommonly like horses poking their noses out. Perhaps he should offer them carrots? Auguste thought benignly. The Dolly Dobbs was being housed next to the repair house, as was usual for motors requiring special attention.

'What you have seen is only the shell,' Tatiana whispered. 'It has been brought here early to receive its very special equipment. It was even stripped of its battery of accumulators for the journey.'

Auguste displayed an intelligent interest in his wife's career. 'You mean it is an electric car? But they have been invented already.' The open landaulet was unlike the tall electric broughams he was used to seeing in London streets.

He instantly regretted his rashness. Tatiana's eyes lit up as she drew breath for a *full* explanation. 'Of course, but they are limited in their use by their range. They can manage only about fifty miles before the battery has to be recharged or changed. So in practice they are limited to town work or to country houses with their own electric lighting plant. It is true,' she continued with the same enthusiasm that Auguste would devote to a *bavarois*, 'the number of garages in the country is increasing now and batteries can be changed easily, but that is no help if the battery is exhausted on the open road.'

'So the Dolly Dobbs will carry a spare battery?' Auguste tried again, ignoring his throbbing eye.

'A *spare*?' Tatiana was amazed at such ignorance. 'Weight versus range is the whole problem. How can they carry another battery? They would travel even less distance. Of course, if the secret Edison battery being developed fulfils expectations . . .'

Auguste's attention wandered. Motoring was much like cooking, after all. Too much flavouring and a dish was ruined; too little produced the same result. 'So what is different about the Dolly Dobbs?' Auguste brought himself back with some effort from a memory of his *écrevisses à la Maisie*.

'The same as that between a *soufflé à la Mrs Marshall* and a masterpiece by Auguste Didier.'

Auguste looked at Tatiana suspiciously for any sign of irony. 'It is true my *soufflé des violettes* is of great quality, though perhaps vanilla is not—'

'Harold Dobbs has *solved* the problem – or so he claims.'

'You mean whether vanilla is essential to bring out the flavour—'

'I do not mean that, Auguste.' Tatiana looked annoyed. 'The problem of the range of the electric car.'

'How?' her husband asked penitently.

'Would you reveal the secret of a new recipe before tasting it?' Tatiana replied loftily. In fact she did not know, much to her chagrin. 'But you will see the car for yourself at the trials.'

'I will?' Auguste was instantly suspicious.

'It is to be a rally and social event as well as the official Motor Club of Great Britain road trial for the Dolly Dobbs. The whole club will leave in procession from Hyde Park Corner. We shall drive our motorcars along the Dover road to Martyr House near Barham Downs on the far side of Canterbury, where His Majesty will greet us. He is staying with the Earl of Tunstall.'

'And the Countess?' Auguste could not resist innocently adding, since Isabel, Lady Tunstall, was well-known in society for her lack of adherence to the marriage vows.

'As you say, and the Countess.' The wild oats of His Majesty might all now be cast but there was still room for respectably cultivated wheat in his social itinerary.

Auguste greeted Tatiana's news with even more foreboding. In his experience any event with both His Majesty and himself involved was likely to go seriously wrong, usually to the detriment of Auguste Didier. He must resist Tatiana's pleas to accompany her on the Léon Bollée at all costs, he decided. 'Delighted though I would be to meet Bertie again, I fear, *chérie*, I have arranged to discuss *Dining With Didier* with my publisher.' There was a great deal more of his projected ten-volume magnum opus in his head than there was on paper, but it proved a most useful 'Bunbury', to employ Mr Oscar Wilde's method of evading unwelcome appointments.

'You must cancel it.'

'*Je m'excuse?*'

'There is the banquet.'

'What banquet?'

'The one you are to prepare in the gardens of Martyr House next Thursday.'

There was a brief silence.

'I could not tell you before, Auguste,' Tatiana added placatingly. 'Bertie has only just thought of it.'

Various verbs that combined well with Bertie rose to Auguste's lips, but what was the point of letting fly with them?

There were distinct disadvantages in marrying into even the outer purlieus of the British royal family, but the chief one was the restriction on his cooking. An artist should be free, not ordered as to where he could or not practise his art. Did the Pope order Michelangelo to paint only for him? No. Yet His Majesty King Edward VII had made it a condition of his marriage to Tatiana, a remote Romanov and hence his cousin, that he should not cook for gainful employment; he might (like Alexis Soyer, Auguste seethed) cook for charity, he might cook at private homes, and he bally well *had* to cook for the King whenever so commanded.

When Tatiana opened her Ladies' Motoring Club earlier this year, Auguste had been overwhelmed with pleasure when she asked him to be honorary chef at important dinners and banquets, of which tonight was one. Cooking banquets for the King was a different matter, not because he had any doubts as to his ability to outshine any other chef in the country (save his old maître Escoffier perhaps), but because he and his friend Chief Inspector Egbert Rose of Scotland Yard had found that the King and themselves, once in proximity, had an unfortunate tendency to run into calamity. On several occasions the calamity had been murder, and Auguste had been forced into the role of detective. He disliked it; he was a chef, not a Sherlock. He saw the apprehensive eyes of his wife, however, and nobly replied, 'How delightful.'

Relieved, Tatiana laughed. 'I will drive you down.'

'Won't you be driving the Dolly Dobbs?' He could at least avoid this ordeal.

'No. Agatha – the Duchess of Dewbury – is to drive it, since she is its inventor's patron.'

Auguste faced the inevitable. The banquet must be prepared in meticulous detail and transported from London; he might make a last-minute appeal to travel earlier. And even if it was refused, if Hortensia Millward heard of the trials it could hardly fail to prove a most spirited journey. Mounted highwaymen at Blackheath were a distinct possibility. Auguste cheered up, even if it would mean the waste of a July day when he might be in their small Queen Anne's Gate garden discussing recipes with Mrs Jolly, their cook.

'Very well. I will prepare a banquet to excel over all banquets. And furthermore the dinner tonight will be my finest. You shall enjoy every morsel.'

'I hope so.'

'Why do you doubt it?' Auguste was somewhat indignant.

'I have my committee meeting first.'

'But what is so unusual about *this* meeting?'

'The agenda.'

'And that is?'

'Hats and Hester Hart.'

The treasurer of the Ladies' Motoring Club, Lady Bullinger, crammed her cap on to her coiffured hair as firmly as she wished she could crush that upstart Hester Hart. The man's cap, goggles, serviceable large fingerless gloves and tightly-fitting buttoned mackintosh coat made an odd match with her blue evening dinner dress, but Maud was a practical woman, and the evening was damp.

'What are your views on snakes, Snelgrove?' she demanded of her maid as the latter handed her the hatbox containing a more suitable head-covering for fashionable dining.

Snelgrove had only seen snakes in the reptile house of the Zoological Gardens; no gallivanting over the Continent in a racing car like her ladyship, but she had her answer ready.

'Keep an eye on them, milady.'

Lady Bullinger snorted. 'Quite right, Snelgrove.'

That was what she would do to Hester Hart. One couldn't go anywhere this season without falling over that woman, seeing her face grinning out from the pages of the *Illustrated London News*, posed at Palmyra, dallying in Damascus, jolting through Jericho, and, worse, lording it over London. Every time she was forced to greet the woman in the Motoring Club or out of it, she had the temerity to hint that she had not forgotten their earlier acquaintance. Well, nor had Maud. She wasn't ashamed of what she'd done. On the contrary, she was proud of it. All the knighthoods in the world couldn't have taken the buttons out of that family. All the same, Maud was a practical woman. It might be better not to antagonise Miss Hart, as society now seemed determined to lionise her. By next season she would be forgotten, but for the moment it was wiser to tolerate her.

Like HMS *Warrior* under full steam, Lady Bullinger headed down the stairs of her Wimpole Street town house, imperiously waved the motor servant out of the driving seat and into the rear, and took the wheel of her new 6-cylinder Napier touring car herself.

As she roared into Oxford Street, she momentarily forgot she was not in her Napier racer now, and strained the newly permitted speed of 20 mph to the limit. She seized the speed lever to change to a lower speed, wishing it were Hester Hart's neck. She turned her mind to happier subjects. Soon she'd have all the opportunity she wanted to drive fast, when she began practising in earnest for the International Women's Race in France in October. There was no doubt now that she would be the representative for England. Who else was there? No one.

Maud gave a triumphant squeeze to the hooter, and two elderly gentlemen in Piccadilly leapt for safety. She was looking forward to dining with Phyllis and Roderick this evening after the meeting. True, her godson could have done better for himself than affiancing himself to a musical comedy actress, but the gel was at least presentable in society. Unlike Hester Hart.

Some mile or so away in Mayfair, Maud's sister-in-law, the Duchess of Dewbury, secretary to the Ladies' Motoring Club, studied herself critically in the mirror. She was preoccupied with her own blonde charm at forty and had little time to spare to meditate upon Miss Hester Hart. That old business was over years ago. She, Agatha, was at the peak of her mature beauty, and whatever pretensions Hester Hart might have, beauty could hardly be amongst them. Her skin was over-tended by sun and under-tended by cold cream, her hair unblessed by regular applications of rosemary rinse, and her face was as long as that of the camels on which she no doubt traversed the deserts. Camels, the Duchess reflected, had rather softer faces than Hester Hart. But then poor Hester, although almost forty, had never married. She had never known how to make the best of herself, not that there was much to make with that father, as round and fat as the buttons he made and a familiar manner that no doubt went down well at his local Oddfellows' Friendly Society meetings but which failed to find acceptance in refined London society. Still, she might as well be kind to the poor woman, now she was a fellow member of the Ladies' Motoring Club. Vaguely she wondered why Hester had joined, and what make of car she might drive. Would she be a Racer, like herself and Maud, seeking excitement and adventure in this developing sport, or a Rabbit, like Isabel Tunstall and Phyllis Lockwood who saw the motorcar as a kind of fashion accessory?

She suspected the former – in which case Maud might have to look to her laurels. Poor old Maud. Fortunately her own position was secure as patroness of the Dolly Dobbs. Which motor should she take this evening? Exciting though her little Horbick two-seater was, it would involve sending her maid ahead to the club to attend to her hair and complexion on arrival. It would have to be Harry's Mercedes.

Phyllis Lockwood, committee member, executed a pirouette in the bedroom of her Belgravia home and thought how beautiful she was. Her latest musical play had just finished its run and she was therefore out of the public eye until the London season began again in the autumn. Her only task was to pose for postcards at Messrs Ellis and Walery for her devoted public. Fortunately this meant she had all the more time to enjoy with Roderick and they could marry at the beginning of the season. She was so glad that her great-great-grandmother was the seventh daughter of a baron and thus her career as an actress did not preclude her marriage into London society, with a wedding in St George's, Hanover Square. She adored Roderick; with his black hair and romantic looks he could have stepped straight off the stage of a musical play himself, although he was a racing driver, not an actor. She had joined the Ladies' Motoring Club to please him. After all, motor racing was a most exciting sport – if one did not have to take part in it oneself. Fortunately, Tatiana had made it clear that the club was to promote interest in all kinds of motoring, not just racing.

Tatiana was adorable. It was entirely to please her that Phyllis had agreed to join the committee. It was, she told herself, a public duty. All the same, she was not entirely happy to be classified as one of the Rabbits. Though why not? Surely all women needed of a car was its ability to travel from place to place and to provide an opportunity for its owner to look attractive while doing so. This, she had found, was hard when the wind blew and clouds of dust blinded her, clung to her cheeks and chin and flew into her nostrils and mouth, despite the silk shields. And goggles were so very ugly. The only answer was to put a veil over one's face, but then one wasn't seen at all. It was all very difficult. Why couldn't those silly car manufacturers stick something up in front of the driver to stop such inconveniences? They didn't seem to consider ladies' complexions at all.

Tonight, she remembered as she climbed onto her new Fiat, they were to discuss hats. That would at least be interesting. And wasn't there something on the agenda about that dreadful woman, Hester Hart?

Isabel, Countess of Tunstall, committee member, watched her husband depart on the Lanchester for their Kent mansion, Martyr House, with relief. For a moment she had feared he had wanted to remain for dinner, and that would be awkward because Cousin Hugh was in town, and to dine with him as a family relation (and *very* close friend) would be not only respectable but highly desirable. After all, he did live in the country at Richmond so until she had purchased her Royce she had few opportunities to see him. Motorcars were undoubtedly extremely useful. No one would think it strange nowadays to see a lady driving a motorcar unescorted. It was considered sporting, and what the sport was was surely up to the driver. Indeed the Ladies' Motoring Club had revealed a consensus that such were the contortions of the body required for motorists, it should be officially (by the rules of society) deemed a sport, thereby obviating the need for corsetry – until one arrived at one's destination, when it should be donned (unless of course the destination included a close gentleman friend). Isabel almost giggled, then remembered what damage this could wreak on lily-white madonna-like faces that carefully cultivated calmness and serenity.

Tonight was the committee meeting, and that eccentric woman Hester Hart would be on the agenda. Isabel had a moment's uneasiness. She had not yet encountered her at the club, but some years ago she had been introduced to Hester – had she been formally introduced? She couldn't remember. What she did remember was that something unpleasant had happened, something to do with His Majesty when Prince of Wales, but whatever it was could not possibly be of any importance now, could it?

Auguste, ready for the evening in tail coat and white tie, was watching Tatiana and her maid in their nightly battle to array his wife in full evening dress. The battle was between Eloise, who wished her mistress to do full justice both to her beauty and to her own prowess as a maid, and Tatiana who wished to get the whole ordeal over as quickly as possible in order to return to the more interesting aspects of life such as motorcars. He was aware that most husbands were never permitted to view such intimate scenes but he found it a rare chance to talk to Tatiana as well as a fascinating look into the deeper mysteries of social ritual. It was like the preparation of a grand dish, perhaps a *caneton*. There were the bones, covered with luscious flesh which in turn was crowned by a sauce perfectly chosen for the dish and the occasion. Tonight Tatiana's sauce was wide-sashed ivory silk with a satin underskirt and colourful embroidered panels. Once the sauce was selected, then came the garnish. Tatiana had a tendency towards impatience over jewels, flowers and fans, but he had counselled her into wisdom. The correct garnish was essential, for appearance was a key to taste and taste to the conveyance of the true message of the dish.

'Why do you not want Hester Hart to join the committee?' Auguste watched fascinated as Tatiana wriggled impatiently and Eloise struggled with the fastenings of a Romanov diamond necklace said, Tatiana had once told him casually, to have belonged to Catherine the Great.

'You always know if meat or fish are bad even though they may be disguised by sauces or spices. How?'

'By instinct, which of course is not instinct, but the experience of a thousand other such dishes.'

'That's how I know too. I've met a lot of Englishwomen. Many I like, many I do not, either personally or as a type, but Hester Hart is different. Every time I meet her I smell trouble, Auguste. She is charming to me, she's lively to listen to, interesting to look at, the toast of London, and yet, and yet . . .'

'"I do not like thee, Dr Fell/The reason why I cannot tell,"' Auguste quoted for her.

'She does not add up as a dish, Auguste. She has explored Syria, Iraq, Northern Africa, and many other places, all on her own. She is a great and intrepid traveller, and yet now she has decided to *settle* in England.'

'London and England have much to offer.'

'But the taste for danger does not die so easily, Auguste. It lives on and has to be fed.'

'That is why she has joined your club,' he pointed out reasonably. 'She will travel in fast motorcars instead of trekking or going by camel or horse. She will be a Racer, though, not a Rabbit.'

'Sometimes I feel I have more in common with Hortensia Millward than with my committee,' its president announced. 'Why did we pick two Racers who talk only of gradients, grease cups and Gordon Bennett Cups, and two Rabbits who don't know a worm-gear from a goose-neck?'

'What trouble could Miss Hart cause if she were on the committee?'

'I don't know. That's the danger.'

He watched Tatiana throwing on the last items of garnish with less attention than he would have paid to the placing of an olive, and thought longingly of the moment that they would be home again and the process be reversed.

'And the hats, my love. What danger can they pose?'

'You'd be surprised,' his wife informed him darkly.

How could ladies get so heated over such an issue? Auguste wondered. Then he remembered Plum's, the gentlemen's club where he had been chef for several years, and the passionate arguments over the ritual of Plum's Passing. If gentlemen could come to blows over demolishing a meringue replica of Napoleon, could ladies be expected to be different over hats? He fervently hoped so, because in Plum's case it had led to murder.

* * *

Auguste cautiously ventured into the club kitchen. True, he had left it in safe hands, but one could never be *absolutely* certain until one's own eye was satisfied. Was all ready? The sauce for the *filets de sole*, the chiffonade for the consommé, the *homard à la Mornay*, the *poularde à la Nantua*, *poularde Alexandra*, the *crème Anglaise* – ah, yes, he deduced this was prepared by the fact that Pierre's sugar nippers were lying on the table. Perfection would elude him while such details were overlooked. Routine was as important as the creative part of cooking. Or was it? he wondered. Pierre was an inspired cook, with a flair that owed nothing to conventional training. He had told Auguste he had been trained at the Marseille Hôtel Grande, but Auguste had his suspicions that his stay there had been brief and Pierre's miraculous affinity with both fish and fowl owed more to the back streets of the city than the hotels it boasted in Baedeker's Guides. Had Napoleon been lucky enough to sink exhausted by the roadside anywhere near Pierre Calille, he would have had a dish far superior to chicken Marengo.

'There is something wrong with the tongue?' Pierre appeared at his side, face strained and anxious as he saw Auguste peering into the tinplate press.

'No, Pierre,' Auguste replied hastily. Pierre took criticism hard. Indeed, who could complain at the satisfying red tongue within and its exhilarating aroma of pungent spices? 'I was thinking of Napoleon.'

'Ah.' Pierre's anxious face relaxed into its usual placid contours. 'A great man of the people.'

In the interests of dinner, Auguste forbore to point out that the peoples of Italy, Egypt, Germany, Poland, Russia, etc. might not agree with this definition.

'You have much experience of murder, I am told,

monsieur,' Pierre continued. 'Do you believe he was poisoned by the British, as rumour says?'

Why was it that once an unwelcome thought decided to enter one's mind, everybody and everything was only too happy to remind you of it? 'No. The English had nothing to gain from his murder, and they are a ruthless but practical nation. Unless,' Auguste added fairly, 'a trivial cause arouses their passions.'

Like committee meetings and hats, the unwelcome thought of murder helpfully nudged. Or even Hester Hart.

'Any other business?' Tatiana had planned the most infinitesimal of pauses before launching, thankfully, into the security arrangements for the Dolly Dobbs. She did not receive it.

'That hat!' boomed Lady Bullinger instantly. 'The obvious solution is a gentleman's cap, like I wear. Plenty of room to stick the badge on.'

Tatiana's heart sank. She was fond of Maud but she was undoubtedly formidable both in temperament and reputation. Fortunately she drove in so many races she was unable to grace the club as often as she'd like, a fact her husband Sir Algernon probably welcomed as well for much the same sort of reason.

'But a cap won't take a veil, Maud,' Agatha pointed out.

'Who needs one?'

Tatiana tried hard not to gaze at Lady Bullinger's weather-beaten complexion.

'Why not something very large to keep off the rain, full-brimmed with flowers and perhaps feathers cut into motorcar shapes on top,' Phyllis suggested brightly.

'We'd take off like kites in the wind, Phyllis,' Agatha pointed out kindly.

Tatiana had a pleasant vision of her committee borne off instantly into the sky and left permanently on a cloud. Individually each member of it might be reasonable, together decisions were as hard to reach as when Auguste agonised over a new recipe.

'Not if it doesn't have a tall crown.' Isabel considered her fellow Rabbit's proposition seriously.

'It has to carry the *badge*.' Maud thumped the table. 'A cap's what's needed. I can pull mine over my ears.'

'I'm sure my ears don't need covering,' Isabel informed them. She touched one lightly to indicate how petal-like they still were despite their thirty-five years.

'Are you implying that I have *large* ears?' Maud thundered in astonishment.

'How about a tricorne?' Agatha suggested. 'It's very fashionable. We could tie a veil round that.'

'We'd look like upside-down Christmas gifts,' Phyllis giggled.

The Duchess cast her a look of great dislike. 'Then I vote for Maud's cap.'

'But *your* ears are beautiful,' Isabel remarked innocently.

'How about a tam o'shanter?' Tatiana said hastily, seeing Maud was about to erupt.

'Very *sporting*,' Agatha said approvingly.

'I don't want to look sporting, I want to look pretty,' Phyllis declared.

When all else fails, change the subject, Tatiana thought quickly. The atmosphere was getting even tenser than she'd feared and surely that could not all be due to hats. 'There is a suggestion on the table that Miss Hester Hart, being of such international repute, should be asked to join the committee.'

There was immediate silence as four committee members inspected the ink blotters and paper before them with intense interest.

So she was going to have to break it. Tatiana steeled herself. 'In principle, I feel it is not a good plan to invite such a new member to join us before we can call ourselves truly established as a committee.'

'A lady in the public eye such as she is could do the club nothing but good.' Phyllis had least qualms about speaking first. 'There is talk of Ellis and Walery issuing a postcard of her in Arabian costume, and darling Roderick says she is a most remarkable lady.'

'You did not seem to think her remarkable when you contributed that article to *The Ladies' Companion* last year about how the true role of women was to provide comfort and beauty for gentlemen, and that women who galloped across deserts on camels or horses must be lacking in true womanliness,' Isabel pointed out.

'I never said that,' Phyllis wailed. 'Anyway, someone wrote it all for me.'

'The club needs more *real* drivers like Miss Hart,' Lady Bullinger trumpeted, 'and fewer of those who refuse to venture out in their motorcars when there's a cloud this side of the Equator.'

'I have to think of my complexion,' Phyllis cried, stung at this broadside from darling Roderick's godmother.

'All that stage lighting, no doubt,' Agatha murmured. 'It's a trifle bumpy.'

Phyllis glared. 'I vote for the suggestion.'

'I don't,' Isabel said. She had remembered just how Miss Hart's plans for the Diamond Jubilee in '97 had cut across her own, and the last thing she wanted was the same lady in a position of power now.

'I do,' Lady Bullinger declared magnanimously. 'Give the woman a chance.'

'Do you know her?' Tatiana asked curiously. She had the impression that on the few occasions Hester had so far visited the club, Maud had almost pointedly tried to evade her.

Lady Bullinger looked stubborn. 'Well enough.' She cleared her throat to indicate the discussion was over.

'And I vote against her,' said Agatha. 'I feel there would be far too much public attention focused on her, and not on the motorcars.' Especially the Dolly Dobbs, she thought. 'So you have the casting vote, Your Highness.'

Tatiana disliked being addressed as Your Highness, preferring Mrs Didier, though reluctantly bowed to the way of the world and allowed her royal rank to be used for official club purposes. She also disliked being put in this position. 'I vote no.'

'I don't think Hester will like it.' Phyllis suddenly looked nervous.

'She won't know unless someone chooses to tell her,' Isabel pointed out comfortingly.

'No one would discuss private committee business, surely,' Tatiana said firmly.

'It has happened,' Agatha murmured.

'If the cap fits,' Maud rumbled, and Agatha looked furious.

'Ah yes, let's return to the issue of the hat,' Tatiana broke in hastily. It might be her imagination, but she remembered Auguste saying that one could *smell* a dangerous situation devloping like the rising aroma of garlic and spices fried in oil.

* * *

The dining room of the Ladies' Motoring Club was palatial, light and airy, unlike so many gentlemen's clubs he had seen. Auguste had instantly approved. With its pale green walls, Adam fireplaces and elegant columns, it was a suitable setting for Didier dishes.

The arrangement of the tables had been the subject of much discussion when the club had opened in March. Should there be a communal table, or separate tables? Compromise had been established with a communal table at luncheon and separate tables in the evening, so that gentlemen should not be foisted on those ladies seeking immunity from masculine company. This principle had been bent a little to permit a permanent male maître d', though his staff was female. A restaurant, it was agreed, was primarily a social venue, not for technical motorcar discussions, and all opposition vanished when Luigi had presented himself for the position. Eyes that melted as softly as butter into a hollandaise, was Tatiana's description of him to Auguste, who was more impressed by his gifts of diplomacy. Now, he was as indispensable as the fluted pillar in the centre of the restaurant.

Unfortunately Auguste was all too well aware of the paragon's shortcomings. The liquid eyes turned to flint and diplomacy deserted him whenever he came face to face with Pierre. Pierre was of mere peasant stock, while he, Luigi Peroni, apparently came from a family once closely related to the former dukes of Milan. Whether this relationship was blessed by the clergy, and how such a scion of a noble house was reduced to earning a living, Luigi never explained. The liquid eyes said it all. Like the mouse in Mr Carroll's delightful story, Tatiana explained to Auguste, Luigi had a long and sad tale.

The feud between kitchen and restaurant was the reason Auguste insisted on being seated conveniently near the kitchen. When they first saw the cook dining with their president, new members of the club had eyed him askance, then viewed Tatiana pityingly when they discovered the relationship. It was gradually accepted, however, that if His Majesty could countenance his marrying into the royal family, they should be able to tolerate a mere dinner in his company.

'I should have made the sorrel sauce myself,' Auguste suddenly exclaimed.

'Auguste, it is *perfect*. I *know* it is.' Tatiana sighed.

'How can you *know*,' he agonised, halfway poised between being seated and being upright, 'until you have tasted it?'

'Because everything you cook is perfect, and because you would not have left it if you had not had confidence in your chef. That is why you have one.'

He considered this. 'But do you not remember the time I deserted the rhubarb sauce and it tasted like stale *water*?'

'That was an unfortunate accident. No one could have anticipated your sauce chef would discover at the critical moment that his wife had taken the butcher as her lover.'

'But I feel something is about to go wrong.' He sat down with this dire warning.

'If so, it will not be with your cooking. It is much more likely to be concerned with hats. Phyllis decided she wanted a high-crowned Romney hat perched on her golden curls, and carried Isabel and Agatha with her. With veils tied round we'll look like white chimneypots. Maud is furious.'

It was true, Auguste conceded, that the dinner seemed to be going well. Lady Bullinger was dining with Phyllis Lockwood, for once without her fiancé Roderick Smythe.

Agatha and Edward, the Duke and Duchess of Dewbury, were with two strangers. No, not strangers. The man was her protégé, Harold Dobbs, inventor of the Dolly Dobbs, so the other lady, who looked a little like a crazed terrier, must be his wife Judith. Isabel, the languid, beautiful Countess of Tunstall, was also at their table together with the gentleman he had first taken to be the Earl since he was here so frequently, until Tatiana had enlightened him. He was her cousin, Hugh Francis, and Tatiana was convinced that all languidness vanished when they were alone together. Tonight the young and giddy Miss Dazey was with them; it was her first season in society and, as they all knew to their cost, her first on a motorcar. She took both at the same dashing pace. Unknown to her parents, she had also developed a passion for young Leo, Fred Gale's good-looking assistant.

By the time the entremets arrived, Auguste had relaxed and barely cast them a glance for imperfections. All around talk seemed to be of the Dolly Dobbs and speculation as to what magic it could possess that could give it a greater range than twenty-five miles out and twenty-five miles back. *Magic?* Magic was not for motorcars; it was for entremets, and entrées. Happily Auguste looked forward to the presentation of the *cerises à la reine*.

He looked round for Luigi, and to his horror saw him locked in hissing angry argument with Pierre who was making a completely illegal and unscheduled appearance in the dining room.

'*What* is this, and why are you here?' he demanded furiously, leaping up, prepared to investigate calamity.

Luigi was happy to enlighten him. 'It's the cherries, Mr Didier. I'm sorry to say I've a complaint that they're burned.'

'If *he* comes to my place of work, then I can come to his,'

Pierre informed his superior sulkily. 'They are *not* burned.'

'Let me taste them,' Auguste ordered grimly.

He was eagerly handed a dish of *cerises à la reine* and, all pleasure in the prospect vanished, he tasted the dish. It was stronger than usual, too much kirsch perhaps, but burned? Perhaps that was— Auguste was suddenly aware that no one was paying either him or the cherries their due attention.

The eyes of the whole room were riveted on the entrance to the restaurant where, posed at the top of the three steps, was a late diner. The face was familiar to Auguste – it had much been in the *Illustrated London News*, even though he had not been present on her earlier visits to the club. It was an interesting face, if not conventionally handsome. It belonged to Hester Hart who was clad ostentatiously in Arabian dress. It was not her dress, however, that was causing such a sensation this evening. She was possessively clasping the arm of someone very familiar to the Ladies' Motoring Club. It was Roderick Smythe, famous racing driver and fiancé of Phyllis Lockwood; he stood self-consciously but pink with pride, looking everywhere but in the direction of the Bullinger-Lockwood table.

Astonishment ranged from the mildly curious to outright shock, Auguste observed, once he was over his own surprise. Harold Dobbs looked frightened, Lady Bullinger furious, the Countess highly amused, Hugh embarrassed, and poor Phyllis Lockwood was white with horror.

Luigi, diplomatically impervious as ever, showed the new arrivals to a table as far from Phyllis's as possible. But Hester went out of her way to choose a route that led them past her rival. Ignoring all rules of polite dining, she stopped and cried loudly for the edification of the room. 'Hugh, how delightful. And Edward too.' A pause, then: 'And dear Agatha, Isabel and Maud. So wonderful to see you again. And Phyllis too of course.' The latter greeting was perfunctory.

'I was right,' Tatiana hissed. 'She's trouble.'

Unable to disagree, Auguste abandoned the cherries and took refuge in the *pêches Maintenon*. They, at least, were exquisite.

Chapter Two

Hester Hart bit into her muffin. It was not fresh. This Mayfair house was rented, servants included; she had made the mistake of viewing the former but not the latter. However, nothing could spoil her good humour today. She had been satisfied with the results of her carefully planned appearance last night. She had been far from satisfied to hear that she was not to become a committee member but this had served to harden her resolve as regards those responsible for the decision. It was as hard as the muffin on her plate.

She rang the bell, and her cook-general duly appeared though rather tardily.

'More muffins, if you please, Smirch. I would prefer them warm when they arrive, and to be of today's baking.'

Hannah Smirch's feet were hurting her, and the fresh muffins had been reserved for herself. She had realised at once that Madam did not know how to treat servants, and she and Peters, 'the man', had decided the sooner this madam left their house the better. And that wouldn't be long now, or her name wasn't Hannah Smirch.

Hester, oblivious of the dire fate ahead of her, contemplated her next move. The success of her first move in the game (in which the rules were known only to herself), together with the slight setback of her not becoming a committee member, decided it for her. She would marry Roderick, a gambit which would have many advantages and present few difficulties. She did not include Phyllis among the latter, although Roderick was thirty-five to her own – well, thirty-nine. Compared with Phyllis, however, she had much more to offer a virile, mature and good-looking man: wit, attractiveness, achievement and accomplishments in intimate matters that could hardly be matched in the prim beds of London ladies. She grinned at the memory of Roderick's delight when she had first blushingly yielded her virtue to him (or so he thought). One did not travel in the East for nothing; even Sir Richard Burton in search of material for detailed explanatory footnotes for his unexpurgated edition of *The Arabian Nights* did not, by virtue of his sex, have easy access to harems, and within them the most fascinating ideas could be gleaned on *ghunj*, the art of moving during the sexual act (some of which she had speedily put into practice).

Yes, marriage to Roderick would be quite tolerable; he at least had an interest in sexual matters, thanks to his participation in the Paris-Vienna, Paris-Berlin, and countless other Continental road races, in which she gathered from him the rewards along the route could take many forms according to individual choice. Most Englishmen would be satisfied with a foot-warmer en route, she thought scornfully, but Roderick had due regard for the comfort of other parts of his body.

Contemplating marriage to Roderick had brought her to her second plan. Thanks to the foolishness of darlings Maud, Agatha, Phyllis and Isabel, not to mention Tatiana, in not electing her to the committee, she had now fully decided on her own future career. She, too, would become a Racer. She had driven motorcars all over Europe and as far as Turkey; her negotiation of what passed for roads both there and in the rest of the world was second to none. Mules, camels, horses, all required driving – what more was the motorcar than a glorified horse? And that thought reminded her of yesterday's demonstration by the Horse Against Motor Car Society, to which she had been a witness. There she had seen an old foe, well worthy of joining the list of those to rue the day they had upset her. Yes, all in all, the next few weeks were going to be extremely interesting for Hester Hart.

Wednesday proved less than interesting for Auguste. Not called upon today for his services in the club kitchen, he was reluctantly struggling with *Dining With Didier*. Why did the recipes that flowed so easily from his brain in a kitchen refuse to communicate the same enthusiasm when he set his pen to the page? When their cook Mrs Jolly had first blessed the Didier home in Queen Anne's Gate with her presence, her son Charlie seemed the ideal Boswell for Auguste's Dr Johnson. Unfortunately Charlie's enthusiasm for eating compared with writing was the same as Auguste's, and when he developed a passionate interest in Annie Parsons, the club's head kitchen maid, which in turn had led to his offering his services to Annie's father who ran a fish stall in Bermondsey Market, it seemed as if *Dining With Didier* was destined for ever to be denied to the world.

'Auguste!'

He was saved from the torment of indecision over whether *chanterelles* required a sauce. Tatiana was here. True, she was not looking happy as she sank into a chair; even her muslin dress looked limp. It was one of the disadvantages of the club for Tatiana that she was obliged to wear conventional feminine attire rather than the curious working clothes of bloomers, smock and man's cap that she adopted when she had first opened her School of Motoring two years ago. Since the School of Motoring still flourished next door to the club, she kept the aforesaid curious attire at the club to change into – a great disappointment to those working and living by St James's Park District Railway Station who had grown accustomed to the strange figure hurrying by twice a day.

'A bad day, *ma mie*?' The question was almost redundant as he saw her face.

'Yes. For the club, for me, for *everyone*. Everyone wishes to talk about how terribly Hester Hart has behaved but how she is no lady and it should therefore be expected.'

'Perhaps she merely met Roderick Smythe on the way to the club?' Auguste suggested fairly.

'Phyllis arrived this afternoon in tears,' was Tatiana's mournful answer. 'She seemed to blame *me*. The problem with being president is that whether you were involved in something or not, everyone is entitled to think you might have been. She had confronted Roderick.'

'What did he have to say for himself?'

'She followed him from his home to his barber's in Jermyn Street and then, from what I can gather, pounced on the poor man as he sat there having his hair trimmed – to the great delight of the barber's shop, clients *and* staff. Having the famous Phyllis Lockwood gracing their premises brought in so many gentlemen in need of a sudden shave that there was a queue. Then Phyllis simply harangued him.'

'What did he reply?' Auguste felt a sneaking man-for-man sympathy for Roderick.

'He pointed out that if he was as worthless as she claimed, someone as beautiful and famous as she could not possibly want to marry him.'

'And what happened next?' Roderick Smythe was obviously

a subtler man than Auguste had given him credit for.

'Phyllis agreed, and handed him back his ring.'

'Then why was she in tears?'

'Auguste, have you *no* idea how a woman's mind works? Because she does want to marry him, she loves him. I told her to have patience, Roderick would soon tire of Hester. A very tiring woman, I'd say.'

'Did she listen to you?'

'No. Unfortunately Maud arrived at that moment. As you know, she's Roderick's godmother. I gather that although she voted for Hester to join the committee, having her marry her godson is a different matter. It was very strange. She was vehement about it, much more than I would expect. She even counselled Phyllis to sue for breach of promise.'

'With half the gentlemen in London having witnessed that it was she who broke the engagement?'

'I know. But having Maud raging around like a bull in a kitchen is not good for the club. On the other hand, Roderick is one of our top international racing drivers, and he's very popular. It was thanks to him the Motor Club of Great Britain agreed to hold the official road trials for the Dolly Dobbs at one of our events, so how can I intervene in his private life?'

'And how is the dear Dolly Dobbs?' Auguste saw an opportunity to distract Tatiana.

It worked. 'With all this going on today, I haven't had much time to inquire. Fred and Leo have been working on it all day, with Harold Dobbs clucking around like a mother hen. Not to mention Mrs Judith Dobbs.'

'She is a member?'

'No, but where Harold goes, Mrs Dobbs goes too if she can possibly manage it. That's another situation that worries me, Auguste.'

'Judith?'

'No. The Dolly Dobbs. It's all too quiet.'

'I thought electric cars were meant to be silent.'

'Don't be silly, Auguste,' was all he received for his pains. 'I meant I think Hortensia must be planning something. We can't leave it in its stable locked up until next Thursday because it has to be tested to make sure it's running properly. So we were planning to bring it out on Saturday.'

'What do you think she could do to it?'

'I don't know. That's the problem with the Hams. Do keep an eye open for suspicious characters hanging around the stable. They feel very strongly about doing away with motorcars.'

Auguste sympathised. He had often wondered what the poet John Milton, a former resident of Petty France, who had lent his name to the club's premises without being consulted, would have made of being linked to infernal machines. Perhaps it would have inspired a second *Paradise Lost*. He decided that a splendid dinner *à deux* would console Tatiana and was glad that he had asked Mrs Jolly for samphire sauce with the beef this evening.

It failed to work. At breakfast on the Thursday morning, a meal that in Auguste's view should be a tranquil experience, an appetiser for the delights of the repasts to follow, Tatiana was still gloomy. She nevertheless, he noticed, managed to work her way as usual through the array of chafing dishes – kidneys, kedgeree, eggs, tomatoes, mushrooms. How did she manage to remain so slim? He tried to impress her with dire predictions as to what might happen in later years but she merely laughed, despite the fact that those later years were beginning to creep over the horizon, he in his mid-forties, she in her mid-thirties.

Suddenly Tatiana stopped laughing. 'Auguste!' she exclaimed. 'This is terrible.'

'The eggs are not perfect? But Mrs Jolly—'

'Not food. Oh, Auguste, look!' The *Morning Post* was thrust under his nose.

'What at?' He found himself staring at an advertisement for William's Shaving Soap. 'His smile speaks louder than words,' he read.

Not louder than Tatiana's '*Look!*' Her finger pointed to an article headed 'Miss Hester Hart'.

He skimmed through it and gathered that Miss Hart had been chosen as the representative for England in the International Women's Race to be run on the Circuit des Ardennes in October. That the race should be run at all was a great concession by the French government after the tragedies of last year's Paris-Madrid race; it was therefore a great honour to participate.

'But what is so terrible about that?' he asked cautiously.

'Maud was counting on being chosen.'

'Had she been formally asked?'

'No, but she has represented the club in many other racing events and naturally she expected to do so this time.'

'And this is an important race?'

'Important?' Tatiana was indignant. 'To be chosen for the first such international contest for women alone is like being asked to cook for Monsieur Escoffier himself.'

'I see.' Auguste was impressed.

'And there's worse if you read on,' Tatiana said hollowly.

Auguste did. Even he realised the import of the next piece of information. '"Miss Hart will also be driving the new experimental Dolly Dobbs motorcar on its official road trials to be held . . . " But you said Agatha was to drive it.'

'I know. She would never, *never* have changed her mind, and Harold Dobbs would be in no position to change it for her even if he'd wanted to. Auguste,' her voice quavered, 'I really *do* smell trouble.'

There was nothing he could say. So could he.

Lady Bullinger stalked to the instrument her husband had installed for the servants' convenience in conjuring up instant supplies of smoked salmon from Senn's Delicacies whenever he chose to visit London. Emergencies were emergencies, and some, like today's, could not be dealt with by butlers. She snatched the appliance off its hook, careful to hold it well away from her ear in view of the warnings about the damage these monstrosities could cause to the hearing, and bawled into it, 'Connect me to the Duchess of Dewbury.'

Agatha had been reading her *Morning Post* at exactly the same moment, and her voice came almost immediately on to the line as she hurtled to snatch their own instrument from the butler's hand. Her usual tinkle was a definite screech. 'Have you read it?' she cried.

'It's a joke,' Maud trumpeted, 'to annoy us.'

'Hester never makes jokes.'

'I shall summon Roderick immediately. He must tell the Motor Club that it is quite out of the question for that woman to drive in an international race. I shall be participating myself.'

'I suspect you will find,' Agatha said sadly, with just a little relish, 'that Roderick had something to do with this woman being chosen.'

'Nonsense!' Maud barked. 'He knows how I feel about it.' But was it nonsense? The more she thought about it, the more possible such total betrayal seemed to be. He was obviously besotted by the woman and had lost all judgement. Well, Maud Bullinger would be a more formidable opponent than that woman thought. She needed allies, however. 'Agatha, what about the Dolly Dobbs? What is that Dobbs fellow thinking of?'

There was a pause. 'I have no idea. But I shall find out.'

'You seem to be taking this very lightly, Agatha.' Maud was disappointed not to hear bellows of rage to echo her own.

'Do you think so?' her sister-in-law's voice tinkled. 'At the moment I should very much like to murder Miss Hester Hart.'

The lady telephone operator, listening in avidly, shivered deliciously. This confirmed all her worst suspicions as to what went on in ducal residences. Should she inform the police?

Two telephone appliances were replaced on their hooks simultaneously as they planned revenge on the woman against whom they had committed much the same sort of offence fifteen years ago.

Some way away in Bloomsbury, another marital breakfast was taking place, this one in silence since the couple had little in common as regards the day ahead. One was preparing to discuss the ancient ruins of Babylon, and the other to go into battle on behalf of horses. Suddenly a subject of common interest arose, though Hortensia, preoccupied with four-footed friends and the latest outrageous scheme to train horses to accustom them to motorcars, failed to notice her husband's reaction.

'Look at this,' she cried, waving the newspaper excitedly and throwing it under her husband's nose. 'It says at the end that the new monster, Dolly Dobbs, is to be driven not by the dashing Duchess but by Hester Hart, whoever she is. Have you heard of her?' Hortensia read little except about horses and their enemies.

John Millward choked on his toast. Yes, he had heard of her, all too often. He had even glimpsed her among the onlookers when Hortensia insisted on his taking part in that terrible demonstration. He was a mild man who usually wished no harm to anyone, and the feud to which Miss Hart referred at every opportunity in learned circles or anywhere where she thought he might be known had been on her side entirely. The point at issue had been a matter of professional integrity for him, not personal vindictiveness. He had been in Cairo in '98, preparing for the opening of what proved to be the tomb of Amenophis II, when Robert Koldewey had asked his opinion of Hester Hart; he was choosing his team for the Babylon excavations that had produced the ruins of the Tower of Babel. Millward had felt bound to say that though the lady had a penchant for appearing in the newspapers and vaunting her travels – and all credit to her for the latter – she had no background in historical research. The next thing he knew was that he was peacefully having a pipe in Shepheard's Hotel when a virago hurtled through the door, set about him with a parasol and accused him of impugning her honour. A lobby full of English-speaking gentlemen listened with great interest, and since then most of the civilised world apparently believed that he and Hester Hart had spent starry nights under the desert skies, wrapped in passionate embrace – an impression she did everything to strengthen.

He lived in fear that Hortensia would come to hear about this. Had he been a horse she might have done, but as things were, their marriage remained sublimely intact. He was immensely grateful for this, for he adored his wife, though he could not have analysed quite why.

'I wonder what this Dolly Dobbs horror is like in action,' Hortensia mused eagerly. 'I've heard that on Saturday the Ladies' Motoring Club are holding hill trials in Richmond Park, followed by a garden party. Perhaps it will make an appearance there. Let's go.'

'No!'

Hortensia looked surprised. 'You love horses, don't you?'

'Of course,' John replied weakly, wondering whether he might pretend to receive a summons to ancient Assyria on Saturday.

'So that's settled.' Hortensia was well satisfied.

Auguste arrived early at Milton House on the Saturday morning, not through choice since Madam President was still preparing, not herself, but her Léon Bollée motorcar, which meant some time would elapse before the pantaloons would be exchanged for more suitable attire for a princess. She had, she informed him, still to check that the accumulators were charged, that lubricators, grease cups and water tanks were full, and tenderly pack spare exhaust valves, inlet valves, sparking plugs, inner tubes, plus a tool kit that Isambard Brunel might have envied. He, Auguste, had merely to check that buffet food for nearly two hundred people was leaving Petty France in perfect condition and would arrive in Richmond in the same state. A simple task in Tatiana's view.

His task well in hand, curiosity sent Auguste to the rear courtyard where Hester Hart would shortly be arriving for the first public airing of the Dolly Dobbs. Within the repair house he could see Leo moving about, and Miss Dazey, jauntily dressed in a dashing blue dust coat and cap, as his faithful shadow. Outside, however, he suddenly noticed a stranger sprawled full length along the gully of the roof between the motor house and the repair house, and doing his best to peer in at the heavily barred skylight. A spy!

'Who are you?'

At his shout the man twitched like a nervous rabbit, scrambled to the rear of the roof and disappeared. Grimly, Auguste ran to the side of the motor stable in time to catch the intruder by the arm before he could slip away. He was dressed in an old top hat and huge apron. The former he raised, and cleared his throat.

'Morning, guv'nor,' he ventured.

'And good morning to you,' Auguste replied amiably, relaxing his hold. 'You are a window cleaner?'

The man's face relaxed. 'That's it, guv'nor. Sort of odd job man.'

'A very odd job man. All such gentlemen here are known to me. You are not one of them.'

'Got the wrong house,' the man said hopefully, in what he obviously believed was a nonchalant manner.

Auguste caught his arm again as he began to walk away. 'Not so fast, *mon ami*. You are a Ham.'

'No, Auguste.' Contrary to his predictions, Tatiana had arrived, becomingly clad in broderie anglaise and embroidered linen dust cloak. Apart from the dark hair already escaping from its pins, and the fact that she appeared to have only one glove, Tatiana was ready. Her toilette was not foremost in her mind, however. 'This is no Ham. You're Mr Thomas Bailey, aren't you? Mr Dobbs's greatest rival.'

The man flushed. He must have been much the same age as Harold Dobbs, around thirty, but whereas Dobbs had the look of an absent-minded butterfly-collector, Bailey – once he abandoned the pretence of being an odd job man – was a much shorter man, with the air of a fanatical Napoleon set on world conquest.

'I am merely displaying a professional interest,' Bailey announced loftily.

'Then I suggest you display it at Hyde Park Corner next Thursday where we begin the official trials.'

He seized this as welcome dismissal. 'Very well. But I have my suspicions,' he added mysteriously as he left.

'Isn't anyone guarding this motorcar?' Tatiana inquired crossly, hurrying into the repair house.

Attracted by the sound of voices, Fred Gale had just clambered up the circular staircase from the repair house basement. He shook his head indulgently as he saw Miss Dazey devotedly peering over Leo's shoulder as he cleaned one of the new pneumatic tyres with a jeweller's scratchbox. 'Now, now, miss, this is no place for you.'

Leo, relief on his face, greeted Fred and Tatiana as his saviours.

'Leo doesn't want me here either. Isn't he silly, Mr Didier?' she greeted him cheerfully, as Tatiana went to talk to Fred.

Looking at her, Auguste could only agree, while Leo muttered, 'I've got work to do,' in the time-honoured way of all harassed men.

'Working on darling Dolly, I expect.' Miss Dazey paused provocatively at the communicating door to the Dobbs's motor house. She put her hand on the knob, causing Leo to spring forward, detaching the hand, and providing his body as a human shield against her invasion of Dolly's secrets. 'We'll all see it in a moment,' Miss Dazey pointed out, hurt.

'But not till Mr Dobbs says,' Leo said firmly.

In answer, her arms crept round his neck and, spread-eagled as he was, he could do nothing to prevent her planting a kiss on his cheek. 'It's at a very delicate stage.'

'It is not a soufflé, *mon ami*, it is only a motorcar,' Auguste pointed out, laughing, just as Harold Dobbs arrived with his wife.

'The Dolly Dobbs is more than a motorcar.' Its proud inventor brimmed over with pride. 'Like Icarus and Daedelus, I reach for the sun.'

'You're wonderful, Harold.' The faithful Judith, clad in an old-fashioned mackintosh hood, three times as large as Napoleon's tricorne, stood staunchly at his side.

'Is Miss Hart here?' Harold demanded.

'Not yet.' Tatiana joined them. 'And Mr Dobbs, just why have you changed your mind about the Duchess driving your car next week? And do you propose Miss Hart should drive it today as well?'

Harold went pink. 'Certainly. Miss Hart is a professional driver,' he said unhappily. 'The Duchess quite understands.'

'Does she? Then why is she marching across the courtyard in such a determined manner?' Tatiana inquired.

Harold took one nervous glance at Her Grace and rushed down the staircase leading to the basement, swiftly followed by his wife.

Agatha swept in in primrose silk and a fine temper. 'Where is he?' She looked round, and when Tatiana indicated the basement, she marched to the staircase. 'Come up here, you foolish little man.'

After a moment Harold sheepishly emerged, bowing to the Duchess and removing his cap.

Agatha wasted no time on formalities. 'Is the Dolly Dobbs ready for me? If so, conduct me to it.'

'Er . . . '

Agatha whirled round to address Tatiana. 'Kindly ignore that rubbish in the *Morning Post*, Your Highness. I shall be driving *my* car.'

'Mine,' squeaked Harold in a semblance of spirit.

'I do not intend to argue with you, sir. Take me to my car.'

Defeated, Harold went to the communicating door, followed by a triumphant Agatha, and opened it.

Greeting them on the threshold was Hester Hart. 'My dear Agatha.' Her handsome face, topped by a rakish tam o'shanter, and topping an unbecoming lilac dust coat boasting two long rows of silver buttons, looked amused. 'Surely you leave driving to the servants? So I shall drive and you can take your rightful place in the rear seat. The motor servant's seat is low. I shall not impede your view.'

Auguste was riveted and stepped forward as if to intervene. Tatiana's hand restrained him. Hester advanced into the repair house, preventing Agatha from seeing the car. Harold pressed himself against the work bench in pursuit of invisibility, Mrs Dobbs was looking mystified, Leo had vanished and Miss Dazey after him. Fred was apparently engrossed in tidying his set of duplicate keys. The Duchess stood stock still, and Tatiana trembled for her club. All eyes were on the Duchess. She said nothing for a moment, and then, amazingly, she ceded victory. She was even smiling.

'My dear Hester,' she said sweetly, 'if Harold wishes you to drive *our* motorcar, then drive you shall. Far be it from me to seek to spoil your hour of glory. Or Harold's. I am quite sure you are the better driver.' She glanced at the bright sunshine, snapped up her chiffon-frilled parasol with its clusters of forget-me-nots as though the damaging rays of the sun were her only concern, and walked briskly away.

Even Hester was surprised. Then she regained her composure. 'What a charming woman Agatha is. One of my oldest friends.'

'Something very strange is going on,' whispered Tatiana to Auguste, as Harold, confidence regained, marched through the communicating door to the Dolly Dobbs. 'When the serpent hisses, he usually has something to hiss about.'

'Is the serpent Hester or Agatha?'

'Both.'

Only Harold and Hester were allowed inside the holy of holies. Tatiana, Auguste, Mrs Dobbs, Fred, Leo and Miss Dazey were forced to gather outside, and Harold Dobbs took one step further down in Tatiana's estimation. By now Auguste's curiosity about what the Dolly Dobbs would be like now it was completed was sufficient to overlook the fact that it was a motorcar.

As Fred Gale was at last allowed to throw back the doors of the motor house, the sound of the Dolly Dobbs's horn tooted in triumph, and the car itself, Hester at the wheel, began to move forward with Harold, almost weeping with excitement, running beside it.

Tatiana clutched Auguste's arm. 'What on earth are *those*?'

If this was a motorcar, it was the most extraordinary-looking one Auguste had ever seen. High up, perched on each of the front mudguards, was what at first sight appeared to be an enormous phonograph horn. At the front of each one was a gaily-coloured windmill with eight blades each painted in a different colour. A sprightly weathercock clung daintily to the curved dash in front of the steering pillar. It rather resembled the last pantomime dragon Auguste had seen at Drury Lane.

After her first surprise, Tatiana ran forward to inspect this monstrosity, which was evidently nothing new to Hester who sat smugly in the driving seat.

'What *are* they?' Tatiana demanded, stopping by the 'phonograph horns' and their accompanying apparatus.

Harold glowed. 'They are wind machines. I have discovered the secret of perpetual motion.'

'The name of Dobbs will be written in the history of science,' shrieked Judith, the mackintosh hood falling over one eye in her excitement.

'The laws of physics do not permit perpetual motion,' Auguste pointed out dubiously. Surely where Ancient Greece had failed to supply an answer, it was very unlikely that Upper Norwood would succeed.

'It is very simple,' Hester announced loftily, instantly assuming proprietorial rights. 'Wind blows in as the car moves forward and is converted by the dynamo and motor into electricity to recharge the battery as fast as it discharges.'

'The voltmeter will always show around two volts per cell,' Harold explained. 'I got the idea from my daughter Dolly's paper windmill which she bought at the Zoo. That's why I've painted the propeller blades these colours – to please Dolly.'

'Suppose there is a tailwind, or no wind at all, or the wind is not coming from the front?' Tatiana asked doubtfully.

'Naturally Mr Dobbs has thought of that,' Hester snapped. 'The weathercock tells me if the wind has changed. I have a handle here on my left,' she bent down and jerked it and the huge cowl on the left mudguard promptly swung round through 360 degrees, 'and on my right.' The right-hand cowl obediently followed suit. 'Dolly Dobbs can catch the wind from whatever direction it comes from. If there *is* no wind, merely driving the car forward will create it. I shall be honoured to drive this wonderful invention on its official trials.'

Only because, Auguste reflected, of the glory it would reflect on Hester Hart. He agreed with Tatiana: he did not like Hester Hart. She had charm, but then so did Medusa.

'You'll certainly attract notice,' Tatiana commented, still convinced there must be a flaw in Harold's theory and longing to see the car in motion. 'We've kept the car's appearance today a secret, but if Mr Bailey managed to see anything before we stopped him just now, it's possible—'

'Thomas Bailey *here*?' Harold interrupted. 'Are you sure?' He went very pale.

'Yes,' Tatiana said blithely. 'I recognised him at once. Isn't he rumoured to be working on a new car too?'

Harold clutched his brow feverishly, ignoring Tatiana's question. 'Take her back into the motor house,' he unwisely ordered Dolly's driver in a strangled voice.

'Nonsense,' Hester retorted.

'*Take it back!*' Harold was so agitated he appeared to be about to pull Hester Hart down bodily. She cast them a look, jumped down from the car and marched inside the motor house, beckoning meaningfully to Harold and banging the doors shut after them.

With bated breath, they waited while the sound of raised voices came from within.

'I back Hester,' Tatiana said with glee.

'So do I.'

'I don't.' Judith glared at them. Her faith was justified, for five minutes later they both reappeared. Harold had won, for he climbed on to the driving seat of the Dolly Dobbs and reversed her into the motor house. Hester Hart, without another word but with lips angrily compressed, walked over to where Roderick Smythe had drawn up in the yard.

Seeing her face, he leapt from the car and ushered her

devotedly to the driving seat of his new Crossley.

'What do you make of *that*?' Tatiana asked as they drove away without a backward glance. 'I never thought I'd see Harold Dobbs get the better of Agatha *and* Hester.'

'Yet he does not seem happy with his victory,' Auguste observed. Far from it; he looked extremely nervous. Why had the mention of Bailey so alarmed him? And what had the Duchess in mind? Remembering her unusual behaviour, he was convinced she had a plan for revenge. Next Thursday promised to be even more interesting than he had hoped.

'Pierre, have you packed the *sauce remoularde* for the *mousse de crabe*?'

'*Naturellement*, Monsieur Didier,' Pierre answered him patiently. And the horseradish sauce for the quails, and the *sauce chocolat* for the bavarois, and the apricot syrup for the chestnut soufflé pudding, and the hundred and one other details that a luncheon buffet and tea in the grounds of a country house at Richmond would require.

After the hill trials on Petersham Hill in Richmond Park, in which the ladies would compete for the best times between two points, the Dysart Arms in Petersham Road, and the Star and Garter Hotel's main entrance on the hilltop, the best twenty would compete again on 'Test Hill' in Richmond Park, between what Tatiana had referred to as the 'usual oak trees'.

Auguste was not entirely happy. The Dolly Dobbs episode did not bode well for convivial club gatherings today. Moreover, Pierre's patisserie inclined to the oversweet. As well as cream, his *millefeuilles* positively oozed honey. Delightful, but unusual. He watched the staff in the last throes of hectic preparation. Once he would have been a bustling part of it, this final onslaught, but now his role was supervisory only.

Today's banquet was Pierre's responsibility, next Thursday's would be his. Yet Pierre did not seem overjoyed at his privilege.

'Something is troubling you, Pierre?' he asked eventually. 'The cold duck, perhaps?'

'That dog.'

'Dog?' Auguste was unable to recall any recipe requiring such ingredients.

'Working with Luigi Peroni is no pleasure, maître.'

'Any trouble today is more likely to stem from Miss Hart, I fear.' Auguste had spoken unguardedly. Gone were the days when his life belonged solely to this side of the green baize door.

'Mr Smythe has returned to Miss Lockwood?' Pierre asked with interest.

'No, but the debut of the Dolly Dobbs has been postponed until next Thursday.'

'She cannot have been pleased.'

'She was not.' Auguste hesitated. 'You must help me keep a watch on the motorcar until next Thursday, watch for *anyone* trying to get into the motor house.'

'Miss Hart would surely not harm the motorcar.'

'No, but others might.'

'Or harm her?' Pierre asked anxiously. 'She is a splendid woman.'

Auguste glanced at him curiously. 'Yes, but she is the prune in a dish of delicate peaches. Too harsh, too dark. She overshadows all around her.'

The last baskets left the kitchen for the motor vans outside. To Auguste, who had reluctantly agreed that motor vans were the most sensible form of transport for a precious buffet, their radiators and lamps seemed to be grinning at him with some secret knowledge as he emerged into the courtyard where the cavalcade was lined up.

Winter House, whose grounds ran down to the river bank, was a Georgian brick mansion which had belonged to the Francis family ever since it had been built. The present incumbent, Hugh Francis, cousin and lover of Isabel, Countess of Tunstall, was a bachelor who undoubtedly merited the description of a 'swell'. It said much for his cousinly (or other) devotion that he was prepared to allow over a hundred motorcars to bump over his grass. Such considerations were trivial beside the attractions of Isabel.

Auguste's nose for trouble, however, was twitching like a diviner's hazel twig over a waterfall. This waterfall must be underground, however, for looking round he could see nothing to justify his anxiety. The ladies and their passengers had now arrived from the hill trials, and Tatiana's whispered information that Hester Hart had won the hill trials in the Crossley with times of 1 minute 42 seconds on Petersham Hill and an astounding 1 minute 48 seconds on Test Hill had not so far ruined the day. Nor had the thrilling news that Maud had side-slipped on to the grass behind her, or that poor Phyllis's benzine tank had been filled with water at an inn by a misguided ostler. Auguste told himself modestly that his buffet, even though he was just supervising this one, could always be counted on to cheer the most aggrieved of spirits.

It had clearly done so this time. He glanced round at the colourful assembly on the lawns, dust coats discarded and parasols sprouting like exotic cabbages. He had been wrong. All would be well.

'What are you going to do about that woman, Agatha?' Maud

Bullinger bit viciously into an éclair. 'You're not going to let her drive the Dolly Dobbs, are you?'

'Are you going to let her drive in the International Women's Race?' the Duchess countered.

'Out of my hands.' Maud looked at her heavy fingers as though she'd like to strangle the lady.

'And mine.' Agatha smiled brightly.

'You're up to something, aren't you?' Maud suddenly realised.

'There are more ways to kill a cat, as the old saying goes.'

'Be careful, Agatha,' Maud frowned. 'We don't want that old story raked up again.'

Both women rearranged their faces as the Duke ambled towards them. 'My dear,' his Duchess informed her sister-in-law, 'I quite forgot I hadn't dropped the sprog; I almost dropped it when the Horbick started running backwards but then I remembered . . . '

Edward, Duke of Dewbury, put an expression of polite interest on his face and decided to track down old Hugh for the latest cricket score. Women never talked about anything of interest.

Some wasted little time in talk at all. Isabel was in bed with Hugh in an upper room in Winter House. She had long since exhausted her interest in discussing average speeds, times and pneumatic tyres. She had taken part in the hill trials solely for the sake of form; she cared not a whit that Hester Hart had won. She cared rather more that the lady was to take such a prominent part in next Thursday's run to Canterbury. As mistress of Martyr House, she expected to star in her role; instead, that woman would be – if this Dolly Dobbs vehicle performed well – graciously received by His Majesty, who might well learn from her the story of how he had earlier been deprived of that privilege. Depending on his mood, he might laugh or he might dismiss Isabel from his court for ever. And *that* wasn't going to happen.

'Darling, where are you?' Hugh's voice whispered in her ear.

Isabel was suddenly aware that she was wasting precious minutes of Hugh's foreplay, all because of that woman, and exerted herself to show due appreciation as became her role of sultry and seductive mistress.

'Nonsense.' Hester smiled fondly at Roderick. 'I know you are as impatient as I am. Let it be today.' She used the look that had melted hearts from the Euphrates to the Yukaton.

For once Roderick was less than eager. His eye strayed to Phyllis Lockwood who was forlornly twirling her parasol and talking to Sir Algernon Bullinger, a far from animated conversationalist. Hester's eye strayed that way too, and her ill temper increased. Victories should be consolidated, whether in hill climbs or personal life. 'I shall think you are regretting wanting to marry me if we don't announce it today.'

Roderick was horrified. 'Never, *never*.' What, do without those exquisitely tormenting tricks of Hester's? He had, however, drawn the line at having his johnnie stung by a bee before he began. He'd had many interesting amorous experiences during his racing career but Hester had crowned them all; she was the Queen who had conquered the Desert of his Life, as he had romantically put it to her. No, he couldn't let her go. With some effort, he turned his back on Phyllis and devoted himself to Hester who was now talking to Tatiana. With ladies, even princesses, Hester used less charm than with gentlemen.

'I'm still prepared to join your committee,' she informed Tatiana challengingly.

'I'm afraid that's not possible this year now the vote has been taken.' Tatiana tried to look regretful.

Auguste, watching with some anxiety from his privileged position behind the *pièce montée* (in the shape of a car), saw Hester's lips tighten. It was fortunate he was not close enough to hear Hester's reply to his wife: 'You are right to be afraid, Your Highness.'

'I am among friends,' snarled Hester from a rostrum conveniently provided by a grassy bank. Hugh had agreed she might address the assembly albeit somewhat ungraciously, but her 'friends' were congregating extremely slowly. 'Under the stars, under an Arabian sky, how often have I longed for England's green fields—'

To Auguste's delight, Hester's address was abruptly terminated by what seemed to be a cloud of dust travelling up the drive, emitting war whoops. As the dust cleared, he saw it was caused by a dozen or so horses galloping at full stretch, led by what appeared to be Buffalo Bill himself in front, with Annie Oakley at his side. All dozen riders were brandishing placards like tomahawks, all reading 'Down With the Dolly Dobbs'. The Hams had arrived to save the day.

'Listen to me,' Hester shouted in vain as the troop drew to a halt and her audience was surrounded by a circle of horses and dismounting riders in Wild West costume. All save Buffalo Bill himself who, much to Hortensia's surprise, promptly if inexpertly tried to hide behind his charger.

Auguste hurried forward just as Hester spotted John Millward. 'Have you yet taken tea?' he inquired politely, edging between Hester and her prey.

Hortensia grinned at him. 'Good fodder, is it?'

'Both for you, madam, and the horses.'

'Any old *foie gras* will do for me. Then lead me to this Dolly monster.'

Auguste began to like Hortensia. 'I'm afraid Dolly stayed at home.'

'Never mind,' she replied cheerfully. 'We'll puncture some tyres instead.'

'Stop trying to hide, John,' Hester Hart said grimly.

Buffalo Bill bravely emerged from behind his horse. 'Good afternoon, Hester.'

'John is a very *old* and *close* friend of mine,' Hester cried loudly to the assembled company. 'Not so much now as in the old days,' she cooed. 'Remember the caravan to Palmyra, John?'

'What caravan?' Hortensia demanded curiously.

'There was no caravan,' John squeaked.

'You are being a gentleman, John,' Hester pouted.

'I see no lady.' John surprised himself with his own repartee.

Hester turned white with fury. 'Get out of the way, you fool,' she yelled at the unfortunate Pierre who was trying to intervene with a plate of éclairs at Auguste's instigation.

Auguste controlled his indignation, unlike Hester.

'Very well,' she shouted. 'All my kind *friends* are gathered here now. I am very moved, remembering the old days, when we were all so much *closer*. It has moved me to two decisions. I shall grant Roderick his dearest wish and become his wife.' She looked round venomously at the horrified faces. 'Secondly, I know the modesty of all my friends forbids any request to see their past kindnesses to me recorded in print but I do now feel they deserve recognition. Fortunately, I have preserved all my diaries, and now I have accepted an offer to publish my memoirs.'

Edith Rose flushed proudly as their maid Ethel, scared out of her sixteen-year-old wits at serving not only a French sir and madam but a princess to boot, staggered in with a large dish and proceeded inexpertly to ladle portions into plates.

'Not Mrs Marshall's *soupe à l'Augustine*? Edith, you spoil us,' Tatiana said valiantly.

'I can't compete with your Mrs Jolly, of course,' Edith replied modestly.

'Mrs Jolly could not produce this,' Auguste assured her sincerely. Firstly, Mrs Jolly would have been instantly dismissed if any of Mrs Marshall's recipes had appeared on his table. Great lady and famous cook she might be. So had Alexis Soyer been. But not to Auguste Didier, maître chef; his professional allegiance was to Maître Escoffier. Secondly, incomparable cook though Mrs Jolly was, Edith, who had no doubt struggled all day to prepare this, had included an ingredient that Mrs Jolly, by the nature of her employment, could not use: love. What could be happier for himself and Tatiana than an evening at the Highbury home of his friend Chief Inspector Egbert Rose of Scotland Yard? For the moment he dismissed the thought of what had prompted his desire to see Egbert. No dinner should be ruined by such matters; instead it was devoted to discussion of the two weeks they were shortly to spend together at Eastbourne. It was not until they were settled in the small conservatory Edith loved so much, watching the dying light over the garden, that the subject could be broached in a general, not official, way, since ladies were present. Not too general, as far as Egbert was concerned.

'Haven't brought me a body, have you? You haven't got Pyotr Gregorin propped up in the rear seat of that motorcar of yours, have you, Tatiana?'

Auguste shuddered. Even in jest the name of Gregorin reminded him all too vividly of the other disadvantage of marrying into the Romanov family. Gregorin, a member of the Czar's dreaded Okhrana, had a personal mission to remove Auguste Didier from the world for his temerity in marrying Gregorin's niece. Like the anarchists, Gregorin employed patience as a weapon, but Auguste had little hope that the mission would be abandoned. Nor had Egbert, and periodic jests were his way of ensuring Auguste had not relaxed his guard.

'Nothing to do with Gregorin, Egbert. We want your advice on how to prevent a murder,' Tatiana replied quickly, well aware of Auguste's struggling emotions.

'Not my department. You want that fellow Freud for that. The *id*.'

'The what, Egbert?' Edith asked, puzzled.

'*Id*.'

'Oh.'

'Let me explain.' With relief, Auguste expounded on Hester Hart and the storm clouds gathering over next Thursday's trials, not to mention the furore the threat of memoirs had produced. The chill that had come over the senior members of the club for the rest of yesterday afternoon had been noticeable.

Edith broke the silence when he had finished. 'She doesn't sound a very *nice* lady, Egbert.'

'Unfortunately, the Yard doesn't deal in niceness, or nasty atmospheres, and that, I gather, is all you have to go on.' He looked at Auguste.

'My nose,' Auguste replied with dignity.

'I've every respect for it but even your nose can't tell the difference between a bad egg and a murder. Let's take what you've told me and analyse it. Is it Hester Hart or this Dolly Dobbs car that's the key to this smell of yours?'

'I don't know,' Auguste confessed.

'Then you'd better make your mind up. If it's the car, you've come to the wrong person. I don't deal with cars put out of action, only people. And a ladies' motoring run doesn't seem a very likely occasion for that.'

'Even when the event will have His Majesty at the end of it?'

A long silence, then Egbert said savagely, 'Not again, Auguste, not *again*.'

Chapter Three

Ill temper permeated the kitchen like over-boiled Brussels sprouts. How could it spread so quickly? Auguste fumed. Surely it could not be mere chance that made Pierre snap at Annie who burst into tears, which made the vegetable chef, who was sweet on her, shout at one of the scullery maids who promptly took it out on the other two, which emboldened the pastry chef to impugn the honour of the sauce chef's mother and the meat chef to choose this Tuesday morning to fight out with the fowl and game chef the relative merits of their specialities. An atmosphere of bad temper was unpleasant to work in, and what was worse was that food manhandled by warring parties all too readily picked up the implications and refused to obey any of the known laws of cuisine. And in two days' time His Majesty the King of England and Emperor of 400,543,713 people would be expecting a banquet served at the usual Auguste Didier peak of perfection.

Instant action must be taken. It was Pierre's responsibility to do so, but Pierre, last glimpsed brandishing his kitchen knife over his head to illustrate his point to Annie, now seemed to have vanished. He, Auguste, as usual must solve the crisis.

'*Attention!*' he screamed at his seething cauldron of a kitchen.

There was a surprisingly instant silence.

'Why,' he continued formidably, 'is the jelly for tonight's *truites froides* shivering in fright? Why is the celebration cake mixture clinging in terror to its bowl and *why* are the snipe for the *côtelettes de Bécassines à la Souvaroff*, specially imported for His Majesty's favourite dish, threatening to fly back to their native habitat? *Why?*'

The silence remained unbroken, since his staff correctly assumed any answer would not be highly regarded.

'I will tell you why,' Auguste continued. 'It is because cooking is a work of art as well as routine toil. The joy of the artist is mysteriously transferred to his creation. So is his misery. The poet, the painter, the gardener, the musician know this. *Why don't you?*'

Again, no answer was forthcoming.

Auguste looked round grimly. 'It is ten o'clock. Monsieur Bernard, the sommelier, is not yet here, so I shall authorise Signor Peroni to open two bottles of the Widow Cliquot's restorative product. This will permit each of you to indulge in a glass of orange juice and champagne. After that, there will be sunshine in your souls, and that is an order.'

To a chorus of gratified approval, Auguste went in search of the maître d'. He was not hard to find; the sound of Italian curses could be heard in the serving room adjoining the restaurant, and from the virulence of the response Auguste guessed they were being hurled at his missing chef. This was too much. He appeared as an avenging Jupiter at the doorway of the room.

'And what is the trouble today?' he inquired solicitously. 'Tarragon, perhaps?'

Neither enlightened him.

'Please excuse me, Monsieur Didier,' Luigi said stiffly with his best maître d' bow. 'A personal difference of opinion.' The air crackled with hostility.

Auguste, his mission and opinion of those who could waste time when the delights of preparing banquets beckoned having been made clear, returned to the kitchen puzzled. The few words he had understood had borne a remarkable similarity to 'Dolly Dobbs', 'Hester Hart' and 'Lady Bullinger'. He supposed it was only natural that the passions of the establishment for which they worked should transmit themselves to the staff, but it was strange that this particular motorcar should be quite so eagerly discussed. He could not recall the kitchens at Stockbery Towers, where he had worked for some years, coming to blows over the merits of the ducal horses and carriages.

The mood in the kitchen improved as the morning progressed, including Pierre's, to Auguste's relief. By the time he met Tatiana for luncheon at Queen Anne's Gate, however, he was still carrying a nagging grievance with him that his staff did not seem to appreciate the delights of preparing a banquet fit for a king. Luncheon was an informal meal to which he usually looked forward, for it could produce delightful surprises concocted from the fertile paradise of Mrs Jolly's creative brain. Today it was her chicken pie, but even the magic of discovering a new taste in it – could it be ginger? – failed to produce a sense of all being right with the world.

'You're troubled, Auguste,' Tatiana remarked at last.

'Aren't you?' He could not explain why the thought of Thursday still loomed like an enormous pile of unwashed saucepans, much higher than the prospect of meeting the King normally engendered. After all, Egbert had reluctantly agreed to accompany the cavalcade to Canterbury, and knowledge of his job and rank should put paid to the possibility of untoward events.

'Yes, but I don't have a black bear sitting on my shoulders like you.'

It occurred to Auguste that his wife seldom did. 'Why not? It's a wife's duty to share her husband's ill humour.'

'I spent the first thirty-three years of my life without you, of which six separated us by a ridiculous barrier because I was a princess and you were the cook. Now I can be with you all the time. What have I to be in an ill humour about?'

The chicken pie regained its full glory. The footman entering five minutes later was scandalised to find his employers locked in a passionate embrace. He reluctantly excused them this improper behaviour on the grounds that neither of them was English.

'All the same,' Tatiana added, sedately resuming her seat, 'I have plenty of reasons for bad temper. Harold Dobbs came to see me *and* Judith . . . '

The Dobbses' breakfast table in Upper Norwood was usually a noisy affair. Judith Dobbs firmly believed, against normal practice, that the gentleman of the household should benefit from proximity to his children instead of being forced to leave for his work before the family breakfasted. Harold had no objection, since his mind was mostly absent anyway; it was glorying in far-off fields where the name of Dobbs took its place beside those of Newton, Watt, Stevenson, Maxim, Hancock, and possibly da Vinci. Harold did not include Cugnot, de Dion or Daimler in the list of those who had served the world on wheels or wings, for to his mind foreigners played little part in the miracle of the motorcar. As far as Harold was concerned, the motorcar was conceived and perfected in England, despite the unfortunate hiccup of the Red Flag Act which drove cars off the road for thirty years. Progress had leapt from William Murdoch's 1784 steam carriage to Harold Dobbs, and in two days' time the full glory of the Dolly Dobbs would be revealed to the world. The tiny fly trapped in the immaculate polish of Harold's future buzzed worryingly, but he immediately swatted it. A mere technical detail could not affect the true artist, save that unfortunately he had had to let that Hart woman drive. He couldn't explain to the Duchess of Dewbury just how this came about but she, like him, he comforted himself, was dedicated to the Dolly Dobbs, and Hester Hart would bring even more publicity for it than a duchess. Harold's optimism about the future regained its usual rosy hue.

Motorcars rose above personal feelings. He had a vision of a future motorcar literally rising, like Hiram Maxim's flying machine. Perhaps they could travel on water . . . His mind wandered, just as Dolly took advantage of his abstraction to tip the contents of the toast rack on to little Billy's lap. Fortunately the maid brought in the morning's post, excusing Harold from involvement in the ensuing fracas. In domestic matters, Judith always felt herself one step away from control, trying in vain to be the perfect mistress of the household that *The Lady* magazine made sound so easy and which was only darling Harold's due.

Darling Harold uttered a yelp of distress.

'Dolly was only playing,' Judith said nervously.

'No, no,' Harold managed to say, choking. 'This – the letter.'

Judith took it. The word letter unduly dignified the communication. Its thick block capitals written apparently without benefit of blotting paper read: THE DOLLY DOBBS WILL NEVER

RUN. Any hope that this might be an objective evaluation of its engineering merits was dashed by the writer's apparent afterthought: I WILL SEE TO THAT.

'What do you think it means?' Harold quavered, helpless in the face of the unthinkable: that someone in the world was not as devoted to the Dolly Dobbs as he was.

Dolly burst into tears, waiting hopefully for her mother's usual instant support. It didn't come, so she bawled, '*I'm* Dolly Dobbs. Why won't I run?'

Billy seized the opportunity to retaliate with a lapful of scrambled egg but to his annoyance was ignored by all but Dolly.

'It means,' Judith said decidedly 'that we must see Mrs Didier immediately.'

Immediately was in the hands of the London, Brighton and South Coast Railway, but obviously realising the importance of the Dolly Dobbs, it deposited them at Victoria Railway Station in plenty of time to ruin Tatiana's morning . . .

Hats, Tatiana decided, revealed mood as well as character. Judith Dobbs's white felt, its front brim curving up like a galleon's prow with a particularly pugnacious figurehead underneath, warned her that trouble was on the way even before the letter had been thrust under her nose by Harold, who seemed incapable of speech.

She read it, greatly perturbed, though her words were comforting. 'Surely this is merely a threat, perhaps from a Ham. One of the members, surely, for I can't think that Mrs Millward would descend to such levels.'

'There are others,' Judith pointed out darkly. 'Jealousy is a powerful force.'

'You mean rivals? I hardly think Thomas Bailey would do such a thing.'

'No. *Women.*'

Tatiana had an instant vision of the Duchess sitting down sedately on a Chippendale chair in Dewbury House, penning this nastiness and handing it gravely to the butler. Or did Judith, she wondered even more wildly, think that nameless hordes of women fighting over the glories of Harold Dobbs's person would take vengeance by such threats? Judith must be calmed, and the Dolly Dobbs made secure, she decided. 'I'm sure it's not a serious threat but I will place a twenty-four-hour guard on the motor stable.'

'Armed,' Judith demanded. 'A stout knobkerrie.'

'Pistol,' Harold at last managed to contribute.

'With a large torch and whistle only,' declared Tatiana firmly.

Mrs Jolly's raspberry charlotte began to look less inviting as Tatiana regaled Auguste with the events of her morning and he was plunged once more back into the nebulous unease. Usually he could pinpoint the cause of disquiet; on this occasion he could not.

'I've spoken to Fred and Leo,' Tatiana told him. 'They'll watch night and day between them. Roderick Smythe insists on taking part too. He was at the stable when I arrived, already covering up the skylight with rubber sheeting and checking the bars.'

'How did he hear of it?'

'That's the worst of it. Hester Hart had a letter too; she promptly threw a fit of high dudgeon and her trusty squire was at her side offering her his trusty sword. Not that that lady needs anyone's trusty sword but her own. She's got more stamina than a camel, and nothing is going to come between Hester Hart and her driving that car on Thursday.'

'Who do you think sent the letters, Tatiana?'

'I've no idea. I can't imagine Hortensia or Thomas Bailey doing such a thing, fanatical though he is.'

'Didn't you tell me he was working on a new car of his own?'

'Yes. But so is half of England. And Thomas is not driving on Thursday, so why should he get so upset about another car doing so? Anyway, even if he succeeded in putting it out of action, Harold could build another.'

'He was concerned enough to snoop round the stable.'

'Professional curiosity. I think it's more likely to be a Ham.'

'Perhaps not. The club has not been a happy place since Hester came. We thought it was because of her but now it seems the problem is both Hester Hart *and* the Dolly Dobbs.'

There was a silence, as the same thought occurred to both of them.

'Agatha couldn't possibly be responsible,' Tatiana burst out. 'She's a—' She broke off, appalled. 'Oh, Auguste, I was going to say "a duchess"! How *could* I? Duchesses have the same passions as everyone else.'

'Perhaps, but you are right in that duchesses would need to feel their position very thoroughly threatened before risking their reputations by such childish threats. Being deprived of driving a motorcar hardly seems to qualify.'

'But those memoirs Hester threatens to write. Suppose, just suppose, the Duchess features in them and her reputation *is* threatened?'

'Then why bother to threaten Harold as well?'

'To hide the real reason.'

Auguste wasn't happy with this. 'No, Harold must be involved somehow, for it is still a mystery as to why he let Hester Hart oust Agatha, *and* why he wouldn't let the car appear last week.'

'Harold is so vague, he may just have changed his mind because Hester let loose her battery of charm on him.'

'He wasn't vague when he heard Thomas Bailey had been prowling around,' Auguste observed.

Tatiana sighed. 'Do you remember the excitement you felt over the banquet you prepared for Monsieur Escoffier's birthday, and the *pièce montée* of Gwynne's Hotel you felt impelled to prepare for Madame Emma Pryde?' Auguste blushed. 'And the very special ball supper for Kalinkova? And—'

'There is no need to continue, my love. Of course I remember.'

'The same passions are aroused by motorcars, as I have often tried to explain. They are more than mere conveyances; they are creations of man's imagination and free artistic spirit, a testament to man's achievement.'

'Hortensia and her supporters don't see it that way,' Auguste muttered.

'Whenever fanatical devotion is involved, you will find it counterbalanced by its opposite. In Hortensia's case, her devotion to horses leads to excessive hatred of motors.'

'Or of Hester, if she has heard the rumours about her husband.'

Maud Bullinger was accustomed to taking risks, especially ones that had been carefully planned. Every time she stepped into a racing car the same thrill swept over her. She had it now. She buttoned her gloves and sallied forth. Her philosophy of life, had she ever entered her own kitchen, would be that omelettes required the breaking of eggs. She'd averted disaster from her family once over Hester Hart and she would do it again. Hester might then retire from the race with a metaphorical puncture and go back to the desert for good, where she could queen it over the natives on the proceeds of those buttons. How dare the woman presume to represent *this* country in an international race? Driving camels, perhaps. Maud snorted in acknowledgement of her humorous thought and mounted the Napier's rear seat. Today Higgins should drive. She needed to plan strategy.

Twenty minutes later she marched into the Carlton Hotel, prepared for battle. The ferns in the Palm Court rustled in fright.

In his Albany rooms, Roderick Smythe nervously prepared for ordeal by Maud. Give him the Paris-Vienna race any time. He knew motorcars, he understood them from accumulators to yokes. The greasiest, muddiest road failed to cause him to side-slip. He only wished he could side-slip old Maud. He was the idol of the crowds on the racetrack, known for his dare-devil adventures. There was Avignon on a Paris to Marseille run when he'd disappeared into a local inn with the outward-going control who was a neat little lady with a twinkle in her eye in place of the usual stolid gendarme. While they were enjoying their *entente cordiale*, thirty motorcars arriving under escort from the inward control failed to have their time of exit stamped and the whole race had to be invalidated. The chaps all had quite a laugh. Roderick disliked being the object of contumely and there was no doubt at all that he was not popular in London. Phyllis on the other hand *was* very popular and rightly so. She was a darling. As Hester had pointed out, however, it was Phyllis who had broken the engagement. He, Roderick, was the aggrieved party, and indeed despite the glories of Hester he was forced to admit he was far from happy. His nights, or the parts of them that English society turned a blind eye to as suitable between as yet unmarried couples (after the servants had gone to bed and before crossing sweepers and milkmen were about) were an exquisite torment of pleasure. Life with Hester was like driving at sixty miles an hour, the wind on your face, living life to the full. That this also meant gnats and dust in your eyes despite the goggles was something he momentarily forgot. Life with Phyllis would have been a bland bread pudding compared to Hester's exotic Nesselrode dessert.

He decided he was much misunderstood, and he suspected the situation was about to get worse. He had an uneasy feeling Maud had been hankering to drive in the International Women's Race herself. 'Let the best woman drive,' Hester had declared, and after seeing her on his Napier, he had no doubts on that score. She had explained it to him in bed the night before her test drive for him, and when he saw what she could do behind a steering wheel, he quite agreed. Perhaps Maud wouldn't. But there was no way Hester could be talked out of it now, was there?

As he entered the Palm Court, Maud sailed towards him like the Boadicea into battle.

'Ah, Roderick. How delightful.' Maud smiled.

'It is indeed, Aunt Maud.' He advanced cautiously and bowed.

'Such a pity Hester was deprived of showing us the Dolly Dobbs on Saturday,' she remarked to open the conversation, once seated at the table. 'But now she is to live in England, she'll have many more such opportunities. I'll introduce her to the organisers of the English ladies' circuit races.'

'You don't mind about the international race?' Roderick nearly dropped his brandy and soda in his amazement.

A hearty bellow. 'Of course not, dear Roderick.' She had every appearance of honesty. 'I did at first, I must confess. An old thing like me –' she swallowed, at forty-eight she was only thirteen years older than he was – 'looks forward to an event like that. But now I know it's still in the family since she's to be my god-daughter-in-law, I'm only too happy. I have enough on hand driving in races in this country. In fact, I had in mind to enter the Scottish Automobile Club's reliability trial next May. Glasgow to London. I'd like a few tips. I'm after the gold, and a nonstop certificate. I've heard there'll be a Mors and an Ariel there. Perhaps you can give me some . . . '

Roderick, flummoxed by this new Maud, managed to say he would be only too delighted to give his aunt whatever help he could.

'I hope Hester wins in October,' Maud continued. 'You'll be married by then, eh? Hope so. Looking forward to seeing more of her on the circuits. She and I can be a team.'

'Yes.' Roderick grew enthusiastic and Monsieur Escoffier's menu regained its appeal. 'Splendid, Aunt Maud.'

'She's a bally good driver. I watched her hands. They're the giveaway. She has the hands of an expert. I expect she'll be driving in the Gordon Bennett eliminating trials next year.'

'Of course not, I shall be doing that,' Roderick replied, slightly shocked. He had had his moment of glory in Germany in June in the Gordon-Bennett Cup race. Averaging forty-one miles an hour over an eleven-hour day wasn't at all bad in itself, considering that was after handicaps in the form of two stray dogs and one stray peasant, the last of which entailed side-slipping the Wolseley into a stall of cabbages but which nevertheless won him a kiss from the comely innkeeper's wife.

'Come on, Roderick. You can both enter. Nothing like a bit of healthy competition.' Maud was as hearty as the caviare and blinis now before her. 'Newspaper men, photographers, even those newfangled moving pictures will all be out there to see Hester win. Phyllis will realise then that there's more to motorcars than posing against the mudguards.'

'Why Hester, Maud?' Roderick asked slowly.

'What do you mean, dear boy?'

'Why should *Hester* win if I'm racing too?'

'Ah, she has the knack. It's like horses. There's an element of fate. You can tell by looking at them which has it going with them, and which hasn't. You're an excellent driver, Roderick, you're a man after all –' it cost her a lot to say this – 'but Hester has the *look* of a winner.'

'I'm sure she won't want to drive after our marriage.' The *cailles aux feuilles de vigne* lost all appeal.

'Why not?'

'Babies and so forth.'

'I do hope so.' Warmth floated towards him over the lobster salad. 'I do look forward to a god-grandson. But it might not be possible. She was at school with Agatha, you know. Her age . . . ' Lady Bullinger diplomatically lowered her voice, then broke off altogether.

'I know she's a little older than me, of course, but after all, love is the most important thing.'

'Hear, hear, Roderick. The sentiment does you every credit,' agreed Maud. 'Love makes the pneumatic tyres of marriage race round, eh?' She laughed heartily, then said in amazement, 'Why, look who's here!'

Roderick, now finding Monsieur Escoffier's best efforts far

from agreeable, glanced up to see a vision of loveliness in pale pink gauze and muslin approaching hesitantly. Had he thought further, he might have been reminded of the entrance of the heroine in *Pink for Miss Pamela* but his eyes were doing his thinking at the moment and they were fully occupied.

'I heard you were dining here, Maud. I didn't realise Roderick—' Phyllis broke off piteously. 'I'll leave of course.'

'You'll do no such thing.' Chivalry well to the fore, Roderick leapt to his feet to hold her chair for her. He had been about to say he was just leaving, anxious to rid himself of disturbing memories of Phyllis in his arms. Something made him change his mind.

He was to regret it. Two minutes after Phyllis had proclaimed her appetite to be small and ordered a *filet de boeuf poêle à la Piémontaise*, there was another interruption. Hester Hart did not bother to pose in pink for their benefit. Firstly she was in muddy mustard yellow which a sales lady had ecstatically described as the colour of the desert, and secondly she was far too angry. She could hardly believe it when her special informant at the club had told her that Roderick was lunching with Lady Bullinger behind her back. She didn't trust that woman an inch. Roderick had told her he was lunching at *his* club. Moreover, that wilting Ophelia was here, Phyllis Lockwood.

'Is there room for a fourth?' Hester inquired dangerously.

'Oh, of course.' Phyllis blushed and looked appealingly at Roderick to save the situation. Maud, delighted at fate's happy strokes, did not want it saving.

It occurred to Roderick that sparks flying from dark eyes might be more exciting than misty blue ones but they were a lot more dangerous. An engine on fire could leave you by the roadside waiting for a Good Samaritan who might never come.

* * *

Having taken luncheon at Richmond during a cousinly visit, Isabel prepared to take her leave.

'I take it you're travelling to Martyr House,' Hugh said casually.

'Darling Hugh, I simply have to be there for the whole of tomorrow. However,' Isabel paused temptingly, 'I plan to come to town again for tomorrow evening, and then I have the perfect excuse for you to accompany me on the run on Thursday, rather than leaving you to travel by railway.'

Hugh thought this out carefully. 'Good. We can dine together at the club tomorrow night – if you're kind enough to invite me.' He laughed.

'Certainly.' Isabel was surprised, but only too willing.

'What's His Majesty going to say if you're not there to greet him?' Hugh was not a modest man but even he could see the attractions of his monarch might outweigh his own in Isabel's beautiful but undoubtedly ambitious eyes.

'He doesn't arrive until Thursday morning at ten o'clock, in plenty of time to receive the club as it arrives.'

'But he'll expect to find you there already. You're the hostess.'

'My work's done,' she told him lightly. 'I've redecorated the whole of the east wing for the one night he'll be staying with us. *And* organised the ball for the evening. So I shall be kind to the Dowager and let her be hostess to His Majesty. In her youth she had a brief, er, friendship with him, and I'm quite sure is hoping to renew it.'

'Will she succeed?' Hugh was amused, not at all convinced by Isabel's unselfish motives.

'With Mrs Keppel looming her metaphorical shadow over him? It's hardly likely.' Isabel spoke bitterly, for now that Alice Keppel had assumed such importance in His Majesty's private life, it had become much harder to maintain her position in his favour, let alone improve it. She had wrestled agonisingly over the decision to return to London tomorrow. That she would do so had little to do with her mother-in-law's wistful memories and much to do with Hester Hart. Isabel's greater need was to be close to that bally woman now that she was about to write her memoirs, and to assure her she was her friend. Just in case she remembered that old story . . .

Writing was power. No one could come between you and the written word, and only the laws of defamation between you and the printed word, although in this case, Hester thought with satisfaction, no one would dare expose their foibles to further public gaze in court. Look what had happened to poor Oscar Wilde, and to Lady Colin Campbell in her deliciously scandalous divorce case, when they exposed their grievances to public scutiny. Both outcasts from society, however unjustly.

Hester gazed at the pile of blank paper with satisfaction. First, she would publish these memoirs, then the diaries of her travels. How certain people would love to get their hands on the diaries on which the memoirs would be based. But they wouldn't, she'd seen to that already. She laughed to herself at the thought of it. Tomorrow, she decided, she would give a talk in the club; they wouldn't be able to resist it. They'd all come and she would make them squirm. She would start the memoirs today. There were two sets of diaries, one written for publication, and one recording the agony of her school years, the horrors of her coming-out year, and more, much more.

She would bequeath the diaries to a library where no living person should touch them for at least seventy years. There'd be no danger of solicitous families burning them then. Think of all the treasures lost to posterity when Sir Richard Burton's wife burnt his journals after his death. It wouldn't happen to Hester Hart. They were her masterpiece, and she needed to control what would happen to them. As soon as she married Roderick, she would make a will. Meanwhile she must ensure the diaries' survival. She could almost recite them from memory, she knew them so well; they were her life.

'There is a poetry impregnated into the Arab by the desert. No desert is barren to them, for it is their homeland whose beauties they love, whose scents are borne to them on the wind, wherever they might be. Ever since I first read Robert Wood's *The Ruins of Palmyra*, I had thirsted to visit the place, and when I arrived that golden evening, I found the Arab's true soul, poetry, passion, hospitality, conversation, all one gracious whole, inspired by the God he worships. All is Allah and Allah is all . . . '

Yes, she would be a great writer, once those diaries were published. But today she would commence her memoirs. Should she begin like Harriette Wilson: 'I shall not say why and how I became at the age of fifteen the mistress of the Earl of Craven'? The first sentence was important; it must attract attention. Something on those lines . . .

'I shall not weary my reader (beyond the dictates of necessity) by explaining how the leaders of English society conspired to break my heart, so that scorned and rejected I was driven to tramp the desert wastes of the world alone.'

The bitter words of her diaries had festered in her mind for twenty-five years, since she was a girl at school, written, despite her passion, in regulation copperplate. 'I hate *everybody*'; the diary of '81 – 'How stupid and horrible they all are,' and the worst of all because it was not bitter but exultant – 'I, Hester Hart, am to marry the heir to . . . '

* * *

'But, Your Grace,' Thomas Bailey expostulated feebly. He seemed to be doing a lot of that recently, and here on a fragile Sheraton chair in Dewbury House, it was remarkably ineffectual.

'Don't be a namby-pamby, Thomas,' Agatha instructed him briskly. 'It's settled. I shall drive the Brighton Baby in the procession. Why not? I am a member of the Ladies' Motoring Club, I am entitled to drive whatever motorcar I choose.'

'But is it *advisable*?'

'My dear Thomas, have you anything to be ashamed of, either in your motorcar or in your actions?'

He thought for a moment. 'No.'

'Then I shall do it.' Agatha paused a moment to gather charm to her aid, with that flash of the eye that had so intrigued Harry (though only on first meeting it). 'Think of the wonderful opportunity to have both the Baby and yourself discussed in the newspapers, perhaps even pictured in the *Illustrated London News*.'

Thomas did think, and reluctantly surrendered. All he wanted to do was design motorcars and then drive them, but even he realised that in order to have the money to do this, other people had to be involved.

'Now you'll be able to get married, Thomas,' Aunt Gertie had said at his father's funeral seven years ago. 'That's a nice little nest egg for you.' An immediate vision of his job on mechanical toys in Gamages department store floated before his eyes, followed by one of Ethel in haberdashery, with her permanently red nose and wistful eyes. He promptly realised they belonged together. Aunt Gertrude was right. He had taken Ethel to Brighton on an August Bank Holiday, intending to propose over a nice cup of tea after the pierrot show. Then Ethel had insisted on having her fortune told first, asking for a penny to put in the palmist's slot machine, and also insisted he put one in himself. Out of his new-found wealth of £25, he did so, nobly forgoing an opportunity to sneak a penny into the Lady Having a Bath machine. He stared at his future life as confidently announced on the flimsy piece of paper rendered to him by the machine: *Take a plunge in the ocean of life. The winds of fate are with you.*

The vision of Ethel for Evermore was immediately replaced by one of his twelve-inch motorcar model designed by himself.

'Mine reads,' Ethel commented happily by his side, '*Hopes may be dashed, but the future is bright.*'

He had not proposed to Ethel (who had now married the owner of an electric lighting shop) but given in his notice to his surprised employers who had marked him down for promotion in ten years' time, and he became a gentleman of leisure for seven whole days. Thomas was as fanatical as Harold Dobbs but more practical. He realised during this week that £25 would not last for ever, nor would it stretch to the costs of converting his beloved brainchild from paper to solid form. He promptly took a lowly position with a cycle manufacturer about to launch themselves into *voiturettes*, and this step had eventually resulted in his life's dream being realised at the age of thirty. He was still unmarried and Aunt Gertrude had ceased sending him her usual knitted egg cosies for Christmas.

Now he bowed to fate once more; its winds seemed to be calling him again, and, after all, something had to be done about that ghastly fellow Dobbs, so it might as well be now. He was obviously a rotter, a villain of the deepest dye, and Her Grace was quite right to have taken steps to deter him from taking part in the run on Thursday.

Her Grace rose, to indicate the audience was at an end. She watched him as he awkwardly retrieved his cap from the butler and remarked lightly, 'Something more must be *done* about the Dolly Dobbs. Don't you agree, dear Thomas?'

'Outside, lad,' Frederick Gale ordained.

'Inside.' Leo was unusually obstinate.

'You've got no blood in your veins, you youngsters. They didn't win at Rorke's Drift by holing themselves up in cosy motor houses; they manned the barricades.'

Leo wasn't interested in old soldiers' tales of over twenty years ago. He was more interested in fending off Miss Dazey. Warm though these dog days were at night, he didn't fancy being stuck here all alone at her mercy. True it was only for tonight – Mr Smythe would stay tomorrow – and it was highly unlikely that a nicely brought up young lady like her would be prowling around after midnignt, but he didn't put anything past Miss Dazey. It wasn't that he thought she had designs on the Dolly Dobbs; electric cars were too quiet for her, she liked roaring and spluttering along in noisy cars that scattered pigeons from their path like dust in a drought.

'Scared of a female, eh?' Fred guffawed, analysing the problem with the same acumen he exercised over a starved carburettor or one of the governor's springs gone missing. 'What do you think she'd do to you? Grab your John Thomas in the dead of night?'

Leo reddened. 'No. She's a nice girl. But what am I to do about her? I can't arrive on an Eaton Square doorstep and tell her parents I've come for their daughter's hand in marriage. Look good, that, wouldn't it?'

Fred guffawed again. 'No harm in a kiss or two, is there?'

'With her there is,' Leo replied darkly. He knew only too

well. She'd surprised him in the motor pit one day, creeping through from the basement storeroom underneath the repair house and running up the circular stairs by the side of the pit platform. He'd been cleaning Lady Bullinger's underframe and tyres – well, not hers, her Napier's – with a bucket in one hand and a waterbrush in the other. She'd crept up on him and rattled one of the chains he'd taken off and put in the cleaning pan. There she was, dropping the chain, arms round his neck, smelling of Floris and paraffin. Lucky he had his Carless and Lees safety lamp with him or they'd have gone up in flames. As it was, he was helpless, nowhere to put the bucket down even. Unfortunately he'd enjoyed the experience.

'Outside for you, lad.' Fred lost patience. Discipline never came amiss. 'You can have a chair and a blanket, but no falling asleep. You can take a ten-minute nap tomorrow to make up.'

'What if it rains?' Leo countered belligerently.

'Take one of the rubber sheets we throw over the cars.'

'Thank you, Mr Gale,' Leo muttered savagely, cursing all engineers, designers, drivers and motorcars, particularly the Dolly Dobbs. To his mind, it was to a real motorcar what a pantomime horse was to a Derby winner. Still, he'd reserve judgement till he saw its paces.

Leo felt a fool sitting outside, after Fred went home, waiting for ladies or their escorts to collect their motorcars. Most of them were driven by Fred himself round to the front courtyard as they were called for, but after midnight when they normally went off duty the motorcars were left here and ladies or gentlemen escorts collected them from their respective motor houses. This evening four remained. Gloomily he waited. At twelve thirty Mrs Didier brought a cup of hot cocoa out from the ktichen, before she went home, which revived his spirits a little. Only seven and a half hours to go. He slipped into the workshop and brought out a large screw wrench, which made him feel safer.

The Horbick disappeared first. To his surprise, since she was normally a stickler for somebody else doing the work for her, Her Grace came to drive it out herself. Trim little job, like the Duchess herself. Two cylinders, shaft-driven, good on hills, so he'd heard.

'Leo, how good of you to wait up.' She did not look over-pleased, however. Perhaps Mr Didier's dinner had not been up to scratch.

'I'm on guard,' he said awkwardly.

'How very amusing. Do you think poor Dolly will escape from her motor house?'

He didn't like being laughed at but he could hardly tell a duchess so. 'I'm watching for spies,' he muttered.

'Like me? How *very* amusing.' She did not sound amused, however, as without further ado she waited for him to unlatch the door and handed him the starting handle. 'Is the battery charged?' she snapped.

'Yes, Your Grace.'

'Grease cups? Lubricators? Water tanks?'

'All full, Your Grace.'

After she had departed, Leo sank back in his chair thankfully. Even Lady Bullinger was easier to deal with. Or so he thought till she marched up to collect the Napier in a no-nonsense cap, goggles and thick veil.

'Start it up and take it round to the front, Leo, if you please.' The peremptory note in her voice precluded any query as to why she could not perform this function herself since she would be driving it to her home.

'I can't do that, Your Ladyship. I'm on guard.' The more he said it, the sillier it sounded.

'*Can't?*' Her voice rose to a bellow. 'I don't know what you think you are being paid for, young man.'

She did not insist, and with hardly a look at the locked Dolly Dobbs motor house she reclaimed her Napier. The six cylinders fired in correct order with military precision, number one, number four, two, six, three and five, as though anxious to display their mistress's skill as a *chauffeur-mécanicien*. Leo almost saluted as the Napier slid smoothly out of view. Two to go, he thought with relief.

Luigi was next to appear from the back staff entrance, and looked surprised to see Leo. 'Drive Miss Hart's motorcar round, will you?'

Leo had no time for Luigi who saw no point on wasting charm on the likes of him. 'I'm guarding the Dolly Dobbs – for Miss Hart.'

Since Leo showed no sign of moving, Luigi was forced to demean his rank. In high dudgeon he climbed on to the driving seat, only to find the motorcar failed to start.

'It's a Serpollet,' Leo said, pleased.

'So what?'

'It's steam-driven. The burner takes a while to get going.'

When it obliged and slid silently past Leo, Luigi's lips were tightly compressed, though his thoughts, in fact, were not on the young engineer at all.

Past two o'clock now, and Leo felt his eyelids closing. He jerked awake to find not the beautiful Miss Lockwood but a gentleman at his side peering through the keyhole of the Dolly Dobbs motor house. It was a gentleman he instantly recognised, for all he was in evening dress now.

'What are you doing?' he shouted.

The man straightened up. 'I've come for Miss Lockwood's Rover.'

'You're one of them horse people, aren't you? The ones who attacked Mr Gale. I saw you.'

'Yes. No. I mean . . . ' John Millward was not cut out for a life of crime. 'Perhaps I was, but tonight I'm dining with Miss Lockwood and I've come to drive her motorcar round.' Both his engagement and his ability to drive motorcars were unknown to his wife.

'Then why were you peering through that keyhole, Mr Millward?' Leo grew bold.

'Mere curiosity,' he relied weakly. 'Having seen it in its raw state, I was interested to see it, ah, cooked, so to speak.' He laughed lightly but unconvincingly.

Driving the new Fiat with its friction shock absorbers and multi-plate clutch, Millward looked as if he was behind a runaway horse, Leo thought. It was an odd motorcar for Miss Lockwood, much too fast. Fred said she thought the blue paint suited her fair hair.

Shortly after he left, Leo became painfully aware that the cocoa had brought about the need to relieve himself. Secure in the knowledge that all motorcars had disappeared, he retreated to the rear of the motor stable. As he got there he registered he was wrong. A curved-dash Oldsmobile had drawn up beside it and, leaping from the driving seat was Miss Dazey, hatless and with stars in her eyes.

'Leo darling.'

He backed away. 'Miss Dazey,' he stuttered, 'how—'

'Everyone but you calls me Daisy. And yet we are sweethearts.'

'We aren't.'

Even in the dark he could see her eyes fill with tears. She

was too near, much too near. 'Just because you're an engineer and I'm a Hon?' She laughed. 'Don't be foolish. I'm a New Woman. Do kiss me. And then you can drive me home.'

Leo was appalled. 'I can't,' he stuttered.

'That's not very gallant. All sorts of fates worse than death might overtake me.'

Leo was pulled in different directions; by the dictates of heart, body – and suddenly ears. He rushed round to the front of the stable to find yet another person peering into the Dolly Dobbs motorhouse.

'Excuse me, madam.' It came out as a squeak.

She screamed, taken by surprise. 'I'm looking for my husband.'

Then he recognised her. 'He's not in there, madam.'

'Quite. A horse would be whinnying by now, or at least emitting a warm living atmosphere. A motorcar is silent metal, and you have the nerve to insult this by calling it a *stable*.'

'He's not here.' Leo stuck to the salient point. A brilliant notion struck him. 'Do you by chance have a motorcar, madam?'

'How dare you, young man.' Hortensia Millward was insulted.

'In that case you can accompany Miss Dazey home in hers, and her chauffeur can drive you home from there.'

'But—'

'I could tell Mrs Didier you've been here . . . '

Exhausted with his efforts, Leo nevertheless stayed awake for the rest of the night. Inside her stable Dolly Dobbs slumbered peacefully and safely until the morning.

Chapter Four

Auguste quietly whistled the aria of his native Provence from *La Traviata*; he was a relatively happy man. This was his favourite stage of preparation for a banquet, the morning of the previous day. Wednesday spread out before him like a luxurious canvas on which to paint his masterpieces. He knew all too well that as the day wore on, tension and perhaps passions might be roused, exacerbated by the heat of the ovens, for His Majesty would expect his banquet to include at least five hot dishes, even though it would be held *en plein air* in the grounds of Martyr House. Rain? It would not dare. St Swithin himself on his saint's day last Friday had declined to send rain, thus, in accordance with the old belief, coming down firmly in favour of His Majesty's banquet being unsullied by such a disaster. Plum pudding was disaster enough in itself. His Majesty – and His Majesty's figure – always demanded its presence on the menu for shooting-party luncheons, and Lady Tunstall had intimated to Auguste that he would expect it to feature in a July 'picnic' as well.

Auguste thought wistfully of a picnic alone with Tatiana, Egbert and Edith, but for that they must wait until the club closed for August. He wanted, he realised with dismay, to be away from Milton House; even tomorrow would bring fresh air into the stale larder of his mind. He felt stultified here, unable to give of his best, and he put it down to the bluebottle of discomfort which still buzzed around the club, especially as he remembered the unwelcome news Tatiana had sprung on him about this afternoon. Hester Hart, it seemed, was determined to cause trouble.

Pierre shared his discontent. He never approved of whistling in the kitchen, Auguste had noticed, and he promptly stopped in the interests of the banquet. Too late, perhaps.

'What is this?' he asked, aghast, as he peered over Pierre's shoulder.

'Daube of beef, maître. For tonight.' Pierre scowled, his face streaming with perspiration.

'In *July*?'

Pierre shrugged. 'These English aristos will eat spotted dick in August and demand strawberries in January. Why not give them what they want? Take their shekels, my son, praising Allah, is my philosophy.'

'Mr Kipling,' Auguste retorted, 'is not a cook. I fear you need more justification than that for daube of beef. What else is on the menu this evening?'

Pierre looked sullen. 'Lobster salad, roast saddle of mutton—'

'Dull,' Auguste pointed out.

'But safe, maître. Tomorrow will be a long and onerous day for the ladies. Most will not dine here this evening, but quietly at home. Tonight those that dine here should have plain food, in order to appreciate the glories of tomorrow when they will eat the glories of a maître.'

'You are indeed a philosopher, Pierre.' Auguste was gratified. 'But why do you say onerous day? Because of the run to Canterbury, or meeting His Majesty?'

'Neither. Because of this motorcar, the Dolly Dobbs.

Something unpleasant may happen. Why else is it being guarded by night?'

'A precaution, Pierre.' And a very necessary one, in his view. The Dolly Dobbs had aroused passions, some understandable, others less so – such as the curious reaction of its inventor when Thomas Bailey was mentioned, and the Duchess's sudden acceptance of the situation that Hester was to drive it.

'This is not a happy place to work now,' Pierre announced sombrely. 'This pig Luigi has something to do with it. Of that I am sure.' He brought his knife down on a chicken with great enthusiasm. 'He is a spy.'

Auguste laughed. 'For whom? For Italy?'

'No, no, I am serious. For ladies, who pay him for information. Where easier to gather it than in a restaurant with his position?'

'What kind of information?' Auguste asked, startled.

Pierre shrugged. 'Whose husband dines with whom? What so-and-so thinks of so-and-so. Yesterday he was boasting of how he kept Lady Bullinger informed of Miss Hart's movements, and similarly told Miss Hart of Lady Bullinger's plans.'

'Do you have any proof?'

'Why should I need it? I am not a policeman.'

'No. And we must remember this is a kitchen,' Auguste said firmly. 'My wife tells me that afternoon tea will be required in the lounge this afternoon as well as the restaurant. She has told you?' He hoped Tatiana had diplomatically suggested someone else should make the pastries today. Lumps of heavy fat and sugary honey would not help the coming ordeal.

Pierre heaved a sigh. 'Yes. Cucumber sandwiches and cakes

are being made, ices prepared. Though it is difficult with the ices that are needed for tomorrow. What is the reason for this special tea?' It was not like Pierre to make sugar mountains out of such grains of annoyance in a chef's life.

'Miss Hart has decided to give a talk on her travels in Syria.'

'*Merde.*' Pierre's face darkened. '*More* sandwiches. And I shall have to be present to serve it, since that pig Luigi will be in the restaurant.'

'The ladies will need all the reassurance and comfort your sandwiches and tea can provide, if Saturday's experience is anything to go by,' Auguste said diplomatically.

'My best pastries,' Pierrre announced.

Auguste's heart sank.

Fascinated, Auguste watched as Hester Hart swept like Queen Zenobia of Palmyra herself through the ranks of her enemies in the lounge to take up a dominant position at the far end of the room, and Tatiana rose to join her. What was it about this woman, he wondered, that although she was apparently set on antagonising the whole club, she was still managing to get her own way? Even Tatiana, usually a diplomatist, had failed to deter Hester from her plans today. Tatiana had thought no one would attend; he had disagreed, and was right – the room was full. Even Agatha sat elegantly at the very front, with Maud next to her. There was Phyllis Lockwood too. One committee member only was missing.

'Where is Isabel?' he had asked Tatiana before Hester's arrival.

'On her way from Kent. She'll be here for the run tomorrow.'

'But then she won't be there to receive Bertie!' Auguste was dumbfounded.

'The Dowager is doing the honours. Once upon a time she was his mistress, so gossip goes, when he was a very young Prince of Wales.'

Given the choice between a hostess aged sixty-five, former mistress or not, and one mature beauty aged thirty-five or so, Auguste had a shrewd idea which His Majesty would prefer. He hoped Isabel's charm would be up to the King's displeasure, but remembering one of his own encounters with the lady, whose unfathomable eyes had suddenly become all too fathomable when they were left alone together, he supposed it could be. It was a risk, however, and he wondered very much why Isabel was running it. He had put her down as a lady to whom social position was all, and whose brains in this respect could be counted on to overrule the heart.

Hester Hart was a good speaker, Auguste conceded, her tall, spare figure, dark eyes and impassioned movements bringing a little of the deserts of Syria into the midst of the *crème* of London society. There was no doubt that whatever private failings she might have, she had accomplished much. Lady travellers were a much unheralded group, as she was only too eager to point out, driven, she claimed, like outcasts from their own society to appreciate other wider horizons. Like Palmyra.

'Palmyra was one of the outposts of the Roman Empire,' she enthused, 'and for centuries before that the centre of caravan trading routes from the mysterious east to the Anti-Lebanon, Jerusalem, Jebel Lubnan, Antioch, Petra, and the Dead Sea. The ruins of its glorious colourful past create a present of its own . . . Damascus, capital of the desert, breathes in the desert air. I visited bazaars and harems, ate with Bedouin and Pashas . . . '

All the same, Auguste noted with amusement, relieved that there was nothing too contentious in her speech, the questions afterwards from her audience centred not on philosophy but on practical matters.

'What do you wear on a camel? Are you truly alone on your travels? I can't go to Bond Street unaccompanied!' Agatha trilled. 'Aren't you *afraid*?' She glanced round as if to reassure herself that she was in a truly feminine society. Obviously she did not count Pierre, himself and three footmen presiding quietly over the arrangements for tea at the back of the lounge. Auguste was amused.

'Naturally I travel with a caravan,' Hester replied loftily. 'And there are muleteers, and my dragomen of course. But they are hardly relevant.'

'But in the *desert*,' Phyllis asked, shocked, longing to know what the sanitary arrangements were like.

'One hires the labour one needs,' Hester said shortly. 'It is of no importance.'

'And the harems?' barked Lady Bullinger. 'Approve of them, do you?'

'They are most interesting ladies, so knowledgeable on some subjects.' Hester looked round maliciously. 'The art of sexual lovemaking, for instance.'

There was a stunned silence.

'You *talked* about it?' Phyllis squealed. A delicious shiver ran through the audience.

'One can hardly discuss British politics in a harem.'

'But you are a maiden lady,' Lady Bullinger barked at her future god-daughter-in-law. 'Hardly a fitting subject.'

'This is going to be the century of the woman. We may like men but we don't need them.'

'Not even Roderick?' Phyllis's voice rang sweetly out.

Not such a rabbit, was Auguste's instant thought, as another delicious shiver ran through the assembled ladies, delighted to see Hester put in a difficult position.

Not for long. 'My fiancé has a co-driver for life, not a rear seat passenger.'

'So you do need a co-driver,' Agatha asked innocently, 'for all you travel alone? Or is Roderick a sort of dragoman to you?'

'He is not!' Hester shouted.

'Then why ask the poor man to guard that car all night? Why not do it yourself? I feel sure Queen Zenobia would have done.'

'I am *driving* tomorrow,' Hester pointed out curtly. 'I have a responsibility to the Dolly Dobbs, dear Agatha.'

'Is that how you managed things in the desert? Asking others to do what one does not care to do oneself? You will find that matters are conducted differently in London society.'

'So I discovered years ago.' Hester Hart's eyes glittered. 'Have you all forgotten? If so, you will not have long to wait before you are all reminded.' She smiled, but it was not a sweet smile. 'And you will find, my friends, that I remember exactly how things are conducted in London society, partly because I recorded it day by day in my diaires. I know them by heart. Shall I recite some passages now, or will you wait for my memoirs?'

'Shall we have tea, ladies?' Tatiana, desperate, rose to her feet. She forgot to thank the speaker but no one noticed in the sudden enthusiasm to collect cucumber sandwiches.

Tea? Iced water might be more appropriate, Auguste thought, for these raised temperatures. Those were the darts of the picador to madden the bull. The ladies had been baiting Hester. Would a matador appear to deal the final blow?

Only Luigi appeared, however. He had apparently decided the restaurant could do without him, and that Pierre, being incompetent, needed his guidance. It was true that under his magic touch, combined with Earl Grey tea, flushed cheeks and angry voices calmed into the semblance of normality. As normal as a box of lucifer matches requiring only a touch to set them alight.

'I wish you were driving with me on the Bollée, Auguste.' Tatiana, shimmering in cream silk, was in the last stages of her garnish in preparation for dinner at the club.

'There is a very dull menu tonight. Mrs Jolly could make a most delightful—' He rapidly changed the subject.

'No, Auguste. Tonight we must dine at the club.'

'But what could happen this evening? Hester won't even be there. She said she was dining at home, to prepare for tomorrow.'

'I would still like to be there.'

Auguste surrendered and stopped feeling treacherous about his relief at travelling with the banquet on the royal train tomorrow. His duty in support of his wife would be performed this evening. As they walked in through the iron gates of Milton House, however, he realised it was going to be a more onerous duty than he had imagined.

'Look!' Tatiana seized Auguste's arm.

Stepping down from the Fiat's driving seat in front of the club was Roderick Smythe. This was hardly surprising. What shook them was to see his companion, who was looking distinctly smug. The tip of Phyllis Lockwood's tiny shoes showed beneath the flimsy blue evening dress, which could be glimpsed under her dainty motoring dust coat as Roderick carefully helped her down from the passenger seat. A very large flowery hat was cunningly placed to reveal as much as possible of her golden hair and pretty face.

Unfortunately for Roderick, as Auguste now shuddered to see, Hester had exercised her woman's privilege of changing her mind about dining at home and was glaring out from the restaurant window. Then her face disappeared. With one accord, Auguste and Tatiana followed Roderick and Phyllis who were, unaware of their imminent fate, already walking into the club restaurant, divested of their travelling coats. Tatiana was too late to warn them.

It was not Luigi who greeted Roderick; it was Hester, the feathers in her hat tilting like Roman emperors' thumbs of death towards her prey. Phyllis's grip on Roderick's arm tightened, either in panic or possessiveness.

Roderick's opening defence was not impressive. 'I thought you were to dine at home, Hester.'

'So you chose to sneak here behind my back?' Hester's raised voice paid no concessions to the presence of other diners, for whom the dull menu had suddenly received an injection of spice.

Phyllis deflected the thumbs with ease. 'Not behind your back, Miss Hart. You asked him to guard the Dolly Dobbs overnight. Don't you remember?' There was an admirable note of solicitous inquiry in her voice.

'That's right.' Roderick was only too anxious to agree.

'Then kindly change your plans, Roderick. I have no need of a turncoat to guard my motorcar. I shall do it myself.'

'Hester, I can explain—'

'How about you, Miss Lockwood? Can you explain why you are dining with *my* fiancé?'

Phyllis burst into tears, a technique she frequently found to be effective when at a loss for words. 'He's *my* fiancé. He loves *me*, don't you, Roderick?'

Roderick apparently found the question too much to answer, for he did not reply.

'Do you, Roderick?' Hester inquired silkily. 'I was under the impression, last night in bed, that you loved *me*.'

Forty pairs of knives and forks, including those of Maud, Agatha, Isabel and Hugh, halfway through their meat stew, were instantly suspended. Their holders were reeling with delicious shock at hearing their *bête noire* mention the word 'bed' in public with no concern at all for frightening the horses.

Standing behind the eternal triangle, Auguste saw Roderick looking from one of the women in his life to the other and, like many a man before him, failing to come up with a solution worthy of the situation. He removed Phyllis's arm, brushed past Tatiana and Auguste without a word, and seizing his hat strode out angrily without even tipping the cloakroom attendant. As he did so, he became aware of two sounds; the first was Phyllis in hot pursuit, the second was Hester's hurled, 'Don't bother to return tonight for your ring; I'll send it back tomorrow.'

The three members of her audience most concerned were delighted. Their entertainment ended, however, as Hester continued, 'I'll have my revenge on the lot of you. I've waited long enough.'

'I don't think it advisable that you should remain here overnight alone,' Tatiana said firmly, as she took coffee with Hester in the lounge an hour later. Not for the first time she was thinking that motorcars were considerably easier to control than people, punctures notwithstanding. Especially people like Hester Hart who insisted on breaking all accepted rules of society. Once Tatiana would have been in full agreement with such sentiments; now she had modified her views. She disagreed with rules that did harm, but agreed with those that caused no harm and made daily life run the smoother.

Hester decided against returning a stinging retort. She had no quarrel with Tatiana, rather to her surprise; Tatiana Didier was, after all, related to the King and was unlikely to have much in common with the world of button manufacture. 'You need not concern yourself, Mrs Didier. I am used to guarding myself as well as my property.'

Overlooking the fact that the Dolly Dobbs was not Hester's property but Harold's and, she supposed, Agatha's, Tatiana ceded to the inevitable. 'Then you must lock all the doors and remain inside the motor house, Miss Hart.'

'It is too warm. I have the instincts of a cat –' how right she was, Tatiana thought – 'I wake on an instant. I also have a pistol.'

'I don't like the idea of that.'

'Perhaps not. However, I am aware I am not popular in the club.'

She sounded proud of the fact, Tatiana thought with distaste. 'You are too outspoken. London does not approve of private matters being aired in public places. The club may be all female, but it is not a harem.'

Hester's face darkened. 'If that is a reproof, Mrs Didier, I do not accept it. Society needs a fresh wind from the desert to blow through it.'

'Be careful, Hester.' Tatiana was genuinely concerned. 'Like the desert, I imagine, it has its own methods of defence.'

Hester laughed. 'When you have faced the perils of the Jebel Druze, a London Ladies' Motoring Club does not seem so very terrifying.'

'I'm sure your travels will also have taught you that danger can lurk in the most unlikely of places,' Tatiana said quietly. 'I shall ask Mr Gale to keep watch outside if you insist on carrying out this vigil yourself, while you remain inside.'

'No.'

'No traveller can afford to overlook the importance of common sense.' Unless their vanity gets in the way was Tatiana's unspoken qualification. 'I am responsible for this club, and I simply cannot allow any member to remain here alone when a threat of violence has been made.'

Hester gave in ungraciously. 'Very well. Fred Gale can sleep outside and I'll sleep inside. After all, as Maud pointed out, I am a maiden lady.'

It was the first sign of humour that Tatiana had ever detected in the redoubtable Miss Hart.

Auguste was in the midst of a heated amicable discussion with Pierre over his desire to serve Cardinal sauce with the lobster mousse. Auguste held firmly that the sauce should contrast in this case, not complement or extend existing flavours. 'Curry sauce,' he was urging. 'Mild, but—' He broke off, alarmed, as Tatiana came rushing up to him. 'What is the matter, *chérie*?'

'It's Hester. She's adamant about guarding the Dolly Dobbs herself. Now she has told Roderick she won't marry him, she doesn't want him or any man to help her – or rather the car. I insisted Fred stay tonight, but I'm still worried about tomorrow. Please, Auguste, come with me by motorcar to Canterbury. Pierre can manage without you, can't you, Pierre?'

'*Oui, madame.*'

'Of course I will come.' His heart sank, but there was no choice. Tatiana was deeply worried, and, he feared, with good reason.

Tatiana left to find Fred, and Auguste tried to regain his earlier enthusiasm for the final stages of preparation. It was hard, however, and eventually he tore himself away from lobster mousse and went over to the motor stable. 'To smell the stock,' he informed Leo to his mystification.

Fred had left to take some rest before his vigil began. There were only four cars left. The separate motor houses were not yet locked, and Auguste walked into them one by one. The smell of machinery was always the same. A slight smell of benzine and of metal polish combined with a dull, dead atmosphere, not the warm living breath of the horses who had lived here before. For those who loved motorcars, he supposed this pungent smell *was* alive and evocative. He preferred his kitchen, where every saucepan, every scrubbing brush, every potato heralded the excitements to come on the morrow. He supposed to motorcar enthusiasts each motorcar had its own personality, reflecting that of its owners. Here, alone, at night, they spoke most vividly. Lady Bullinger's Napier was a mighty roast sirloin of beef. Isabel's new Royce was a subtle blend of spices from the Orient, Agatha's Horbick a daintily arranged noisette of lamb on a purée of peas *à la française*. Lastly, in the next house to the Dolly Dobbs, was Miss Dazey's curved-dash Oldsmobile, looking as out of place as a carp surrounded by turnips. Of Hester Hart's Serpollet there was no sign.

And here was the cause of all the trouble, the Dolly Dobbs. Here the open passageway connecting the rear of all the motor houses had had temporary doors attached but the one to the repair house was still open and he could see Leo working at the bench. Here was the Dolly with all the hopes and dreams placed on her about to be fulfilled tomorrow. Or were they? Suppose it was a case of the King's New Clothes in Hans Christian Andersen's story, a fantasy motorcar? If one looked at it objectively, could those outlandish windmills inside their monstrous hoods really work? The theory sounded possible, but then the theory taken to its logical limit, Tatiana had pointed out, would mean Harold had indeed discovered the secret of perpetual motion. Mankind had been seeking this for centuries; could a man like Dobbs really have succeeded? It remained to be seen. Tomorrow.

Despite his antipathy to motorcars, Auguste found he was interested in whether the Dolly Dobbs worked or not. Canterbury was fifty-five miles from London Bridge, the beginning of the Dover Road along which they would travel. Add to that a few miles for starting from Hyde Park Corner, plus about seven miles from Canterbury to Martyr House, and the run would be over sixty-five miles, well in excess of the capabilities of current electric motorcars. If Dolly succeeded, the glory would reflect on Tatiana's club; if it didn't, would the reverse be true? Suddenly he realised he was as eager to see the motorcar's success as Harold could have wished.

He peered beneath Dolly's wheels into the suspended pit and the circular staircase going down to the basement, in which a few stores and sand buckets were stored. Alongside him was the massive block and tackle equipment suspended on frames attached to H-shaped girders on the motor-house roof. Its purpose, Tatiana had told him proudly when the premises were converted earlier this year, was to pull engines out of the motorcars. Horses, he had traitorously thought, required no such maintenance. Not quite knowing why, he went down the staircase and through the interconnecting doorway to the basement of the repair house where Fred stored the larger spares and tools. Did he expect to find Thomas Bailey or some other spy hiding there? If so, he was disappointed. There was nothing living there. He ran up the steps into the repair house where Leo was working on what appeared to Auguste's inexpert eye to be a pile of waste rubber.

'What time will Fred be back?'

'Around twelve, he said, Mr Didier. I won't go till he gets here, whether Miss Hart comes or not.'

Telling himself he felt reassured, Auguste returned to the kitchens. His mind was still not entirely on the intricacies of ice creams, mousses, terrines, raised pies and the thousand and one details of trying to organise a banquet to take place at a distance. It was a hard job to refrain from intimating that Pierre might have forgotten the horseradish sauce, or the marinated olives, but even more impolite for him to sneak around checking himself, especially as Pierre was fully conscious of what he was doing. He would have to leave those tasks until Pierre and the staff left, which they had agreed should be no later than twelve thirty in view of the fact that they would be in again at five for a frantic two hours of packing and last-moment tasks before leaving to join the royal train at Victoria.

Auguste was still amazed at the lack of thought devoted by diners to the hours of work that went into the preparation of the delights they took so much for granted; the hours of straining purées through muslin, the time spent on the spun sugar that adorned their *pièces montées*. Yet it was all necessary. Particularly for tomorrow. His Majesty had an uncanny knack of noticing the thousandth and first detail, were it to be forgotten. He was always polite in pointing it out but it would be remembered.

At twenty to twelve Tatiana appeared once more. 'Only Maud, Agatha, Isabel and Hugh left in the lounge now, thank goodness. They have every appearance of staying for ever. What's happening in the motor house?'

'Leo is there. Neither Hester nor Fred has arrived yet but I will be here to see all is well. You must go home to sleep and prepare for tomorrow.'

Tatiana wearily shook her head. 'Not till everything and everyone is settled in the motor stable. I'll stay here until you leave. I won't get in your way. I could do some washing-up.'

'You could *not*,' Auguste said firmly, alarmed. The staff had been outraged at Madam President's appropriation of their tasks when she was discovered helping the scullery maid out on one occasion.

She laughed. 'Very well. Perhaps I could help you cut things up instead.'

He eyed her suspiciously. 'You could not.'

'May I make some cocoa, then?'

'You may.'

Hester Hart arrived at five to twelve and drove her Serpollet into a motor house. She inspected the remaining three motorcars and identified them. Like the Serpollet, she was steaming, in her case at the injustice done to her by Roderick and Phyllis. Just because Phyllis Lockwood had a baron in the family many generations back, who had performed some service in losing the American colony for England, her pedigree was deemed superior to hers. Phyllis was *persona grata* here, despite being a mere picture-postcard actress, and she, despite all she had achieved, was *non grata*. It was like school all over again. Well, when her picture appeared in the *Illustrated London News*, posing with the Dolly Dobbs, and when she sat at His Majesty's side as the triumphant driver thereof, their faces would rapidly change. Some of His Majesty's best friends were in trade, just like her own father.

Hester threw one of the rugs Fred provided for passengers into the rear seat of the Dolly Dobbs and stalked into the repair house which Leo was about to leave.

'Where's Fred?'

'I'm here, miss.' Fred appeared at the outer doorway. 'You can go now, Leo.'

Leo thankfully obeyed.

'This is what I'm going to do,' Hester peremptorily announced. 'I'll throw the door of the motor house open but stay inside until all the motorcars have gone. You keep out of the way. I want to talk to my fellow competitors. After that, I'll sleep and you can take over.'

'Open? But the motorcar's a secret, ain't it?'

'That's my business. Yours is to get on with your work until I'm ready.'

Fred, his views on women drivers unprintable, disappeared into his basement where he took pleasure in hammering very loudly, and Hester sat herself on the rear seat of the Dolly Dobbs from which she had a splendid view through the open doors of the motor house. She waited for her 'friends'.

Lady Bullinger marched round the corner of the main building into the yard and noticed the door of the Dolly Dobbs motor house was open. There was no one about and temptation was too great. She hurried to the open doorway.

'Something you wanted, Maud?'

'That woman' was seated inside the monstrosity, grinning out at her like Medusa. It gave her the fright of her life, and she rapidly changed her plans.

'No,' she said baldly. 'Just curious about the Dolly Dobbs. No harm in that, is there?' She stared fascinated at the vehicle.

'Not at all. I'm delighted to see you. I was feeling a little lonely after my tiff with Roderick.'

There was a pause. 'I can probably help,' Maud eventually said gruffly. 'We're friends, after all.' It might have sounded like a plea. If it was, it was misplaced.

The viper struck. 'After what you did to me, Maud?'

Isabel crept up more silently, somewhat annoyed that Hugh had not insisted on collecting the Royce for her. However, it gave her an opportunity to peer in at the Dolly Dobbs. She jumped as she saw Hester Hart's face grimly glaring at her.

'Goodness, Hester. You quite frightened me. I thought the motor house seemed to be unguarded.'

'How kind of you to be concerned, Isabel dear.'

'I was going to guard it myself.' Isabel was eager to please.

'I'm sure you were, Isabel. Just like you always guard and care for everything and everyone.'

'I admire motorcars.' Isabel never recognised sarcasm.

'And their drivers, I'm sure. Like Hugh – or is your preference still for coachmen?'

Isabel lost colour. 'I don't know what you mean.'

'You must have a short memory, Isabel dear. I shall enjoy a chat with His Majesty tomorrow.'

Agatha tripped confidently and excitedly up to the open door. At last she could gain access to her own car, the Dolly Dobbs. And then decide her plans.

'Good gracious, Agatha, you have a starting handle in your hand. How very violent.'

Agatha was speechless, staring first at the Dolly Dobbs's occupant and then at the Dolly Dobbs herself.

'Interesting, isn't it?' Hester went on, disappointed at receiving no reaction. 'Of course, you haven't seen it before. Such a pity since you gave Harold the money to build it.' Still she received no real reaction. 'What's wrong with it?' she demanded suspiciously.

'Nothing,' Agatha said slowly. Then she began to laugh, managing to hiccup, 'It's beautiful, quite beautiful. I wish you every success with it, Hester.'

'I'm sure you do. Just as you've wished me success in everything in life.'

Agatha stopped laughing.

By twelve twenty Hester Hart had locked the doors of all the motor houses, including her own, and Fred had taken up his station outside the repair house, wrapped in a rug. He had been settled perhaps five minutes when he looked up to see he was no longer alone and struggled to stand up, tripping over the rug as he did so.

'So you're on guard duty, Fred.'

'Yes, sir.'

'Well, you can go. I've decided to come after all.'

'Mrs Didier told me to stay.'

'She's not here, and she didn't know I was coming back. I *am* Miss Hart's fiancé, it's my duty to be here as arranged.'

True enough. Fred thankfully took his leave since there was no one left in the club to ask. Mrs Didier must be long since gone, and Mr Didier with her.

'Leave your keys,' Roderick said.

'Spare set in the left-hand drawer, sir.'

Smiling his thanks, Roderick went into the workshop and through the adjoining door. 'Hello, Hester.'

Tatiana, emerging with some cocoa for Fred and Hester,

was just in time to see Fred leave, much to her surprise. 'Where are you going?'

'Mr Smythe came to stand guard after all. He told me I could go, and I didn't know you were around, ma'am. I didn't think you'd object.'

She had no grounds for objecting, so she let him go. After all, if Roderick and Hester had made up their quarrel, it was no business of hers.

She looked at the two mugs of cocoa on the tray, uncertain what to do. She decided to take them to the stable. Roderick must be inside but she wanted to be reassured he was still there. The door to the repair house was open. As she approached, she could hear Hester and Roderick talking in the adjoining motor house. Obviously what had happened earlier in the evening was under animated, even acrimonious discussion, and discretion being the better part of valour, she retreated. She would return on her mission at a more convenient time.

By the time she returned to the kitchen, Pierre and the staff had vanished, and she went to find Auguste. He was deep inside one of the larders in the passageway to the rear door, investigating a refrigerator. He grinned shamefacedly. He had assured her he would be finished by the time she returned.

'I just wanted to be sure the curry sauce was of the right consistency.'

'How long will you really be?'

'Twenty-five minutes,' he suggested cautiously. 'I shall have to grind coffee and whisk the egg whites for meringues, purée the—'

'Very well.' She fidgeted in the kitchen, lifting lids and covers until Auguste could bear it no longer. 'What is wrong, Tatiana? Are you impatient to go?'

'No. I suppose I'm anxious about Hester Hart still. Fred has gone and Roderick has come back.'

Auguste considered. 'Let them sort out their quarrel. They'll hardly attack the Dolly Dobbs themselves, and if they are both there, no matter whether they are speaking to each other or not, no one else will attack it. And if anyone comes to attack *Hester*, he'll stop it. The last thing he'd want to do is attack her himself.'

'All the same I'll take some more cocoa over before we leave.'

'You're right. Cocoa is soothing for the stomach. No one could quarrel over cocoa.'

It seemed Auguste's belief was to be tested. As Tatiana set off across the yard at one o'clock, she realised the discussion had developed into a full-blown quarrel. She heard Hester's shouting, shrill voice, 'Marry *you*? You fool, as if I ever would,' and instantly retreated. Cocoa could do little here, and lovers' quarrels had nothing to do with the Dolly Dobbs or, therefore, with her.

Thankfully she escaped with Auguste five minutes later out into the peaceful starlit night of Petty France.

Chapter Five

Today presented a sartorial problem: was he cook or gentleman? Auguste pondered. Gentlemen were not called upon to present themselves in kitchens at six thirty in the morning, which suggested working clothes were called for, but on the other hand cooks did not have to be presented to His Majesty King Edward VII five hours later. He compromised with his new grey flannel lounge suit, swathed in the white protective clothing of his trade, and sending more formal clothes by train. He must remember, he told himself, to change hats; a terrible vision of His Majesty being presented with the sight of a bowing suit from Savile Row topped with a chef's hat propelled him from bed so that his brain could occupy itself with more practical matters. Even so, as he bathed, soap and sponge were mingled with visions of huge jellies wobbling into splintered fragments and hayboxes soaked with sauces and gravies from inadequately sealed containers.

Motorcars and His Majesty – the combination was far from attractive, and combined with the onerous duties of the banquet, and supporting Tatiana, he had to suppress a craven desire to creep back under the sheets and forget all about Thursday. Tatiana was already up, and from the cheerful noise in the dressing room the daily battle had begun between Eloise's wish for her mistress to do her credit and Tatiana's to jump on to or under a motorcar at the earliest opportunity. Eloise had insisted on travelling to Kent with the other ladies' maids, where arrangements were to be made at Martyr House for them to repair the ravages of road travel to their mistresses' toilettes before luncheon, and for the ball this evening.

Pierre would already be at Milton House together with his staff – and, unfortunately, Luigi. Auguste had a pang of uneasiness, but surely nothing could erupt between them at such an important moment. Pierre could be depended upon in a crisis – such as the time the ortolans had overcooked at a dinner held in Monsieur Louis Renault's honour. Luigi, however, struck Auguste as the kind of man who would stick like marzipan during fine weather and at the hint of a storm vanish like oysters from a July menu.

At six thirty Auguste walked through the gates of Milton House, leaving Tatiana busy preparing the Bollée in their own motor house with Charlie Jolly. Eloise had insisted on the latter's presence to prevent her mistress inspecting the underside of the Bollée's frame dressed in lilac foulard and white linen.

A satisfactory sight met Auguste's eye. Baskets, hampers and boxes were already being packed into waiting motor vans, and three hired Napier station buses awaited the accompanying staff. He entered the kitchen where a lingering smell of venison stew delighted his nostrils; the hayboxes were being packed with (well-sealed) casseroles. Jellies and ice creams, still in moulds, were conveyed as tenderly as new-born babes in baskets and ice cabinets to the vans. In the midst of the kitchen Pierre superintended his charges with an expert eye.

'Are there any problems?' Auguste asked anxiously.

'*Non, monsieur.*'

'And the *salade*?' A particular point of concern if their delivery from Covent Garden had failed to arrive. 'It is ready?'

'*Oui, monsieur.*' It was obvious from Pierre's taciturnity and grim expression that Luigi had arrived.

Pierre could in any case be forgiven some gruffness for this was no ordinary shooting party luncheon or picnic, and the resident servants at Martyr House could probably be counted on to gloat rather than assist in a crisis. Their moment of glory would then appear the more brilliant at this evening's ball supper, which was their responsibility. By that time Auguste would definitely have made his appearance as a gentleman, for even Bertie, King and Emperor, had reluctantly conceded Auguste could not present both meals without offending his hosts. This morning he was a chef, however. The transposition between the two worlds pleased him; he was sometimes acutely aware he was now fully accepted by neither, but there were virtues in detachment.

Luigi, Pierre, Monsieur Bernard and the rest of the staff in the royal train (in the baggage wagons) would be leaving Victoria Station at eight; the cavalcade of motor vans was to depart from Petty France at seven thirty to allow time for unpacking under the suspicious eyes of the King's detectives – in case, Auguste supposed, of explosive strawberry *bombes*. He himself was planning to leave at about eight o'clock for a solitary walk to Hyde Park Corner for the eight-thirty departure of the Ladies' Motoring Club. Fortunately Tatiana was taking his all-enveloping coat, cap, goggles and mask with her; a walk through London streets clad like Count Dracula did not appeal to him.

At twenty past seven Luigi strolled into the kitchen. 'Are you not ready?' he inquired solicitously of Pierre. 'My part is done, so is Monsieur Bernard's, and the vans are able to leave.'

Luigi was an excellent connoisseur of wines, Auguste grudgingly conceded, but he dominated the elderly Bernard; however, he displayed only the slightest tendency to favour Italian over French wines. Today he and his staff were in charge of table decoration and service, and his task was not a light one. Nevertheless Auguste had firmly scrutinised the final choice of wines.

'Naturally I am ready, dog,' Pierre informed his enemy curtly.

Auguste's heart sank. 'Today, gentlemen, we work *together*; tomorrow you may kill each other.'

'I shall be happy to oblige, monsieur.' Luigi shrugged amusedly, as Pierre shot by him with a scowl and a sauce hamper.

When they had left, Auguste relaxed. He had half an hour in which to ensure with the aid of two kitchen maids and one under meat chef that those ladies not participating in the run could, if they wished, dine at the club. It would be plain roast beef— *horseradish*. There on a side table was the prepared horseradish sauce for luncheon today. Pierre had overlooked it.

Auguste rushed up the steps into the courtyard to see the last of the vans driving merrily round the bend of Petty France. The King would never forgive this crime. It was almost treason since the King had specifically demanded the presence of pressed beef on the menu. What to do? Run to Victoria? Tatiana would worry if he was late. He must take it himself on the Léon Bollée. Oneself was the only person who *never* let you down, Auguste told himself bitterly.

By eight o'clock he had finished his duty by tonight's menu and hurried to the water closet and lavatory stand to prepare himself for the journey ahead. He passed the larders and scullery on the way but resisted the temptation to check that no other forgotten treasures lay within. He refused to nurse a ham in his arms all the way to Martyr House. He was halfway through the call of nature, however, when it struck him that it was remarkably quiet. Although the club would not yet be open, he would have expected to hear some kind of activity from the motor stable across the yard, even though Fred and Leo were going straight to join the cavalcade in case of mishaps. The Dolly Dobbs must have left while he was in the kitchen – after all, it ran silently, and the sound of voices in the rear yard would not have carried to the kitchen with so much noise going on. Would it?

Auguste found himself running up the steps to the rear yard instead of back to the security of the kitchen, just to reassure himself. He found the stable closed and deserted. Dolly had left for her maiden voyage. Nevertheless he walked quickly over to the motor house, just as Harold Dobbs came rushing round into the yard, shouting bitterly and wildly of the inefficiency of the London, Brighton and South Coast Railway.

'Where is it?' he cried querulously, breaking off from his diatribe.

'What?' Auguste asked fatuously. What else, after all, could Harold Dobbs be interested in?

'The Dolly Dobbs. Has it left already? Without *me*? Is that woman planning to drive her *alone*? Is she bent on ruining my debut?'

'I don't know.' One answer sufficed for all questions.

Harold threw himself at the door and rattled it in vain.

'It's padlocked,' Auguste pointed out helpfully. 'I expect they all are,' he added as Harold worked his way down the row with the same negative results.

'Get the key,' Harold howled.

'I don't have one.' Auguste might be cook as well as gentleman, but he was *not* a motor mechanician.

'You must. Its Motor Club trial begins in twenty minutes.' Harold was as white as a floured pastry board. He rushed back to the Dolly Dobbs door and, bending over, applied his eye to the keyhole. Auguste regarded his plumpish bottom with intense dislike. Motor designers were worse than motorcars. Harold stood up, trembling.

'She's in there,' he whispered.

'*Who?*' Alarm now shot through Auguste like a wave of nausea.

'Dolly Dobbs, of course,' Harold moaned. 'But there's something wrong with it. Are Miss Hart and Thomas Bailey conspiring against me?'

All Auguste's former forebodings, superseded by the demands of the banquet, swept back. 'Why should Miss Hart—'

'I see it all,' Harold interrupted, following his own thoughts. 'That's why she—' He stopped short.

'Why she?' Auguste prompted sharply.

'Wanted to drive it,' Harold finished unconvincingly.

'Then where is she?' Presumably she and Roderick would have needed to take it in turns to return home to change, but they were leaving it very late to join the run. Auguste knew from bitter experience just how long it took to check a motorcar before one set out on a journey, and even if the battery had been changed earlier this morning, twenty minutes would not be enough for the final check. All thoughts of Hyde Park Corner and the run vanished, as, commanding Harold to stay where he was, Auguste rushed back into the kitchen shouting for a screwdriver. The two kitchen maids and the underchef gazed at him blankly, wondering what marvellous new dish might require a screwdriver to achieve perfection. Fortunately the solid figure of Charlie Jolly ambled into the kitchen, for once as welcome a sight as his mother. 'Padlock,' Auguste shouted. 'Need screwdriver.'

Charlie's brain worked a great deal faster than his body, so when he moved it was with agonising slowness.

'Hurry, Charlie, *hurry*.'

This word always disagreed with Charlie. Nevertheless he flourished a screwdriver within moments and followed Auguste back to the stable.

'There.' Auguste pointed to the door hinges. 'Off with them.'

Charlie had the feet and hands of an artist, and he worked deftly and swiftly. One of Charlie's great qualities was that he never asked why. Mrs Jolly never wasted time asking why steak and kidney pie was demanded in July; she just provided it. Charlie took after her. Even so, Auguste danced up and down with impatience, while Harold, apparently in a state of collapse, moaned softly to himself, at intervals inspecting his pocket watch like Mr Carroll's White Rabbit. At last the door of the motor house swung free and Auguste pushed past Charlie. 'Keep Mr Dobbs away,' he instructed him.

'Why?' Harold cried, hurling himself at Charlie. Charlie was the stronger, but Harold was the taller and could see past him to his beloved Dolly Dobbs. '*What's that?*'

The first thing Auguste saw was that something large and heavy now adorned Dolly's steering and driving area. As he ran forward it was immediately obvious that Dolly would be driving nowhere today and probably never again. The huge iron block and tackle equipment had been swung with sickening force across Dolly's bows, destroying steering pillar and wheel, levers and voltmeter, damaging both far hood and windmill, and smashing the nearside hood, windmill and dynamo, up against the remains of which the iron block now rested. Behind him, Charlie, with eyes for more than the Dolly Dobbs, gripped Harold firmly in an armlock, as with the strength of ten he tried to hurl himself on Dolly's corpse.

But Auguste had no time to waste in sympathy for a motorcar. He was concerned with what lay sprawled on the ground behind it. Nausea welled up in him as with sickening fear all his premonitions proved justified. It was an inert body, the body of a woman.

'*Silence, s'il vous plaît*,' Auguste shouted with such force that even Harold was hushed. Would there be life in that still body? Would it be smashed like the motorcar? Heart in mouth, Auguste walked closer, trying to still his pounding heart so that his eyes could take in all he needed. There were, to his relief, no smashed brains or pulped flesh, only blood round the body. And, he now noticed, splashes of dried blood on the walls and the floor by the doorway. Alive? How could she be? Hoping against hope that he was wrong, he knelt down gingerly to touch the body. It was already cooling but not yet cold, and as far as he could tell from looking at the face and jaw, rigor mortis was just setting in.

Hester Hart had not gone home to change, she was lying dead, face down, still in the warm walking skirt she had obviously donned for her vigil.

Now that the nightmare had proved reality, Auguste desperately tried to call all the instincts of the detective to his aid and not those of the man. Had Hester died by a glancing blow from the iron block? Out of the question from the position of the body. He dared not move the body to search for other cause of death. Egbert would not be pleased. Then with fresh horror he remembered: Egbert was not sitting in his office at

Scotland Yard but with Tatiana in the Bollée, waiting patiently for Auguste to arrive at Hyde Park Corner. There was no possible way he could now reach Hyde Park Corner in time, Auguste realised, feverishly hauling out his pocket watch; it was twenty-five minutes past eight already. Thoughts raced chaotically through his mind like meat through a mincer, and like minced meat had to be organised for use.

'Charlie, go into the club and telephone for Inspector Stitch at Scotland Yard to come here immediately. Tell him I am trying to reach Inspector Rose.' Egbert would be travelling the Dover Road on a fruitless errand, for there was no longer a Dolly Dobbs or Hester Hart to guard.

What about Harold Dobbs? He should not be left alone with the body while Charlie was absent. Impatient though he was, Auguste knew he must stay here. Then rescue appeared as the meat chef made an incautious appearance in the yard. He was promptly summoned to Auguste's side and ordered to guard Harold until Charlie returned. It was almost irrelevant. Harold, sitting on the ground sobbing convulsively, looked as incapable of action as Dolly herself.

The motorcars at Hyde Park Corner were assembling at an hour not normally acknowledged by fashionable ladies, had not the presence of His Majesty at Martyr House persuaded them to rise in what many considered the middle of the night. There had been much to be decided. Not only had ball dresses and morning dresses for the return drive tomorrow to be packed but a decision made on whether mourning garments should be included on the off chance that some member of the royal family might pass away during the day, thus forcing the entire assembly into deepest black. Furthermore, the essential despatch of maids by railway train to be in Kent to minister to their needs on arrival had had the unfortunate result of depriving their mistresses of their services in the vital hour before their own departure. In consequence, as the motorcars took their places, lined up in double rank on Constitution Hill, the atmosphere was not nearly as clubbable as Tatiana might have wished, though she hardly noticed in her own anxiety.

'Where is Auguste?' She turned worriedly to Egbert, sitting shrouded at her side in the clothes Edith had ordered as suitable for the perils to health of a July drive: his winter full-length mackintosh, her Great-Uncle William's deerstalker, a knitted scarf that usually saw duty when winter necessitated a draught from the sash window being blocked off, and goggles carefully smoked over a candle lest the rays of the sun affect his eyes. He also had a hot water bottle, despite his reassurance that cars were provided with footwarmers nowadays.

'Surely he could not have forgotten and gone by train,' she continued.

'Easily. If he had his mind on carbonades and not carburettors.' He was rather enjoying himself, despite his garb. He couldn't see anything very terrible happening in this procession of London society, it was a day in the country even if the King was at the end of it, and he could partake of at least one Auguste Didier banquet. Moreover, he could enliven Edith's weekend with a description of the outlandish clothes these women dolled themselves up in, which far outstripped his own. He could hear her now: 'Tell me about the *hats*, Egbert . . .'

'Good morning, Tatiana.'

Maud Bullinger loomed up beside Egbert, giving him the fright of his life. This one looked like the close-up of a beetle's face in the nature study book he'd bought his niece for Christmas, what with her enormous goggles and hat secured by a black chiffon veil, at present thrown back.

'Good morning, Maud.' Tatiana climbed down and walked round to the pathway to greet her, thankful that at least one participant seemed in good humour.

'Are the Motor Club men here yet?'

'Yes. They're over there,' Tatiana indicated the opposite side of the road, 'waiting to measure the first mile. There will be two more just outside Chatham, to measure a mile at Gad's Hill, and the last two will be on Barham Downs.'

'Ha,' Maud commented cryptically. 'Madam not here yet, I see.'

'No. I'm concerned.' Tatiana frowned. 'We depart in five minutes.'

Lady Bullinger gave a short, jolly laugh. 'Knowing Miss Hart, she'll leave it till the last possible moment to make a spectacular entry.'

Tatiana looked down the line of cars at the club she had founded with such excitement only months ago. Why had she imagined peace and harmony where all were devoted to the cause of motorcars? The long line of limousines, tourers, two-seaters, voiturettes, landaulets and broughams stretched into the distance. Petrol, steam, or electrically-powered, at the wheel of each of them sat one of her members. She saw that wheels gleamed, satin dust coats shone, paintwork on cars and ladies alike was brightly polished. Her sun shone again. 'Don't they look *wonderful*?' she breathed.

It was all worth it, Hester Hart or no Hester Hart, Dolly Dobbs or no— Where was Hester? And where was Auguste? Her worries returned. One latecomer arrived but proved to be Isabel with Hugh beside her. Only three more to go. Phyllis, the Duchess – and Hester. The first drove by to join the line with a happy squeak of the hooter.

'No wonder she sounds so happy,' Tatiana commented to Egbert. 'Look who's with her.'

'Who is it?'

'Of course, you don't know. That's Roderick Smythe.'

'The racing driver?' Even Egbert had heard of him.

'Yes. Whatever has happened? Hester won't like this one little bit. He was going to drive his new Crossley at the end of the procession but he's with Phyllis in her Fiat.'

'She looks a very pretty lady to be with.'

'Indeed she is. There's only one problem.'

'And that is?'

'He's engaged to Hester Hart.'

As she ran down the line to greet Phyllis, Egbert watched her go, admiring her enthusiasm. Privately he could understand Auguste's views on motorcars, but he could also see they were useful. Leaping into a hansom did not achieve the same immediate results, particularly when their drivers had to be haggled with as to whether their book of distances covered the journey in question. He wondered whether he might get a motorcar if they ever became cheaper. At the moment they were the toys of the rich. He tried to imagine Edith perched on top of one of these shining monsters, swathed in chiffon like a Hallowe'en phantom. So far she had not been enthusiastic. Dusty, dirty contraptions had been her verdict after a trip in her sister's husband's brother's de Dion, hence her concern for him today. In his view, travelling by foot, omnibus and railway train taught you more than a box on four wheels. You were in the middle of life, not shut away from it. But times changed. It was nearly forty years since he was a crusher on the beat on the Ratcliffe Highway. Villains had changed, transport had changed, the century had changed, and now he was a chief inspector with Twitch, his private name for Inspector Stitch, still faithfully plodding behind him despite his persistent attempts to dislodge him from the trail.

'No sign of Auguste?' he asked as Tatiana hurried back. It was eight thirty.

'No, nor the Duchess nor Hester. But we'll have to go.' She bent down to pick up the starting handle to hand to Egbert, and gave one last look down the line.

'*There's* Hester!' she exclaimed with relief, signalling to the Motor Club officials. Joining the queue of cars was the familiar shape and bright red of the Dolly Dobbs. 'Thank goodness. We're only missing Agatha and Auguste now, and that –' as the engine spluttered into life – 'is just too bad.'

Egbert Rose jumped up into the passenger seat again, relieved he still had his right arm. He wasn't used to cranking motorcars and Edith had sombrely read out an article in her magazine about the dangers of allowing your husband to indulge in such occupations, lest he break his arm if the handle swung back. He had survived his first ordeal, and the Bollée swept off with a triumphant toot round Hyde Park Corner. As the wind caught his face he was suddenly grateful for the deerstalker, though he still felt like a fish out of water. Even Auguste Didier banquets lost their appeal as he realised over sixty windy, dusty, chalky miles lay ahead. Why hadn't he sent Twitch?

'Didier's hopped it, has he?'

Inspector Stitch was well-satisfied. He was no friend of Auguste's, and deduced his absence from the scene of the crime meant he was involved in it up to his neck, or his name wasn't Stitch. True, he found the image of Auguste as a murderer hard to reconcile with his being intimately connected to the royal family, of which both Stitches, Alfred and Martha, were unshakeable admirers, but he lived in hopes that there had been some terrible mistake and that Auguste and Tatiana's marriage would be declared null and void, thus rendering Stitch's world once again unsullied.

'He wanted to catch Inspector Rose before he reached Canterbury, so he said,' Charlie explained.

'Why?' Twitch bristled with suspicion.

'Maybe so he could tell His Majesty himself,' Charlie suggested helpfully.

This was unwelcome news to Stitch. His name did not carry the weight it should have done with His Majesty, and devoted admirer though he was, if His Majesty was in the case, then the further out Stitch was the better.

'Taking the Dover Road, are they?'

'The very one.'

'I'll have them stopped, and get the Chief back here.'

'But—'

'Leave it to the police, son.' Stitch moved portentously into the motor house where the police doctor was examining the body, and proceeded to act like the competent and thorough policeman he was.

Auguste attempted to organise his jumbled thoughts and emotions. Here he was, sitting in a railway train bound for a village he did not know, in the hope of stopping the cavalcade before it passed through. He had waited impatiently at Charing Cross while an army of bowler-hatted gentlemen had marched their way off Platform 1 towards their offices for the Saturday morning, hoping that his memory of poring over the road map of Kent with Tatiana was accurate, and that at Welling the railway station was almost on the Dover Road.

As the station names passed by, New Cross, Blackheath, Well Hall, he realised with thankfulness that his thoughts were beginning to take shape. First he must consider how the iron block had swung with such sickening force on to the Dolly Dobbs's vital innards. By accident? By Hester's hand? By another's? Was that why she now lay there dead? Motorcars raised dangerous passions – he remembered his last sight of Harold Dobbs who had hardly seemed to notice that a human being had lost her life, only that his beloved motorcar was ruined. He could build another motorcar; the life was lost for ever.

How Hester had died would not be resolved until the police had inspected the body. Auguste had his own views though. She lay face down, the back of her body apparently uninjured, despite the dried blood he had noticed on her clothes and on the floor. A gun? Hadn't Tatiana told him Hester carried one? Stabbed? He would soon know. And then came the question why? More people had reason to dislike her than Auguste could have believed possible, but how many of them felt strongly enough for murder was another matter. Perhaps it was an accident, he thought without great hope. He tried to keep his mind clear, for it could achieve nothing until he had more facts, yet against his will stray memories flitted in and out of his mind. Some were connected with Hester Hart, some were not, and they were all unwelcome.

In the end, he banished them by an even more unwelcome thought. In two hours' time His Majesty would be ready to greet the first arrivals of the cavalcade. If it was murder, not accident, every one of the people now on the run might need to be questioned, and quickly. He could envisage His

Majesty's face all too clearly. He would deem the murder a personal insult dreamed up by Auguste Didier. Auguste battled with conscience. Could he – terrible thought – leave the banquet to Pierre and return to London with Egbert? No, that would be deemed a personal insult too. The sheer awfulness of his situation overcame him. His cup overflowed with horror when he realised as he leapt down from the railway carriage at Welling Station that *he had forgotten the horseradish sauce.*

'Down there, mate.' There was a jerk of the thumb from the ticket collector in answer to his question as he handed his ticket in. 'Left under the bridge, and Bob's your uncle.'

Whether Bob was his uncle or not, Auguste was thankful to see as he pounded down the slope and turned under the railway bridge on a rough track that the old Roman Watling Street, now re-used as the Dover Road, was indeed close. He stood on the corner and looked to left and right. The station was set in a waste of sandstones and protective palings. In both directions the Dover Road yawned straight and comparatively empty, save for horse vans. To his right under another railway bridge he could see stuccoed cottages; to his left, some way off, villas, and what was obviously the centre of the hamlet. Opposite was farmland. There was nothing to indicate whether a cavalcade of fifty cars had recently passed. He looked westwards again towards London. The cottages must be near the delightfully named Shoulder-of-Mutton Green, and in the distance he could see wooded hills stretching up into a blue haze, surmounted by a tower of some sort. That must be Shooter's Hill, beloved of highwaymen. Perhaps with luck the steep hill had caused problems for some of the motorcars and the cavalcade had stopped. It was just gone nine thirty, a long time for a drive of perhaps fifteen miles out of London, though it was, he told himself, a time of day when roads out of the city might be busy. Then he realised with joy that the haze was now a huge cloud of dust, and it was growing larger. He was not too late. Never had he been so glad to see the Bollée coming towards him. He jumped out into the road, waving his arms.

'Auguste!' There was a shriek, either from Tatiana or the motorcar, as Tatiana was so startled that she almost forgot to apply the brake, so that when she did so the car indignantly side-slipped as Auguste leapt for his life, fortunately in the opposite direction. Behind the Bollée, forty-eight motorcars drew up with varying degrees of promptness and distinct lack of pleasure from the steamers.

'Have you taken all this trouble to catch me up, *mon amour*?' Tatiana was delighted.

'No, I mean yes. I'm afraid, Egbert – ' Egbert had already jumped down from the Bollée, recognising the look on Auguste's face – 'that what we feared has actually happened. Hester Hart is dead, and the Dolly Dobbs smashed.'

'A road accident?'

'No. They never left the club.'

'Oh, but you're wrong,' Tatiana interrupted. 'The Dolly Dobbs is here at the end of the procession. I saw it arrive, so Hester must be driving it.'

'My love, I am not wrong,' he replied gravely.

'But I *saw* it.' She jumped down and, ignoring the questions hurled at her as she passed, ran to the end of the cavalcade.

Left alone, Egbert turned to Auguste. 'Murder?' he asked.

'I don't know. Twitch should be there now. The body was face down so I couldn't move it. But it was cooling, so there was no doubt she was dead. The block and tackle had swung and smashed the car's controls but I don't think it possible it caught her too.' He explained his reasons.

Egbert thought quickly. 'Right. I'll go back. Where are we?'

'The village of Welling. There's a railway station behind me. You'll need to take Fred Gale back with you. He's in charge of the motor stable.'

'Right. And I take it, if it's murder, half the suspects are trundling along here?'

'Yes.'

Egbert Rose did some fast thinking. In normal circumstances he'd have turned the whole lot of them round, dukes, duchesses, Uncle Tom Cobley and all, but these, as he was fully aware, were not normal circumstances. The King was waiting for them to arrive, and arrive they must.

Tatiana came running back, her face pale with horror. 'Auguste, Egbert. I was wrong. It wasn't the Dolly Dobbs. It was Agatha with *Thomas Bailey*.'

'Does it matter?' Auguste asked. If driving with Bailey was her revenge on Dobbs, she had been overtaken by events.

'It matters very much. Suppose it has something to do with Hester's terrible death?' Tatiana's cup was full. 'The car Agatha is driving is an *exact replica* of the Dolly Dobbs.'

Even Auguste could see the enormity of this, and its relevance. 'Tatiana is right, Egbert. It could be important.'

'It's quite awful.' Tatiana was distracted. 'Thomas claims he has been working on this car for years, and since Agatha was deprived of driving her Dolly Dobbs, he allowed her to drive this one. I only caught a glimpse of it earlier and naturally I thought it was the Dolly Dobbs. It isn't. It's the Brighton Baby. And what am I to do about the Motor Club trial? Neither Agatha nor Thomas informed the officials that this isn't the Dolly Dobbs.'

'Keep out of it,' was Egbert's instant advice. 'Sort it out later. There's more important things to worry about.'

'You're right, Egbert,' Tatiana said gratefully. 'I'm getting it out of proportion. It's been a terrible morning with my worry over Auguste, then worrying why Phyllis had turned up with Roderick—'

'*What?*' Auguste exclaimed.

'Yes, I was surprised too,' Tatiana said. 'Since he was guarding the Dolly Dobbs last night, I supposed he'd had a quarrel with Hester this morning—' She broke off, looking at their faces. 'Oh.'

'Stay here, *ma mie*.' Auguste quickly ran after Egbert who was already marching purposefully down the cavalcade.

'Point him out,' was all Egbert said as Auguste caught him up. The goggles and mackintosh had vanished, but the deer-stalker remained.

As they approached the Fiat, Auguste could see Roderick sitting in the passenger seat next to Phyllis; his motoring hat and goggles shielded his expression but it was clear that Phyllis was doing all the talking.

'Mr Smythe?'

'Yes.' His tone was guarded and lacked its usual lofty superiority.

'Chief Inspector Rose, Scotland Yard.'

'Scotland Yard?' exclaimed Phyllis delightedly. 'How *interesting*.'

Roderick did not appear so enraptured, for he said nothing.

'Some bad news, I'm afraid. About your fiancée.'

'That's me,' Phyllis supplied helpfully.

'Miss Hester Hart has been found dead.'

'Dead?' Roderick's voice emerged as a squeak and Phyllis

gave a yelp that would never have been allowed on the boards of Daly's Musical Comedy Theatre.

'You were with her last night to guard the Dolly Dobbs, I understand.'

Roderick's head turned from Egbert to Auguste helplessly. 'No – yes. *No*.'

'Suppose you come back to London with me,' Egbert suggested. 'You might remember which it is.'

Without a word Roderick climbed down, just as Phyllis belatedly realised what was happening. She jumped down herself in a flurry of skirts, lace and veils, and not even remembering her parasol ran round and hurled herself into Roderick's arms. 'You didn't do it for me, did you, my darling?'

'No.' Roderick came to life immediately if ungallantly. 'I had nothing to do with it. Whatever it was,' he added. 'I'm not under arrest, am I?' He tried a light laugh which failed. Despite Egbert's denial, his hand on Roderick's arm suggested the opposite, and had its effect on the cavalcade as they walked back towards the station lane. The news rippled from motorcar to motorcar and by the time it reached Tatiana, Hester had been strangled in a fit of jealous rage and Phyllis and Roderick were under arrest for dastardly conspiracy.

'I will explain to Tatiana that I'll travel to Martyr House by railway later today,' Auguste told Egbert, preparing to leave for London.

'Not you, Auguste. You're going there *now*.'

'Now?'

'That's right.' A gleam in Egbert's eye. 'Someone has to tell His Majesty.'

He was travelling not only without the horseradish sauce but without his goggles, which he found he had forgotten to put in the Bollée before he left for the club, and was forced to borrow Tatiana's spare pair which he was miserably aware were quite clearly ladies'. It was not the way Auguste would have hoped to make his appearance at Martyr House, and he squirmed as the cavalcade passed groups of village children gazing open-mouthed as the motorcars lurched over and into the tramlines; two cars got stuck and, to the ecstasy of the mocking children, had to be pushed out by Leo and two male passengers in the absence of Fred.

The small shops of Welling gave way to splendid villas, bright with geranium beds in front of them, then a mile or two of market gardens and orchards before Bexley Heath came into sight. Or, rather, what sight could be obtained through dust clouds and goggles. One crisis at least might be solved here. Auguste persuaded Tatiana to stop at Penney Son and Parker Ltd, a promising emporium proudly proclaiming itself 'The London Grocery and Provision Stores, Families Waited on Daily', in the forlorn hope of finding fresh horseradish and cream. He came away with three bottles of Mrs Marshall's commercial version of it, which did nothing to improve his mood.

'Poor Hester.' Tatiana broke a long silence as they passed through a cloud of chalk over the River Cray. 'I did not like her but for her to meet such a violent end is terrible.'

'It might have been an accident or even suicide.' Auguste was unable to convince himself, let alone his wife.

'But you don't think so.'

'I'm afraid murder seems all too possible.'

'I know we've feared trouble but I never thought it could be so bad. I know I should not consider such matters, but I can't help wondering what will happen to the club now.'

'It will probably double in membership.'

'Auguste! It's not like you to be so heartless.'

Heart was what his wife had never lacked, he reflected, as he justified himself on grounds of honesty. Hester Hart's death was a shock, and a sadness which the waste of human life always aroused. But she had seemed a bitter woman who would trample on whom she pleased for her own ends. Perhaps, however, she was justified in being bitter – and perhaps there were those here today who had caused it.

Elsewhere in the cavalcade, Hester Hart's death had replaced all other topics of conversation, even displacing His Majesty and such interesting matters as the merits of pneumatic tyres and the new belt-driven transmission. Hushed voices paid respect to the dead but the excitement suppressed within them was attributable to other emotions.

'You knew her once,' Sir Algernon rumbled, closing his eyes as Maud drove headlong into the cloudy white chalk dust slipstream of the cars in front.

'Yes.' Maud's heavy foot hit the brake.

'Wasn't there some to-do or other over her?'

Maud ignored him as she expertly regained speed to take the 1 in 14 hill out of Dartford in fine style.

He tried again. 'I didn't know she was a member of your club.'

'Never thought to tell you, Algy. She'd changed, you see. Thoroughly nice woman now. Or rather was.' Maud thought with satisfaction of the pleasure ahead driving in the October International Women's Race. Fate took its revenge at the fork where Watling Street left the Dover Road. She had a puncture. With a scathing glance at her unmechanically-minded husband, she climbed down. Leo was already struggling with a tyre some way back so she'd change the wheel herself. It was a small price to pay fate, on the whole.

Sailing past in her Fiat, Phyllis allowed tears of self-pity to trickle down her cheeks behind the veil. She was *alone* in a motorcar. If Roderick had not turned up so unexpectedly this morning and insisted on driving with her instead of in his Crossley she would have had her motor servant with her. Now she had no one. What would happen if she had a puncture? It would be so ignominious to have to ask Leo for help, and even he seemed to have disappeared. The horrors of her position overcame her as she realised she was dangerously close to the motorcar in front, and she clutched the wheel as though it were the lead of a mad bulldog. She told herself if she allowed herself to cry, she would be in no fit state to curtsy to the King with her charming smile. Why *was* she crying? she suddenly wondered. After all, Hester was dead and there was nothing more to worry about. Except punctures. And unless Roderick was arrested for murder.

'There's someone else stopping us,' Tatiana exclaimed disbelievingly, beginning to brake. 'On Gad's Hill, of all places. We'll all be running backwards if we're not careful.'

'It's not Mrs Millward, is it?' Auguste peered through his now filthy goggles with their even filthier lace side shields.

'Not unless Hortensia is disguised as a police constable.'

'Police constable?' he echoed in surprise. Had Egbert issued a reprieve for him? It was rather late to summon him back to London now.

The constable, middle-aged, lean and excited, more used to rubbing out tramp markings on his beat than having urgent messages from Scotland Yard, smartly saluted Auguste. 'Chief Inspector Rose?'

'No.' All, Auguste instantly realised, was explained. Twitch had been at work.

'Where is he then?' The constable's politeness faded and suspicion replaced excitement.

'He has returned to London.'

'How could he know he was wanted?'

'I told him.' Auguste cursed all police constables who aspired to the Detective Branch.

Suspicion increased. 'What have you got to do with it?'

'I found the body of the dead woman.'

The constable pounced. 'Then why aren't you back there too? Escaping from justice, are you?'

'Because—'

Tatiana decided to intervene with a rare call on her rank. Auguste could be annoyingly obstreperous at times. 'I am the Princess Tatiana Didier, and this is my husband. We are on our way to a reception given by His Majesty. He will not be pleased if we are late.'

A princess? The constable lost some of his confidence. Nevertheless, his duty had to be done.

'I'd best come with you then to see for myself.'

This was all he needed, Auguste thought. Now he would arrive at Martyr House with a policeman behind him intent on arresting him on suspicion of murdering Egbert.

Tatiana again saved the day, her despairing eye on two Motor Club of Great Britain officials waiting to time a measured mile by what they believed to be the Dolly Dobbs.

'I wonder if you would mind, Sergeant, travelling with Miss Lockwood – the musical comedy star, you know. She is a very *young* lady, and nervous about travelling on her own.'

The policeman turned brick red. He had no objection to travelling with Miss Lockwood; he'd seen her in *Pink For Miss Pamela*. He'd been up in the gods then and now he'd be sitting next to her. He took his place in the Fiat with alacrity –

just in time for Phyllis's first puncture of the trip. She turned to him, removed her goggles and let tears form in the lovely eyes. 'I wonder if you'd mind, Constable . . . '

'I wonder why Phyllis needs a policeman with her.' Isabel broke the inexplicable silence that had fallen between herself and Hugh ever since they'd heard the news of Hester's death. 'Do you think she thumped poor Hester over the head in jealousy? Or that she was in collusion with Roderick to do it?'

'You don't seem too upset at Hester's death,' Hugh observed, watching her closely – not that her expression was visible under the veil.

'No,' Isabel replied with surprise. 'Why should I pretend? I didn't like her very much.' It was an understatement. She was almost faint with relief.

'My first murder took place near here,' Auguste observed suddenly as they sped along the Dover Road between hop-fields and cherry orchards towards Faversham.

'I'm glad that policeman can't hear you say that.' Tatiana managed a laugh.

'I've known Egbert nearly thirteen years. I met him at Stockbery Towers on the downs in eighteen ninety-one.'

'And now you're an experienced detective.'

He considered this. 'Perhaps.' He wondered why he always felt ambivalent about this role which had been none of his seeking.

'Will Egbert want you to help him on this case?'

He considered this too. 'I can hardly refuse if he asks me.' Nor, he realised, did he want to. He was already throwing ingredients into the casserole of this murder, and besides, he was angry that Tatiana's beloved club had been the scene of so much violence and hatred. As they passed over Harbledon Down and the magnificent view of Canterbury spread out before them, he reflected on the joy this point in the journey must have brought the pilgrims to the cathedral's shrine. Their own journey would be a darker one. 'I hope he does. I want it over *quickly*. Is that selfish of me?'

At the back of both their minds was tucked away the thought: what about Eastbourne? Would the trip they were all four looking forward to so much take place? If Egbert was allotted the case, it must be solved. Eastbourne was now less than two weeks away.

The journey passed slowly as even the mechanically perfect Léon Bollée laboured up the hill out of Canterbury, and then the wind caught them in all its fury on the exposed and virtually treeless Barham Downs. At last a battered signpost displayed the legend Barham. Martyr House was almost upon them.

'At least we haven't had any trouble from the Hams,' Tatiana remarked more cheerfully as she turned the steering wheel towards Barham.

One motorcar was not to be so lucky.

'Your motorcar is driving splendidly, Thomas,' Agatha informed him briskly. He had been very quiet since they had heard the news of Hester and the Dolly Dobbs and could hardly be raised to enthusiasm even by this praise. 'It's done over sixty miles now,' she continued. 'Doesn't that mean we're over the limit of what the accumulators could have achieved on their own?'

'Yes.' He belatedly added, 'Your Grace.'

'Splendid, for we're approaching Barham Downs where the last Motor Club trial will be. After they've taken the time at the end of the measured mile, we'll tell them this isn't the Dolly

Dobbs. And no apologising to them, Thomas.' She wagged a warning gloved finger at him, then removed it to pull the lever controlling the hoods round to face full front to catch the wind driving head on towards them over the Downs.

Half a mile further on, the Brighton Baby slid to a halt, in full view of two Motor Club officials.

There was a pause. Then, 'What is wrong with this contraption, Thomas?' The Duchess's voice was dangerously quiet as, aghast, he sought an answer. He had leapt down and was running frantically round his beloved Baby. 'Is it a broken cable?'

'No.'

'Is it a fault in the motor or dynamo?'

'I don't think so.'

'Could it by any chance be the battery?'

'I think it must be.'

'*Why?*'

'The voltmeter fell below seventy-five volts.'

'Kindly explain yourself, my man.'

His voice rose in panic. 'I think it must be the wind.'

'There is enough wind on this heath to power a railway train.' Agatha's voice was clipped.

'But not the right kind of wind.' Thomas eyed the approaching Motor Club officials with dread fascination.

'Right *kind*?' she purred.

'It's coming from the wrong direction. It must be too strong.'

'Forgive me if I'm wrong, but the point of the levers is to turn those windmill hoods to obtain all the wind they can get.'

He gazed at her, his face white. 'I might have forgotten to reckon with the wind resistance factor.'

'It seems to me the wind is resisting you all too well,' she snapped, turning to speak to the Motor Club men with a winning smile. They were not won, and a few minutes later, with the Brighton Baby's fate officially sealed, she switched her attention back to the cowering designer.

'And how,' she asked sweetly, 'do you propose we travel from here to meet His Majesty?'

The local group of Hams led by Hortensia Millward, who had been biding its time hiding in the straggly line of trees and undergrowth lining the road, burst out, only too willing to tell her.

King Edward VII advanced cordially towards the Bollée as its occupants descended. This, he had decided, would be a pleasant, informal event. What could be more pleasant, after all, than a procession of motorcars driven by at least some pretty ladies, welcoming them all and then tucking in to an Auguste Didier banquet on a perfect July day? Especially when Tatiana was organising the event.

'Good morning, Bertie.'

How did she manage to look so calm? Auguste wondered admiringly as Bertie kissed her, complimented her on her looks, her gown, and her Bollée. He almost went so far as to compliment her on her husband, such was his good humour.

'If I might have a word, Your Majesty,' Auguste murmured, returning upright after his bow and then taking the final plunge, 'after you have received all the drivers, of course.'

'Certainly, certainly. Nothing wrong, I hope. Haven't left the horseradish behind, have you?' Bertie chortled.

While he was awaiting execution for incompetence, Auguste slipped into the marquee. In there there would be comfort, and there was. Even to his anxious eye, all seemed to be going splendidly. Greenery and roses adorned the tables in elegant trails, silver gleamed, glasses shone. More important still, the food appeared a model of pleasing colour and succulence. Hot food was ranged ready to serve along the back of the marquee, cold buffets along one side, and wine, desserts, cheese and fruit along the other. Moreover Luigi was with Bernard standing on one side of the tent and Pierre on the other, *without* an atmosphere that needed to be cut by a specially sharpened knife. Auguste debated whether to tell them about the tragedy now or after the banquet, and decided in favour of now since they would undoubtedly overhear gossip during the luncheon. He called them together, to tell them Hester Hart had been found dead and the Dolly Dobbs smashed. There was instant silence. Everyone had heard of the problem of Hester Hart.

'No. We don't know yet how she died, but the Dolly Dobbs was put out of action in the motor house and she was found dead beside it.'

'Did the police come?' asked Luigi sharply.

'Yes. They are coming here later as well. They will doubtless wish to speak to us all, but the important matter for the moment is the banquet. Let us ensure that it goes with the perfection it deserves.'

Ten minutes later, his soul soothed by the calming sight of mousses, quails in aspic, *filets de sôle*, and a hundred other dishes blending into an exciting panorama of gastronomic delight, Auguste went back to face his less pleasant duty of giving His Majesty the news. He was just in time to see the arrival of the Brighton Baby. It had come with much less horsepower than all the other cars, but what it had came from real horses.

Hortensia Millward, flushed with pride, marched in the vanguard of four horses towing the broken-down motor containing one distraught inventor and one irate duchess whose victory over Hester Hart had been ruined.

'Why's he coming?' the King asked in surprise at the news that Egbert Rose would be arriving later. Then fearing this sounded inhospitable, he said with his usual courtesy (it was his expression that could whittle Auguste into the ground quicker than a tent peg), 'I'm delighted, of course. No one planning to assassinate me today, I hope?' There was caution in his voice for he associated Egbert, and therefore Auguste, with such attempts in the past.

'No, sir.'

'It's about a sudden death,' Tatiana broke the news gently.

'Here?' There was instant alarm in the King's voice.

'In London.'

Bertie beamed in relief. 'Splendid.'

'But it affects the Ladies' Motoring Club. Hester Hart was a member of it.'

'Hester Hart?' The King frowned. She was that woman in the press who kept wandering off to the desert. And something had happened years ago, when he was still Prince of Wales. He tried his best to remember, but failed. He met so many women. 'What sort of death? Apart from its being sudden?' He fixed Auguste with the eagle eye he had come to know. It could spot defenceless prey from a thousand feet.

'It might be murder, sir.'

There was a pause as His Majesty grappled with the word he always associated with Auguste. Then he decided to be magnanimous. After all, the body wasn't here, only the damn suspects, from what he could gather. 'Another case for Inspector Didier, eh?'

The banquet passed without mishap, with even a regal compliment on the horseradish sauce. Éclairs, jellies, ice creams and circular sandwiches smoothly followed at four o'clock. Champagne punch flowed. The name of Hester Hart had not been heard for at least thirty minutes when Egbert arrived.

'Was it murder, Egbert?' Auguste asked soberly.

'Oh yes. A whacking great stab wound in the chest.'

Chapter Six

Martyr House, a severe and to Auguste's eye rather dull seventeenth-century mansion, was large, but even so it seemed to be overflowing with bodies. Live ones fortunately. Most of the guests were staying at neighbouring houses but the provision of retiring and temporary dressing rooms for the ball this evening seemed to have converted the house into a scene worthy of Bruegel's brush. Or perhaps, Auguste thought as he led Egbert to the cubbyhole which had been allotted to his investigation by the somewhat grudging Isabel, Lewis Carroll's pen could do more justice to it. It was a scene built of a pack of cards, and here was Egbert in its midst, perhaps to bring them fluttering down in a heap. Auguste only hoped His Majesty didn't decide to enter this Wonderland of a situation by crying 'Off with their heads'.

It was a strange juxtaposition, seeing Egbert in his familiar Scotland Yard bowler and dark suit marching stolidly past those glittering birds of paradise. They hardly cast him a glance, so intent were they on discussions of such vital matters as last week's ball and next week's soirée, combined with average speeds, petrol consumption, and the high wages of nearly £100 a year demanded by chauffeurs. He had hardly heard the name of Hester Hart, though during the afternoon the Dolly Dobbs had most certainly been a talking point – or rather Thomas Bailey's imitation. Or was Dolly the imitation? There were undercurrents at work here, at which he and Egbert could only guess and into which they would have to delve to reach the truth.

These smiling ladies in their muslins and gauzes looked as if their delicate lace-gloved hands had difficulty holding bone china teacups, and yet each one of them was adventurous enough to drive a motorcar, even if they were Rabbits, not Racers. To be a Rabbit demanded an adventurousness greater than most women saw any need for.

Egbert took one look at the bare cell he had been allotted in the kitchen block. 'The labourer is worthy of his hire,' he announced briskly, and marched straight out again. 'Where's the Countess?'

Auguste consulted his pocket watch. 'It is six o'clock. She will be dressing for the ball.'

'I'll see the Earl then, even if he's in his suspenders and long johns.'

Twenty minutes later, installed in the library, a room rarely disturbed by the owners, Egbert was eyeing a tray of tea with satisfaction. It was after six, so even this gesture suggested how low Scotland Yard figured in the social scale of Martyr House, Auguste thought, but refrained from comment to Egbert.

'Auguste,' he set his cup down, 'we've got to solve this one quickly.'

'We, Egbert?'

'For Tatiana's sake. You know the club, you know the people.'

'I suppose it couldn't be suicide?'

'Someone came along and moved the body if so. *And* the weapon. It was murder. Question is, why? Was the motive the death of Hester Hart, in which case why put the car out of action, or was the motorcar the intended victim and Hester Hart inconveniently in the way?'

'Or both,' Auguste suggested. 'But why would someone wish to destroy the Dolly Dobbs when another one could be built tomorrow? It is true that for some people a great deal depended on today.'

'Any more than what you told me about last Sunday?' Egbert consulted his notebook. 'This Duchess had her nose put out of joint.'

'She put it back. Dobbs's rival brought his own motorcar here today and the Duchess drove it.'

'She still had a motive though. Revenge on Hester Hart.'

'Her vengeance *was* the Bailey car. The Brighton Baby is identical to the Dolly Dobbs, and the Duchess let the Motor Club officials test it under the impression it was the Dolly Dobbs.'

'Reason enough for both of them to want the Dolly Dobbs out of action.'

'Both Harold and Hester received threatening letters this week, warning them against driving the Dolly Dobbs.'

'Nasty.' Egbert made a note. 'Anyone else have reason to smash the car? We can exclude Dobbs for a start.'

'Perhaps.' Auguste thought back.

Egbert cocked an eye at him. 'You sound doubtful.'

'A pinch of salt or pepper can transform a dish, and you always tell me never to discount anything. Suppose Dobbs knew about the Brighton Baby being identical to his own car?'

'He'd have had all the more reason to go through the trials first.'

'Yes, yet he behaved very strangely last Saturday after he knew Bailey had been snooping around. He refused to allow the Dolly Dobbs out of the motor house. Even Hester could not persuade him.'

'I suppose it's possible, in the heat of the moment.' Egbert was still doubtful.

'But was it in the heat of the moment?' Auguste asked. 'The murderer went prepared for murder.' A sudden thought. 'Or did the weapon come from the repair house?'

Egbert eyed Auguste appreciatively. 'Twitch has had Fred Gale and Leo go through that repair house like a dose of salts. If there was anything missing we'd know. There wasn't.'

'It might not be missing.'

'Twitch thought of that too. He's sized up the wound, drawn it out, and had every single article in the repair house that might fit lined up. Chisels, knives, anything. No bloodstains. None that show, anyway. We're doing a further check with some of them to see if a camera can pick up anything. But Twitch doesn't think so. He's a good man, Twitch. Within his limits.' The limits were those to which Egbert's patience could be put.

'Hester told Tatiana she always had a gun with her. Was there no sign of it?'

'No. Interesting, that. Perhaps she forgot to take it.'

'Just when she knew there was a chance she might need it? That's not likely, Egbert. How about the Dolly Dobbs? Could the block have hit it by accident, do you think?'

'Not a chance. It would take several swings to get the momentum going to hit the controls that hard.'

'It would take strength too. Beyond a woman's capabilities.'

'There you're wrong, Auguste. I got Fred Gale to demonstrate. It wouldn't take that much strength, and they're all used to driving motorcars, after all.'

Auguste was silenced, remembering his own thoughts a little earlier on the strength of delicately-gloved hands.

'The doors were padlocked this morning. How did the murderer get in?'

'Ah. Now we're back to our Mr Roderick Smythe.' Egbert had all the satisfaction of a cat with a mouse firmly in his sights. 'Fred Gale didn't bother with locking up because Miss Hart *and* Smythe were there. When Smythe went – if he did – he claims he didn't bother locking up because Hester said she'd do it.'

'How could she padlock herself in?'

Egbert thought for a moment. 'She'd only have to padlock the Dolly Dobbs door, enter the repair house, close that one and then bolt the inner door to the Dolly Dobbs stable after her.'

'Then how did the murderer get in?'

'You're not thinking, Auguste. You need a good cup of tea. She let him or her in, of course.'

His head was spinning, and Auguste struggled to puzzle it out. 'But the repair shop door was padlocked this morning, not bolted inside. Had Fred been there?'

'No. He left the car fully charged last night. The murderer clicked the padlock home without a key, and Hester couldn't bolt it because she was dead.'

'Of course.' Auguste suddenly felt exhausted. It had been a long day.

Egbert poured tea for him and pushed the cup towards him. 'Have some.'

He sipped. It was terrible, but it was comforting. He took another sip which was better. 'There is a lot we don't know about Hester. Why did she join the club and then go out of her way to tell them about her memoirs? And, even more interestingly, her diaries?'

Egbert was suddenly alert. 'I must need more of this tea

myself. I'd forgotten about them. Twitch will find them. He's at her house now.'

'They may reveal other motives, besides that of the Dolly Dobbs.'

'They may, but for my money Roderick Smythe still has some explaining to do.'

'Is he still at the Yard?'

'No. He's changing for dinner upstairs. He's back here.'

'*Here?*'

'I've no evidence yet,' Egbert said irritably, correctly interpreting Auguste's expression. 'Better here than on a cross-Channel steamer. He's an arrogant chap and was shouting all over the Yard that the King was waiting to receive him. Not to mention Phyllis Lockwood.'

It was Auguste's opinion that Phyllis was fully able to manage on her own. Her arrival with a policeman at her side had not gone unremarked by His Majesty. The constable had changed a tyre, refilled a boiled radiator, and shooed off a herd of sheep who had inconsiderately barred Miss Lockwood's way when she took a wrong turn on Barham Downs. Once arrived at Martyr House, he had been leapt on by His Majesty's private guard to ensure he really was a policeman, and without so much as a caviare canapé he had been driven to the nearest railway station for immediate despatch back to Strood, whence he came.

'What's his story about what happened last night?'

'Frederick Gale says Tatiana asked him to stay with Hester because Smythe was no longer coming. That right?' Auguste nodded. 'He came back from a nap at twelve o'clock and Hester Hart was then inside the Dolly Dobbs motor house.'

'Alive?'

'So he says.'

'Of course she was alive,' Auguste remembered. 'Tatiana heard her talking to Smythe.'

'Did she? I'll have a word with her. Smythe's story is that he came along shortly before twelve thirty hoping to make up the quarrel with his fiancée and stay on guard himself, so he told Fred to hop it. Fred was doubtful about going but as he knew nothing about any quarrrel between the two of them, and the original intention had been for Smythe to stand guard, he couldn't see any reason to object. So he went home, glad to get a night's sleep before the big day. This morning he and Leo went straight to the cavalcade with their motor vans.'

'Why did Smythe change his mind about staying?'

'He claims Hester told him quite amicably that she was fully capable of guarding the Dolly Dobbs on her own, that their quarrel was resolved and their engagement reinstated.'

'That does not quite accord with what Tatiana overheard.'

'I'm not too surprised. I can't see Hester Hart being so amicable if she was anything like you've told me. Smythe says he had a good night's sleep and only drove down with Miss Lockwood because his own motorcar wasn't drivable. He'd been intending to follow the cavalcade, with Fred and Leo, as the dustcart after the Lord Mayor's Show.'

'Strange for a racing driver to be so inefficient with his own motorcar. Does he have witnesses to the time he arrived home?'

'His manservant says just before two. He says one o'clock, but he spent some time in the motor house alone hoping to get the Crossley going.'

'Alone?' Auguste repeated.

'Quite alone. On the other hand,' Egbert grunted, 'there's no evidence against him except that he was last on the scene.'

'Fingerprints?' Auguste asked hopefully. He knew that the Fingerprint Department at the Yard established three years ago was at last beginning to pay dividends and that there was hope the courts might take notice of such evidence.

'Twitch is working on it.'

Leaving Egbert to struggle into the tail coat and trousers he had reluctantly brought in honour of his King, Auguste yielded to the temptation to slip down to the kitchens before changing for dinner himself. Ostensibly this was to check that the remains of his luncheon and tea were not in any way hindering the progress of the resident chef's ball supper and that his own club china and glass and ornaments had not intruded – by sheer mistake – into the assets of Martyr House. He also, he admitted, had a professional curiosity in seeing another's kitchen at such a critical moment in the preparation of a meal of which His Majesty was to partake. True, His Majesty always had the foresight to send one of his own chefs down to superintend the food to be served, and sometimes to cook it. When he was not long married, Auguste had had several clashes with these otherwise admirable gentlemen, as to whose authority reigned supreme. His victory was his first taste of the power that status of social position can bestow, and when he belatedly realised the reason for the chefs' speedy surrender he had spent much time in rebuilding the delicate bridges of spun sugar needed to heal wounded feelings and open a route to a tarmacadamed smoother future.

By a kitchen, so shall you know a house. He did not like the smell of this one. There seemed to be wealth without taste, beautiful objects that instead of warming heart and eye lay and hung lifelessly, as if stifled in a house without love. Indeed it probably was, if the rumours about Isabel were true, and from what he had seen of the Earl, he was an amiable but aimless gentleman who could no more stamp a personality on the household than a dried-out stick of sealing wax. The only member of the family who could claim connections with humanity was the Earl's mother, who had enlivened Auguste's teatime with a spirited account of her early, and close, friendship with His Majesty. The kitchens, however, lacked even this glimpse of warmth. Its staff moved like pawns on a sterile chessboard, the smell of food battling with, not enriching, its surroundings. Auguste knew precisely the kind of supper that would emerge from this kitchen: competent, expensive and *dull.* Lobster salads would be just that, a series of ingredients put together to answer the description, not created to form an excitement of its own; *oeufs à la neige* would be floating cardboard meringues in a sea of stagnant custard. However, he had another reason for being here, an important one, one which he had been at a loss to define until the events of the day had brought them to the surface and crystallised them into a question.

There was no sign of his staff here, and upon inquiring for Pierre's whereabouts he was directed to the vast area of larders and stillrooms at the back of the kitchens. Most of his staff were busy repacking boxes and hampers, but from the very cubbyhole Egbert had rejected he overheard the familiar strains of a quarrel between Pierre and Luigi. It was too much, and he burst into the room.

'And what is the problem *now*? The banquet went splendidly, did it not? You worked together admirably. Can we not at this difficult time stay united?'

'I am telling this dog how splendid a lady Miss Hart was. That no one would wish to murder *her*. It must have been someone who wanted to harm the motorcar.'

'And *I* have told *him* –' Luigi smiled with a maddening complacency – 'that many people would wish to murder Miss Hart. When you're *in* a restaurant you hear a great deal that those who are confined to kitchens miss. Let this oaf dream on. Whatever I say, he will contradict it. He has no brain.'

'Only a heart, which you lack, dog.'

'Suppose we *all* remember that Miss Hart is dead,' Auguste said quietly, 'and that quarrelling about her can achieve nothing. Remembering what might be helpful to the police might, however, achieve something.'

'That is true,' Luigi said slowly. 'And I might remember very interesting things.'

Egbert Rose felt constricted by his dinner shirt and white waistcoat, though unlike His Majesty had had no reason to leave his bottom button undone. He had been all for bringing a white dicky but Edith had insisted on taking it out of the suitcase and putting in her father's best dress shirt, now bequeathed to Egbert. She had pointed out, with some justice, how awkward it would be if the edges of the dicky popped out as he bowed to His Majesty. In the interests of the smooth furtherance of the case, Egbert had submitted, but now he shifted in it uneasily as he stood by the door of the ballroom in which all the guests were now assembled; they were waiting for His Majesty's arrival.

He remembered the first time he had met Auguste; that had also been the first time he'd been plunged into the midst of the aristocracy in a murder case. It had been at Stockbery Towers in '91. He'd been surprised by what he had found then, even shocked, but the aristocracy were, he now knew, no different from Edith and himself or anyone else. There were villains amongst them and good-hearted people, just the same as there were anywhere. What made them seem different, he thought as he surveyed the glittering evening dresses and jewels before him, was that they all conformed to some artificial code to which you had to learn the key. Though was it so artificial? All groups had their own language, from street sellers and rat-catchers to Metropolitan policemen. The aristocracy did have one asset, he conceded, which rat-catchers and chimney sweeps lacked. They had power, and Egbert never under-estimated that.

He listened as the Earl called for silence, and believing that this meant His Majesty, not Egbert Rose, was on his way, they obeyed.

'Hester Hart was murdered,' Egbert informed them as the Earl motioned he was free to speak. 'Most of you knew her; she was a member of the Ladies' Motoring Club, and she was murdered by someone who was either a member or who knew the ways of the club. That someone also either knew she would be there that evening or they had designs on the Dolly Dobbs and didn't care who was there.'

The ripple of unease communicated itself as fast as news in the Seamen's Rest that a crusher had come through the door. Egbert registered the looks of shock around him. Auguste would have said he felt like a turnip thrown into a ratatouille, but that's just what Egbert intended – to shake them up a bit.

'Many of you were dining in the restaurant last evening, most of you knew of the Dolly Dobbs, so that means some of you must have information to give me. I shall be in the library this evening, while the ball is on, so you can come to see me there. Otherwise I'll call on you in London.'

As he finished his brief statement, his eye travelled round, wondering who was who. Which were the women who might have good reason to dislike Hester Hart? His eye fell on a middle-aged woman with a long face and determined jaw, standing by an inoffensive, scholarly-looking man. Now them he did recognise. How on earth did Hortensia Millward and her husband get invited to a Ladies' Motoring Club ball?

'Good evening, Tati. And Auguste.' A belated thought.

Auguste glowed, for this was the first time he had ever been addressed as Auguste, not Didier. Unfortunately it was soon clear His Majesty was preoccupied, and it had slipped out by accident.

'This murder,' His Majesty began querulously.

'What about it, Bertie?' Tatiana glanced nervously at Auguste.

'That fellow Rose says he's going to be in the library this evening, interviewing people. Odd thing to happen at a ball, but murder is murder, I suppose.' He glared at Auguste as though daring him to disagree.

'You're always very understanding, Bertie,' Tatiana consoled him helpfully.

'I try to be.' This was news to Auguste. 'Does it mean Rose thinks the murderer is actually *here*?'

Auguste hesitated. 'It means he or she *could* be here, sir, simply because it is probably someone associated with the club, even if not a member. No one would break in from outside without at least a contact in the club.'

'What about that horse woman?'

'Mrs Millward?' Tatiana was astonished. 'How would she even know which motor house the Dolly Dobbs was in?'

Auguste decided not to court trouble by mentioning Thomas Bailey had found no difficulty.

'Good.' The King cleared his throat. 'I've had it on my mind, you see. I invited her.'

'To the motor stable?' Auguste was muddled.

'Here.' His Majesty glared. 'I remembered John Millward will be on the next honours list, so I invited them this afternoon. Then as I was dressing I suddenly thought, suppose they're murderers.'

Tatiana glanced at Auguste. His Majesty must be comforted, and distracted. 'This house is used to them,' she said lightly.

'*What?*' His Majesty looked round nervously for John Sweeney, his private detective.

'This house, or rather the mediaeval house it was built around, was one of several that belonged to one of the murderers of Thomas à Becket, so Isabel Tunstall told me.'

'Let's hope he's not walking around, eh?' The King roared with laughter.

Dancing with Isabel, Auguste decided as he exchanged polite pleasantries (it would hardly do to ask his hostess while clasped in his arms where she was at the time of the murder) was like gliding over an already iced cake with the point of an icing bag. Maud Bullinger had proved a bumpier experience, like smoothing pastry over plums. He had felt like a mere garnish to Agatha's neat tournedos of a waltz, and a fish scorched by a salamander after he had been released by Miss Dazey. He had then taken the floor with Isabel, watched suspiciously, he nervously noticed, not by the Earl but by Hugh Francis who appeared to be as devoted to Isabel as mutton to haricots. He was grateful that his next duty was to his wife.

'Bertie does not seem too upset,' Auguste whispered to her.

'It's not Bertie whose club has been ruined.'

'The club is only the location, not the cause of the crime,' he comforted her. 'It will survive.'

'What is the cause?'

'People, as always.'

'And those people are here tonight,' she said soberly. 'You will find out who has done this terrible thing, won't you, Auguste?'

'*Chérie*, I will.'

He meant it, but it was not going to be easy. To begin with, he must eradicate the cause of the smell of something amiss which had pervaded his kitchen for the last two weeks. The smell had not stemmed from Hester Hart but had arisen within himself, his own private stockpot, for it stemmed from where he had believed himself secure. It was time, he decided, to slip away while supper was being served. The kitchens would be quieter.

He found Pierre in the servants' hall enjoying a plateful of roast beef. Not for the Martyr House servants anything so common as lobster salad; they roasted, even in July, meat for their own suppers.

'Our own venison stew, of which much remains, is of no interest to you?' Auguste inquired lightly.

Pierre was not put out by Auguste's sudden appearance. 'A cook is entitled to tire of his own wares,' he countered.

'But not of mine,' Auguste pointed out, a little hurt. 'Pierre, I have something to ask you. When you have finished, we will go to somewhere more private.'

Pierre eyed his remaining roast parsnips wistfully and put them aside. 'Let us go now, Monsieur Didier. Whatever it is you have to ask, I have something to tell *you*. Something that will interest both you and this Scotland Yard inspector. I would like to explain to you first.'

Auguste, taken aback by the accuracy of his own suspicions, accompanied him into the cubbyhole once more, but Pierre gave him no chance to speak first.

'I knew Miss Hart before I came to the club. That is what you wanted to ask me, isn't it? I knew her very well, and that is why I admired her so greatly and why I grieve so much for her death.'

'Then, Pierre, would I be right in thinking that your apprenticeship as a chef was not served in the Hôtel Grande in Marseille?'

'Yes, monsieur. My father worked in the kitchens for a time. As a child, I washed dishes, even peeled vegetables there on occasion. But my training, if you can call it such, was in my father's restaurant in Marseille, and in my travels.'

'And your father's restaurant, I imagine, did not cater for French customers or provide French cuisine?'

'Only in the sense that Algérie is considered part of the French Republic.'

'And your father is of the Arab race, is he not?'

'You are correct. And my mother is Turkish. I was born into a land of Christian beliefs but brought up as a Muhammadan. Our family name is Khalil with a K, but my father adopted French spelling.' He hesitated. 'Might I ask how you guessed?'

'From your cooking. You are skilled in the cuisine of many lands but in the end one's origins betray one.'

'*Asl*,' Pierre commented ruefully. 'It means a man's origin, and we Arabs believe it influences conduct for ever.'

'Your love of mint does, certainly. Your fascination with sweet and sour in unusual combinations, your use of honey, and an approach that combines crudeness with occasional great subtlety. Moreover –' Auguste was a little hurt – 'you obviously disliked my whistling, and I know Arabs strongly disapprove of it.' He had also thought it strange that Miss Hart had spoken so rudely to Pierre last Saturday; if that was how she treated the servants at the club, he had thought, she was in no position to complain of her treatment by those who considered themselves superior to her. 'Now, please tell me how you met Miss Hart. I cannot believe it was in a couscous restaurant in Marseille.'

'It hardly matters where I met her. What I must tell you urgently is what I was to her, so that you can find her murderer *quickly*.' There was vehemence in his voice.

'You were her cook?'

'Her dragoman. Cooking was only part of it. For over six years I accompanied her on her travels, beginning in Algérie and elsewhere in Africa, then east through India, Syria, Persia, Jordan. I understand the Muhammadan attitude to women, to strangers, to money, to food, and to life. What was invaluable to her was that I could also understand hers. The Muhammadan holds women in high respect, monsieur, despite the fact that their women are kept at home. The foreign woman who travels, while not of their religion, should be safe, but it is necessary for them to have a dragoman, for not all Arabs keep the faith. There are brigands who would murder rather than have the trouble of bartering. Also,' he laughed, 'Miss Hart was not a good cook.'

'And how did you come to be at the club?' Auguste asked sharply. He was annoyed with himself for not having pursued his doubts before.

'Miss Hart asked me to come,' Pierre explained simply.

'Why? Surely she had no need of a dragoman here?'

'This is what I asked her immediately. I would not have been surprised if she had employed me as her cook at her new home, but a ladies' motoring club seemed very strange. Then she explained. I was in a sense to be her dragoman in the club too. She wanted me to defend her. And look how I have failed her.' His face contorted in agony.

'Defend her against what?' Auguste asked more gently. 'Did she know her life could be in danger?'

'Perhaps not, but she was in some sort of danger for she was marching into unknown territory, she said, and I was to be there to help if needed.'

'And did you?'

'I did what she asked me. Anything I heard about her, good or bad, I was to relay back to her.'

'How?'

'I sent letters, and sometimes met her outside the club. My writing is good,' he added proudly.

'But how did she know that a ladies' motoring club could be a dangerous place *before* she joined it and started causing trouble?'

'Because I know she intended to find danger. She sought it as eagerly as she sought adventure in the desert. She sought revenge; it was a long thought-out plan and the reason for her return to England.'

'You know? How?'

'She told me.'

'When, where and what?' Auguste was sharper than he intended. This could be the key he had been hoping for to the secret of Hester Hart.

'Everywhere. In the desert, monsieur, in the ruins of Palmyra, in Petra, in Egypt, in ancient Babylon. A dragoman is more than a butler or cook, whose wages are paid for duty done. He is a partner in an adventure. In the desert one needs a companion, for its beauty is too immense for man to be alone. The infinite stretches ahead, behind, to east, to west, and words flow easier than here in England. In the desert there is stillness and natural beauty to rest the eye; here there are a thousand distractions to occupy every moment. Hurry is from Hell, says the Arab. Hurry is the honeyed path to Heaven, says English society.'

Auguste hardly dared to ask. 'While Miss Hart talked to you of this great adventure, her revenge, did she mention any names in particular?'

'Indeed she did, monsieur, and that is why I knew I must tell you of them immediately, for my own sake as well as hers.'

'*Your* sake?'

'Because she is dead, monsieur, and I too have a life I cherish.'

Chief Inspector Egbert Rose was impatiently awaiting the arrival of anyone at all. All that had happened so far was that the door had cautiously opened to reveal the most junior footman who had put down a tray of lukewarm roast beef in front of him. He had been disappointed. It tasted like Mr Pinpole's beef; he suspected his local butcher of advertising in Smithfield for the toughest beef in England to sell to Edith, and now he knew Pinpole was not alone. Mr Pinpole's brother must be a cattle farmer down here. Meanwhile no one from the ballroom had bothered to take time out of their busy dancing schedules to come to talk to him. Had his visit here been a waste of time? Not entirely, he reflected. In fact, it suggested quite a lot to him. He studied the list Tatiana had given him with the participants of the run and their passengers, plus the notes which Auguste had made at the side on some of them. On the whole, Roderick Smythe was still well up on his own list of those to be carefully investigated.

He'd quarrelled early in the evening with the deceased, he'd come to the motor stable to guard the motorcar when she'd said he wasn't wanted, and he'd told Fred Gale to go home. Rose was inclined to believe in simple answers where he could – until eliminated, at the very least. He had known Auguste long enough to prove that some cases were far from simple in their resolutions but it still remained a good jumping-off point.

He looked up hopefully as there was a rap on the door and it opened. It wasn't a duchess, or a countess; it was only Auguste again and some cook fellow judging by his long apron.

'Come to apologise for that beef, have you?' he grunted.

For a moment Auguste was sidetracked, seeing the remains of dinner and instantly wishing to put the matter right. After he had explained and introduced Pierre, Egbert looked at him with what Auguste called his 'Factory face' – Factory being slang for Scotland Yard.

'Kept quiet about this, haven't you?'

'Miss Hart asked me to do so, monsieur, and then when I heard the terrible news at luncheon today, what else could I do? I was there to serve luncheon to the King. I could not rush away to tell Mr Didier then.'

Egbert sympathised; he had his own problems with His Majesty. 'How did you get the job at the club?'

'Miss Hart asked me.'

'Yes, yes,' Egbert said impatiently, 'but *how*? Mrs Didier wouldn't have taken you without a character.'

'*Pardon?*'

'Recommendation from your previous employers,' Auguste explained.

'Ah. Miss Hart helped me.'

'Forged them, did you?' Egbert asked grimly.

Pierre blushed hotly. 'I am a good cook, monsieur, and an honest man. Miss Hart testified to that.'

'They don't always go together. Look at Sweeney Todd.'

'Who?' Pierre turned to Auguste.

'A gentleman who was not overconcerned with the contents of his pies,' he explained. 'Egbert, I can vouch for Pierre's pies.' Auguste suddenly wondered whether it had ever occurred to His Majesty that Sweeney was not the most propitious of names to employ as a private detective. Distracted by this happy thought, he missed Egbert's next comments to Pierre. When he came to, Pierre had already embarked on the list of those who had upset Miss Hart.

'First there is Miss Lockwood. While we were travelling last year, Miss Hart received a copy of a magazine article which much distressed her. It was written by Miss Lockwood, and it was that that made up her mind to return home to—'

'Not her sweetheart?'

'That I do not know,' Pierre replied simply.

'And who else is there?'

'There were many, but three in particular she never forgave. She mentioned them time after time. She had attended the same school as one of them and moved in the same circles as all of these ladies, she told me, but yet she was treated as an inferior, mocked and laughed at, although her father was a knight, honoured by the great Empress Queen Victoria, and he was very rich.'

'English society is strict,' Auguste agreed. 'My wife says sometimes it takes so long to be accepted, it can't happen before you are dead.'

Egbert looked at him. 'Miss Hart *is* dead.'

'I apologise, Egbert.' Auguste was contrite.

'Al-Islam believes that the lowest may aspire to the highest,' Pierre said.

'Not in England.'

'Who else?' Egbert asked impatiently, glaring at Auguste.

'There is Lady Tunstall.'

'She a friend of yours, Auguste?'

'Not particularly.' He did not add more, but intimated to Egbert that he would elaborate once they were alone.

'When Miss Hart had been travelling for several years,' Pierre continued, 'she returned to London for periods still hoping, she told me, to expunge the memory of a terrible event that had forced her to leave London, and to be accepted by society again. She had recently had much acclaim for her travels in Egypt, and so there was a chance. She was determined to be received by the Prince and Princess of Wales. She had an ideal opportunity, for the Princess was interested in Egyptian tombs and as one of the celebrations for the Golden Jubilee of Queen Victoria she was to hold a special dinner for explorers, at which Miss Hart was to be one of the guests.'

'And what happened?'

'She was dropped from the invitation list at the last moment. Lady Tunstall, who is a very beautiful woman, was a close friend of the Prince of Wales and persuaded him that Miss Hart was not a suitable person to attend.'

'But His Majesty wouldn't agree to that if it was an official dinner. He is a man of principle.'

'She told him, so Miss Hart later discovered, that Miss Hart was quite mad, and travelled much abroad because of her notorious – forgive me – sexual life here. Worse, she was addicted to fabricating fantasies about love affairs with famous gentlemen. She mentioned the name of Harriet Mordaunt. I did not understand that.'

Egbert glanced at Auguste. They understood all too well. One of the less savoury incidents in the Prince of Wales's career was when he had been forced to appear in the witness box during an unpleasant divorce case in which the truth of Harriet Mordaunt's claim that the Prince of Wales was her lover was to be tested. It caused much excitement and scandal, and the last thing the Prince of Wales would have wanted was to be troubled by such a scandal again – especially without cause.

'Miss Hart intended to take revenge against Lady Tunstall by recounting the story in her memoirs, together with the story of how she had eloped with the family coachman at the age of seventeen.'

'Did she?' Auguste was diverted, earning another glare from Egbert. 'How did Miss Hart know?'

'I have no idea.'

'What about the defamation laws? Wasn't she worried?'

'No. She was a rich woman, and in any case she could start to travel again, taking her money with her. But no one, she thought, would dare to sue because the allegations would be true and she could prove them.'

'What about Lady Tunstall's allegations against *her* to the Prince of Wales? Were they true?'

'Yes and no. There was a scandal, but Miss Hart was innocent.'

'Or so she said.'

'But she *was*,' Pierre shouted hotly. 'That was why she was so bitter against Lady Bullinger and the Duchess of Dewbury.'

'Tell me about it,' Egbert said.

'Miss Hart often talked about them, for it eased her bitterness, she said.' There was pride in Pierre's voice. 'After school Miss Hart's father wished her to enter London society, and to please him she did so. She was attractive, she said, but she scared gentlemen because of her interest in travel. Englishmen, she believed, sought only a mother for their children, a hostess at their table, and a woman in their bed.'

Egbert thought of Edith's staunch faith in him and wondered why people generalised so much.

'She spoke of society, of course,' Pierre qualified, 'and of the kind of gentleman her father so much wished her to marry. He wanted her to have a title if possible, to add to his riches. But there was one gentleman who fell greatly in love with her and she with him.'

'Titled?'

'Oh yes. The heir to a dukedom.'

Of course, Auguste thought. Of course.

'And what happened?' Egbert demanded.

'His sister, two years younger than he was but the stronger character, objected strongly to Hester marrying her brother.'

'Why?'

'Because of her birth. Trade, Miss Hart would say when she spoke of it so bitterly.'

'Half of them were butchers once, on the battlefield if not in the slaughterhouse,' Egbert muttered.

'And Miss Hart was intelligent, too,' Pierre said. 'The English aristocracy, she told me, distrust intelligence in men or women.'

'And what happened?'

'The sister selected a friend of hers as a suitable future duchess, and between them they concocted a plan. They did everything they could to dissuade the brother, but Miss Hart just laughed at them when she found out. He would not be dissuaded, so they then took stronger measures. They forged letters in Miss Hart's handwriting and gave them to a young man who moved in the best circles. He pretended to be inebriated and boasted in one of your gentlemen's clubs about his love affair with Miss Hart, and when the brother challenged him, he showed him the letters.'

'And he believed it, just like that?' Auguste could not believe it. It sounded straight out of a Sherlock Holmes story.

'Not at first. He loved Miss Hart. But the young man then became inebriated regularly in restaurants, at balls, at the opera, even boasting of her charms –' he blushed – 'in bed not only with him but other gentlemen of his acquaintance. In due course the friend, a lovely and apparently shocked young lady of twenty-five, purported to have heard the rumours and asked the duke-to-be whether they were true. It got to the point where for the sake of his family's reputation he could not afford to marry Miss Hart, innocent or guilty. Society believed they were true, and Miss Hart was forced to go abroad. The sister is now, of course, Lady Bullinger, and the young lady the Duchess of Dewbury.'

'And who was the young man?'

'I do not know his name.'

Auguste was about to delve further when Egbert changed tack.

'Miss Hart mentioned diaries at the club. Did you ever see them?'

'Of course. She wrote them every night. She had begun at school and kept them up wherever she could.'

'And all you have told us would be recorded in them?'

'Certainly.'

'Twitch will have found them by now,' Egbert said. 'Wait here.' He went into the entrance hall and put through a call to Scotland Yard, returning a few minutes later.

'No diaries were found in the house.'

Pierre looked astonished. 'But they must be there. They were in a large chest, she told me.'

'Perhaps she's given them to someone to look after for her. Her parents?'

'Both are now dead. There is no family home. She was going to buy one when she married.'

'Could she have given them to someone else?'

'There is only one person to whom she would have entrusted them. Me, and I do not have them.'

'A bank?'

'Perhaps, or—' Pierre exclaimed. 'It is just possible that dog Luigi has them.'

'Why should he have them?' Auguste asked, bewildered.

'I suspect Miss Hart used him for information,' he said darkly. 'It was my job but I failed to tell her in sufficient time about the Dolly Dobbs's arrival for her to accompany it. It may be she was punishing me by paying Luigi to provide information too. I told her he is a rogue, and not to be trusted.'

'But she did trust you?'

'Yes, but I am a man of honour. I could not approve,' he admitted reluctantly, 'of all Miss Hart did, though you will recall I have always defended her to others. I tried to dissuade her from her plan of revenge because of the danger to herself. She may have feared I would destroy the diaries if she gave them to me.'

'And would you have done so?'

He considered. 'Possibly.'

'Very loyal of you,' Egbert commented sourly.

Pierre took it at face value and inclined his head in acknowledgement.

'Did you see Miss Hart the evening she died?'

'No, monsieur, I wish I had,' he said vehemently. 'But by the time I knew she intended to guard the car, I also knew Fred Gale would be there. I was working in the kitchens all the evening – Monsieur Didier will confirm that.'

'He left shortly before Tatiana and I did, at about twelve thirty,' Auguste confirmed.

'And this morning?'

'I arrived early to let the staff in and then worked until it was time to go.'

'A pieful of motives,' Egbert commented after he'd gone, 'presented to us on a plate. She must have died in the early hours, anyway, as you told me the body was cooling, so it's immaterial if Pierre was in the kitchen alone early this morning.'

'Powerful motives, too, Egbert. All recorded in those diaries. Did Twitch check to see if there had been any callers at Miss Hart's house before himself?'

'He didn't say but I'd wager Mr Pinpole's best joint that he asked.'

'What about her servants there?'

'Hannah Smirch, cook-general, and a general handyman called Peters, both hired along with the house when Hester Hart returned to this country in April. They don't seem as enthusiastic about their mistress as this Pierre of yours.'

'Then they might be bribed not to mention any other visitors yesterday.'

Egbert considered. 'Possible.'

'And Pierre suspects Luigi of being a paid informer for members of the club.'

'One way and another, that club of Tatiana's seems to be nurturing quite a few vipers in its bosom.'

Many of these vipers were circling in stately fashion on the dance floor to the strains of a merry waltz played by a German band from Margate overcome at the honour of playing for His Majesty, even if that Majesty was nowhere to be seen. When Auguste returned to the ballroom, he found it hard to believe that only last evening these people dancing the night away to Strauss were concentrating their hate on Hester Hart, an evening that had ended in her murder.

Isabel circled complacently in the arms of her cousin Hugh. Maud Bullinger overwhelmed a slightly-built lad, doing his best to enjoy his duty. Agatha bobbed and jerked in the arms of Roderick Smythe, Phyllis danced with a reluctant John Millward, blissfully happy in the knowledge that her beloved was restored to her. Miss Dazey chatted brightly to her partner while wondering jealously where Leo might be, and Hortensia discoursed on the merits of her new mare to Sir Algernon Bullinger who found his evening unexpectedly enlivened. Thomas Bailey, in disgrace, sat in a corner of the servants' hall with a notebook and pencil, feverishly scribbling mathematical calculations which intimately affected the Brighton Baby, and an ashen-faced Harold Dobbs moaned over the injustice of it all at home after a whole day at Scotland Yard.

Chapter Seven

All motorists were mad, Auguste decided, and lady motorists were the maddest of all. He had come out to find Leo, but was arrested by the spectacle outside the Martyr House stables on the Friday morning. Unlike Milton House, these stables housed motorcars along with horses with whom they had settled down to an ill-assorted but companionable partnership. The horses, Isabel had informed him without a glimmer of humour, were periodically sent to Coventry to learn the ways of motorcars in that home of manufacturing. This morning, however, the horses' noses were decidedly out of joint. The Earl's Lanchester was already drawn up in front of the main entrance of the house waiting for His Majesty's appearance (it would have a long wait, in Auguste's experience; it was only ten o'clock) while the horses' yard was entirely full of the motorcars belonging to those who had stayed overnight in Martyr House, together with those of the outboarders who had come to rejoin their comrades for the cavalcade home. Luncheon was to be served before their departure, for which the ladies had Auguste's full sympathy. Even with income tax at 5½d in the pound, the Earl could surely afford better staff.

The yard seemed to have become an open-air garage, batteries were being reinstalled after charging, oil was being checked, water tanks filled, a queue waited for the benzine house, and Leo was rushing from car to car (his faithful Miss Dazey trotting at his heels). The Duchess, to Auguste's dismay, was sitting in the driver's seat of their Léon Bollée with ominously proprietorial pride. Last night all these serviceably-clad ladies were delicate flowers in satin and silks on the ballroom floor. Now they were an Amazonian army.

Egbert had been responsible for delaying departure till after luncheon, to Isabel's great displeasure. Had His Majesty remained, she would not have objected, but to entertain her fellow club members, she had intimated to Egbert, was an imposition. Egbert, however, had not been amused at being made a monkey of last night, and blandly ignored all cries of protest when he informed the party at breakfast that the boot was now on the police's foot and they would await his convenience. Cries of complaints to the Commissioner were also ignored; the nearer you rose to the top of the pyramid, Egbert reflected, the less pressure could be applied from above.

Tatiana was taking breakfast with His Majesty, a rare honour which Auguste did not regret missing. Auguste could imagine Bertie's guffaws as they swapped stories of the royal families of Europe, especially those of Russia. It was Bertie's opinion that they were riding for a fall more injurious than anything Hortensia Millward's horses could inflict if they failed to acknowledge that the Czarist empire, too, had entered thc twentieth century. Auguste disliked guffaws at breakfast and much preferred taking breakfast with Egbert to enduring the company of the Martyr House breakfast room – despite the fact that Egbert, quartered in the housekeeper's linen room, was in sour mood after missing a great deal of sleep. Footsteps had creaked up and down the passageway all night.

'I remember,' Auguste observed with a straight face, 'that the corridors of Stockbery Towers were equally busy at night.'

Egbert was, once again, not amused. Auguste was instantly sent to check his own staff's movements on the Wednesday night. By the time he returned to inform Egbert that only two of them had visited the far larders near the entrance, and ten visits had been paid to the privy, all of them before twelve o'clock, the kedgeree was cold and the coffee lukewarm.

'Twitch has had the pathologist's report now. She was killed between about twelve thirty and two thirty, and Tatiana can vouch for her being alive and quarrelling with Smythe just before one. He says he only stayed fifteen minutes or so, which as he knows full well wouldn't have given him time to quarrel with Hester, kill her, and smash the car.' Egbert paused. 'Apart from him, looks like you were last on the scene, Auguste.'

Egbert looked well-breakfasted, Auguste noted grumpily. He disliked interrupting his digestion. In his opinion life processes went on in three main areas of the body, one of which was irrelevant at the moment, but all should be allowed to finish their course uninterrupted. This morning his brain and his stomach were alternating in a fashion highly detrimental to both. What's more, Egbert knew it and was enjoying it.

Auguste had come out to the stables to settle his temper and his stomach and to find Leo before seeking out Luigi in accordance with Egbert's demands. He dragged Leo away from an eight horsepower Wolseley, despite his protestations about compression leaks. He was holding a lighted taper aloft like Florence Nightingale's lamp, but Auguste had no compassion on this particular errand of mercy and promptly blew it out.

'While you were guarding the Dolly Dobbs, Leo, did you notice anything or anyone odd that you haven't told us about?' Auguste asked.

'Nothing.' Leo didn't mention Miss Dazey. 'They just came to collect their cars, that's all. And that horse lady turned up looking for her husband,' he suddenly remembered.

'Mrs Millward? But why should her husband be there?' Even as he spoke, Auguste had a vision of John Millward on the ballroom floor with Phyllis Lockwood last night.

'She didn't say. But he was there. He came to collect Miss Lockwood's car. I didn't tell her that.' Leo looked worldly-wise.

'Very sensible, Leo.' What was Phyllis Lockwood thinking of? John Millward surely would not look at any woman younger than three hundred years old apart from his wife. Would he?

In a somewhat more spacious bedroom than Chief Inspector Rose's, another shared breakfast was in progress. The boiled eggs under their dainty cosies were, however, of little interest to Maud and Agatha. Agatha had summoned her sister-in-law to a conference, one to which Maud raced as keenly as in the Paris-Bordeaux of '99.

'Now dear Hester is no longer with us –' Agatha poured tea carefully into Maud's cup – 'what are we going to do about you know what?'

'The diaries?' Maud never appreciated delicate china.

Agatha nodded. 'The police will be searching for them, I fear. That policeman looks as indefatigable as Edward's bloodhound.'

'I told you we should have gone to see him last night, Agatha.'

'Do try the toast, Maud. I really cannot recommend dear Isabel's eggs. That would have looked over-eager on our part. He is a public servant; it is his place to request an audience of *us*. Now we know Hester cannot have progressed far with her memoirs, it is the diaries that are at issue.'

Maud ruminated. 'Roderick will know what to do.'

'Excellent. Burn them, I suggest,' said Agatha thoughtfully. 'Really, I do feel Isabel's kitchen could have peeled this peach. What is happening in this world?'

'This murder is a terrible thing,' Luigi informed Egbert sanctimoniously, as if the chief inspector might disagree. He had not been pleased to realise Auguste was to remain in the room, and Auguste decided to leave all the talking to Egbert.

'You knew Miss Hart well, did you?'

'Naturally. In the restaurant I saw her on many occasions.'

'As maître d' you must hear quite a lot, too.'

'If so, I am discreet. I am from an old-established family of the Milan aristocracy.'

Egbert grunted. Pedigree was no way to his heart. 'Did you talk to Miss Hart in the dining room on the evening she was killed?'

'Only polite courtesies. Monsieur Didier will confirm that Miss Hart was not in a happy mood, having had a public altercation with her fiancé and broken her engagement to him.' He glanced confidently at Auguste, who nodded.

'How late were you at the club that night?'

'The restaurant closed early since there were few diners, at twelve. I must have left about,' he considered, 'twelve thirty.'

'Through the kitchens?'

Auguste's last remaining amiability towards Luigi vanished as he replied, 'I am not a menial. I left through the main entrance. The night porter will vouch for that.' He hesitated. 'When was she killed, please?'

'Between one and two thirty.'

'Ah.' He looked at Egbert's unfriendly face. 'I hope the night porter will confirm the time I left. He is not always at his post, and I cannot be certain I saw him.'

'That may be your misfortune.'

'Why should I wish to kill Miss Hart?' Luigi burst out, injured. 'Or smash the Dolly Dobbs? I have no interest in motorcars.'

'An interest in money, though, so we've heard. That right? We're told you passed information on to Miss Hart, and I daresay for other members too. All out of the kindness of your heart, was it?'

'That peasant Pierre!' Luigi's face took on the colour of his beloved Chianti. 'He goes too far. This time I will tell you something about him. Did you know—'

'That Pierre Calille was Miss Hart's dragoman on her travels?' Egbert finished for him. 'Yes, he told us. Rather more forthcoming than you.'

'He *told* you?' There was a blank surprise on Luigi's face.

'So now you can be just as frank. You don't want us to think you've something to hide in a murder inquiry, do you?'

Apparently he did for he said nothing for a few moments, then virtuously declared, 'Miss Hart had many enemies at the club. I felt I should keep her informed of anything she should know.'

'And how grateful was she?'

'She gave me presents from time to time,' he replied a little less eagerly.

'How many other ladies gave you presents?'

He was slower to answer now. 'Lady Tunstall, Lady

Bullinger, the Duchess of Dewbury, and Miss Lockwood.'

'Very generous of them.'

Luigi was shaken from his usual poise. 'I have done nothing criminal. I merely passed on innocent information – who was dining with who, where. That sort of thing.' He proceeded to give some examples in his sudden anxiety to help.

'Did Miss Hart give you anything for safekeeping on her behalf?'

'What sort of thing?' he asked cautiously.

'Her diaries, for instance. They're not at her home.'

'Diaries?' he repeated. 'No. She might have given them to Pierre – no,' he changed his mind, 'he is a peasant; she would entrust nothing of value to him.'

'We'll be searching your home, of course.'

He flushed. 'Do you refuse to take the word of a gentleman?'

'Always,' Egbert informed him heartily. 'Now if it is not too ungentlemanly for you, you can go away and write me a complete list of all the information you passed on and to whom.'

'Arrogant blighter, isn't he?' Egbert remarked when he had left.

'He was smirking with relief, I think.'

'It may be short-lived.'

'Miss Lockwood is innocent!'

'No doubt she is. Come in, Mr Smythe.'

The racing driver was poised dramatically, if sulkily, in the doorway, a lock of his black hair falling over his forehead in blatant defiance of his macassar oil. Gone was the cowed man Auguste had seen being led off to Welling Railway Station.

'And so am I,' her defender added. 'Phyllis is the dearest, sweetest little thing that ever walked this earth.'

Auguste blinked. This was somewhat of a departure for a man who was only too eager to turn a cold shoulder on Miss Lockwood while providing the other for Miss Hart to lean on.

'And Miss Hart no longer does walk this earth.' Egbert cut his tribute off sharply. 'I want you to tell Mr Didier the story that you told me at the Yard yesterday.'

Roderick cast Auguste a look of intense dislike. 'After that quarrel with Hester which you overheard,' he began meaningfully, 'I took Phyllis to dinner at the Carlton, and afterwards decided I should go back to the motor stable, make up the quarrel with Hester, and guard the car in her place.'

'So although Phyllis is the dearest sweetest little thing, you preferred to marry Hester Hart?' Egbert asked.

'I respected Hester greatly,' he replied with dignity. 'My feelings for Phyllis are quite different. I believed I had let down Hester badly by my behaviour and that as a gentleman I should apologise. I went back and we did resolve our quarrel. Hester quite understood that I still felt affection for Phyllis, and admitted she had been overhasty in speaking to us the way she did. We were reconciled, but she told me there was no need for me to lose my night's sleep as she had every intention of remaining there herself, and it would not be proper for us both to be there. She had only agreed to let Fred Gale stay because Mrs Didier had insisted on it. Now she was insisting on staying there alone, so I came away.'

'And next morning you went straight to Miss Lockwood to ask if you could drive down with her?' Auguste asked.

'Only because my own motorcar was incapacitated.'

'The funny thing was, Auguste, that when our sergeant went to see this incapacitated motorcar, the engine started up like a dream. Mighty pleased with himself, he was, for being able to drive a motorcar which had defeated the famous Roderick Smythe.'

There was a moment's pause. Then, 'Dirt on the spindle,' Roderick cried with a glad shout. 'Of course. And it cleared itself.'

'Most obliging of it. You say you left Miss Hart, alive, at about quarter to one. Tell him, Auguste.'

'My wife heard you quarrelling with Miss Hart,' Auguste said quietly, 'and that far from agreeing to marry you, she absolutely refused to. That was at one o'clock, so my wife must have been mistaken, if you are right.'

Roderick turned red, then tried a light laugh. 'Mrs Didier must have misunderstood. Hester and I did shout a little at first, but then we realised how much we loved each other. Perhaps she did not hear that part.'

'Doesn't explain the time, does it? Not covering up for anybody, are you? You seem very keen to defend Miss Lockwood.'

'Whatever reason would Miss Lockwood have to harm Hester Hart?' he demanded belligerently.

'The same as quite a few people perhaps. Those diaries. Seen them, have you?'

'No. I knew Hester kept diaries but I've never seen them.'

'She didn't give them to you for safekeeping?'

'She did not.' He was growing increasingly uneasy; yesterday had been a nightmare and today had begun little better.

'Where did you first meet Miss Hart?' Egbert asked casually, and Auguste was surprised to see this question threw Roderick's composure even more.

'In—' He stopped. 'In the Motor Club of Great Britain headquarters. In April.'

'Not earlier?'

'I don't think so.' He tried another light laugh. 'I may have done. One meets so many . . .' His voice trailed off.

Phyllis burst into tears. A short burst. 'Darling Roderick wouldn't hurt a fly. He tells me you think he murdered her, just because he realised he loved me and not her.'

'He claims he was reconciled to her.'

Her large blue eyes brimmed over. 'Perhaps I was wrong. Anyway, he can't marry both of us, can he? I mean, he won't have to now. Just me.'

'Quite, Miss Lockwood.'

Phyllis smiled shyly. 'I suppose that gives me a sort of motive. But I couldn't have done it, really I couldn't. I can't stand loud bangs. I couldn't pull the trigger on a water pistol.'

Egbert looked at her suspiciously. Bangs? 'Miss Hart was stabbed, not shot.'

'*Was* she? I quite thought she was shot, because of the gun she always carried.'

'It wasn't with her body when she was found.'

'Roderick said she always carried a Colt pistol, so I quite thought she was shot. That proves I couldn't have done it, doesn't it?' she added brightly.

Egbert did not comment.

'She may have left it at home,' Phyllis continued helpfully. 'After all, she had come out expecting only to dine that night when she was so horrid to us; she wasn't planning to stay all night to guard the car, so she may have left it at home, but it is odd, isn't it, because she must have had time to run home – well, not literally run – to get it.'

'She did go home,' Auguste said. 'She had changed her clothes, and it is odd.'

Egbert agreed. Twitch had not mentioned a gun being found at Hester Hart's home. 'Where were you on Wednesday evening, Miss Lockwood?'

'Oh, we had a lovely evening, although Hester was so nasty to us, just because Roderick had brought me to the club for dinner. We had been engaged, after all. *She* stole him from me, though Roderick has explained it to me.'

'How?' Auguste was fascinated as to how he had managed to wriggle out of his predicament.

'Roderick told me she more or less *forced* him into marrying her. She knew something really nasty about his godmother whom he's very fond of and said unless Roderick married her – I mean Hester, not the godmother, that's Maud Bullinger, you know – she would tell *everybody* about it. I was puzzled because she then threatened to tell everybody about it anyway, but Roderick is such an old-fashioned gentleman, he agreed straightaway.'

'Not very gentlemanly towards you.'

'Don't you think so?' She looked sweetly surprised. 'But he loves me, he really does, and always has. It was only because—'

'Yes, yes.' Egbert cut her off hastily as the phonograph recording threatened to begin again. 'Where did you go when you left Milton House?'

'To the Carlton. We had a divine little soufflé of—'

'And after that?'

'He took me home, and went home himself.'

'No. He went back to Milton House. I take it you didn't accompany him?'

'Oh *no*.'

'Or decide to follow him?'

She stared at him, tears threatening to well up once more. 'Oh, *no*! Why would I?'

'You, too, had good reason to dislike Miss Hart; perhaps you wanted to ensure the engagement was not reinstated, as Mr Smythe claims it was.'

'She trapped him.' The sweetness vanished.

'You were dining with Mr Millward on the previous evening. Why was that, Miss Lockwood?' Auguste asked politely.

'He's a friend of mine.'

'Not of Miss Hart's, though.'

She stared at him. 'Poor John,' she said tremulously, 'you don't understand. He was in such distress. His wife, you know . . .' She cast her eyes demurely down, and refused to say more.

'I don't see Phyllis Lockwood missing her beauty sleep, even for darling Roderick, let alone John Millward,' Egbert commented after she had left.

'*Mon ami,* remember her profession.'

In the home of a good horse-loving family, Hortensia for once was not thinking about form and flanks but about her husband. He was off his fodder and that was unusual. Then she remembered what she'd been going to ask him.

'Where were you on Tuesday evening, John?'

He turned pink. He was always a bad liar. 'At the club.'

'Oh.' She didn't pursue the matter, to his relief, and he assumed she had just forgotten to inquire *which* club. She had not, and her concern increased.

'My dear Inspector.'

Agatha sailed into the library, as though welcoming Egbert to an At Home. 'And Mr Didier. How delightful. And how is dear Tatiana this morning?'

Auguste was tempted to reply that she was as well as might be expected after a murder, but simply bowed instead, as the Duchess graciously agreed to be seated.

'Poor Hester.' Agatha sighed. Obviously, like royalty, she felt she must speak first, Auguste noted.

'Did you like Miss Hart, Your Grace?' Egbert asked.

Agatha considered. 'I don't believe I gave much thought to the question. Her lectures were stimulating.'

'You had known her a long time, I believe, long enough to be threatened by the announced publication of her memoirs.'

'Good gracious, no.' She decided in favour of humour rather than the outrage she felt. 'People don't *threaten* duchesses. It is one of the great advantages of the position.'

'So you didn't meet her earlier in your life?'

'I can't recall. Why? Should I have done?'

'She was at one time going to marry the man who is now your husband.'

'Oh, is *that* who she was? Do you know, I thought there was something just a little familiar about her face. She was infatuated with my husband – or, rather, with his title. It was all very sad, poor girl. Luckily my husband – though he wasn't my husband then of course – realised that it would never do. She went abroad, and then he met me.'

'Hadn't he met you before that? Weren't you instrumental in making him realise it would never do?'

'Really, Inspector, what are you implying? I fear I find you quite impolite.'

'I fear I have to be at times, Your Grace. I can speak to your husband, if you prefer.'

She stared at him coldly. 'I doubt that very much. I shall advise him to have nothing to say to you, if you are to twist what I say in this appalling manner.'

'Then I'll have to rely on what Miss Hart's diaries tell us.'

She was ready for that, Auguste observed. 'Poor Hester, always such a dreamer. She wrote such a lot about so many things and not one of them true. Have you found the diaries? One's lawyers may have such a splendid time. They are not at all impressed by fairy stories without evidence to back them up.'

Egbert decided to change tack. 'You were originally planning to drive the Dolly Dobbs, weren't you?'

'Yes, until poor Hester badgered Harold into letting her drive. I quite understood, of course.' Then she glanced at Auguste and belatedly remembered his presence at a certain occasion when understanding had not played any part at all in the proceedings. 'I was naturally disappointed at first.'

'Why did he change his mind?'

'I see now the woman must have blackmailed him, threatening to describe his car to Thomas Bailey.'

'And you resented it?'

She laughed winningly. 'Perhaps a little. Until Thomas Bailey came to me.'

'He came to you, not the other way about?'

'He is of the servant classes, Inspector. How could I visit him? He asked me to drive his new motorcar, the Brighton Baby.'

'And you agreed, knowing that it was exactly the same as the Dolly Dobbs?'

'So I have now heard. I had absolutely *no* idea, I assure you. I simply suggested to Thomas, as Hester did not appear in time to join the run, that he let the Motor Club officials think the Brighton Baby was the Dolly Dobbs, as none of us had any idea what Harold's car was like. I gather they had the same idea about the hoods and the windmills. Harold was so scared his great idea would be stolen that he kept his secrets even from me. If you recall, Mr Didier, Dolly did not emerge on the day it should, and no wonder, if it was a copy.'

'No. I didn't say copy, Your Grace. I said exactly the same. There's a difference.'

Agatha was not interested in semantics.

'When did you last see Miss Hart, Your Grace?'

The eyebrows arched. 'That evening in the restaurant when we were all treated to the most exciting scene.'

'Your motorcar was still in the motor house when Leo went off duty at twelve. Did you collect it yourself?'

'I cannot – ah, yes, I believe I must have done.'

'But you didn't see Miss Hart?'

'I am glad to say I did not. I am quite sure the motor house doors were all shut.'

Lady Bullinger, who followed her sister-in-law in the library, gave all the appearance of being the more dominant of the two, though Auguste did not underestimate Agatha's sweetened steel.

'I didn't like the woman,' Lady Bullinger barked, 'but I wouldn't have wished that death on her. Very sorry to hear it.' She sat down heavily in the chair Egbert held for her.

'Would you be one of the ladies Hester Hart referred to in her diaries?' he asked.

'We moved in different circles, Inspector. I knew her, but I doubt if she recorded the fact.'

'You and Her Grace may be mistaken.'

'You haven't been accusing the Duchess of Dewbury of murdering the woman, have you?'

'I'm not accusing anyone at this stage, Lady Bullinger. Your godson in fact was the last person to see Hester Hart alive.'

'Is that why you hauled the boy off to London like a common criminal? We all saw Hester after he did.'

'I beg your pardon?'

'She was on public display in the restaurant, my man.'

'Roderick Smythe returned after midnight to the motor stable.'

'Nonsense.'

'He was seen and he admits it.'

'The boy was still infatuated,' she said after a few moments, having assimilated this. 'Probably went for a goodnight kiss and left.'

'The boy is thirty-five,' Egbert pointed out.

'A boy at heart,' she maintained doggedly. 'He wouldn't have touched a hair on her head.'

'Miss Hart was going to marry your brother at one time, wasn't she?'

'He did know her,' she replied instantly and dismissively. 'I gather Miss Hart over-dramatised the extent of their involvement. When he met and preferred Agatha, she went abroad.'

'Without any help from you?'

'I'm George's sister, not his nurse. I may have met Miss Hart then, I can't recall.' She paused. 'She's a first-class driver, you know.'

'Ah yes,' Egbert said thoughtfully. 'This race in October . . .'

'I was glad to have her on my team,' Lady Bullinger said stoutly.

'Did you have a chat about it on Wednesday night, when you went to collect your motorcar?'

'I did not.'

'But you saw her?'

'I could hardly help it. She was sitting in the back seat of that ridiculous motorcar. And she was still sitting there, alive, when I left.'

'With the motor house door open?'

'Naturally. Otherwise I wouldn't have been able to see her.' Her tone implied if this was the standard of Scotland Yard inspectors, it was hardly surprising that crime was so prevalent in London. She congratulated herself as she emerged that she'd carried that off rather well.

'When will you be in town again, Isabel?' Hugh asked as casually as he could, as Isabel pretended to be fascinated by Leo's contortions in providing the Royce with its necessities of life. 'And why,' he suddenly asked, 'are you preparing the Royce?'

'My husband suggested I drive you back, Cousin Hugh.' She moved out of Leo's earshot. 'Aren't you pleased?'

'Delighted,' he answered truthfully. He glanced at her. 'You're worried about those diaries, aren't you?'

'Wouldn't you be?' Hugh was her cousin, he must know the old story. He even knew about the Jubilee dinner; she'd never kept secrets from Hugh, even though he was now her lover as well as cousin.

'Where do you think the diaries are?'

'I've asked Luigi, but he claims not to know.'

'Perhaps you haven't paid him enough.' Hugh thought carefully. 'We'd better offer more.'

Isabel thrilled to the sound of the 'we'. She needed help. Uncritical and unreserved help.

* * *

When she entered the library, her walk suggested that Egbert and Auguste should shudder at the approach of her languorous beauty. Her equanimity was restored.

'Am I a suspect?' She sank gracefully into the chair, her body arched at an angle far beyond that demanded by her S-bend corsetry.

'Not yet.' Egbert was not prepared to exchange banter.

'How exciting. I expect you'd like to know where I was on Wednesday evening. I came up to London so that I could take part in the run early on Wednesday evening and dined in the club. I may have seen Miss Hart. I can't recall.'

'Your motorcar was still in a motor house at eleven thirty.'

The eyelids flickered. 'If you say so, Inspector, I'm sure it was. I dined late.'

'And you walked there to collect it?'

'My dining companion did, I believe. No, I'm wrong. It was me.'

'And what then?'

'We drove to my home. I believe we were there about a quarter to one.'

'And then?'

'*He* went home, Inspector.' There was a yawn in her voice. 'And no, I did not return to the club to murder dear Hester. I wish I'd thought of it, but I decided to get a good night's sleep.'

'You had reason to wish her dead then?' Egbert asked mildly.

Isabel was aggrieved that her pleasantry had misfired. She tried earnestness instead. 'I did not like her but I did not seriously wish to kill her.'

'Not even if she revealed in her memoirs how you'd ruined her chances of being accepted into the Prince of Wales's circle?'

She stared at him coldly. 'I may possibly have advised His Majesty some years ago that Miss Hart was not a suitable person for His Majesty to meet. Why not?'

'Unjustly?'

'In society unfortunately that is irrelevant. What is relevant is reputation.'

'And yours might have been threatened if her memoirs had been published? And still might.'

'The diaries,' she said slowly. 'You have them? They are full of lies, I assure you, Inspector.' And when he did not reply, '*Do* you have them?'

The Brighton Baby had the motor stable yard all to itself. It had been banned from joining the cavalcade of *real* motorcars which had now moved round to the front of the main house. Of its dejected designer only the rear half was to be seen as Auguste approached; the other half was buried under the hidden parts of his beloved motorcar. Gradually Thomas became aware of two boots at his side which showed no inclination to walk away, and he reluctantly withdrew himself.

'It *will* work,' he cried defensively. 'It's just a matter of a few adjustments.'

'That wasn't what was on my mind.'

Thomas sat down on the running board dejectedly. 'You don't want me to explain exactly how having too much wind provided so much resistance to the car that it went slower because it overcharged the batteries, buckling the plates, which meant loss of voltage? I've worked it all out. Look.' He waved a sheet of paper at Auguste hopefully.

'No. What *we* want to know is whether you put the Dolly Dobbs out of action.'

Thomas looked astounded. 'Certainly not. I wouldn't demean myself. Nor –' as he belatedly made the connection – 'did I kill Miss Hart. I wouldn't dream of such a thing. I'm a professional motorcar designer.'

'We're told that the two motorcars are identical.'

'So the Duchess has told me. How could I know?' he asked pathetically.

'I saw you peering through the roof at the Dolly Dobbs,' Auguste reminded him.

'Yes, but I couldn't see much. How *identical*?' he asked.

Never had Auguste expected to be in the position of having to discuss the technicalities of motorcars. 'The Dolly Dobbs, like your Brighton Baby, is designed to recharge the batteries in motion with the help of wind power. It, too, had hoods and windmills—'

'Propellers,' interrupted Thomas sharply.

'Isn't the coincidence rather strange?'

'These things happen.'

'There is surely some competition to be first in the field.'

'Of course,' Thomas replied simply. 'But I didn't destroy the Dolly Dobbs just for the sake of the trials. I didn't *know*. The Duchess came to me and told me she'd heard I had a new car and she wanted to drive it. As for coincidence, I would say great minds think alike, except I don't know whether Harold Dobbs's *is* a great mind.'

'There's no question of you stealing his idea then, or writing threatening letters to him?'

Thomas looked nervous. 'Why should I? I have been working on my Baby for five years. The idea is ridiculous. Have you asked him if he stole the idea from me?'

'Not yet, but we will.'

'Mr Didier,' he called after Auguste as he departed, 'I

suppose I couldn't drive you back to London, could I?'

'You could not.' Which, as Auguste reflected, was probably true.

'Good morning, Mr Didier,' Hortensia called, dismounting happily. 'We're here to bid the happy band of motorcars farewell. A small demonstration of two.'

'Splendid. You can begin with blocking the path of His Majesty's motorcar,' Auguste replied gravely.

Hortensia laughed. 'We never expected when we set out to barrack the Dolly Dobbs that it would end with meeting the King. Rather fun.'

'If it doesn't put paid to my chances of meeting him again in the New Year,' her husband added gloomily.

'When did you travel down to Kent, Mrs Millward?'

Hortensia barked with laughter. 'You've got your detective voice on, haven't you? I've heard about your cases. You suspect us of putting the Dolly Dobbs out of action, don't you? We travelled down here by early morning railway train yesterday. The local Hams met us with a splendid carriage and pair, and we were in plenty of time to greet our chugging petrol horrors.'

'And where were you both the night before?'

'At home,' John supplied promptly.

'Together.' Hortensia grinned. 'Sorry, Auguste.'

'And the evening before?'

Neither of them replied.

From the noise it was clear that His Majesty was about to depart, and Auguste hastened round to make his farewells. Bertie had the air of one whose duty had been overdone and who spied freedom near at hand. He was far too cordial in the farewells he was paying to the assembled occupants of Martyr House. Auguste hurried up to stand respectfully near the car.

'Auguste?' He was fixed with a belligerent eye.

'Your Majesty?'

'I don't like to see Tati upset, and she is. I've invited her to Goodwood to cheer her up. And you, of course,' he added courteously before returning to the subject in hand. 'Find out who murdered that woman, there's a good chap.'

The good chap, watching the Lanchester drive away, felt relieved that he was to travel back with Egbert by train. Tatiana had insisted on his doing so. What was the point, she said, of his enduring a drive back on the Léon Bollée when he could achieve much more by a discussion with Egbert. Moreover, she conceded, judging by the number of punctures on the way down, a train might arrive quicker than the cavalcade. Agatha, she announced gloomily, had offered to travel back with her. The Duke had an appointment with a cricket match.

Directly the King had gone, the Ladies' Motoring Club climbed enthusiastically on to their own motor cars. Cranking handles were turned, engines began to roar, the Kentish air was full of fumes. Hortensia pointedly held her nose as the motorcars began to pass her. At the end of the procession, but markedly not part of it, a lonely electric motorcar, its propellers turning defiantly, slid silently past with its solitary occupant: Thomas Bailey. Auguste and Egbert went back into the house to collect their luggage and were surprised to find they had a companion walking quickly up behind them. It was John Millward.

'I wanted to tell you . . .' He was extremely nervous and pushed his spectacles up his nose agitatedly several times.

'Yes, Mr Millward?' Egbert stopped.

'I wanted to tell you I knew Miss Hart. My wife is not fully aware of what happened.'

'You were at the club on Tuesday night dining with Miss Lockwood. Is this connected?'

Millward looked as if he could happily jump into one of his beloved sarcophagi. 'You know about that? Yes, it is connected. I disliked Miss Hart.' He looked as nervous as though this alone was sufficient for Egbert to clap handcuffs on him. 'I am an archaeologist, as you know, and when I was working in Cairo, a fellow archaeologist, Robert Koldewey, asked my opinion of Miss Hart because she had applied to join his excavations at Babylon. I gave it to him frankly and of course unbiased.' He glanced at Egbert as though this was too much to be believed. 'Nevertheless, Miss Hart resented it and the next thing I knew I appeared to have a public reputation as some kind of Don Juan, tampering with her affections and, some rumours said, her body. It was most distressing. Fortunately the rumours did not reach my wife.'

'And there was no truth in them, I presume?' Auguste could not resist asking.

John Millward gazed at him. 'If you had a wife like Hortensia, would you have an affair with Miss Hart?'

Auguste could see his point, though not perhaps in the sense he had meant.

'Did Miss Hart record all this in her diaries?' Egbert pressed him.

'That's what I'm worried about. If Hortensia found out . . . Will you tell me?'

'At the moment they seem to be unaccountably missing. Now you tell *me* just why you were dining with Miss Lockwood.'

He hesitated. 'I can say nothing. I am a gentleman,' he offered hopefully.

'You were sweet on her? She on you?'

'No!' His voice came out as a squeak. 'She had heard the lies Hester had been spreading about our supposed affair and she wanted me –' he almost choked in his indignation – 'to go to Mr Smythe and persuade him they were true and that Hester wasn't a fit person for him to marry.'

'And did you?' Auguste was agog.

'Of course not. But it was most unpleasant. She threatened to tell Hortensia of Hester's story if I didn't. I didn't know what to do,' he ended ingenuously.

'Miss Lockwood,' Egbert remarked some time later, comfortably installed in an Elham Valley Railway carriage, 'is a ruthless young lady. All the same, my money's *still* on Smythe.'

'Money?' Auguste's mind cleared, despite the wholly unsatisfactory luncheon. How could they not have considered it? It was like preparing the hollandaise and omitting the asparagus. 'Egbert, Hester Hart was a rich woman, the only child of wealthy parents.'

Egbert grunted in self-disgust. 'The first rule, who gains?'

'To be precise, who inherits?'

Egbert stared out of the window at the Kent countryside flashing past. Sheep, hops, apple orchards . . . Give him Highbury any day. 'I don't know, but I'm looking forward to getting back to London to find out.'

Chapter Eight

Auguste always enjoyed visiting Egbert's office at the Yard, tucked away on the top floor overlooking the Thames. Down below was the vast organisation of the Fingerprint Department, archives, registers, photographs, Black Museum, and countless other aids for the suppression of crime. This was a Thinking Room, untidy, small, yet the still, quiet centre of Egbert's spider web. Egbert had once told him that the first case brought to New Scotland Yard was an unsolved murder in the foundations – a woman's mutilated body had been found there after the site had been bought – and his job was to ensure it was the last.

Inspector Stitch was Egbert's link with his web. It was his *métier*, and increased his devotion to the task of assisting Chief Inspector Egbert Rose. In his nightly prayers, offered up side by side with Martha Stitch, he concluded with a grateful prayer to the Deity that he had such an understanding superior, one as devoted to the advancement of Inspector Stitch as was he.

Twitch, Egbert often pointed out, had his uses. Auguste, only tolerated by Stitch as one of his superior's eccentricities, agreed the sauce you knew was a useful standby. Stitch's view was that Auguste should more rightly slink into the building through the rear entrance via the Convicts Supervision Department.

When they arrived at the Yard late on Friday afternoon, Twitch appeared immediately in the small office; his nose was as acute as Auguste's in sniffing out Egbert's presence.

'Ah, Stitch, what kept you?' Egbert inquired evilly. 'This Hester Hart business, any trace of a solicitor's address amongst her possessions?'

'Yes, sir. I took the liberty of making an appointment for you tomorrow morning.'

'Excellent.' Egbert was well aware, as was Stitch, that usually Stitch would have carried out this interview himself but in any case where His Majesty was even remotely concerned, Stitch believed in playing for safety.

Stitch permitted himself a slight smile of satisfaction at such praise.

'I take it there was no sign of a will anywhere?'

'No, sir. There was a small safe, and I opened it as the keys were found in her bag. Nothing of interest.'

'And no diaries?'

'No, sir. No trace of them. Only three pages of something headed My Life. All about buttons, it was. I've been back to the house since you telephoned, but that Hannah Smirch –' Stitch was aggrieved – 'ain't what you'd call an obliging lady.' There'd been some tempting-looking muffins and a pot of tea in that kitchen, but never a word of would you like some.

'How about a gun? We were told she always carried a Colt with her.'

'Nothing in her bag, nothing in the house, sir.'

'It seems to me,' Egbert said grumpily, 'we're told a lot of things about Miss Hart but the evidence is slower to make an appearance.'

'Was there nothing on her key ring or in her handbag to indicate where the diaries might be, Inspector Stitch?'

Auguste asked as deferentially as he could manage. A look of injured reproach was all he got for his pains.

'I'll show you, sir.' Twitch swivelled his eyes back to the chief inspector in case the Frenchie got the wrong impression over the destination of the mark of respect. Twitch returned with the serviceable large black dorothy bag which Auguste remembered seeing Hester carrying at the club, and opened it wide, removing the items one by one. A cheque book, a sovereign purse, a separate coin purse, a bunch of keys, a monogrammed cotton handkerchief without benefit of the usual embroidered roses, a comb, and a small leatherbound book which Egbert picked up.

'A prayer book?' Auguste asked curiously.

'No. It's the *Rubáiyát of Omar Khayyám*, FitzGerald's translation.'

'That's unusual.'

'Why? You see it everywhere.'

'Hester Hart did not strike me as a romantic lady, and this is a sensuous poem.' Auguste took it from him.

'Any clues in it to where the diaries might be? Every second letter marked – that sort of thing?'

'No, *mon ami.* Nothing at all. Not even her name.' He flicked through it and replaced the book on the table.

'And those keys, Stitch? You've accounted for every one?'

'No, sir.'

'No?'

Twitch blushed at making this unusual confession. 'These,' he indicated three small brass keys and a larger one.

'What about next of kin?'

'There were a few early photographs but most of the personal stuff was to do with her travels.'

'Letters?'

'Nothing of much interest yet. It's a rented house, so she's either stored them elsewhere or she travels through life very light indeed.' Stitch was rather pleased at this way of putting things, almost poetic, he thought.

'Nevertheless, I'd better have a word with your Mrs Smirch.'

He'd better not expect any muffins, was Stitch's instant thought, but he expressed the sentiment differently: 'She needs a firm hand. And that Harold Dobbs is a rum one too. Sat in my office and cried.'

'Very touching. For Miss Hart, himself, or his motorcar?'

'He didn't inform me of that, sir. He claims he was at home with Mrs Dobbs at the time of the crime.'

'And Mrs Dobbs confirms it?'

'Yes. Mind you, she admitted he was in his workroom from teatime until the early hours so she didn't actually see him till the morning. But I can't see he'd risk running up to London, murdering Miss Hart, and rushing back again. He'd miss the last train.'

'There's always the milk train, but I still can't believe he'd knock his own horse out of the race, even if the Dolly Dobbs was deliberately *copied* from the Brighton Baby and he had just found out the Duchess would be driving the Baby in the cavalcade. Which came first, the chicken fricassée or the egg soufflé?' Egbert ruminated. 'Whichever it was, it's going to take a fair time to sort all through their records to get at the truth.' At the back of both their minds was Eastbourne.

'There's a simpler way,' Auguste pointed out. 'An inventor's first step would be to take out a patent on the design.'

'Sometimes, Auguste, I know you're wasted on beef puddings. Tatiana won't mind if you spend a Saturday morning at the Patent Office, will she?'

* * *

Tatiana was still at the club when Auguste returned to Queen Anne's Gate for dinner. Nobly delaying his enjoyment of Mrs Jolly's carp salad, he walked round to the club to find her, since Egbert had said he might call round to talk to her. He tracked her down to the small room on the first floor which she used as an office. She looked up with relief as he came in. 'I thought you might be another newspaper man, or Maud, wanting to talk about the October race and the need to get the hat settled and produced. The last bright idea was a tricorne with a Romney-style tall crown, with a steering wheel in gold perched on top.'

'*Ma mie,* I am not in the least like Maud, nor do I want to talk about hats. And why –' it occurred to him – 'should she? Isn't the murder more important?'

'The odd thing is, Auguste, that *no one* seems to want to talk about the murder. I find it very creepy. Agatha chattered brightly all the way home. You would think nothing had happened in the last few days apart from her meeting the King, the dance last night, and Goodwood next week. And, of course, the Hat. I got so cross I deliberately talked about the Brighton Baby. I've never seen Agatha so put out. She took the motorcar's failure as a personal slight. I feel almost sorrier for Thomas Bailey than for Harold Dobbs, and not,' she added truthfully, '*very* sorry for either of them.'

'What's your diagnosis of the coincidence of the two motorcars being identical, *ma fleur*?'

'I can't understand it. How *could* one be a copy of the other? Harold has kept his under lock and key ever since he began it, and so has Thomas. Harold says he has been working on it for five years, so does Thomas. I'm afraid it's going to make a big story for this new *Car* magazine to be published in August, and a laughing stock of the club for supporting crazy inventions.'

'We will make very sure it does not. We will solve both the murder and the mystery behind these two cars quickly. During August the club will be closed, and in September we can begin again. Society's memory is short.'

'You are a great strength, Auguste,' Tatiana said gratefully. 'But somehow I can't think it will be as easy as that. I'm not helping. I haven't had the courage even to look at the wreck of the Dolly Dobbs, even if that policeman on duty outside would let me in.'

'Have any of the members gone round to the stable since they returned?'

She shook her head. 'We got back about five o'clock, had tea, and then everyone went home, except for Leo and –' she smiled – 'Miss Dazey. Fred has gone off duty.'

'Then let's go together and look at the car.'

She accepted reluctantly, and they walked over to the motor stable. 'I can't bear to think of anyone I know being implicated in this. I can't imagine anyone killing Hester, and I can't imagine anyone wanting to smash up a motorcar.'

On the latter, at least, Auguste disagreed with her. Having with some difficulty persuaded the policeman that a chief inspector of Scotland Yard would be less than pleased if they were refused entry, they entered through the repair house where they found Leo sitting disconsolately without an occupation. There were no club customers and he was not allowed to work on any cars.

Averting her eyes from the chalked outline near the door, Tatiana went straight to the far side of the Dolly Dobbs, where the crushed windmill and distorted hood clung precariously to their mudguards, and forced herself to inspect the damage.

'Must be an interesting case to keep you from your dinner,

Auguste.' Egbert had come up behind them. 'Evening, Tatiana.' The bowler was removed and replaced.

'Egbert, I'm glad to see you.' Auguste had been prowling around the motor house. 'That may be where the body was found, but I think she was actually killed here,' he pointed to just inside the door to the repair house. 'The body was then turned and pulled to where the murderer hoped it might not be seen.'

'You may be right.' Egbert examined the blood splashes Auguste pointed out. 'Or maybe she was pulled out of the way so that he or she could move the block and tackle into place.'

'I still think a woman would need a lot of strength to do that,' Tatiana said, hoping to exonerate her members.

'Swinging the ropes to get the block moving would be hardest. After that it would be relatively easy. If you've finished here, let's go back into your club to talk.'

Auguste realised Egbert was thinking of Tatiana's feelings and was grateful. She was obviously eager to leave the stable and return to the comparative normality of the club.

'Hester Hart was in the motor house when you heard her speaking to Roderick Smythe, was she?'

'Oh yes. Fred, to my surprise, was leaving, and told me Mr Smythe was here instead. I was about to walk in through the repair house with some cocoa when I heard a quarrel going on.'

'And it was definitely Roderick Smythe?'

'Yes, I recognised his voice, and it was definitely anger in the voices, not just excitement, so I went back and tried again half an hour later, just before we left. She was shouting at him that she had no intention of marrying him. Obviously cocoa was not a good idea, so I went away again, though it never occurred to me her life might be in danger.'

'Lovers' quarrels rarely end in death,' Auguste comforted her.

'This one did, and I might have prevented it.'

'We don't know it was a lovers' quarrel,' Auguste said. 'And even if it was, he might have walked off, as he claims, and any one of half a dozen people could have done it. They would be expecting to find Hester alone there, and that's what happened once she'd quarrelled with Smythe.'

'Smythe is still the last person to have been on the scene and that means he's got some more explaining to do,' Egbert said dogmatically. 'It's my belief we're going to solve this case in double-quick time.'

'But Goodwood is only a few days off,' Tatiana said seriously.

'What has horse-racing got to do with it?'

Auguste smiled. 'It's the end of the London season, Egbert. After that, most of your suspects will vanish to the countryside, or seaside, or abroad.' Including, he hoped wistfully, themselves.

Messrs Ferdinand and Buffer's comfortable Lincoln's Inn offices proclaimed that Hester Hart was not as averse to the traditions of old England as her behaviour had suggested. Mr Ferdinand, an affable gentleman of Pickwickian build and mien, received a chief inspector of Scotland Yard as though it was an everyday occurrence in those law-abiding offices.

'Miss Hart?' He carefully adjusted the tails of his formal morning coat as he resumed his seat. 'A terrible business. Have you solved it yet?'

Egbert wondered how he would like it if asked if he'd settled a case akin to Lord Palmerston's problems with Schleswig-Holstein. 'Terrible,' he agreed cordially. 'How did you come to be her solicitors?'

Mr Ferdinand looked somewhat offended. 'We are solicitors to the family. Ferdinand and Buffer acted for dear Sir Herbert.'

'And you have Miss Hart's will?'

'Miss Hart did not make one – to my knowledge, and against all my advice.' Ferdinand managed to look both regretful at such blatant flouting of his wishes and confident that his knowledge was all-encompassing; if, however, he implied, Miss Hart had been misguided enough to choose another solicitor for the purpose of a will, then she must have taken leave of her senses, which would invalidate it anyway.

'There's none been found at her rented London house and –' Egbert took pity on Ferdinand – 'no mention of another solicitor. Odd considering the dangerous travels she's been undertaking for the last fifteen years.'

Ferdinand looked affronted. 'I have already said that I advised her to make a will. Frequently. Indeed, after Sir Herbert's death four years ago, I considered it essential. Miss Hart, however, travelling much in the East, strongly believed that destiny was in the hands of Allah; if it was important that her will should be made, then Allah would protect her until such time as there was someone with whom she wished to share her worldly belongings. As, indeed, seemed to be the case, for when she returned on this last occasion, she was considering making one.'

'In whose favour?'

'She did not say. She informed me she was planning to marry, however, and I deduced it was therefore Mr Smythe.'

'He's our obvious suspect, Mr Ferdinand.'

Ferdinand was shocked. 'Mr Smythe is a most amiable young gentleman.'

'You'd be surprised how many amiable young gentlemen I've put behind bars. How much is Miss Hart's estate worth?'

'Quite a lot. An income of ten thousand pounds a year at least. The sale of Bromley House, Sir Herbert's residence, alone brought a capital of fifteen thousand, and the value of Hart's Buttons of which Miss Hart holds a majority of the shares at one penny three-farthings is a further fifty thousand pounds.'

'And *no will*?' Egbert was incredulous.

Ferdinand went pink. 'I cannot force my clients to take my advice,' he said huffily.

'Any more income?'

'Very little. Sir Herbert was the only son of a Lancashire chimney sweep, and his prospects were therefore unlikely to be good. However, one day, slithering down the wrong chimney stack, he arrived, like Mr Charles Kingsley's Water Baby Tom, in a lady's bedroom where he came across a broken glass button on the floor and was immediately seized with the idea that superior buttons might be produced if portraits of our late dear Queen's children could be incorporated within them. He began in a small way and within two years he had made modest headway. Then came the unexpected tragic death of the late Prince Consort. Immediately his new factory rushed out superior quality black buttons decorated with an oval black and white silhouette of Prince Albert, and his fortune was made, as they say.' Ferdinand beamed, looking more like Mr Pickwick than ever.

'A most stirring story,' Egbert commented gravely.

'Hester, his only child, was born the following year, eighteen sixty-four, by which time her father was already a rich man. Those were the days. Shall we ever see their like again?' He sighed. 'I had a great regard, and I may say affection, for Sir Herbert.'

'And for his daughter?'

'Since you ask, no. Poor Hester did not inherit her father's confidence in his own abilities and she did not possess a social position of sufficient standing to give her that confidence. Nevertheless she was determined to go out and win her own buttons, so to speak. And very well she has done for herself,' Ferdinand said approvingly, then stopped speaking rather quickly as he recalled her death.

'And to whom, if she did not leave a will, does the fortune pass now?'

'I haven't the slightest idea,' Ferdinand announced gleefully. 'I know of no relatives on her father's side, save a cousin who died in the South African War, and I know nothing of her mother, who predeceased her husband, save that she was his first factory "hand" and his model. We are advertising in *The Times* and making investigations at Somerset House.'

'The funeral won't wait for that,' Egbert commented.

Mr Ferdinand lost some of his cheerfulness. He was professionally averse to matters that would not wait.

A morning's study in the splendid new public reading room of the Patent Office confirmed everything Auguste had ever suspected about the eccentricities of the English. Every year about ten thousand happy inventors had their applications granted for patents on such essential items as burglar traps, bust improvers or foul breath indicators. There were also a great many ladies and gentlemen devoted to the technological future of the motorcar. The ladies tended to concentrate on the provision within them of face-protectors and footwarmers, the gentlemen on motorcars that could travel up staircases (presumably to be parked by the adoring driver's bed) and horse – and human – removers to clear unwanted debris from the sacred motor vehicle's path.

With the invaluable aid of the Patent Office reference systems, Auguste was able to hurry to Scotland Yard at midday on Saturday with the eagerness of a dripping Archimedes leaping from his bath to report his new theory on the displacement of water. 'I think you should have a further talk to Mr Dobbs, *mon ami.*'

'What have you found?' Egbert looked up hopefully.

'There is a patent on Mr Thomas Bailey's Improved Electrical and Wind-Powered Motorcar dated tenth March eighteen ninety-nine, *and* renewal. I made the most exhaustive searches and there was nothing in the name of Harold Dobbs. Moreover, I was not the first person, I was informed, to be recently interested in checking the patents for motorcars. At least two ladies, on separate occasions, recently spent some time there on the same pursuit.'

Upper Norwood would not have been Auguste's ideal venue for a Saturday afternoon in July. He had more in mind a quiet discussion on their balcony with Tatiana overlooking the park, perhaps even a fleeting visit to his own kitchens. Mrs Jolly had mentioned a new recipe for venison that had intriguing possibilities. Mace entered into it. However, Egbert was insistent that he should accompany him, and making only the proviso that he must be back at the club by five o'clock in order to check the Saturday night dinner – and perhaps, he thought wistfully, even *cook* some of it – he submitted gracefully.

Harold Dobbs was, surprisingly, in happy mood, pottering in the large shed that dominated their garden, his inventor's domain. It fitted Harold, Auguste decided. It was haphazard, untidy, and decidedly eccentric. A drawing of a motorcar that looked as if Sir John Tenniel might have put his hand to it in a very off moment was pinned over a newspaper portrait of General Gordon at Khartoum, while a similar one of his late monarch Queen Victoria had various amounts of pounds, shillings and pence scribbled in its borders – presumably Dobbs's costing budgets. Bits of motorcars still to be made lay everywhere. In the middle of the floor was a large space roped off for no apparent reason. Dobbs saw Auguste looking at it.

'My new motorcar,' he said happily.

'There's nothing there,' Auguste ventured cautiously.

'It's in my *head.*'

'No more Dolly Dobbs, eh?' Egbert remarked genially.

'My heart went into that motorcar, and it was broken beyond repair.'

'The car or your heart?' Auguste could not resist asking.

'Both. How could I rebuild it *now*?'

Auguste sympathised. If a *pièce montée* of his creation had been flung to the ground, smashed into pieces, its delicate spun sugar strands a heap of crumbs, how could he recreate exactly the same artistic triumph? Personally, he could not see motorcars in quite the same light, or the Dolly Dobbs as a triumph, but he was prepared to admit a similarity in outlook.

Egbert was not so tolerant. 'That's what we're here to discuss.'

'I don't want to rebuild her,' Harold said piteously.

'That couldn't be anything to do with the fact the Dolly Dobbs is a copy of Thomas Bailey's Brighton Baby, could it?'

He stared at them nervously. 'How could it be? I've been working on the Dolly Dobbs for five years. How could I have known what Bailey was doing? Anyway, who says it's a copy?' he added too belatedly to convince.

'Those who've seen both of them. Mrs Didier, Mr Didier, the Duchess, Leo, Fred Gale—'

'It's coincidence.' Harold was red in the face.

'Then why didn't you try to patent yours? Bailey did. Is that why you smashed the machine up yourself, so that you didn't have to drive it publicly once you knew the Duchess was driving in the Brighton Baby?'

'That's certainly why you would not allow it to come out of the stable last Saturday, isn't it?' Auguste asked.

'You don't understand,' Harold moaned. 'I'm an artist. How could I lay a violent hand on my own beloved Dolly? The reason I didn't apply for a patent is much simpler.'

'And that is?' Egbert pressed as Harold came to a full stop, looking wildly from one to the other, hoping for appreciation for the artist in him in vain.

'I forgot.'

'Forgot? For over five years?'

'I'm rather absent-minded.' An air of slight complacency entered Harold's voice. 'I was so enthusiastic about building my Dolly I'm afraid it never occurred to me that anyone else could possibly be as clever as me.'

'Yet you didn't seem too surprised when we told you the Brighton Baby *had* been patented. You knew about that.' Egbert was never moved by the plight of artists.

He swallowed. 'Miss Hart told me. Now you'll think I murdered her.' His voice ended in a shriek as the full horror of his position struck home.

'Why should we?' Egbert inquired as gently as a pike after a minnow.

Harold gave in. 'She was blackmailing me. She'd found out that I hadn't patented it. I think she was determined to drive Dolly, she liked her so much,' he explained ingenuously. So she went to the Patent Office just on the off chance she might find something interesting. She told me Thomas Bailey had a similar idea to mine, and that if she couldn't drive the Dolly, she would tell him before the trials.'

'And how did you hope to get away with it once details were published?'

'I suppose I hoped Bailey's was different and wouldn't work.'

'It didn't.'

'*Really?*' Delight took over his face. 'So I can rebuild Dolly.'

'Only if it's different to the Brighton Baby, or yours won't work either,' Auguste pointed out.

'Of course it will work,' he answered feverishly. 'I wonder if I should go to see Mr Bailey. If I don't, he'll rebuild *his* and all my work will be wasted.' He was already moving towards the door.

'But you're starting on a new car,' Auguste pointed out.

'Dolly's reputation must be cleared first. Where's my hat?' He looked round vaguely for Judith.

'Not so fast, Mr Dobbs,' Egbert said none too cordially. 'Don't forget that Dolly's reputation gave you an excellent motive for disposing of Hester Hart.'

Harold Dobbs's mouth opened, shut, and opened again. 'I suppose it did,' he agreed unhappily.

Pierre looked up eagerly as Auguste came in, though whether this was excitement at the possibility of a discussion on the superiority of French *sanguines* mushrooms over English parasols or desire to discuss the topic of Miss Hart Auguste could not tell. Obstinacy made him decide to concentrate his immediate attention on cuisine, not on the missions with which Egbert had charged him. He was, after all, a maître chef, not primarily a Scotland Yard consultant detective, he reminded himself. Egbert all too frequently overlooked this fact.

'What is there still to do?' he asked, donning his long apron. 'Are the pies glazed?'

'*Oui, monsieur.* Is there news about—'

'And the *poussins* with the veal and pork truffled stuffing ready for the oven?'

'*Oui, monsieur.* Has the murderer—'

'The Calvados and apple sauce for the quails?'

'*Non, monsieur,* but I will do it. Have you—'

'No, *I* will do it.' Auguste was happy again. He was part of that warm, cocooned world in which heaven and hell had briefly made appearances and disappearances; the ecstatic joy of creation versus the imps of mischief in the form of imperfect supplies and smoking stoves. The world was called a kitchen, and he was king of it. For a little while, at least.

Eventually he took pity on Pierre – or, rather, on the club restaurant's forthcoming dinner. Pierre had at least one eye on him, if not both, and the food might suffer. Some dishes could sulk as effectively as humans, often more disastrously.

'Did Miss Hart ever speak of her family to you? Living members, that is?'

Happiness glowed in Pierre's face. 'She spoke little of her family at all, monsieur. I gained the impression she had left England to break away from her family as much as her so-called friends.'

'But she was a wealthy woman, thanks to them.'

'I do not know.' He shrugged. 'She was concerned for money. She carefully checked what I spent in the markets but I do not think she was short of money. How could she be? She travelled where she wished.'

'And when she was not travelling, where did she go?'

Pierre considered. 'Sometimes she would return to England, sometimes stay in Paris, I believe. I was not with her then, of course. I returned to my father's restaurant in Marseille, or took temporary positions in other restaurants in France, or Algeria, and sometimes Turkey. That is how I gained so much experience. As you will know, monsieur, in countries where food is highly esteemed, the peasant or the seaman is as exacting in his demands as the nobleman.'

How true. The best judge of an *omelette aux truffes* Auguste had ever met lived in a charcoal burner's hut in the Alpes-Maritimes.

'Now tell me, monsieur, have you found this murderer yet?'

'A *daube* is not cooked in thirty minutes, Pierre.'

'But he, perhaps she, may escape. Leave London. Leave *England*.'

'Then we will know who it is, and track him or her down,' Auguste told him patiently. 'And meanwhile you can help.'

'Me?' Pierre's face lit up. 'Anything to trap the dog who did this.'

Auguste produced the copy of the *Rubáiyát* which had been found in Hester Hart's dorothy bag. 'Have you any idea what this was doing in her bag? Was it a favourite of hers, a present from someone?'

Pierre took it and examined it. 'No, I do not think so. She was very fond of poetry and frequently carried it with her; she may have bought this, or had it given to her. It looks quite new.' He opened it, and read. '"But still a Ruby kindles in the Vine/And many a Garden by the water blows." A very nice poem,' he said approvingly. He handed it back to Auguste, and as he did so the page fell out.

Auguste bent to pick it up, glanced at it and replaced it. 'I like it too, Pierre. You should read it.'

'If Miss Hart liked it, I shall.'

'Did Miss Hart carry a gun while she was with you?'

'Always.'

'Did she use it?'

'To threaten brigands frequently, and once to shoot an intruder in her tent. The captain of the caravan. It was a difficult time, we were lucky to escape from his companions.'

'Did she carry it with her here?'

'I cannot be sure, of course, but knowing her I would think she did.'

'Then why would it not have been in her bag in the motor stable?'

'That seems strange. I do not understand. But then Miss Hart had her own way of doing things.'

'It's the last time I go with the house,' Hannah Smirch declared, limping painfully into Hester Hart's former study and dining room.

'I beg your pardon?' Auguste asked the question for both of them, as Egbert immediately began to look through the desk. Not, he explained later to Auguste, in case Twitch had overlooked anything but to get the smell of the evidence himself. Twitch, in Egbert's opinion, never overlooked anything except the Thames from his office window, and even the Thames thought twice about it with Twitch's eye on it.

'With the house,' Hannah repeated. 'It's rented, and Peters, that's the man, and I go with it. Not any more, I don't. It's not right. Tenants getting themselves murdered. The landlord should be more careful. I can't be getting all upset with all these people marching in and out. Police indeed.'

'We won't be long, Mrs Smirch,' Auguste said pacifyingly, before Egbert could reply. He was well used to a long succession of Hannah Smirches in the course of his profession.

'You'll be wanting muffins,' she continued gloomily. 'That's all you police think of. I've got better things to do than run around all day serving you muffins and tea.'

'Before you start them,' Egbert weighed in, 'I want to know what happened to the chestful of diaries that Miss Hart kept here.'

'You're about the fourth person to ask me that today, and I'll tell you the same as I told them. She had it here up to a week or so ago. Now I don't know where it's gone. And before you ask, nor does Peters.'

'What other people?' Egbert asked sharply. 'Police?'

'With a feathered hat like that stuck on her head? Said she was Miss Hart's cousin but didn't give a name.'

'Cousin? Describe her, if you please.'

With a martyred look that would have done justice to St Catherine, Hannah Smirch obliged with an excellent description of Isabel, Countess of Tunstall.

'Who else?'

Maud Bullinger had not been so coy about her name, John Millward had apparently masqueraded as a lawyer but was identifiable not only by the description of his person but by the fact that he was the only one to arrive in an old-fashioned hansom horse cab.

'How could the chest have been removed without either you or Peters seeing it go, Mrs Smirch?'

'Must have gone on my afternoon off.' Her look implied that any reasonable employer would give her Sunday off too, so she wouldn't be troubled with all these police. 'Madam didn't say anything to me about it, or to Peters, though most likely it come out through my kitchen while he was asleep in his room. Lazy good-for-nothing. Catch Madam hauling it down the front steps. A stickler she was for "How Things Are Done, Mrs Smirch."' She mimicked Hester's high, strained voice.

'She was a great traveller, social conventions would not trouble her, surely,' Auguste observed.

'Wouldn't they?' Hannah replied darkly. 'Except when it come to *him*, of course.' She eyed them, obviously hoping they would insist on hearing more.

Auguste obliged.

'I'm not one to speak ill of the dead, mind, even if she did complain about my muffins, but sometimes *he* stayed over.' She gave them a look heavy with meaning. 'Mr Smythe. Madam said to make the guest room up, but I can tell a rumpled sheet when I see one.' She nodded to herself, confirming her own worst suspicions.

'She was planning to marry him, wasn't she?' Auguste asked innocently.

'Not afore time. A den of sinful iniquity this house has been.'

'Has he been here since Miss Hart died?'

'No. I wouldn't let him across the threshold. I didn't like him, no more I did that foreigner chappie.'

'Pierre Calille?'

'That wasn't the name. Louis Gee something. I had to show him into Madam quite often.' She heaved a sigh. 'He always drank wine. He didn't go round demanding muffins, I'll say that for him.'

As they left, Auguste nursed a fantasy in which Hannah Smirch might have murdered Hester for criticising her muffins. After all, if he as a maître chef was entitled to rage against those who did not appreciate his *cailles farcies,* why should Hannah Smirch not rate her wares as highly?

Chapter Nine

'The case of the disappearing chest, Tatiana.' Egbert settled himself on the Chesterfield in the drawing room at Queen Anne's Gate, indulgently glancing at the amorous activity of the numerous goddesses, nymphs and infant cupids rampaging around the Angelica Kaufmann ceiling above him. Busier than Stockbery Towers, he had remarked to Auguste when he first saw it. He liked this ceiling though; they looked as if they were enjoying themselves, which appeared to be against the rules in English society. The warm golds of the ceiling were reflected in Tatiana's choice of décor and made this a comfortable place to be on a Sunday working lunchtime.

'Like Maskelyne and Devant?'

'I'd welcome their assistance.' Egbert was beginning to think only a couple of magicians could sort this case out.

'Mrs Smirch, *ma mie*, the all-too-solid housekeeper, claims the chest has vanished into thin air,' Auguste told his wife. 'One day it was there, another it wasn't.'

'Is Mrs Smirch entirely reliable?' Tatiana inquired.

'Has she had her palm greased with silver, do you mean?' Egbert considered this. 'It didn't look too greasy to me. What do you think, Auguste?'

'I think it more likely that Hester Hart deliberately chose Mrs Smirch's afternoon off, and organised Peters's absence too, in case they should prove susceptible to silver. Miss Hart was a well-organised woman.'

'And so is Mrs Jolly,' Tatiana mentioned. 'I fear if we don't appear in the dining room right away, her luncheon might perform the same trick as the chest.'

Auguste leapt up anxiously. Tatiana was not jesting. On one terrible occasion they had had to make do with cold food because the game pie was deemed by Mrs Jolly to be overcooked, and no amount of cajoling could magic it back to their table.

Today, however, Mrs Jolly was obviously prepared to do her best to further the course of British justice, Auguste realised thankfully as he eyed the comforting assortment of cold plates on the sideboard which Mrs Jolly had provided, and the even more comforting smell of roast duck wafting up from the kitchens to their ground-floor dining room. It needed only Mrs Jolly's olive sauce to make his satisfaction complete. They had a harmonious triangular arrangement. If Auguste proposed a dish, Mrs Jolly amended it, and Tatiana accepted it – with a few interventions of her own, usually eccentricities from her Russian upbringing or culled from reading of Far Eastern delights.

Today all was well. What could be more English? Potted lobster, young celery salad, roast duck, olive sauce, stewed cucumbers, young potatoes, raspberries with whipped strawberry cream, splendid English Stilton cheese, followed by dessert of fresh fruit and a savoury. Auguste still could not entirely reconcile himself to the English habit of concluding a meal with a savoury taste instead of sweet, but in Egbert's honour Mrs Jolly produced her special Scotch Woodcock savoury and he was content, though feeling somewhat guilty at the thought of Edith ploughing valiantly through Mr Pinpole's tough beef alone. It was with regret that he remembered he must return to his desk, not retire to a comfortable deckchair in their Highbury garden.

'Before you leave, Egbert, I must tell you about the gun.' Auguste regretted having to spoil the afterglow of such a meal. 'Pierre confirms that Miss Hart always carried one when he knew her, and presumes she did in London also.'

'Our villain can't have known that, or why not use it to kill her?' Egbert made a superhuman effort to drag himself back into the case.

'Because of the noise?' Tatiana suggested.

'At that time of night there would be so few people around that even if someone came rushing to investigate, there would be time for the villain to escape.'

Auguste was dubious. 'I'm not sure. The murderer would have to shoot Miss Hart *before* destroying the Dolly Dobbs, and then move the block and tackle along the roof girders to the correct position to swing the block in. It would take some time.'

'Most of our suspects were familiar with that motor house. They'd know how the block and tackle worked.'

Tatiana said nothing. Looking at his wife, Auguste suffered with her. This was her motoring school which she had carefully built up into the crowning glory of the club this year, over which she had worked so hard, and the members of which were, many of them, her friends. And now this!

'It would take courage to carry out the destruction of the car,' Auguste maintained, 'knowing that the alarm might be raised by the gunshot.'

'In that case,' Egbert asked, reasonably enough, 'where *is* that dratted gun?'

'Pierre did not know. Nor did he know anything about this

book –' Auguste produced the *Rubáiyát* – 'save that Hester Hart liked poetry, so it must have been a recent purchase or gift.'

'I don't think many people felt like giving Hester Hart gifts.'

'Except Roderick Smythe,' Tatiana pointed out.

'That's true, Tatiana. I'll see what he has to say for himself.' Egbert eyed the sunshine outside wistfully. 'Shame to spend an afternoon like this inside, case or no case.'

'Perhaps a walk in St James's Park would help your thoughts, Egbert?' Tatiana asked with a straight face.

Egbert yielded. 'Do you know, I think it might.'

St James's Park was crowded. A multitude of large hats that seemed to be adorned with more birds and flowers than the park itself possessed sat in deckchairs listening to the military band playing selections from *The Troubadour,* children were dressed up in their Sunday best, sailor suits, frilly pinafore dresses and black stockings, ducks were fed, an army of sunshades battled their way along the paths, sweethearts strolled daringly arm in arm, and on the bridge over the lake visitors to London gazed towards the Horseguards Parade and the Foreign Office then turned to admire Buckingham Palace. It was a beautiful park. Auguste recalled an old story of how a Queen of England had asked the Prime Minister how much it would cost to buy it back for private royal use. The answer had been: two crowns.

'Here is the book, Egbert.' Auguste handed it to him as they stopped to take tea at the refreshment house. 'Be careful, there is a loose page.'

'A page of the book or something inserted?'

'Of the book.' He leaned over and plucked it out to confirm his memory.

'It's unlikely you'd have just one loose page,' Tatiana pointed out. 'It is probably bound in small sections, so there must be one missing or another loose.' She took the book from Egbert. It was an ornate, compact edition, each page artistically decorated with coloured scrolls and vine motifs. 'You see,' she cried in triumph, 'the title page is missing. What at first seems to be the title page is only a preliminary page bearing the title, put in so that it can be attached to the endpapers. In an eight-page section, this loose page would have been printed on the same sheet as the title page.'

'Maybe that excellent duck has clouded my mind,' Egbert replied, 'but what's so interesting about that?'

'Because the title page might have been signed by the giver.'

There was a silence, which Auguste broke. 'Then why did the murderer – if he was by chance the giver – leave the book in the handbag? Why not remove it entirely instead of tearing out the title page?'

Tatiana's face fell, then brightened again. 'Perhaps he tore out the title page earlier. Hester would have noticed if the whole book had disappeared.'

Egbert shook his head, dissatisfied. 'Seems unlikely to me. More probably she bought it herself, and the page got ripped somehow.'

'Perhaps.' Auguste was disappointed. 'After all, if it was Roderick Smythe who gave it to her, why should he remove the dedication, even if he was the murderer? It would be quite natural for him to give a book to his fiancée,' Auguste said.

'Unless he'd intended to give the book to Phyllis,' Tatiana suggested brightly, 'and changed his mind.'

'Wine! Wine! Wine! Red Wine!' Auguste replaced the loose page.

'Haven't you had enough?' Egbert asked.

'That's how the poem continues,' Auguste replied patiently. 'A hymn to the glories of the Grape of Today, rather than the silence of tomorrow.'

'Must be a drinker, then, our friend. A wine-lover.' Egbert stopped. 'Are you thinking what I am, Auguste?'

'Yes. Suppose Luigi thought he stood a chance of her hand in marriage, since she was a rich woman.'

'But that's ridiculous,' Tatiana declared. 'She was going to marry Roderick.'

'Modesty is not Luigi's strong point.'

'But he is a maître d'. I don't see Hester Hart marrying even a top waiter. Not in London. She was always so socially aspiring.'

'Luigi may not have seen it that way. Moreover, he claims to be from an aristocratic Italian family.'

'It's worth following up,' Egbert said resignedly, 'but it may be a red herring. My money's on the obvious – Roderick Smythe. Or Harold Dobbs,' he added, as a small girl ran past, a windmill twirling merrily in her hand.

'I don't see Harold giving books of poetry to Hester Hart,' Tatiana objected.

'Nevertheless, I'm keeping my eye on him. Now about this Luigi. Is he on duty today, Tatiana?'

'Yes, but at this time in the afternoon he is free. He is unlikely to be at the club on an afternoon like this.'

Nor at home, Auguste thought. It was warm enough to enjoy the sunshine but not so hot as to endanger delicate London complexions, despite the cloudless blue sky. He longed all the more for the seaside. London was dusty, country roads were even dustier, but the seaside, approached by railway train, promised clean, exciting air. Already London was beginning to empty for the summer holidays – holidays in society's case from the wearying business of social life. Behind the glittering smiles of appearance, he knew, lay as many anxieties, rivalries and battles as any industrialist or City stockbroker faced. He and Tatiana compromised with the rules, but for those like Hester Hart who vainly clambered to reach the 'heights', the climb was hard indeed.

Roderick Smythe was escorting his once more beloved Phyllis through the Royal Botanic Society's gardens in Regent's Park, anxious that no rough tussock of grass, such as was found on common ground like that of Hampstead Heath, might impede the progress of her dainty feet; moreover a satisfyingly large number of people bowed to them here, whereas on the heath it was all too likely that he would pass unrecognised.

He was reasonably contented; he had been released from Scotland Yard, and once he had put a certain question to Phyllis he would be the happiest man on earth. 'Darling, I've been an absolute fool. Can you ever forgive me?'

Phyllis smiled sweetly at him, passing several sunshade owners and an interested robin. 'Yes, Roderick.'

'By Jove, that's wonderful. I can't think what came over me, deserting you like a rotter.'

'Hester came over you, Roderick. She was not a nice woman. All the same,' she added quickly, 'it's terrible that she's dead.'

'Terrible,' he agreed, though all he was feeling was an overwhelming relief. When the inquest was over, Hester and all the problems surrounding her would be laid to rest. True, there was all that lovely money he'd be missing, but she'd made it clear enough that she wouldn't be marrying him, and even if she had, he suspected a tight hand would be kept on her cheque book, however generous her hands in other fields.

Bed, after all, took up eight hours of the day including sleep, which meant there were still sixteen of the day to fill. Even allowing for racing and driving motorcars, there were still quite a few hours left, and he was by no means sure that the best use of them for Roderick Smythe would have been on Hester, despite her expertise in the other eight hours. With Phyllis at his side, he realised, life was going to be jolly all day.

'Phyllis,' he said earnestly over tea a little later, 'I can't drop on one knee here at this table, but if I could I'd be asking whether there was any chance that you could forgive me enough to let me slip the ring back on your dear little finger?'

Phyllis glanced at her lace-gloved hand. The glove remained on.

'Shall we wait a little, Roderick?' She poured the tea with a steady hand. 'Just for the look of the thing, you know.'

'But you will eventually, won't you?' Roderick asked, greatly alarmed at this diversion from what he had planned.

'Oh, *eventually* I will,' she agreed sweetly. Or at least, she thought, after an arrest had been made. She had to look after her own interests, and it was Roderick, she bore in mind, who had last seen Hester Hart alive. Hester, she remembered all too clearly, had been awfully rude to them earlier that evening, and Roderick did have rather a temper. She had not forgotten the occasion when he had scolded her for wasting time when all she was doing was putting a little woolly jacket on Mr Henry Irving, her little doggie. No, on the whole, she thought she would wait a little. It was no good spending time and effort posing for picture postcards if one's name was to appear the following day linked to a murder charge.

Roderick, to whom the message was all too clear, glumly watched his adored Phyllis demolish two éclairs and a *petit four.*

* * *

Thirty years ago this was a rookery. Now, although the worst of the slums had been removed, the area still looked drab and overcrowded. Nearby Rochester Row and Horseferry Road boasted buildings such as the Guards Hospital, police court, and Wesleyan training college, but huddled around them were terraces of tall, smoke-blackened brick houses. The London grime showed up even murkier in the July sunshine and yet on the Embankment and in St James's Park London society serenaded itself. It was an odd contrast, Auguste thought.

The front door of Luigi's lodgings was opened by a thin, truculent woman of forty-odd, who appeared determined not to rejoice in the Lord's sunshine. 'Mr Peroni's out.'

'I'll see for myself, if you don't mind.' Egbert displayed his badge, and with the air of one who had suspected it all the time she led them up three flights of stairs to the top floor, and flung the door open triumphantly to prove her point.

Luigi had two rooms, one a bedroom, the other a living room, both small, crowded and stuffy. A small statue of the Virgin Mary and an unlit candle in the bedroom revealed a new side of Luigi; several bottles of the club wine store revealed a more familiar side and suggested devoutness stopped short of the Ten Commandments.

'Do you know where Mr Peroni is?'

'Out with his lady friend.' His landlady snorted with disdain.

'And who might she be?'

'I don't know, I'm sure. She doesn't cross this threshold, that I do know. This is a respectable house.'

Auguste looked round the two rooms. Even the briefest glance was enough to show him that no chest was hidden here, nor even a pile of diaries. If Luigi had them, they were elsewhere.

Luigi was evidently primed by his landlady for by the time they caught up with him at the club just after six o'clock, he did not look surprised to see them. 'This is a busy time for me.' He inspected a table, rearranged napkins, and picked off a wilting bloom from the floral decorations.

'I can't believe you'll be run off your feet on a Sunday evening in late July,' Egbert replied. 'We could go to the Yard. You might not feel so busy there.'

Luigi cast a longing look at his safe territory, and decided his mammoth tasks could wait.

'You didn't tell us you'd ever called at Miss Hart's home.'

Luigi looked hurt. 'You did not ask me, Inspector. It is natural, after all. I admitted I gave her regular information, and it would be difficult to talk frequently here without arousing suspicions. I called to see Miss Hart once a week, more if I had urgent news for her.'

'And this money she gave you, how highly did she rate your services? Information, that is.'

Luigi flushed. 'I am not proud of it,' he said angrily. 'An Italian aristocrat should never be reduced to accepting money from ladies. But it is not cheap to live, and I wish to marry – for *bambini*,' he explained virtuously.

'And who's the lucky young lady?' Egbert inquired. 'The one you were with this afternoon?'

Luigi was shocked. 'She is only one of the servants. My fiancée is high-born. Her father owns a hotel.'

Auguste began to like Luigi even less. 'On the Riviera?' he asked.

'Woolwich.'

Not quite so fashionable, but nevertheless it must be a prosperous hotel if it attracted Luigi, Auguste decided, feeling sorry for the mere 'servant' he had been with this afternoon.

Which servant? he wondered, as Egbert produced the copy of the *Rubáiyát*.

'Seen this before?' he asked. Luigi shook his head. 'Take a closer look.'

He obeyed, and opened it readily enough. 'The *Rubáiyát*,' he remarked.

'You've heard of it?'

'Florence, where I worked, is home to many English people, and it is a popular poem.'

'Any idea who gave it to her?'

'It was not me,' he said apologetically; his smile was meant to charm. 'I cannot afford leather bindings.'

Egbert was impervious to charming smiles. 'You could if you used those diaries for blackmail. That is why you went to her home, isn't it?'

The smile rapidly disappeared. '*Me?* Inspector, information is one thing, blackmail quite another.'

'Even more lucrative,' Egbert agreed. 'Where have you hidden the diaries? In a bank? Railway station? Lost property office at New Scotland Yard?'

'Why do you think I have them?' He shrugged as though the matter was of little concern. 'Pierre was her dragoman, Mr Smythe her fiancé. Either of them could have them.'

'Pierre didn't go to Miss Hart's house, according to the housekeeper. You did.'

'And so did Mr Smythe. He went far more than I did.'

'Good of you to be so helpful,' Egbert said grimly. 'But I'm asking *you* where the diaries are. I know they're not in your rooms, I've looked.'

Luigi looked as if he was about to protest, then changed his mind. 'Why should I not tell you?' he cried. 'You think I *want* to be suspected of murder?'

'You could be taking up a new career in blackmail. While those diaries are lying around, quite a few people might feel the need to give you little gifts.'

Luigi stared at him, then suddenly grinned. 'That is a splendid idea. I'll bear it in mind.'

'Morning, Stitch. I've got a job for you.'

Stitch was instantly wary. Cordiality at this time on a Monday morning was unusual from the chief and seldom bode well.

'Somerset House.'

Stitch's worst fears came true. The last time this had happened he'd been made a monkey of by that Frenchie; he remembered it bitterly. He wouldn't put it past Monsieur Didier to have invented some reason to send him off on another fool's errand to get him out of the way on an interesting case. The chief wouldn't do it to him but that foreigner would. He didn't behave like an English gentleman, for all he was related to His Majesty now.

'Hester Hart, father Herbert Hart, born in Blackburn in eighteen thirty-two, mother Maria Trotter, born in Blackburn eighteen thirty-six. See what you can find out.'

'About what, sir?' Twitch inquired woodenly.

'Nearest living relatives.'

'That's before registration was officially compulsory.'

'Always ready for a challenge though, aren't you, Stitch?'

'I am, sir,' Twitch answered despondently. He left the Yard with the feeling that H. M. Stanley had been allotted an easier task when he set off to find Livingstone in the heart of Africa. A few million jungle trees and rivers were as nothing compared with the mighty tomes of Somerset House and the prospect of hunting down parish registers in Blackburn. He thought wistfully, instead of with his customary resentfulness, of the two weeks' holiday ahead at Margate-on-Sea with Martha, when a Panama hat would replace the accustomed bowler, a shrimping net his notebook, and a penny for the 'Burglar Jack' slot machine his entire acquaintanceship with crime and criminals.

Lady Bullinger greeted Monday morning with the same determination as her Napier had greeted Porlock Hill. This was Goodwood week. The fact that horses would necessarily take pride of place there made her arrival by motorcar all the more important. This morning she was to visit the Motor Club of Great Britain headquarters to discuss her representing the country in the International Women's Race in October. This afternoon she would join Agatha for tea at her house, where they had equally important matters to discuss.

After a highly satisfactory morning, she approached her afternoon assignment somewhat later than intended but with equal confidence in its successful outcome.

'Maud, darling.' Agatha flitted in hand-painted silk with apparent delight to greet her.

'Business first, Agatha,' Maud said briskly, once sunshade, goggles and dust coat had disappeared along with the butler. 'What have you discovered about those diaries?'

'They're not with Roderick, so he informs me. He knew of them, but they disappeared.' The Duchess took a delicate sip of China tea.

Maud exclaimed in annoyance. 'And does Roderick not know where they have gone?'

'No. It does seem rather careless of him, Maud. I suppose he can be relied on when he says he doesn't have them himself?'

'How dare you, Agatha. Roderick is my godson. He wouldn't lie to me.' Maud thumped down her teacup, determined to forego the usually rather good seed cake if need be.

'I dare, Maud, because it seems to me that you have got entirely your own way in this terrible affair.'

'Just what do you mean by that?' This was not going the way Maud had planned, yet she couldn't walk away now. Or even drive. Maud, always one for looking facts in the face, acknowledged that she and Agatha were as much bound together over Hester Hart as they had been fifteen years before.

Agatha gave the tinkling laugh that had always annoyed her sister-in-law. 'If I were objective like, say, that police inspector, I might notice that due to Hester's death you are going to drive in the October race as you wanted, and that you have rid yourself of Hester as a god-daughter-in-law – a result which I do appreciate is entirely desirable.'

'Rid myself?' Maud was belligerent. 'What do you mean?'

'Whatever you think I mean, dearest. There is no doubt that you have emerged from this terrible affair rather splendidly, whereas I am a laughing stock on account of that terrible motorcar. Seldom have I been so mistaken in a man as in Thomas Bailey.' She paused. 'It now turns out the Dolly Dobbs and the Brighton Baby are *identical.*'

'But you knew that, Agatha.' Maud was astonished. 'You told me at Martyr House.'

Her Grace's eyes arched upwards. 'I did? I fear you are mistaken, Maud. I cared very little about the Dolly Dobbs and Hester Hart.'

Maud saw no reason to take a hint. 'You cared a lot, Agatha. And you wrote those threatening letters. Do the police know?'

There was a pause, as the steel that had ensured the survival of the British aristocracy for so many hundreds of years came to the Duchess's rescue: when in trouble, unite. 'I suggest, dear Maud, that on the whole our best course is to find those diaries, as I said to Roderick. We don't want the whole world knowing what dear Hester wrote in her private diaries for herself alone.'

'I doubt if we can prevent it,' Maud said stiffly. 'I would remind you there were three of us involved.'

Agatha paused. 'Destroying the diaries is *essential*. And we know where to start, don't we?'

'Not that housekeeper again,' Maud declared. 'The woman was positively rude.'

'No. I believe Luigi has them. So does Roderick. It is most unfortunate; he is not the most discreet – or cheapest – person in the world.'

Hortensia was engrossed in studying form for Goodwood.

'I must say it's a rotten field. I think His Majesty's horse, don't you? Chatsworth.'

John Millward could raise little enthusiasm for horses; he was rather more interested in remaining in London this week but knew that the odds on Hortensia allowing him to do so were considerably longer than on the King's horse. Goodwood always bored him. It was true that the archaeological world in London was closing down for the summer and after that he would be starting a long trip to Cairo. He always endeavoured to miss Newmarket and Lincoln, with a vague promise of being back for Christmas. This year was different, however. He felt uneasy about leaving with those diaries of Hester's floating around. Whatever she had said in them, it would be pure invention but that never stopped people from believing it; furthermore, he had met a publisher this week who told him he wanted to publish Hester Hart's travel diaries since he had lost the chance of the memoirs. John was all too well aware that he would be figuring in them, including, if he were really unlucky, coy references to their imaginary love affair. Hortensia, he was still convinced, simply would not understand, especially after his dinner with the fearful Phyllis last week. No, he had to find those diaries before they were handed over for publication, and he thought he knew where to start.

'Good legs,' Hortensia continued.

John Millward looked enthusiastically at the chicken limb on his plate.

'Very tasty,' he agreed bleakly.

'Where do you think those diaries are?' Hugh lounged back on the cushions spread on the grass in an entirely private part of the grounds of Winter House.

'They're not at her home,' Isabel replied despondently. 'Have a cherry.'

He obliged, watching the way she daintily expelled the stones from her mouth. They appeared to glide out of their own accord in order to avoid over-sullying Isabel's fine white hands. In a fit of absent-mindedness he reverted to his childhood habit of spitting his own out as far as they would go. He chortled as one hit an oak tree, and Isabel looked pained. He didn't mind; he felt he had struck a small blow for the freedom of the male of the species.

'Where else could they be?' Isabel fretted. 'I suspect that maître d' would know; she was always very chummy with him,' she observed superciliously. Typical of Hester to consort with the servants.

'They might be with a publisher already.'

'That's an alarming thought.'

It was indeed, Hugh thought uneasily, wishing he hadn't had it. This whole affair of the diaries and Hester Hart was beginning to get out of control. He was going to have to get involved in the search without a doubt. Once the matter of the diaries was satisfactorily settled, perhaps he'd separate from Isabel, delightful and beautiful though she was. She was his cousin unfortunately, so it wouldn't be easy. He would have to keep on reasonable terms with her; perhaps he could make her think she had broken it off. It was always difficult to know what Isabel was thinking about but he was quite sure that she didn't like being thwarted. Meanwhile, the diaries had to be found.

Harold Dobbs was not out in the sunshine; he was looking at it through his parlour window, unimpressed. Outside in the garden, his children were whooping around like a Wild West rodeo, using the neighbours' somewhat younger children as horses. Why didn't they use them as motorcars? he wondered fiercely. The charge of the Light Brigade would never have failed if Lord Cardigan had used motorcars, especially if they were of Harold Dobbs's design.

Should he or should he not go to see Thomas Bailey? Suppose he mentioned the awkward matter of the patent? Then Judith broke in upon his thoughts.

'It's time you rebuilt Dolly.'

'I can't.'

'Why not?'

'It's not patented, and Thomas Bailey's was.'

'So what? You didn't steal his idea, did you?'

'No,' he said quickly, 'but it means I can't build one again.

Unless Bailey and I see if we can't make it work between us. You see, Judith,' he went off into a string of technicalities during which she adopted her Harold-you-are-a-genius look and mentally composed the week's shopping list. 'Perpetual motion is within our grasp; I am positive I am on the right road. Perhaps wind is not the answer. I shall discuss it with Bailey.'

'I shouldn't.' Judith suddenly finished her list and heard what he was saying.

'Why not?'

'We don't know that he isn't the terrible person who smashed poor Dolly.'

'That would make him a murderer too,' Harold pointed out.

'Someone has to be.' Judith fixed him with a stare. 'And it wasn't you, was it?'

'Of course not,' Harold said righteously. 'You know I was here all that evening and night.'

Judith said nothing. She had slept like a log till morning.

Egbert Rose yawned. Mondays were worse when you had worked on Sunday. He had been here all day, studying forensic reports, Fingerprint Department reports, and his own notes. There was no sign of Twitch who was no doubt still beavering away in Somerset House.

Time to go, and he closed his files thankfully. Edith was expecting her sister for supper tonight, and he always liked her husband Fred, a restful sort of bloke. Auguste was also, in a way, though not like Fred. Fred rarely said anything, and you couldn't say that of Auguste.

The door opened and a messenger shot in with a telegraph message. Egbert regarded it with extreme distaste. He didn't like things you couldn't control. You could decide whether to read letters that came by post, and even whether you answered a telephone, but a telegraph message brooked no delay. It could be from one of the divisional supers, and it could be urgent. He pulled it towards him, read it – and lifted the telephone off its hook.

Auguste hummed to himself. The cares of the day were over and he had the bliss of this special evening ahead. True, Tatiana would be out, but this meant the whole evening could be devoted to delightful experimentation. It was Mrs Jolly's evening off, and by arrangement he was allowed the courtesy of cooking in his own kitchen. He had decided on chicken crépinettes, a recipe he had learned during his apprenticeship under Monsieur Escoffier at the Faisan d' Orée in Cannes, to which he now wished to make some subtle variations. He had tried to interest Mrs Jolly in this fascinating project, but she had refused. She knew what she was good at, and though she could always be persuaded to try something new, she could never be persuaded to try something at which she had previously failed.

He ran upstairs to his dressing room to bathe and change into his cooking clothes, just as the telephone bell rang out. He heard their butler go to answer it, and then with sinking heart heard his footsteps mounting the stairs. The call was for him. With a sigh Auguste followed the footsteps downstairs again, and took up the telephone, always solemnly offered to him on a silver salver.

'Egbert here. What are you doing this evening?'

Relief. 'Tonight I am cooking, in my own kitchen. You are welcome to—'

'I'm afraid you're not. I need you, and later Tatiana.'

'What has happened? *Where* do you want me?'

'The Zoo, Auguste. The Zoological Gardens of Regent's Park.'

* * *

Monday was always the busiest day of the week at London Zoo, mainly because it cost only 6d to get in as opposed to 1s on the other days, and partly because admission on Sundays was restricted to Fellows of the Society and their friends. This ensured that every Londoner from Ealing to the Isle of Dogs would be there on Monday, together with a few members of higher London society who had failed to persuade a Fellow to give them a ticket for the more fashionable Sunday. It was still crowded when Auguste arrived although it was past six o'clock, and some of the smaller children were being dragged bawling out through the gates as he paid his sixpence entrance fee. He wondered idly whether Egbert had had to pay sixpence too.

He hurried through the turnstile, studied the usefully provided Guide to the Gardens plan, then set off towards his goal, pushing through the crowds gazing entranced at monkeys and pink flamingos. Why did the parrot house have to be in the furthest corner of the gardens? Was Gregorin, his old enemy, the reason for the summons? He hadn't thought of him for months; perhaps this was his reward for ignoring the threat. His reason promptly dismissed the thought. If it was Gregorin, Special Branch would be involved, not Egbert. No, this was to do with Hester Hart.

Three solid-helmeted police constables were shooing away curious sightseers, to the great indignation of the lawful occupants, some of whom, it being a fine day, were enjoying an outside airing on their perches and resented being deprived of their due reward in the form of nuts. A black-capped lory screeched angrily as Auguste rushed past, backed up in his complaint by an equally colourful Swainson's lorikeet. Auguste, however, had no evil designs on their living quarters outside or inside; he could hear Egbert's voice coming from somewhere out of sight behind the parrot house, where the public had less cause to walk.

Heart in his mouth and feeling rather sick, Auguste cleared his credentials with the constable and hurried round to join Egbert. He found him standing by a kneeling police surgeon. To his horror he realised they were inspecting species of homo sapiens. Auguste struggled to overcome his revulsion as for the second time in under a week he saw a pool of blood creeping out from under a face-down dead body.

'Who is it?' he asked in a voice he hardly recognised as his own. All Egbert had been able to tell him on the telephone was that the body of a man had been found; there was no identification save a club key on him. He could be the husband of a member or, Auguste swallowed, one of the kitchen or dining room staff.

'Luigi Peroni, and he's been stabbed. No weapon again. Odd thing is,' Egbert indicated a gun, 'there was a Colt lying tastefully by his side. My money's on its being Hester Hart's, so we don't have the trouble of hunting it any longer. Very thoughtful of our murderer.'

All around came shouts of family laughter interspersed with jungle roars from animal cages. Close by, children were scrambling over one another in their eagerness to pay their twopence for an elephant or camel ride. Chimpanzees were clutching the hands of their keepers as they paraded round the lawn; judging by the excited roars, a sea lion was performing for an admiring crowd. Here behind the parrot house, in stark contrast to the life that buzzed around them, a man lay dead.

'And it could have been anyone who killed him,' grunted Egbert.

Chapter Ten

'The parrot house,' Egbert remarked disgustedly. 'What a place for anyone to end their days.' Edith liked coming to the Zoo; it had been part of the holiday ritual for them to escort her sisters' children here at least twice a year, and the lion house, sea lion enclosure and camel rides were old familiar friends. Now that the children were adults, he and Edith still came, tracing out the familiar patterns ready for the new generation of children now coming of zoo age. He didn't like this blot on the gardens of his memory; it was a personal affront.

The police surgeon clambered stiffly to his feet. 'He's been dead about an hour and a half, judging by his temperature. Roughly, that is.'

Egbert looked at the long row of parrots on their outdoor perches by the trees, screeching in the late afternoon sunshine. 'He could have used the gun. Wonder why the villain brought both?'

People were now beginning to make their way home, and as Auguste watched, the gardens began to belong once more to the animals they housed. The roars from the lion house, the chattering of the monkeys, and the cries of birds of prey began to speak more loudly of the jungle they had come from, in these last hours before sundown.

'And why choose this public spot at all? There are many quiet corners in London,' Auguste pointed out.

'But a good place to meet unobserved. The animals are on parade during the week, not their visitors like on Sundays. What gatekeeper is going to remember one face from another? Stitch is over at the main gate now.' Egbert watched as the surgeon and constables covered the body. 'We'll wait till the Zoo closes.'

'I suppose it could not be suicide,' Auguste asked, 'and the weapon removed by someone else?' It sounded unlikely even to him.

The surgeon shook his head. 'I'll know more later. But from the amount of blood I'd say the weapon was driven in too deep and hard.'

'The killer would get blood on him though?'

'Some, but not as much as from a more superficial wound.'

'Was there nothing in his pockets, Egbert, that might lead us to the diaries?'

'I'll send Stitch back to the house again, just in case. Here he is now.'

Twitch was escorting a uniformed man, white in the face at the prospect of his coming ordeal. 'The gatekeeper, sir.'

'I'd like you to take a look at him.' Egbert was sympathetic. 'Nasty business, but it has to be done. Look at the clothes – and the hat,' he instructed as the gatekeeper gingerly approached the body, which the surgeon uncovered again. The homburg had been found lying at the side of his body. 'Remember him? And whether he came in alone or with someone else? Or someone leaving with bloodstained clothing?'

The gatekeeper took as short a look as was possible, and shook his head on all counts. As he departed, a police constable brought up an elderly sandwich-board man. He, too, was nervous, his boards proudly bearing the signs 'Buns for the Bears. Two a penny' clanking together in his agitation.

'He says he saw a gentleman walk round here,' the constable prompted, as his charge seemed overwhelmed.

'That's right. During my easy time when I takes a little walk.'

'This gentleman?' Egbert indicated the still uncovered face of Luigi Peroni.

'That's him.' He edged away as quickly as possible.

'When was this easy time?'

'In my business, after the big animals have been fed at four o'clock, my turnover decreases,' he explained. 'It picks up again just before closing time. It must have been about a quarter to five. There was someone waiting for him.'

'Who?' Egbert asked sharply. 'Man or woman?'

'I believe it was a man, but the merest impression was all I gained. A long coat, a hat, a *presence*. Lots of people come to the Zoo to meet other people. Ladies and gentlemen, if you know what I mean.' He looked hopefully at Egbert.

Egbert did know what he meant. He meant he didn't want to be pinned down.

'I went into the parrot house. I like looking at them. They're restful.' A screech nearby sounded like mocking laughter to Auguste. The bun-seller looked at them, conscious of disappointing, and tried again. 'This place hasn't been the same since Jumbo went.'

'At least we're a little further forward,' Auguste said comfortingly to Egbert as half an hour later the corpse of Luigi Peroni was carried to a waiting motor van. Twitch had been despatched to Luigi's lodgings, and he and Egbert were walking back through the gardens to the main entrance. At their side pink flamingos waded in the evening sunlight, an elephant (not the late lamented Jumbo) extended a hopeful trunk for buns, and monkeys chattered, bringing close lands Auguste would never see.

'How far forward?' Egbert cast a scathing look at a monkey extending the hand of friendship towards him. 'Even the parrot-keeper couldn't tell us anything.'

'The bun-seller believed it to be a man, and surely if Lady Bullinger, the Duchess or the Countess had come into the gardens with murder in mind, they could hardly be mistaken for a man.'

'They wouldn't be wearing their tiaras,' Egbert pointed out grumpily. 'In one of those dust coats, with a large hat, they might pass at a distance for a man.'

'Unlikely,' Auguste replied firmly. 'Moreover, there is something else you must consider.'

'And what's that?'

'You are assuming that the killer of Luigi was also the killer of Miss Hart.'

'That's true.' Egbert was none too happy at having this pointed out to him. 'But it's likely, isn't it?'

'Yes, but coincidences do happen. We know Luigi supplied information for money, but we don't know to how many people he supplied it – or how many he might be blackmailing as a result. He might even have had other enemies who were nothing to do with the club.'

'What about Pierre? He couldn't stand the fellow.'

'Certainly you should talk to him. And there is Luigi's fiancée – and his other young lady.'

'Nicely brought up fiancées don't go stabbing their intended behind parrot houses.'

'Nicely brought up people are as capable of murder as anyone else when they are threatened.'

'Which brings us back to their ladyships, the diaries—'

'And Mr Roderick Smythe,' Auguste supplied for him. 'He is, remember, Lady Bullinger's godson.'

'Ah yes, my Mr Smythe. Where might he be this evening? Any ideas?'

'Yes. On a moonlight drive to Hampstead.'

'Charlie, I have a job for you this evening.' Tatiana summoned all her charm and all she could assume of centuries of Romanov authoritarianism. Jobs for Charlie were not easy to assign, especially at the last moment, and especially on a July summer evening, but in view of Auguste's terrible telephone message, she had no option.

Charlie eyed her narrowly. He was not averse to work but he preferred it to be of his choosing and timing. Nevertheless, he was prepared to listen. His bulk shifted to a pose of amiability.

'I want you to be maître d' at the club restaurant this evening. It won't be very busy.'

Charlie, taken entirely by surprise, was unable to adopt his normal laconic attitude. 'Hell and Tommy, why?'

'Can't you do it? Tatiana abandoned charm for the formidableness of Peter the Great.

'Consider me there already, Mrs D. Luigi ill, is he?'

'Worse, I'm afraid. He has been found murdered.'

Charlie whistled. 'Annie will be upset.'

'Annie?'

'Annie Parsons, ma'am. She's been sweet on Luigi for weeks.'

'I thought she was sweet on you.'

'So,' said Charlie darkly, 'did I. But Charlie, she says, my heart is another's, and off she goes. I suppose that gives me a motive.'

'Charlie,' Tatiana remarked sadly, 'you wouldn't have the energy for murder.'

Hastily she scrambled into her linen dust coat, put on her tam o'shanter, searched frantically for her goggles, and hurried outside to where the Léon Bollée awaited her. Even that glory failed to excite her this evening. After all, who wanted a motorcar that ran so perfectly it was silent? She liked noise and excitement. Perhaps it was time to have a new motorcar. Or perhaps she, like Auguste, was just longing for the end of the season when she, too, could escape the London dust for Eastbourne, which was now assuming the attraction of a Lost Atlantis. But how could they leave the club while the murder of Hester Hart remained unsolved? And now there was another to add ot it.

The malaise clung to her as she drove the Bollée round to Birdcage Walk where the club was to assemble. There would only be fifteen cars – that in itself was a sign that the London season was near its end. After Goodwood this week, it would be over. This Saturday the club would close for a month, after a final dinner for those still lingering in London; the die-hards, her committee, would be among them.

She saw Maud, a formidable figure in blue in her Napier. She had been full of bonhomie now she knew she could race in October. There was Agatha, neat and trim in the Horbick, Isabel, managing to imply beauty even in dust coat and goggles, and there was Phyllis with Roderick Smythe, who seemed glued to her side at the moment. Tatiana suspected Phyllis had had a tussle between not wanting to associate herself too closely with the prime suspect in a murder case and not wanting to face the ordeal of a mechanical defect alone. In fact, Phyllis would have been quite safe from sullying her hands, for Tatiana could see Miss Dazey in her

Oldsmobile and at her side a highly uncomfortable Leo.

There was no Dolly Dobbs. She had heard nothing from Harold since the disaster, and the remains of the Dolly Dobbs were still, to her annoyance, in the repair house. To her knowledge he had not been near them, and she would have to ask him to remove them.

How could she believe that any of these people, her members, her *friends*, had anything to do with murder? Tonight, however, she would have to tell them at some point that a second murder had blighted their club.

'Darling Tatiana,' Agatha cooed as Tatiana drove by and came to a halt behind the Horbick. One of the two steam cars let off a coincidental hoot as they prepared to move off. 'What could be more delightful?'

Normally Tatiana would ecstatically have agreed with her. Today, the spark was failing on the plug of her enjoyment. It was hardly surprising. She had not particularly liked Luigi but he was efficient, popular, and he was a human being who was no longer alive. Should she tell the ladies now? She decided against it. Later this evening she would break the news.

The cavalcade set off past the Guards' Chapel and Buckingham Palace, and up towards Hampstead. Their route was to include Netherhall Gardens, simply for the fun of unofficially racing the motorcars on the 1 in 7.2 gradient. It was something Tatiana had looked forward to but once again fate took a mean hand.

As the cars turned into Netherhall Gardens and halted at the line of the forecourt fence on the east side of the Finchley Road, a familiar sight met Tatiana's eyes. Stationary at the bend at the top of the steepest part of the hill by the drain grating was a bright red motorcar with two enormous hoods on its mudguards, facing towards them like monster eyes.

Tatiana knew it couldn't be the Dolly Dobbs and so—

'Just what do you think you are doing, Thomas?' Agatha demanded, squeezing her hooter bulb furiously.

He couldn't hear the words, but the message was clear enough. Thomas, in cap and huge goggles, jumped on to the Brighton Baby and trundled her bravely down the hill towards them. 'I'm sure I've got the right answer this time,' he assured the Duchess feverishly. 'I've been testing it up and down this hill—'

'The right answer is to forget this pile of rubbish,' Agatha informed him crisply. 'Kindly crank my motor, young man.'

He stared miserably at the cranking handle and obeyed. The Horbick, which hadn't needed cranking since it was hot anyway, roared away up the hill as Thomas jumped for his life.

A fine start, thought Tatiana miserably, seeing the Horbick drive round the bend without any intention of stopping, and signalled to the rest of her flock to forget their race and proceed to Hampstead. At the top of the hill, the danger lamp in the middle of the road had been knocked askew by the angry Duchess, and as Tatiana's wheels rumbled over the next drain grating, it sounded like ominous thunder for the days ahead.

Two hours later, Egbert and Auguste alighted from a motor cab at the lamplit gates of Westland House overlooking Hampstead Heath.

'I've been tempted to buy one of these contraptions,' Egbert remarked. 'Saves finding cabs all the time.' He grinned. *Et tu, Brute?* was the message very clearly emanating from Auguste.

Auguste always enjoyed visiting Lady Westland, the former music-hall star known as the Magnificent Masher, and since it was in her gardens that Tatiana and her club were to dine this evening he had nurtured a secret hope that he and Egbert might be in time to dine with them. As he smelt the aroma from the remains of the hot plates in chafing dishes on the serving tables, he wondered wistfully what he had missed. A furtive glance at the dinner plates being cleared back to the kitchens told him the worst; he had missed Gwendolen's saddle of veal with soubise sauce. He tried to forget it as he explained Egbert's presence and his mission to Lady Westland and her husband, but a slight sense of injustice as well as the lingering aroma remained with him. Gwendolen interpreted his expression correctly. 'I suggest, Inspector Rose, that you and Auguste eat first and interview later, otherwise half the aristocracy of London will end up in Brixton prison cells.'

Lady Bullinger's temper at the disruption to the race up Netherhall Gardens had not been assuaged by lobster and raspberry charlotte, and she took exception to being escorted into Lady Westland's drawing room, adorned with photographs of her in masculine dress in her music-hall days. 'Murder? But what on earth does Hester Hart have to do with where I was today?'

'It's not Miss Hart. It's Luigi, the maître d'.'

She looked astounded. 'Merciful heavens, *why* should anyone want to kill him? And why, may I ask, do you need to know where I was? I don't go around murdering the servants.'

Egbert disliked being boomed at. 'Where were you?'

'At an At Home.'

'At home?'

'No. *At* one.' She glared. 'I was with the Duchess of Dewbury. Where did the unfortunate occurrence take place, may I ask?'

'The body was found in the Zoo.'

'The *Zoo*? Do you suggest I disguised myself as a gorilla?' Maud had evidently decided on hearty humour. No one, however, had mentioned disguise, it occurred to Auguste, glancing at the photographs of the Magnificent Masher.

Agatha appeared equally horrified to hear of Luigi's death. 'That dear man? I am truly sorry, Inspector.'

'May I ask where you were this afternoon, Your Grace?'

'Certainly you may, though if you think I attended the Zoo you are greatly mistaken. I visit only on Sundays. My husband is a Fellow. I was holding an At Home.'

'So Lady Bullinger told us. And she was present?'

'Certainly she was,' Agatha replied promptly.

'And who else?'

This time the answer was not so prompt. 'There was no one else, Inspector.'

'Unusual, isn't it?'

'It's the end of the season,' Agatha replied snappily.

'What time did she leave?'

'About five o'clock to prepare for this evening.' There was no hesitation in her voice. She might almost have been waiting for the question, Auguste thought.

Isabel was equally unperturbed. 'I was shopping, Chief Inspector. At Whiteleys. Doubtless I will be remembered. I spent some time sitting in the hosiery department. I acquired ten pairs of ribbed silk stockings with lace insertions.'

'We'll check with them to confirm it.'

Isabel extended a leg and delicately revealed an ankle. 'There is your proof. Why am I being cross-examined in this impudent way?'

'Luigi, the maître d' of the Motoring Club, has been found dead. You paid him for information from time to time, I understand.'

The beautiful eyes rested on him without enthusiasm. 'Yes,' she admitted at last. The perfect lips closed, and did not re-open as Isabel considered the import of what she had been told. 'My husband is a very jealous man. He has the absurd idea I have – ridiculous though it sounds – a lover. I like to know if he calls at the club. That is all.'

'All? You didn't pay him for a look at Hester Hart's diaries?'

'No!' The eyes widened. 'Did he have them?'

Egbert did not reply, and Isabel wished, oh how she wished, she'd had the sense to insist on Hugh's coming this evening. He had pleaded a stupid engagement elsewhere and she hadn't seen him all day. It was too bad, when she needed him. Tomorrow she would leave for Goodwood and there at least she would see him. *He* would know what to do.

'Luigi?' Bitterly regretting his own faithfulness to his beloved, Roderick's voice rose to an effective shriek when he had replaced Isabel in the drawing room. *'Why?'*

'We believe he knew where your fiancée's diaries were.'

'Why should he?' Roderick was guarded.

'Just what I wanted to know,' Egbert told him cordially. 'Why give them to Luigi when she had you to turn to?'

'She didn't give them to me.'

'So you've told us. What did you give to *her*? The *Rubáiyát*?'

'No. Whatever it is,' Roderick added cautiously.

'Now tell us where you were this afternoon.'

'Why do you want to know? You can't suspect *me* of murdering him for the sake of diaries. What could possibly be in them of concern to me? I only recently met Miss Hart.'

'I like to keep things tidy, Mr Smythe. Especially my notes.'

'I was with Miss Lockwood from about –' he hesitated – 'two to five. We took a turn on the Crossley. Splendid horse,' Roderick added unnecessarily, pushing back the famous lock of hair which seemed to be sticking to a damp forehead. Sweat? Auguste wondered.

'And where did this turn take you?'

'I don't recall. About.'

'Perhaps Miss Lockwood's memory is more vivid.'

Roderick looked unhappy, and was justified. Phyllis Lockwood's memory was not vivid at all.

'Mr Smythe tells us you were out on a drive with him on his Crossley this afternoon.'

'Did he?' The blue eyes opened wide. 'Oh, I'm sure he's right then.' She gave them one of her sweetest smiles.

Charlie Jolly appeared at the kitchen door. 'I'd like a word with you, Annie.'

Pierre, distracted from the interesting problem of whether he should add both truffles and mushrooms to the garnish for the sole, looked up with a frown. 'Annie is working.'

'I'm working here too.' Charlie came right into the kitchen in pursuit of his erstwhile beloved.

'Here?' Annie forgot all about the quenelles in her amazement.

'For this evening, at least. I regret to tell you, Annie, that Luigi is absent; not to put too fine a point on it, he is dead. In fact, murdered.'

Her eyes grew round. 'Dead?'

Charlie put a protective arm round her. 'I regret, yes.'

Pierre stood stock still, clutching a truffle, as he assimilated this information. 'Murdered?' he asked in a curious voice. 'Like Miss Hart?'

'Apparently so. I know no further details.'

Annie began to cry, sniffling into Charlie's shoulder, and Pierre returned to the sole. But his attention was not wholly on it.

Auguste rode back with Tatiana on the Léon Bollée as the cavalcade made its way back to London. He watched her unhappy face and lightly touched her thigh. 'I am sorry, *ma mie*, that your evening is ruined.'

'Has it brought you any closer, Auguste, to finding out the truth? That is the important thing.'

Auguste hesitated. 'Every case is a possible maze. You can appear to be getting closer but until you are at the very centre you can never be absolutely sure that the path will not lead you away again.'

'And do you think that will happen in this case?'

'I hope not. With the murder of Luigi, the path may become clearer, not more confused.'

'I hope so. It's beginning to poison not only the club but our lives. Not to mention Eastbourne,' she added unhappily.

There was nothing he could say that she would accept as other than mere words of comfort, as the Léon Bollée glided serenely down the hill bringing them back into London.

At Scotland Yard Egbert found Twitch waiting patiently for him. 'What's Peroni's landlady got to say for herself, Stitch? Plenty, I've no doubt.'

'That she wouldn't have let the rooms to him if she'd have known he was going to be murdered,' Stitch reported faithfully and without humour.

'Still no sign of where those diaries might be?'

'I've been through everything again. Short of sending them back home to his family in Italy, they've vanished. And no one got there before me, either.'

'All that means is that Peroni might have had a clue on his body as to where they might be, and our villain is biding his time to pick them up, having removed the clue for our benefit. What did you find out about his fiancée? I suppose it's too much to hope for that she's confessed to murdering him in a jealous rage?'

'She's in Biarritz, sir.'

Eastbourne would do for him, Egbert thought savagely.

Stitch produced a modest beam of self-satisfaction. 'This servant person, she's a different matter. She's head kitchen maid at Milton House. Annie Parsons.'

'Well done, Stitch. Any luck at Somerset House?'

Stitch inflated then promptly deflated again. 'You've no idea the time it takes.' He was aggrieved. 'I've checked the father's side. Miss Hart's grandfather, John Hart –' Twitch consulted his notes – 'had a brother Cedric who had a daughter and a son, both dead. As far as I can make out, the son had no nippers, and his sister Maud only had one son who died three years ago. To go further means going back a generation to John Hart's father.'

'Tackle the mother's side next then.'

'Yes, sir. I've started. Her mother Maria was an only child. Her grandmother, Victoria, had a sister Mary. I'm on her track now.'

'Keep at it, Stitch.' Egbert yawned. It had been a long day.

Breakfast, like any other meal, was not a time to be disturbed, Auguste thought crossly. Tatiana, however, had already left for the club this Tuesday morning, so he reluctantly left his devilled kidneys to see what might be amiss with Pierre. He must have heard the news but why should they have brought him to Queen Anne's Gate instead of waiting for his arrival at the club?

Auguste found him in the morning room, agitatedly pacing to and fro, beret in his hand. He came forward eagerly as soon as he saw Auguste.

'I wish to see you, Monsieur Didier. I am told Luigi has been found dead. Is it true?'

'It is.'

'Murdered?'

'Probably.'

'And in connection with the death of Miss Hart?'

'Again probably.'

'Then he was killed instead of me,' Pierre said simply.

Whatever Auguste had been expecting, it was not this. 'Why do you think that? You are not dissimilar in height and colouring, but no one could mistake him for you in broad daylight.'

'No. But the reason he was killed might have been because of Miss Hart's diaries. Knowing Miss Hart paid Luigi for information, the murderer would have thought she gave him the diaries to guard. But I have the diaries.'

'*You* do? But you told Inspector Rose you did not have them.' Auguste was aghast. Egbert was not going to like this, pleased as he would be to know their whereabouts.

'I had to,' Pierre said wretchedly. 'I swore to Miss Hart to tell no one, and we Arabs take such vows seriously.'

'Then what has changed?'

'If Luigi was murdered for those diaries, so might I be. I am the most likely person to have them after Luigi, now that everybody knows I was her dragoman,' he said wretchedly. 'If I give them to Scotland Yard, I can tell everyone so, and then they will have no reason to kill me. Please to help me.'

'Tell me where the diaries are, and *then* I'll consider helping you. You've wasted a lot of time, Pierre.'

'I know,' he replied humbly. 'They're at Waterloo Railway Station luggage office.'

So simple. 'You put the whole chest in there?'

'No. Miss Hart did not want me to come to her house. Miss Hart took the chest herself to the railway station. I met her there and she gave me the ticket. The idea was that this was a temporary measure, until she had married and had thought of somewhere safer to keep them.'

'Give me the ticket, Pierre.'

Pierre hesitated for a moment, then produced it from his pocket.

'Are you sure the diaries are in the chest?'

'Indeed they are. I have seen them.'

'Why? You weren't intending to make use of the information, were you?'

'No.' Pierre was indignant at this slur. 'I knew Miss Hart would have wanted the diaries of her travels to be published if she failed to write her memoirs, so I gave those diaries to her publisher. You can ask them. Bacon, Archibald and Frith is the firm. Only the private diaries are left in the chest.'

'I think that will satisfy Inspector Rose for the moment.' Auguste took the telephone from its hook.

Waterloo Station at holiday time had a sense of a new life beginning, an energy that the city itself now lacked in late July. Buckets and spades swung enthusiastically from hands of all ages, porters shot to and fro with hand luggage, carts rushed hither and thither with trunks being forwarded in advance to seaside hotels. There were no sad farewells, only eager expectations. Hester Hart's chest was just one more holiday trunk to the left luggage attendant, but Pierre eyed it wistfully as it was loaded by a porter into a growler.

Leaving Pierre to walk back to Milton House, Auguste set off in the growler to Scotland Yard. He peered out of the window to see Pierre standing to watch their leaving as though with them went the last of his life with Hester Hart.

'Here it all is. No doubt of that. Listen to this.' Egbert, having expressed his opinion of Pierre, returned to more positive thinking, and picked a diary at random. 'Sixth of June, eighteen seventy-eight. She must have been about fourteen. "I hate them all. They are beastly to me, all of them, and especially Agatha. I'll show them. I wish my father were a *crossing sweeper*. I hate him too. And I hate *buttons*."'

'And here's a later one.' Auguste took up another volume and leafed through it, then exclaimed in excitement. 'Egbert, this is the one that affects this case. Look. Thirteenth of January, eighteen eighty-nine. "I love him so much, and I really think he loves me . . ." And then,' Auguste riffled through the pages, 'eighth of May the same year. "I cannot understand why he has not called upon me . . ." Then in June, "Today I heard the most terrible story, that I am being talked about in all the clubs, and that he has left town. What does it all mean? I know what it means. It means Maud and Agatha have been up to some more of their dirty games. I hate London society. I hate it. There's only one person I trust."'

'They seem to stop as she goes on her travels,' Egbert said. 'No, here's one. "June, eighteen ninety-seven: I am quite sure it was Isabel who prevented my being invited to

Marlborough House. She has always disliked me. One day I'll get my revenge. I'll use that story so carefully hushed up about her eloping with the family coachman when she was seventeen. That never reached the Earl's ears *or* the Prince of Wales."' He closed the book. 'And more of the same, no doubt. You'd better check the travel diaries with the publishers too.'

Auguste's heart sank. 'Must I?'

'Why not? Don't fancy any more diaries?'

'I fear, Egbert, that Miss Hart's publishers are my own.'

'Writing your memoirs, are you?'

'My cookery book, *Dining With Didier*.'

'What's wrong with that?'

'It is not quite as advanced as it should be.'

Egbert guffawed. 'Too much eating, too little writing.'

'I am a perfectionist,' Auguste replied with dignity.

It was Pierre's evening off, and Auguste was relieved. It meant that he could clear his mind of everything save what he did best: cooking. True, this was difficult while Annie was sniffing into the potatoes, but even this he could ignore while he was intent on preparing the madeira sauce for the sweetbreads, not to mention an asparagus and truffle salad. And a soufflé. No matter that it was not on the menu, he would prepare one. He searched his memory for something suitable for the occasion. It obliged. He would cook his former maître's Palmyra soufflé. Vanilla was the main flavouring.

He began to collect the ingredients, cream, eggs, flour, vanilla sticks, sugar, salt, butter, and with satisfaction contemplated the final result. It was usually the case that the subtlety of the main ingredient was the key to the whole dish.

So it was in detection cases as well. In this case, it was Hester Hart. Could it be that the main ingredient had been so subtle that they had overlooked it altogether?

Chapter Eleven

Publishers were formidable people. Auguste adopted an expression of nonchalance as he walked up the steps of Messrs Bacon, Archibald and Frith in Bedford Square. Publishers had inviting-looking brass nameplates on the door, comfortable leather armchairs as you went in, a book or two strewn on the occasional table, even an aspidistra to suggest that they were loving, homely human beings. They were not. Particularly towards authors who had failed to deliver the manuscripts of cookery books on the date promised. At least, he consoled himself as he pulled the bell, he was to see Mr Archibald this morning, not the once affable Mr Bacon who had long ago expressed a burning desire to publish all ten volumes of *Dining With Didier* and, moreover, had advertised this fact to the book trade.

Auguste tipped his hat down to hide his face as the smiling lady clerk directed him up the stairs to Mr Archibald's office. He wondered if Charon had been trained to give a comforting grin as he helped the dead into his boat for the trip across the river Styx to the Underworld. At least they did not run the risk of seeing a grim-faced Mr Bacon materialise before them.

'From Scotland Yard, I believe you said?' Mr Archibald was no Bacon. He was thinner, more anxious; the whole responsibility for the future of the printed word in English seemed to weigh on his shoulders.

'Yes.' Auguste began to recover as imminent danger receded.

'Ah yes, you want to write your memoirs.' Mr Archibald looked pleased at this feat of memory. 'I seem to know the name. Didier, isn't it?'

'The Hester Hart diaries.' His voice came out as a squeak at the terrible vision of board meetings at which the name of Auguste Didier was all too frequently raised.

'Ah, yes.' Archibald's face fell at the prospect of a minnow escaping the venerable jaws of Bacon, Archibald and Frith. 'I placed them ready for you.' He led the way into an adjoining room where a pile of familiar-looking leatherbound volumes lay on a table, and after hovering for a moment as if hoping Auguste might be seized by a sudden hankering to start his memoirs there and then, left a thankful Auguste to his task.

There were fifteen volumes in all, one for each year from late 1889 to 1903. Auguste glanced at each one. In 1889 she had travelled to Egypt, in 1890 South America, in 1893 to India, even a short one for 1897 when she had travelled to Egypt again after the Jubilee, in 1898 to Algeria and then Iraq – that must have been when she first employed Pierre – and in 1901 Palmyra. Auguste made methodical notes of dates and years, and then began to study the diaries. His first reaction was one of envy. How could Hester write so uniformly well and with so few corrections? His own manuscript had been recommenced several times, and even in its current version had been condemned by Tatiana. Not that she had made any comment; she had merely bought a typewriting machine for his birthday.

'"September tenth,"' he read. '"What can I say of Palmyra's pride, it's magnificent colonnade, that has not already been better expressed by Mr Robert Wood. I can but relate how I rode in Lady Hester Stanhope's footsteps into Palmyra and like her was greeted as a Queen by the Bedouin chiefs. As I rode beneath the Triumphal Arch . . ."'

He turned to another volume and looked through: '"My dragoman was watering the mules, and I was alone as I walked over the debris and into the mighty fortress of Kal 'At El Beida . . ."'

A sudden thought struck him and he looked for the volume of 1900. In 1898 she had hoped to join Koldewey's team as he began his excavations of Babylon but rightly or wrongly had been prevented by the intervention of John Millward. Two years later she had visited the excavations to see what progress had been made: '"I held my breath. Here, this pile of rubble being painstakingly reconstructed, this was the Tower of Babel itself. The city dedicated to the worship of the mighty Marduk was rising again, thanks to one man, Robert Koldewey, born in Germany forty-five years ago . . ."' Auguste closed the volume and tried to analyse why he felt dissatisfied.

He had seen Hester Hart speak, he had talked to her, he felt he knew a great deal about her through her early diaries. Why did she not speak to him out of these travel diaries? Where was the girl who had written with such passion, '*I hate, I hate, I hate*'? There was no sign of her here in these carefully-penned diaries with scarcely an alteration. No doubt Mr Archibald's printers would be delighted with such perfection, but to him they were pallid compared with the young woman who had vowed to take revenge on those who had, in her view, ruined her life. Had she written these diaries with the sole intent of establishing her reputation as a traveller by publication? The earlier diaries revealed the private woman, and she, he knew all too well, had remained as set as ever on revenge, a revenge she did not propose to sully her professional reputation with by mentioning it in these volumes.

A sparrow on the windowsill peered in as though anxious to help. Auguste stared at it, reflecting that in earlier times, no sensible sparrow would dare show its face so close to a cook in case it made an unexpected contribution to a pie. This case was a pie, his thoughts rambled on, but not one up to Mrs Jolly's standards. There were too many ingredients, too much flavouring, and he had a feeling that if only he could grasp it, one more ingredient was missing. There had been an over-seasoning with motorcars and these might yet prove to be a more major factor than he appreciated, not to mention a fine layer of Hams in the form of Hortensia's followers. What else did the pie need before he could cover it with the pastry of success? In the pie of Hester Hart, Isabel, Agatha, Phyllis, Roderick and Maud had lined up on the marble-topped table, had been chopped and then pre-cooked to their order.

What more did it need? Surely these diaries must provide the answer? Auguste took his mind back to the entries he had read in Egbert's office yesterday. And then, at last, he *knew* the ingredient he lacked.

He hurried down the stairs, after a brief word of thanks to Mr Archibald and a vague promise to write his memoirs of life on the beat in London with the Metropolitan Police Force. A pair of plump pinstriped legs stood courteously aside to allow him to pass. Auguste looked up to thank their owner. It was Mr Bacon, looking, to his relief, affable.

'Ah, Mr Didier, I'm most gratified. I expect you have called in to leave the manuscript of your undoubted masterpiece *Dining With Didier*.'

Auguste flushed scarlet in a way he had not done since Maman had caught him testing the *confit de canard* in the larder. 'Alas, no, a few finishing touches remain. Perfection, Mr Bacon, perfection.'

'Schedules, Mr Didier, schedules. They, too, are an art demanding perfection.' A note of reproof entered the erstwhile affable voice. 'Perhaps you will let me know when I might—'

He spoke to Auguste's back. Something that might have been 'Forgive me, an emergency at Scotland Yard . . .' floated up to him from the hallway beneath.

Authors! Mr Bacon sighed. The only unfortunate blot upon a publisher's life.

The constable who showed Auguste into Egbert's office in Twitch's absence retreated, leaving Auguste to burst out excitedly, 'Egbert, the diaries. Can we—'

'Just a minute, Auguste.'

'But this is important.'

'Everything's important here. Even Twitch.' It was a bad day. It had started off with Mr Pinpole's kidneys, though on this occasion Egbert, always a fair man, was inclined to exonerate the butcher and lay the blame on Mary, the general – though doubtless she'd been working under Edith's instructions. A hazy memory returned of Edith talking excitedly about a new recipe she'd like to try from Mrs Marshall, kidneys *á la campagne*. In Egbert's view, culinary adventures should never be embarked upon before midday. The whole point of breakfast was that it was *the same*.

'Where is Twitch?' Auguste was momentarily diverted.

'Back at Somerset House. He's held up over Henrietta Trotter.'

'Who?'

'Mary Trotter's daughter. No death certificate and no marriage certificate yet. The lady could be anywhere, dead or alive. He's got the Lancashire police on it.'

'Oh.' Auguste was not anxious to pursue the question of Twitch and Somerset House. For some strange reason Inspector Stitch seemed to bear him a grudge over a past unfortunate experience. 'What about the advertisement in *The Times* put in by the solicitors for relatives of Hester Hart?'

'Every madman bar the Tichborne claimant himself. Nothing, in other words.'

'Oh. Egbert, about those diaries—'

'Forget them. We've got the villain.'

'What?'

'It's Roderick Smythe.'

'But his motive—'

'Forget about motive, Auguste, for the moment. Look at facts. He was the last person to see her alive, he'd quarrelled with her, *and* he lied about his movements yesterday.'

'Where was he? Not driving with Miss Lockwood?'

'Yes, but not in the Crossley and not for long. His man confirmed his story that he left with the Crossley, but he took it to a garage and left it there for a tyre change. Then he went to see Miss Lockwood, and they went out in her car. Not for long, though. She left him in St James's where he claimed he was going to his club. He didn't. We checked.'

'And he has no alibi after that?'

'Part of the time. The butler at Dewbury House revealed he came to join Her Grace and Lady Bullinger at three thirty but left again shortly after four. I can make a guess where he went then: in a cab to Regent's Park.'

'Has he admitted it?' Auguste was taken aback.

'Not yet. He left London yesterday to go to Goodwood. Lodging place not known. Miss Lockwood was only too eager to tell us his movements, and that she'd planned to meet him there. Whether the fair Phyllis warns him is open to question. Fancy coming? I'm leaving shortly.'

'For Goodwood?'

'I ain't offering to take you to the opera,' Egbert said irritably. 'You're slow today, Auguste.'

Goodwood was not only the last social event of the London season but this particular year one of the most important. Tatiana, too, was shortly leaving to stay overnight at Goodwood House, the home of the new Duke of Richmond which the Duke had nobly deserted to allow His Majesty and the Queen full possession as usual for those four days. They took their own house party, hence their invitation to Tatiana. Tomorrow was the all-important Cup Day – all-important from the social viewpoint, at any rate. The horses, Auguste gathered, were in second place.

This year was especially thrilling socially, he understood from Tatiana. The fact that she had bothered to mention a non-mechanical event proved it. There were two major attractions: the new grandstand and the presence of the King, not, Tatiana had laughed, necessarily in that order. Bertie and Alexandra had been absent for some years, in deference to the late Duke's age and infirmity. They were always so considerate, she told Auguste gravely, by which he knew she suspected Bertie liked the house to himself to chat to his racing chums. At least he condescended to sleep in his host's bed, unlike his mother who, Auguste gathered, had always despatched her own bed and washstand appliances in advance of any private visit.

Tatiana had accepted the invitation; he had pleaded his necessary absence at Scotland Yard. Now here he was about to attend himself. What would His Majesty make of that?

'I'd be delighted, Egbert,' Auguste replied. 'I still think you should establish the motive before you tackle Smythe.'

'He'd quarrelled with Hester. That's enough motive for me. He gave her that book, tore out the title page in a fit of temper in the motor house, handed it back and stabbed her. He'll break down once I get to him, that sort always does.'

'Were his fingerprints on it? Or on the gun at Luigi's side?' Auguste asked.

Egbert cast him a scathing look. 'Outdoors. He'd have been wearing gloves. You're as obsessed with fingerprints as Henry himself.' The present Commissioner Edward Henry had been the instigator of the system.

'You told me that by last year over three thousand cases had led to identifications by fingerprints last year, and I consider a murder without a known motive is a pile of ingredients without a recipe.' Auguste felt obstinate. 'If he had no motive other than a quarrel, how did he happen to have a knife in his pocket when he attacked Hester?'

Egbert glared. 'They'd quarrelled earlier in the evening too; he planned it, Auguste. Why else should he go back?'

'First it is a *crime passionnel* caused by a violent quarrel. Now he plans it?'

'You got any better suggestions?'

'Yes,' Auguste said undiplomatically.

Egbert surrendered with grace. 'I might have known it.'

'The diaries, Egbert, let us look at them again.'

Egbert fetched the diaries from amidst the chaos of files and papers meticulously logged in his own organisational mind. Auguste eagerly riffled through them.

'This one. The early eighteen eighty-nine diary.' He read it out again: '"It means Maud and Agatha have been up to some more of their dirty games. I hate London society, I hate it. There's only one person I trust."'

'Who's that?'

'She doesn't say. But what's important is the sentence before. "I am being talked about in all the clubs." Egbert, she can't have meant women's clubs, and anyway Pierre mentioned a man, not a woman. *Who* circulated the story round the clubs? And look at this entry a few days later. "I have not yet found out who is spreading these rumours, but when I do, I'll be revenged. I shall, I shall."' Auguste hurried on through the diary, with Egbert, by now interested, leaning over his shoulder.

'"Tomorrow,"' he read out, '"I take the P and O liner to Cairo. I still have not been able to find out who spread those terrible rumours about me. But if it takes for ever I shall do so. I think he is quite young . . ."'

'And Roderick Smythe,' declared Egbert with satisfaction, 'would have been twenty or so at that time. There's my motive. Thank you, Auguste.'

'But he couldn't—' Auguste stopped. He *could*.

Egbert actually laughed. 'The trouble with you, Auguste, if a theory doesn't have as many twists and turns as old Minos's labyrinth you think it can't be right.'

Auguste applied logic. 'If it was Smythe, then Hester would hardly get engaged to him now, would she, unless she still didn't know. And if she didn't know, then he would have no reason to kill her.'

'She was a tricky woman, Auguste. She might well have known and decided to humiliate him by agreeing to marry him and then rejecting him. And, I remind you, she might only just have discovered the truth. *Phyllis's* revenge. Moreover, it does explain one thing that's been troubling me.'

Reluctantly, Auguste began to see his point. 'What's that?'

'Why she got engaged to him so quickly. She'd obviously

known him earlier in her life, and it had to be someone she knew spreading the rumours or the story wouldn't have held water. So whether she suspected him of being the traitor or not, she naturally sought him out on her return.'

'I suppose, too,' Auguste conceded, 'it would be natural for Lady Bullinger to turn to someone she knew well, like her godson, to help in her plans fifteen years ago.'

'Auguste, you're right. Hester was going to have her revenge on them *all*, and she told Roderick so when he turned up at the Dolly Dobbs motor house.'

Auguste thought of Hester in the club that evening, hurling abuse at Roderick: 'I'll have my revenge on the lot of you. I've waited long enough.'

Yes, it fitted, like an anchovy and mint stuffing for a leg of lamb.

'Shall we all drive to Goodwood?' Tatiana asked hopefully.

'For myself, I would be delighted,' Auguste replied tactfully, 'but for your sake I feel we should take a railway train in the interests of arriving punctually. You know what Bertie is like over that.'

'But my motorcar is perfectly reliable.'

'His Majesty only concedes a puncture as a reason for unpunctuality when it is his own motorcar,' Auguste said firmly.

'You could stay at Goodwood House too,' she suggested, having yielded on this point.

'I think not. Bertie might be reminded of murder.'

'I suppose you're right. Alexandra told me that ever since the murder of the King and Queen of Serbia in their bedchamber last year, he's been looking under his bed every night.'

How does she know? was Auguste's instant thought, but he refrained from voicing it for fear of upsetting Tatiana.

She laughed. 'His valet told her.'

'Egbert and I will stay in Chichester,' he told her hastily.

'Is he going to make an arrest?'

'Possibly.'

'That means Bertie *will* be upset because it will be someone he knows. Poor Bertie. He was so looking forward to tomorrow. He has two horses running, one in the Cup and one in the Halnaker Stakes. I'm tempted to do some nobbling to make sure he wins.'

'You'd better not, with Egbert around.'

'I'd rather face Egbert's wrath than Bertie's bad temper. And he's certainly going to be bad-tempered if you arrest one of the most famous racing drivers there is.'

'How did you know?' Auguste asked, amazed.

'I didn't, Auguste, but you've just told me. Shall I take the broderie anglaise gown or the pleated muslin with the hand-painted motorcars on it?'

Auguste eyed his wife grimly. 'Take the muslin, then I can throw you to Hortensia's mob.'

'Unsettled. That's what the forecast is for today.' Egbert lowered the newspaper, having enjoyed a muffin for breakfast that could have given Hannah Smirch pause for thought. Muffins might be part of an old Dickensian England that had now vanished into a more turbulent century, but there was no reason why they should not travel into the future as well, in Egbert's view.

The day ahead indeed looked unsettled to Auguste's jaundiced eye – he had mistakenly chosen mushrooms and bacon for breakfast, and was by no means sure that the mushrooms had been picked by someone who knew the difference between a chanterelle and an *amanita phalloides*. Time would tell. With luck, he calculated rapidly, he would have time to bid farewell to Tatiana before he relapsed into coma.

The drive by motor cab to the racecourse in drizzling rain did nothing to cheer him, and even Egbert was remarkably silent until a crowded road degenerated into a solidly packed and stationary mass of traffic, at which point he exploded into volubility on the subject of the preferability of (a) horses and (b) foot as a means of transport.

There was one thing the congestion had in its favour. By the time they were admitted into the grounds, the drizzle had stopped. Umbrellas were cautiously being lowered to reveal a display as colourful as a flower show. Here and there skilfully wielded skirt-lifters revealed neat ankles; above them floated muslin, silks, voiles and lace, some gowns still covered with light dust cloaks, doubling up their duties as mud coats.

The noise of the crowds round the bookmakers deafened them, all an incomprehensible jumble of jargon to Auguste. He comforted himself that this was because English was his adopted not native language, but was uncomfortably aware he was at a similar loss at Longchamp. Tatiana had offered, rather enthusiastically, to teach him, but had added it hardly seemed worthwhile since they would visit very few horse races but a great many motorcar races. It had been her intention to teach him motorcar jargon instead, an offer he had so far managed to postpone *sine die*.

They made their way to the new grandstand where Tatiana was sitting with His Majesty's party; the royal party had not yet arrived in its canopied royal box, but Auguste hastily looked the other way in order to avoid the royal eagle eye in case it rushed in at the last moment. He was interested to see that Tatiana wore neither the broderie anglaise nor the accordion-pleated muslin but was clad in bright sky-blue silk shot through with mauve – he believed that was the correct term, unfortunate reminder though it was of the still unexplained gun at Luigi's side.

'The numbers are up for the Corinthian Plate,' Tatiana informed them, shooting her lace parasol up in excitement and then remembering she was in a grandstand. 'I've put money on Rightful. He's got a professional jockey, whereas three of the runners – naturally it would be Agatha who told me – are gentlemen.'

'I'd sooner back a horse,' Egbert informed her gravely, and she giggled.

It lightened the mood, for all three were aware of what they were gathered for, and tense because of the shared knowledge.

'Have you seen Smythe in the grandstand, Tatiana?' Egbert asked, for Auguste had somewhat shamefacedly told him of the slip of confidentiality.

'No. I did see Phyllis earlier, and asked very casually after Roderick, but all she said was that she hadn't yet met him. I'm not sure I believe her, but I *am* sure she didn't suspect my motives.'

There was a stirring in the grandstand and a band broke into 'God Save the King' as the royal party arrived and took their places in the new box.

'Bertie was complaining last night that the royal box isn't big enough to swing a cat – or the Duke of Sparta,' Tatiana whispered to Auguste.

'Why him?' Royal 'jokes' often flummoxed Auguste.

'That's the Duke of Sparta with them now. Next to Princess Victoria. He was Bertie's guest in London and he was supposed to go home on Monday, but he keeps hanging on, trailing everywhere after them. He's driving Bertie mad.'

Despite his lack of interest in horses and his preoccupation with watching for Smythe, Auguste found his attention was on the race now about to begin, and on the spectators. The sun was trying to come out now, and parasols of lace and chiffon were tentatively appearing by the track, like eschscholtzias opening up their petals to the sky. They were needed only to protect the delicate flora and fauna of the hats, which in themselves successfully shielded their respective complexions. The hat in the row below him fascinated him; coloured bunched ribbons and flowers adorned the crown, tiny horses made of feathers chased each other round the outer edge of the wide brim. He wondered if the lady would mind if he perched his binoculars on the brim too; it provided a most handy shelf. The roar of the crowd suddenly rose to fever pitch as the barrier was lifted and the race began. He was aware of Tatiana pulsing with excitement beside him – and also that Egbert had vanished. He could not follow, he was hemmed in, and was forced to wait several minutes until the race was over.

'I won, I *won*!' Tatiana declared happily.

'The horse won.'

'I won,' she insisted. 'My judgement. Now I shall put it all on Chatsworth, Bertie's horse,' she added for those unfamiliar with the *Pink 'Un*.

Auguste excused himself and anxiously went in search of Egbert. He did not find him but did find another familiar face.

'I hear Tatiana's here, Auguste. Made a convert, have I?'

Auguste doffed his hat. It was Hortensia and John Millward.

'Made an arrest yet, have you?' John inquired awkwardly.

'Not yet. It is near.'

'Ah.' He shifted anxiously. 'Have those diaries turned up yet?'

'They have. In fact some are in the hands of a publisher already.'

'She can't do that,' he stammered, horrified.

'Why not, John?' inquired Hortensia.

Auguste hastily intervened. 'She appears to have put nothing in them that would be detrimental to her reputation. They seem to me very carefully edited for her readers.' That was true, he reflected.

'What about my reputation?' John hissed plaintively as Hortensia turned to speak to a friend.

'Miss Hart seems to have taken care to say nothing that might be disprovable. She was seeking approval from the professional world as well as the general reader.'

John brightened up a little. 'But what about the private side of the journals?'

'There does not appear to be anything in the journals that affects you.'

'That's not like Hester.'

'Did you hear that, John?' Hortensia turned back. 'No backers for Tankard. Out of Kissing-Cup, too.'

Auguste tried to look knowledgeable and to slip away quietly. Hortensia's iron grip descended on his arm. 'How can you match this, eh? I heard you were stuck in a wretched motorcar unable to move while we were galloping in a carriage and four down the lane through Birdless Grove, nothing but the sound of hooves and clattering carriage wheels. No petrol fumes, no clouds of dust, no punctures. Why don't you join the Hams, Auguste?'

'Delighted,' he agreed fervently, seeing Egbert ahead of him at last.

'Good,' cried Hortensia approvingly. 'Do you hear that, Tatiana?'

His wife was standing right behind him.

'Where the blazes is he?' Egbert was getting worried. By lunchtime Roderick Smythe still had not put in an appearance. 'I think he's hopped it, and that young lady Phyllis has helped him to do it.'

'I doubt it,' Auguste said. 'I don't think she'd have the courage. I suggest we go to take luncheon ourselves. If he's going to watch any race, it will be the Cup, and that's after lunch.'

'I thought you'd be in favour of eating.'

His Majesty and the Queen had repaired to their private dining room in Goodwood House and their party, including Tatiana, were taking lunch on the terrace. Auguste and Egbert walked to the luncheon tents and tables set out in the plantation. It was crowded with ladies in fluttering muslins and voiles and their immaculately suited escorts, though here and there a coat was slung over a tree branch which gave the place a sporting air. For once, Auguste was slightly torn. He had some interest in accompanying Tatiana, for he wanted to see whether Mr Tschumi from the Buckingham Palace kitchens had come to prepare the King's food while he was here. Bertie always brought his own chef and entourage to avoid 'putting out his hosts', as the press claimed, but in fact was owing to his determination not to risk strange cooks. Tschumi and Auguste might not be English, but they understood the King's stomach and that was enough for Bertie.

'At least all our chickens are together,' Egbert remarked. 'Look at that.'

At one table beneath an oak tree sat Maud and Agatha, their

husbands, Isabel (without her husband but with her cousin Hugh), and in the midst, brimming over with charm and loveliness, Phyllis Lockwood.

'All except Roderick,' Auguste pointed out. 'Unless he's hiding in the branches of that tree.'

'Really, Inspector.' Agatha looked up with a frown as he approached. 'This is a private luncheon.'

'And I'm on a public murder inquiry, Your Grace.'

'But it's Goodwood Cup Day.' Agatha was shocked. 'Even Scotland Yard must realise that.'

'Crime sometimes races quicker than horses.'

'That,' she agreed, 'is so true. The racing today has been disappointing, don't you agree?'

'It's whether Mr Smythe would agree I'm more interested in. Have any of you seen him today?'

'I expected to,' Phyllis said with a brave smile.

'I haven't,' Maud boomed.

'Nor I.'

'Hugh?' Isabel turned to her cousin. 'I haven't, have you?'

'Yes. Saw him this morning, as a matter of fact. Said he was invited to have a chat with His Majesty after luncheon. I suggest you try the royal box, Inspector.'

'Try the royal box,' Egbert repeated in exasperation as they made their way to the grandstand. 'His Majesty's going to like that, isn't he? The most important race of the day, his horse favourite at short odds of six to four, and I barge in and say I want to arrest the man he's sharing his binoculars with. You stay here with Tatiana. I'll guard the exit from the royal box and nab him as soon as he leaves. Smythe, not the King,' he added.

'Which one is Chatsworth?' Auguste craned his neck as the flag dropped, momentarily forgetting Smythe. After all, he had a financial interest on Tatiana's behalf.

'The black colt,' Tatiana answered.

'There are two black horses.'

'Very well. The one that's going to *win*!' Tatiana declared. 'The other is Saltpetre, second favourite at five to two.'

Saltpetre. Auguste approved. At least it was a sensible name. A most useful ingredient in corning and salting beef. That was the horse he would have backed.

'There's a black horse in front.' Now that the field had reached the straight, he was drawing ahead of his competitor by a length or more.

'I hope it's Chatsworth. I put all twenty pounds on him.'

'*What?* As much as that?' August was aghast.

'I know. When I win I can afford to buy a new car.'

Auguste forgot completely about Roderick Smythe now as he grappled with this domestic emergency. He was incapable of words.

'A cheap one,' his wife amended hastily.

The crowd was roaring as after two and a half minutes of racing a black colt passed the finishing post by three clear lengths. It was not Chatsworth.

'There he is!' Tatiana cried suddenly, pointing to the paddock.

'Who?'

'Roderick.'

'Can you see Egbert?'

'No. Only Bertie. Roderick's still with him.'

Auguste groaned, quickly worming his way out of the grandstand and fighting his way through the crowds. There was no sign of Egbert, but Tatiana was faithfully following him.

'Bertie will never forgive you if you interrupt him here,' she panted as she hurried to his side.

'And Egbert will never forgive me if I lose Smythe now.'

'Very well. But leave it to me,' she said. 'I can speak *to* him – you have to wait until spoken to.'

Etiquette hardly seemed to matter when the King might be chatting to a murderer, but Auguste yielded. When they reached the paddock he stopped and let Tatiana precede him past the gatekeeper, adopting a look of what he hoped was enormous sympathy as he straightened up from his bow to His Majesty.

'I'm so sorry, Bertie, about Chatsworth,' Tatiana said with genuine sympathy.

'He didn't even try to make a race of it,' His Majesty grunted. 'Good thing. I've got Perchant for the Halnaker Stakes.'

'I'll back it,' she declared.

'No,' Auguste unwisely cried.

The King fortunately decided to make a joke of it. 'You may be a judge of horseflesh on the plate, Didier, but your wife has all the sense when it comes to live horses.'

'Yes, Your Majesty.'

Satisfied, the King turned away and Auguste relaxed, though not for long when he realised Roderick had vanished. He caught sight of him, pushing through the crowds, his bright informal blazer making him distinctive. Auguste set off in pursuit, desperately hoping that Egbert was similarly engaged and that he would not have to apprehend Smythe himself. He struggled against the tide of spectators making their way to the grandstand and barriers for the Halnaker Stakes. The sun was warm now, beating down in full force, and the thought that he was in pursuit of a murderer took on a dream-like quality, distanced by the glare of the bright sky. He saw Smythe glance behind him and then break into a run, dodging behind the grandstand wall, then he lost sight of him.

He heard a shout from the far side as Egbert ran towards the far wall, blowing his whistle for his supporting constables. Smythe was obviously making for an exit behind the grandstand.

'Stop him,' Egbert yelled, apparently to no one in particular.

Whoever it was, out of Auguste's sight, obliged. By the time Auguste arrived, Smythe was handcuffed. Scrabbling on the ground searching for his newly-won golden sovereigns which he had dropped to answer Egbert's call was Thomas Bailey, to Auguste's amazement.

The reason was quite simple. His aunt lived nearby. He always escorted her to Goodwood. This year he had had his reward. He had backed Saltpetre and now had enough money to work on another motorcar. The Brighton Baby had ceased to interest him. The wind, so to speak, had been taken out of its sails by his new brainwave.

Tatiana had gallantly remained at His Majesty's side during the running of the Halnaker Stakes, and raised her eyebrows despairingly as Auguste returned to find them leaving for the paddock again. Auguste had failed to follow the progress of the race and was therefore unprepared to be shouted at by His Majesty:

'Bolted. Did you see that? No style at all.'

'We have caught him now, Your Majesty.' At least he could impart good news.

His Majesty appeared surprised. 'Where?'

'Behind the grandstand.'

His Majesty appeared even more astonished. 'How the dickens did he get there?'

'I'm not sure of his exact route. Probably he went through the grandstand.'

'Near the royal box?' The King was white with shock.

'Yes.' Auguste was slightly puzzled.

'I could have been killed,' His Majesty pointed out. 'Damned careless, wasn't it?'

'I don't think he would kill *you*, Your Majesty.'

'You can't expect a horse to make exceptions for royalty,' Bertie snapped.

'A horse?' Auguste felt he had gone wrong somewhere.

'I told you, Didier, Esclavo bolted when the barrier was lifted and put Perchant off his paces. Only came in fourth. Tatiana's lost again,' His Majesty added with relish. 'What did you think I was talking about?'

'About a murderer.'

'A murderer?' The King's face slowly changed hue once again.

Egbert had left; Auguste and Tatiana would follow shortly. That is, if he could find her, Auguste thought wearily, having seen Egbert off under the auspices of the local Sussex police.

He tracked his wife down on the lawns of Goodwood House where he saw she was taking tea with a friend. A friend? Immense pleasure seized him as he realised who it was. More than a friend, oh, much more, or had been so once. It was darling Maisie, his sweetheart of Galaxy days, now the matronly but even lovelier wife of an earl, and a good friend to both Tatiana and himself. He kissed her enthusiastically while Tatiana watched somewhat quizzically.

'I thought you didn't like horses, Maisie.'

'I don't. George is here somewhere, introducing his son and heir to the obligations of being a gent – that is, attending Goodwood. Did I see old Egbert here today?'

'You did.'

'On a case?'

'Perhaps.'

'Come now, tell me. I might be able to help.' Meanwhile she helped herself to a large éclair. Auguste regarded her fondly. After all, there was no reason why he should not tell her. A large section of Goodwood had seen Roderick Smythe taken away.

'Roderick Smythe has been arrested in connection with the murder of Hester Hart.'

'I don't believe it. Unless our Phyllis put him up to it.'

'I'm not happy about it.'

'Let me cheer you up and take you both to dinner at the Carlton tonight.'

'Tomorrow. Tonight I have to go to Scotland Yard and all you could do to cheer me up is to tell me you know a lady called Henrietta Trotter who would be approximately seventy years old.'

'Trotter? Ah.' Maisie laughed. 'I knew I could help.'

'You can?' Tatiana was delighted. 'Maisie, you are a wonderful lady.'

'You can take *me* to dinner at the Carlton then. Henrietta died about eight years ago, though. Ever heard of the Nightingale of the North?'

'Of course.' Auguste was puzzled. 'But her name was Alice Whitby.'

'Stage name, my old duck. She was otherwise known as Henrietta Trotter, my mother's best friend, and Aunt Alice to me. She conveniently forgot all about the Trotter long before she was married. Not a name suitable either for the stage or for marrying into the minor aristocracy.'

'Did she have children?' Aromas of all sorts now began to rise enthusiastically in Auguste's mind.

'That stuffed shirt Gerald Francis wouldn't let her off without providing him with a son and heir. Only the one, so he married again after her death, just in case.'

'Francis?' both he and Tatiana said together.

'Not Hugh Francis?' Auguste asked, hardly daring even to hope.

'That's the blighter's name. Know him, do you? Been playing in the haystacks for years with Isabel Tunstall. She's a cousin on his father's side.'

'Maisie, I'm going to kiss you again!' Ah, the memories of that warm, plump cheek decorously extended towards him.

Tatiana laughed.

'Has Roderick Smythe confessed, Egbert?'

'No. Arrogant to the last,' Egbert grunted. 'Do you have to keep appearing through my doorway like a blessed genie out of a lamp?'

'I'm sorry, but perhaps Smythe is innocent to the last too, Egbert. I have news for you.'

'Am I going to like this news?'

'May I please see those diaries again?'

'Now I know I'm not.' Reluctantly Egbert pulled them off the shelf and piled them in front of Auguste, clearing a minute space on the far side of his desk.

'Here it is: "One day I will get my revenge. I'll use that story so carefully hushed up at the time about her eloping with the family coachman when she was seventeen." Egbert, how did Hester Hart learn that story? And who was the one person she could trust – or so she thought – when she left England?' He paused dramatically.

'Why do I have the feeling you're about to tell me?'

'It had to be someone close to *Isabel* to learn the story in the first place. And it had to be someone close to *Hester* to tell her the story. It was the man who has proved to be her cousin – and heir – Hugh Francis.'

'You're sure of this?' Egbert asked sharply.

'Quite sure. *He* was one person she thought she could trust. But could she?'

'You think he was the one who spread the rumours around the clubs?'

'The Francis family was never wealthy, and Hugh, so my informant tells me, always needed money.'

'Then he wouldn't risk antagonising his wealthy relations,' Egbert pointed out. Auguste could hear relief in his voice. 'Doesn't wash.'

'It washes very well. A Sunlight Soap of a case. He didn't know fifteen years ago that he was related to Hester, and neither did she. His mother Henrietta had no more contact with her sister after she ran away to join the stage. I suspect he only found out when his mother died eight years ago, and finding Sir Herbert was a wealthy man and Hester his only child made haste to renew acquaintance with his newfound cousin.'

'Renew?' Egbert queried sharply.

'If he spread those rumours fifteen years ago, he must surely have been seen in public with her occasionally or the mud would not have stuck.'

'Too many ifs, Auguste. Find me some facts. Like I've got on Smythe.'

Stitch returned wearily, bleary-eyed but triumphant. 'I've got her, sir. Henrietta Trotter – married in Hanover Square, you see. I didn't connect her up at first with our Henrietta. And that's led me on to what you might call an interesting development.'

Egbert had had a long, frustrating day. 'It couldn't be called Hugh Francis, could it, Stitch?' Twitch's face fell. 'Mr Didier told me half an hour ago.'

Auguste's conscience smote him. 'But I found my connection through luck, you by sheer hard work, Inspector Stitch. You have provided the evidence on which Inspector Rose will work.'

Twitch remained unmollified. He distrusted Frenchies bearing gifts.

Chapter Twelve

'Like the postman in Chesterton's story, because we were so used to seeing him with Lady Tunstall we never paid too much attention to him,' Egbert observed. He had taken an olive branch round to Queen Anne's Gate.

'What will you do?'

Egbert took out his pocket watch. 'Go home. It's eleven thirty. He'll keep. If he's our man he's congratulating himself he's safe.'

'If?'

'Sorry, Auguste, my money's still on Smythe. There's as much on one as on the other, in fact more on Smythe. You can't arrest a man for being someone's cousin. Or for spreading scurrilous stories fifteen years ago. Mind you, I agree the money alone gives him plenty of motive. *If* he knew they were related.'

'Surely he must have done. He found out that she was still unmarried, and therefore – provided she had made no will to the contrary, a subject she could well have discussed with him – he was her heir. Then to his horror he heard she was going to marry Smythe. He had to strike before he was automatically excluded from inheritance, will or no will. He must have been very relieved that she had never discovered he was involved in the conspiracy to stop her marrying the Duke.'

'I suppose it's possible,' Egbert admitted grudgingly. 'I still think the clubman was Smythe, though. He is Lady Bullinger's *godson*, Auguste.'

'But Francis could be the only one in a position in 'ninety-seven to tell her scurrilous stories about Isabel eloping with the coachman. She certainly knew him – I remember she greeted him the first time I saw her in the club restaurant. *And* he was dining with the Duke then, which implies he could have been part of that circle fifteen years ago. What do you think?'

Egbert yawned. 'I think I'd like to get this wrapped up and us off to Eastbourne.'

Auguste tried not to think of it; it was too tantalising. 'He was at the club on the night Hester Hart was killed; he could well have thought that was his opportunity. He couldn't guess that Smythe would return.'

'You've got it at last, Auguste. We know Smythe *was* there,' Egbert remarked with great satisfaction. 'We don't know Francis was. He claims he went to his club after leaving Isabel Tunstall. The villain's clothes would be bloodstained. You could cause comment walking into Boodles like that.'

'That would apply to Smythe too.'

'But it's my belief Maud and Agatha were in it too. Lady Bullinger lives close enough for him to go straight there after murdering Hester Hart. And don't forget Smythe was part of a cosy little trio at the Duchess's home just before Luigi's murder. It's Smythe, Auguste, *Smythe*.'

'It seems to me, Egbert, there were three ounces of batter in one basin, and three in another. Which made the crêpes?'

Egbert regarded him soundly. 'If I've got to go off hunting hares at Richmond, you're coming with me. But *tomorrow*.' Back at Highbury, Edith had promised to wait up with hot cocoa; it would be lumpy, but on this July night that ordeal seemed a prospect fit for a gourmet.

Auguste hated the moment when theory became reality, when the amateur was plunged into the professional, and Egbert knew it. He was therefore determined not to betray his reluctance to go to Richmond, even though it entailed a drive by one of the only three petrol motor cabs in London. Lacking the inspiration of a Dolly Dobbs, the electric cabs were as reluctant as Auguste to travel as far as Richmond. The Bollée suddenly acquired new charm by comparison with the petrol cabs. The day was sunny, and he had to fight back his desire to be wandering along the towpath with Tatiana, even fishing in a punt on the river by Richmond Bridge, or admiring the view from Richmond Hill, or sampling the excellent wares of the Star and Garter Hotel – in short, anything but going to interview a probable murderer. Possible murderer, he amended, in Egbert's view.

'Mr Francis is not at home.' A young supercilious butler of the new school answered the summons of the old-fashioned bell-rope at Winter House.

'Criminal Investigation Department, Scotland Yard.' Egbert walked in. 'I'll wait.'

The morning room of Winter House displayed little of Hugh Francis's personality, if indeed he had any, Auguste thought. He had never taken to him. Endless foxes being pursued by endless hounds and horses, a shelf of Surtees and the Racing Calendar, and a still-life oil of what looked like a half-eaten deer. It was not to his taste.

To their surprise it was not Hugh Francis who arrived five minutes later; it was Isabel, Lady Tunstall, clad in a lace housefrock, and obviously summoned from breakfast. Isabel believed in attack, not defence, and did not bother to explain her own presence in a bachelor's house at ten o'clock on a Saturday morning.

'Really, Inspector, could this not have waited?'

'It's Mr Francis I'm here to see, Lady Tunstall – for the moment.'

'Mr *Francis*? What can Hugh possibly have to do with Hester Hart? I presume that *is* what these questions are about?'

'Did you know he was related to her?'

For once Auguste saw a genuine emotion on Isabel's face: surprise, then it speedily rearranged itself into its normal social mask. 'I am afraid you have your notes confused, Inspector. *I* am related to Mr Francis. He is my cousin, and I can assure you *I* was not related to Hester Hart.'

'Mr Francis was Miss Hart's cousin on his mother's side of the family.'

A slight doubt crossed her face. 'It is true I am related to him through my father. How close a relative was he?'

'A second cousin, descended from her great-aunt.'

'I am quite sure Hugh has not the slightest idea about this and indeed I also feel sure you are mistaken. Hester Hart was the daughter of a button manufacturer and Hugh could not possibly be related to trade. His family have been army people for centuries.'

'Francis's mother was an actress in burlesque.'

'I'm quite sure you're wrong,' she replied vigorously.

'How can *you* explain the entry in eighteen ninety-seven concerning you?' Egbert continued blandly.

'What is it about?' Her tone was guarded. 'I suppose you mean poor Hester's rantings about being excluded from the Marlborough House dinner. Vastly exaggerated. The woman was unhinged about her absurd social pretensions.'

'No. I had in mind the story of how you eloped with your family coachman.'

Isabel tried a light laugh. 'Dear Hester. So imaginative.'

'Who told Hester Hart about it if not Mr Francis?'

Emotions struggled to take precedence on Isabel's face. She was saved from having to answer the question. Auguste, looking through the window, saw a familiar and distinctive motorcar driving well over the permitted 20 mph speed limit. It was Hugh Francis's Rover, and it was heading out of, not into, the estate.

'There he is,' he shouted, and Egbert rushed to his side.

'I thought Mr Francis had already left,' Isabel said plaintively. She was only too anxious to help. 'He is going either to his club, Plum's, or to Gwynne's Hotel. You know them?'

Auguste knew them very well.

There had to be pleasanter ways of travel than at high speed by motorcar. Auguste was glad he was sitting in the covered hansom-style passenger accommodation in the motor cab and not above their heads like the driver. Hot it might be in here, but at least the clouds of dust being whipped up by their fast progress were not settling on them. How the driver managed to see anything even with goggles was beyond Auguste's comprehension. As they careered over Kew Bridge, it occurred to him with some vividness that he had no idea whether there still *was* a driver. At least with a horse hansom you could see the reins shake occasionally, just to comfort yourself that high behind you, looking after your safety, was a human being. In this monstrosity there was no such comfort. Here it appeared they were on a highway to hell, clattering along in a machine over which they had no control whatsoever, driven by a maniac who might well already have abandoned them to their fate, with only a flimsy door between them and destruction. It was with relief he heard Egbert restore normality.

'Makes you long for Eastbourne, doesn't it?'

Auguste had a sudden imaginary whiff of the sea breezes he, Egbert, Tatiana and Edith would – or should – be enjoying at the Eastbourne Hydro Hotel next week, but that only served to remind him that much water must pass under Kew Bridge before then.

The cab, still mercifully with a driver, braked outside Plum's Club for Gentlemen in St James's Square. The club doorman prudently waited until the dust had subsided before advancing to open the door. When he recognised Auguste, who had been chef there for several years, he almost shut it again, but then remembered Mr Didier now had connections with royalty and was thus, almost, worthy of entering Plum's.

Egbert had no inhibitions about the sacredness of Plum's portals and ran straight in. There was no sign of Hugh Francis's Rover, and having checked with the porter, he ran back to the cab. 'Gwynne's,' he shouted to the driver. 'And wait.'

The driver's heart sank. An even longer job than he had bargained for, and the Yard were notoriously bad tippers.

There was no sign of the Rover in Jermyn Street outside Gwynne's either, but this time Auguste came in with Egbert. To see Emma Pryde, Gwynne's redoubtable owner, was always a pleasure and, unlike Maisie, Emma's idiosyncrasies had failed to endear his former love to Tatiana, a fact Emma seemed rather proud of. He gathered it was a regular occurrence.

'I think you may find, my old cock sparrow,' she answered Auguste amiably as he burst somewhat unceremoniously into her office, 'that he saw you coming. He seemed very eager to leave my company, and that, as you know, ain't usual.'

'Where's he gone, Emma?'

'Ah well, now. I'm bound by the confidentiality of my profession.'

Which profession? he was tempted to ask, since Emma's succession of young and not so young men was well known, but he refrained. Emma's temper was unpredictable and irreversible.

'Emma, this is murder.'

'It always is with you, old cock. I see you ain't planning to stay, so I'll tell you. Out that door where he left his motor.'

Auguste ran into the yard at the back of Gwynne's in time to see Hugh Francis driving out into York Street. He turned and, to the disapproval of several elderly gentlemen and a dog taking their ease in Gwynne's lobby, ran right through and out into Jermyn Street where Egbert had already spotted the Rover and had banged on the window for the driver to follow it. The driver had cranked the engine and was starting to turn in pursuit as Auguste leapt up on the steps to let himself into the interior. He reflected as he sat down beside Egbert that a good walk to Beachy Head each morning next week coupled with a Turkish bath in the hotel's therapeutic amenities might help his agility. There was no doubt one suffered in the cause of gastronomy.

The Saturday morning traffic in Piccadilly was heavy; the congestion ahead around Eros looked as if the whole of London had elected to spend their day stuck in the middle of the Circus. Horse vans, horse buses, motor buses, motorcars mingled together, infuriating Egbert. As they at last reached the Circus, they saw the Rover proceeding into Regent Street towards Regent Circus, and agonising moments were spent steering their way past obstacles, human and mechanical, to follow its route.

'Look out!' Egbert shouted, and Auguste sat with glazed eyes as they appeared to be within inches of murdering an ancient lady in a poke bonnet so set on selling lavender that she regarded roadways as naught. Could the driver even *see* her, set so high up at the rear? His nerves were going to require more than camomile to revive them after this. The driver's position had one advantage. He had a better view of the Rover than they had, as a sudden lurch round to the left into Vigo Street threw Auguste into Egbert's arms. He straightened up. A few moments later they were reunited as the Rover turned sharply into Sackville Street.

'Something tells me he knows we're after him. He's going to play "Here we go round the mulberry bush" round the Circus again in the hope of losing us.'

'No, he's not. He's turning right,' Auguste shouted. 'He's going to go past Green Park.'

'Or back to your lady friend's at Gwynne's. I wouldn't put it past Emma Pryde to hide him in her bed.'

Nor would Auguste, but he had little time to ponder the question as a motor bus braked in front of them and the horrible insecurity of being unable to see if their driver had noticed but able all too clearly to see the back of the bus bereft him temporarily of speech. Why had they done away with the useful requirement of a man with a red flag walking in front of any motor vehicle?

When they had swept round the bus in fine style, narrowly avoiding a large delivery horse van proclaiming its allegiance to Silver Ray's Rum, the Rover was some way ahead, but visible.

'I'm beginning to feel like Custer after the Indians,' Egbert grunted.

Auguste was more preoccupied with meeting a similar death

and destruction as the Rover chose to turn right into Park Lane and their own driver, now getting into the spirit of things, drove straight across the path of a large Daimler.

By the time they reached Dorchester House they were gaining on the Rover, but any hopes they might have had of stopping it in the relatively traffic-free Park Lane were doomed to disappointment. Ahead of them appeared to be a group of suicidally-inclined people marching out of Mount Street straight across their path. Traffic on the other side of the road had come to an abrupt halt; on the far side, in front of their cab, the Rover lurched to the left to avoid collision with the two human lemmings leading the group. To his horror Auguste saw firstly that they were bearing placards, secondly that they were followed by a troop mounted on horseback, and thirdly that they were all wheeling round to provide an impenetrable barricade across Park Lane, and hoisting their banners.

The Horse Against Motor Car Society had come to make a stand. Why did they have to make it six inches from their cab? Egbert yelled in fury. The Rover, and Hugh Francis, were lost to them.

'Good morning, Auguste,' Hortensia greeted him cheerfully.

By Saturday evening the kitchen at Milton House had already taken on a sad air, as if it was aware that for a whole month it would remain unused. For over four weeks no smells save those of Keatings Powder and turpentine would emanate from it; gone would be the warmth, the excitement, the ever-ready stockpot, and the smells of baking pies. Tonight would be the last dinner of the season. After that, the staff would vanish, once the kitchen was cleaned and tidy, and Auguste and Pierre would lock its doors and they, too, would part for a month. Like Antony to Cleopatra, Auguste proclaimed, 'Let's have one other gaudy night, Pierre,' as he was handed the menu for the evening.

'Monsieur?' Pierre looked blank.

'This is the last dinner of the season. The club's first season. Let us make it a dinner to remember.'

Pierre's polite 'Yes, monsieur' suggested he was under the impression that all his dinners were to be remembered.

'Are you leave England for this month, Pierre?'

'Yes, I am travelling to France to see my parents. I have been saving for it. I have not seen them for two years now, and I have to tell them of Miss Hart's death.'

Why did he have to be reminded even here of what still remained to be settled before he could go on holiday? Auguste thought crossly, and made a determined effort to forget it again. Egbert would work out whether the murderer was Roderick Smythe or Hugh Francis far better than he.

There was something soothing about cooking; it ordered the chaos of the brain, and even the most menial jobs, cleaning, chopping, collecting ingredients, provided a calming influence. Sometimes he would do the chopping himself rather than leave it to a vegetable chef, simply to get a sense of the recipe building up, the salutary feeling of his hands mixing flour. After all, unless one performed the basic tasks, how could one fully enjoy the fruits of creation, the pinnacle of his art? Left to itself the brain went on working behind the scenes, a servant *par excellence*, and could sometimes knock at the door and deliver a most unexpected message. Perhaps even now his own brain was working on the question of Smythe and Francis, and would produce that one vital ingredient which would set the seal on the recipe.

He began to crush the raspberries, forcing them through a sieve into a purée for a *coulis*. How satisfying the colour, how rich compared with strawberries. He had seen white raspberries in the market, but they were an oddity like . . . like . . . the diary of 1897. Had his brain obliged? he wondered in sudden excitement. He left it to itself for a little longer in the hope it would oblige a little more fully and explain just what point it had in mind. By the time it condescended to do so, the *coulis* was fully prepared – *like those diaries for publication*.

'Pierre!'

Pierre came running over, leaving the lobster, under the impression that at the very least a cockroach had been discovered enjoying the delights of kitchen life.

'Pierre,' Auguste told him excitedly, 'the diaries. We have read the private ones of Miss Hart's early life, and also the diaries you have sent for publication, but those seemed to me so different in style that they were *written* for publication.'

'I believe that is so.'

'Yet there were two diaries for 1897, the year of the Jubilee; one with private material in it and the other a short one of a visit to Egypt. Isn't that odd?'

Pierre considered. 'Yes. That is the year before I met her, however, so I cannot say why there should be two for that year or why the diaries should be different in style.' He lost interest in diaries, clearly wanting to return to lobster.

'Why should Miss Hart suddenly have written a private diary for eighteen ninety-seven?'

'Because that was the year Miss Hart felt so bitter about. Often she would speak of the horror of ninety-seven.'

The horror of ninety-seven. Auguste put his brain to work again, and tackled the dressing for the salad. His immediate brain tackled the important question of whether to include anchovy in the dressing, and the brain behind the scenes was told to get on with the problem of Roderick Smythe and Hugh Francis, a *crime passionnel* or a premeditated murder, in which the murderer carefully selected his murder weapon.

When Auguste returned to Queen Anne's Gate, Tatiana was already dressed for dinner and ran to him eagerly as he came in.

'I detect you are impatient, *ma mie*. For my lobster Didier?'

She tried to laugh. 'For holidays, and a chance to recover from this horrible month. At least now Egbert has arrested Roderick we may be near the end of it, even if it's not an end I like. And then we can *leave*!'

'It may not be Roderick, Tatiana.'

'Not? Who then?' Tatiana was startled. 'Oh, Auguste, not Agatha, after all?'

'No, Hugh Francis.'

She looked at him blankly. 'Why on earth should *he* wish to murder Hester Hart? To preserve Isabel's reputation?'

Auguste's brain rang a faint bell which he was too tired to answer, so the query was dismissed to join the stockpot of his simmering thoughts. Instead he told Tatiana just how Hugh Francis had entered the picture.

'Is Egbert convinced that Hugh is guilty?'

'No, but he's notifying all the Channel ports in case. But he still believes it's Roderick, and I too – if only, Tatiana, I could put together all the pieces of this jigsaw I would know which one. But I can't.'

'Perhaps Edith's new hat will inspire you.'

'What?' Auguste looked puzzled.

'You know how excited she is at coming to dine at the club this evening – she has bought a new hat for the occasion.'

'I'm not sure that the menu is up to Edith's new hat.'

'If it's not we'll just eat the hat. I gather it has plenty of cherries and a strawberry on it.'

'I'll ensure the lobster à la Edith is up to the occasion then.'

'You've named the dish after her? That's kind of you, Auguste.'

'It has her favourite corraline pepper in it, as beloved by her Mrs Marshall.' Mrs Marshall was only slightly behind Alexis Soyer in Auguste's list of *bêtes noires*.

'Did you by any chance see Harold Dobbs at the club?'

'No.'

She sighed. 'I gave him strict instructions that wreck of a motorcar had to be taken away before we closed for the summer. I asked Egbert, to get his permission. Once Dolly was the most precious thing in Harold's life, now she means nothing to him. How like a man.'

Charlie Jolly winked at Edith as he gravely conducted the party to Auguste's favourite table near the kitchen, now set for four. It cheered her up; it was a friendly wink that told her all these duchesses and countesses were just ordinary people who had chilblains just like she did. Mind you, in her new hat delivered by hand yesterday by Miss Peabody, Milliner to Gentry, she felt equal to anybody.

'What has happened, Egbert?' Auguste hissed as soon as they were all seated and Tatiana had embarked on a discussion of The Hat. Not Edith's which she had already admired, but the club hat. A compromise had been reached. A tam o'shanter had been agreed for the summer, a tricorne for the winter, each to be ornamented with a steering wheel. 'Until the fashion changes,' Auguste heard Tatiana mournfully add.

'We haven't got Francis yet, but the Kent police are keeping a watch on Martyr House, and Lady Tunstall. He may have gone down to Kent with the idea of hiding there awhile before slipping quietly overseas. He won't know that she isn't feeling quite so loving towards him now. I may have to go down there myself tomorrow, if there's no news. Smythe will be applying for *habeas corpus*.'

'Tomorrow?' Tatiana's sharp ears picked up the word with dismay. 'But we were all leaving for Eastbourne tomorrow.'

Edith said nothing.

'With luck I'll get away Monday,' Egbert said quickly. He looked round. 'We've got a roomful of suspects here, Tatiana. Suppose I arrest one or two of them, just to tide things over till we get back from Eastbourne?'

'That's an excellent idea,' Auguste replied gravely. 'I suggest you wait until after you have tasted the lobster Edith, Egbert.'

Edith flushed. 'Lobster *Edith*, Auguste?'

'In your honour.'

'Oh.' Edith went even pinker. 'How very kind,' she managed to say, overcome.

Maud Bullinger, Agatha and Phyllis were dining together, earnestly discussing the terrible news about Roderick, and also a delicious rumour that Isabel had parted from Hugh Francis who had promptly tried to kill himself by driving at over 20 mph down Park Lane. They were not pleased to see Inspector Rose dining at a nearby table. The law should be kept to bowing respectfully at the roadside as far as the peerage was concerned. They were even less amused when the inspector rose to his feet and came purposefully over to their table.

'Even if you are dining with dear Tatiana, this *is* a private restaurant!' Agatha was appalled at such manners, even among the working classes.

'And a very good lobster I've had too. I trust you've enjoyed yours?'

Lobster was not at the top of their list of topics to be discussed.

'I'm wanting to see Mr Francis. Any of you any idea where he might be found?'

'I only know where poor dear Roderick is,' Phyllis informed him, summoning a tear to her eye.

'Why should we, Inspector?' barked Maud.

'I think you should ask Lady Tunstall, Inspector,' Agatha said coldly.

'Shall we say ten o'clock Monday morning?' Egbert replied. 'I'll come to your homes to see what you've remembered about Mr Francis. Unless you prefer the Yard?'

From their silence it appeared they did not. Only Phyllis made an objection. 'But it's the end of the season, Inspector.'

'This is delicious, Auguste.' Edith was well into her dessert when Egbert returned to the table. 'Could I cook this, do you think?'

'It is a little complicated,' Auguste said diplomatically. 'You begin with a soufflé which is—'

'Oh, that's easy then.' Edith beamed. She had had two glasses of red wine, she was looking forward to her holiday, she was only fifty-six, she was sitting not only with those she loved best but with duchesses and ladies, not to mention that Tatiana was a princess; she was aglow with her new hat and the thought of Eastbourne to come.

'Some more wine, Edith,' Auguste said, preparing to pour

the infinitesimal amount into her glass that he deemed wise.

'Oh *yes*. A jug of wine, a loaf of bread, and Thou beside me singing in the wilderness,' Edith pronounced lyrically.

'You can't drink a jugful, Edith.' Egbert was alarmed.

'The *Rubáiyát*,' Auguste said to him. 'It's one of the most famous quotations from it.' Another bell rang in his brain, but like its predecessor was sent to the stockpot, on this occasion because Leo suddenly appeared through the kitchen door.

Miss Dazey, dining with a schoolfriend and pouring out her tale of unrequited love, beamed with happiness and rushed over to him. 'Have you come to find me, Leo? I *was* coming to find you.'

'No. I want to speak to Mrs Didier,' Leo said doggedly, red in the face from the attention he was arousing.

'Oh. But I have something *very* important to ask you.'

A sudden fear seized him. It wasn't leap year, was it? 'I've got to speak to Mrs Didier, Daisy.'

Unconscious of what he had said, he went over to Tatiana, leaving a deliriously happy girl behind him. He had called her Daisy. Even when he'd kissed her that time, it had been 'Miss Dazey, ma'am'.

'Mrs Didier, that Mr Dobbs is here.' He delivered Fred's message.

'What, *now*? It's ten o'clock.'

'He says he's come for the motorcar.'

Tatiana sighed, glad that at least Auguste's inventions weren't as troublesome as the Dolly Dobbs. She excused herself from the table and followed Leo out to the motor stable. On a sudden impulse Auguste decided to accompany them and hurried in their footsteps.

There at the stable were a cross-looking Fred and Harold Dobbs, and to his amazement the ubiquitous Thomas Bailey.

Tatiana appeared as astonished as he was.

'Thomas and I have been having most interesting discussions,' Harold announced. 'Designers and inventors, you see, Mrs Didier, are above petty differences.'

'Such as patents?' Auguste wondered.

'The Dolly Dobbs is no more, nor is the Brighton Baby. However, Thomas and I have had the most splendid idea!'

Thomas looked modest to counter Harold's exuberance.

'We've jointly patented it now, so we can tell you, Mrs Didier. We shall be honouring you with the first trials, of course.'

'Wind-powered?' asked Tatiana tentatively.

'Wind?' Harold loftily dismissed this as a minor aberration. 'No, no, we are Daedalus and Icarus.'

'I beg your pardon?'

'You're going to make a motorcar fly with wax wings?' Auguste asked, delighted he'd come.

'No, no, we are Phoebus.'

'We're going to harness the energy of the sun,' Thomas amplified. 'We call it solar power. We need a huge circular piece of metal to attract the sun's rays and a source of water to produce steam or gas to produce electricity.' He beamed.

'How splendid,' Tatiana said weakly.

Miss Dazey, prowling in the wake of the party, seized her chance as Harold and Thomas began the task of fitting a towing line to the front of the Dolly Dobbs's frame. She plucked at Leo's sleeve. 'What are you going to do in August, Leo?'

'Dunno.' He looked round for support, but there was none. Mr and Mrs Didier were inside the motor house with those two daft inventors. They hadn't the least idea how to build a motorcar. Whereas he— He tore his mind away from such daydreams.

'I do. My parents are employing you as motorcar driver and engineer to drive them to Deauville, stay there, and drive back. I shall be there too,' she added carelessly. 'What do you say?'

Nothing apparently. He was speechless.

'You don't even have to kiss me if you don't want to,' she said cheerfully. 'Only it would be nice once in a while.'

Leo found his voice. 'Like now?' He led her out of sight of his superiors and proceeded to demonstrate great mechanical and artistic skill in a field even more enjoyable than motor repairs.

Everyone had gone. Tatiana was conferring with the porter over last-minute details, Egbert and Edith had gone home to Highbury. Auguste felt an odd reluctance to return to the kitchen; he had bidden his farewells to it before dinner and therefore the soul had gone from it; it would remain an empty shell until life was breathed into it once more in September. Nevertheless he found himself automatically going there to check all was well.

'Goodnight, Mr Didier. See you in September.' Annie Parsons was leaving, all but the last to do so.

The kitchen looked desolate; all signs of dinner were gone, copper pans replaced on their hooks, plates stacked away, utensils back in their drawers instead of lying invitingly by the side of chopping boards. Only a basket full of food open on the table suggested signs of life. He felt a great longing for Eastbourne, as far away as ever. He would have to stay with Egbert until the case was over. Did he not bear an equal responsibility in these closing stages? There might be some snippet of information, some detail he might remember that could tip the scales of justice as far as Francis and Smythe were concerned. Francis had not yet been caught; suppose Egbert followed his inclination and charged Smythe? How would he feel then? The answer was simple: Egbert would be making a mistake, and therefore he, Auguste, had to remain.

He eyed the basket of food on the table, left over from dinner. After Eastbourne, he and Tatiana would travel to France for two weeks, a different land, a different cuisine. It would inspire him anew for the autumn. The best food in the world could be found in England, but the inspiration for cooking it was found only in France. If only the two countries could get together in the interests of the *estomac*. Perhaps that was what His Majesty had had in mind when he proposed the Entente Cordiale.

Take a *saupiquet* for instance, a dish he had discovered while travelling to eastern France – for thus he thought of Alsace-Lorraine, not as part of Germany as they had been since the war thirty-odd years ago. The most delicate sauce was needed, and not too strong a ham. On the other hand the sauce must be piquant; the reduced vinegar, and the meat stock, must be strong enough to complement but not clash with the ham. It was all a question of emphasis.

A question of emphasis . . . The brain left to simmer behind the scenes suddenly reasserted itself. The bells rang, and this time were answered. Auguste turned and ran through the corridors to the main entrance, fearing to find it in darkness. Had he missed her? The porter's lodge was dark but there was an electric light still burning in the lobby. He rushed to Tatiana's office and found her still occupied at her desk in the process of last-minute clearing.

'I need another fifteen minutes, *chéri*,' she pleaded as he burst in.

'Tatiana, tell me everything you heard when you took the cocoa over to Hester Hart.'

'But it's all in the notes, and Auguste, we are leaving on *holiday* tomorrow.'

'The pot is still on the boil, *ma mie*. Please tell me. Exactly as it sounded.'

Tatiana obliged. It was the quickest way. 'I couldn't hear all they were saying on the first occasion, but I heard Hester, of course, and Roderick's voice quite distinctly. They were quarrelling, but I couldn't make out what about. On the second occasion I did hear because Hester was shouting. "Marry you, you fool. As if I ever would."'

'And what did Roderick reply?'

'I didn't hear. I came away.'

'Then how do you know it was Roderick she was speaking to?'

'Because she was talking about marrying him, of course,' Tatiana said patiently.

'Try to remember, *ma mie*. Did she say "*marry* you" or "marry *you*", or "marry you" with equal emphasis?'

'Is there a difference?'

'Yes. A vital one.'

She thought back, reliving it in her mind, disentangling it from the overlay of repetition. 'I'm almost sure she said "marry *you*". You mean the second time it was Hugh Francis, don't you?' Tatiana was suddenly excited, as she thought about it. 'It could have been, I suppose. Yet the first time was definitely Roderick. He would have to have left and Hugh to have arrived all in the course of twenty minutes or so. It's possible, but why should Hugh Francis need to marry her if he would inherit anyway?'

'That, *ma mie*, is the question.'

Auguste returned slowly to the kitchen. Was he hallucinating, overtired, seeing sour milk where there was only pure cream? Should he not leave it to Egbert? No, for tonight the club closed, and holidays began tomorrow. Holidays for everyone.

Pierre looked up as he came in. 'I am sorry, monsieur. I was not here earlier. I was clearing the larders.'

Auguste looked at him first subjectively, the man who cooked so wonderfully that even he could rarely fault him, who had run this kitchen almost as well as he could have done himself, who had good-temperedly and patiently put up with intrusions into what he must see as his own domain and become temporarily loyal servant, not master. Not servant, junior partner was a better term. Then Auguste saw him objectively: an Arab brought up in a Western land, who had travelled much in the East. What was he doing here, in a club in St James's? Did loyalty to Hester Hart really answer that question, when the man's heart lay Eastwards? Auguste was too tired to prevaricate.

'It was you, wasn't it? You thought you'd marry her and when she rebuffed you, you killed her.'

Pierre's face hardly changed. He might have been discussing the best way of cooking lamb. 'No, monsieur, *she* wanted to marry me, then she changed her mind.'

'Why should she?' Auguste found it hard to believe. 'You were a hired servant to her.'

Pierre sighed. 'I will explain – if you have the time,' he added politely.

How unreal to be sitting at this kitchen table with a double murderer who asked if you could spare the time to listen, Auguste reflected. Now that his question had been answered, he felt even more tired, as anticlimax set in. He could not have moved even had he wished to. He felt as bound to his chair as the Ancient Mariner's unwilling listener.

'Out there everything is different.' Pierre seemed not so much to be talking to him as to his own past. 'It is the land of the Arab, not the Westerner, and their ways are the paths of right for them, just as your Bible and law are for you. They, too, have slaves of course, but all freemen have an equality you could not imagine here or in France. There are rich men, there are poor men, there are bad and good, and they are judged by that, not by their parentage. Rich men, and those of ancient families, as the world over, demand respect, but that has nothing to do with worth as a man. In London and Paris that is not the case. Society is a caste that does not admit outsiders, so Miss Hart told me, and I see it for myself. I was her dragoman for six years; she travelled as a wealthy English lady and I as her hired servant, but we were equal in the respect paid to us. The Arab values a man or woman who knows their own trade well; we were partners in an adventure. It is always so in the desert; brothers need one another's support, for, as I told you, not all Arabs are of good will to travellers.

'We talked much during those years; our outlook on life was the same. You saw only the worst Hester Hart; I saw the real woman stripped of the shackles of Western society. She was brave, strong, light-hearted – and happy. Of course we must marry, she said; we had been through too much together not to. It was at Palmyra she said this, a place of destiny.'

Auguste had to say it. He must be objective, not swayed by his liking for the man. 'And you realised if she married you, you would be a rich man.'

Pierre smiled. 'Would you believe me if I replied simply that I do not think that way, though I understand the temptation because I was brought up in France. The English traveller Richard Burton when he travelled in the East commented that the difference between the Arab and the Westerner is that the aim of the Arab is to *be*, that of the Westerner is to *have*. The splendour and the squalor. That, he said, is the Arab life, and one finds it in the desert. It was my privilege to share it with Miss Hart.'

'You asked her to marry you?'

'No. She suggested it. She wore my ring, and we exchanged copies of the *Rubáiyát*, a poem of which Hester was very fond.'

'That was her copy in her handbag? Why did you leave it there?'

'Because I had given that copy to her. I have hers to me. She always carried it, so I knew it would be there. I needed to remove the title page for her own reputation, as well as my protection, for I had written in it. When I saw the pistol in her bag I removed that too. I took it away because it was so familiar to me. Part of my life. I was going to shoot her, but instead it was more fitting to stab her with our dagger.'

'*Our* dagger?'

'The one we shared in the desert. We exchanged vows over it, it cut our meat there, we defended ourselves with it. We had bought it together in Damascus and decided it was a symbol of our unity. To use that was the fitting end for a traitor.'

'*Traitor?* She just changed her mind.'

'More than that, monsieur. She put her own pursuit of vengeance first when she came here. She was a different person to my beloved Miss Hart. She asked me to take this job to help her in her plans. I knew how important they were to her, so I agreed. She would pretend not to know me, she said, and that, too, I understood. Therefore I must not come to her house; I would meet her in the Zoological Gardens.'

'Ah, the Zoo. Now I see.'

'Yes, where I killed that dog Luigi,' Pierre replied matter-of-factly. 'She changed. She spoke no more of marriage, she treated me as a servant is treated here, and you yourself know how that can be. The gulf between society and servants is a river as wide as the Euphrates, and none shall cross it.'

'And that is the reason she cried "Marry *you*?" with such scorn, when you went to her that night?'

'It had not always been like that, monsieur. I knew I had to kill her when she announced her betrothal to Roderick Smythe.'

'Why *had* to? Murder is a matter of the individual will.'

'Not for the Arab, monsieur. My wife had betrayed me, so she had to die. She was an adulteress. The woman to the stone, says Muhammad.'

'Wife?'

Pierre took no notice. 'That evening I heard you say that she was not going to marry Mr Smythe after all. I assumed immediately that saying she would was all part of her plans, and that she still intended to marry me. I hid in the store-rooms, after you thought I had left that evening. I kept the dagger with me so that we could renew our vows. I was very upset to see Roderick Smythe arrive, and relieved when he left not long afterwards. I rushed to her immediately. She laughed at my love. She was not my Hester. She was an English lady after all, who would not marry a servant. So I killed her.' He shuddered. 'I killed my Hester. Up till then I had not thought of myself, but then I realised I must for I was in a Western country which would not look on my deed in the same way. So I smashed Dolly Dobbs in the hope you would think that the motorcar was the reason for the murder.'

'And Luigi?' Auguste was determined not to be swayed. 'Was it *right* by your standards that he should die?'

'When you are among brigands, defence is not a crime. That dog realised, when you talked to him, that I had killed Hester, and was surprised that I had confessed to you that I was her dragoman. Why should I not, after all? It was the truth. Nevertheless he realised I had killed her for he saw me cross the yard from his serving room window. If I had to die for Hester's death, I was determined not to do so while that dog lived. So I agreed to his demand for money and suggested we met in the Zoo for me to hand the money over. I left the pistol as a sign to Hester that she was avenged. She would have been glad that it was where we used to meet.'

'You said "wife" earlier,' Auguste said. 'Were you already married?'

He still did not reply.

'Very well. Then perhaps it is recorded in her diaries.'

'You have the diaries,' he said shortly.

'Not all of them, Pierre.'

He stood up swiftly. 'What are you going to do now, Monsieur Didier?'

'I must tell Inspector Rose.' Auguste spoke without thinking. When he saw Pierre slip his hand under the apron, he knew he had made a mistake. Could he reach a door? No, none of them. His only chance was to talk his way out. This was no Gregorin, after all. This was Pierre, his loyal assistant. Pierre, holding a dagger with a carved handle, a digger that had killed Hester Hart and killed Luigi Peroni.

'I have three choices,' Pierre said calmly. 'I can kill you, I can kill myself, or I could tell the inspector I am guilty. Which shall I do, do you think?'

'You respect me, Pierre. You will not kill me. That isn't in the Arab soul.' Auguste tried to keep his voice steady, tried to sound as if he believed what he said.

'I was brought up in Marseille.' Pierre studied the dagger. 'I could easily kill you, if that is ordained.'

'Pierre, it is not.' Almost with compassion, Auguste spoke quietly for he could see what Pierre could not – Egbert creeping into the kitchen, followed by two police constables. All the tiredness and tension of the last few days rose up and overwhelmed Auguste. He collapsed.

Auguste opened his eyes. The sun was streaming through the window. The bed was empty apart from himself. Tatiana was humming in the dressing room. They were going on holiday. Then he remembered.

'Egbert wants to see you downstairs, if you feel well enough.' Tatiana came anxiously into the bedroom. 'Do you?'

'Are we still going on holiday?'

'Yes. All of us.'

He sat up in bed. The world looked wonderful. He swung his feet to the floor. 'Has he breakfasted?' First things first.

'Mrs Jolly and Egbert have reached an understanding. She is preparing one of her special crêpes with kidneys.'

He could already smell it in his nostrils. Soon he would smell the sea. 'I will be with him in fifteen minutes.'

Egbert greeted him cordially, almost as though he had not been up all night. 'Thought you might like to see these before you go. We found them when we searched his lodgings.' He planted fourteen familiar volumes on the morning-room table.

'Ah!' Auguste pounced. 'The diaries. The private ones for the years Pierre spent with her.'

'Yes. And previous years. Pierre wasn't the first dragoman to be her lover. She entrusted the lot to him. Seemed odd, and I asked him why if they were no longer on chummy terms.

Because he was a servant, he said bitterly, who would naturally obey her commands.'

Auguste picked one up and opened it at random. '"Last night Pierre taught me the Oriental *upavishta*, the sitting posture, so difficult for Westerners, but I mastered it. That makes the thirty-third position in all. He is a man of many parts, and one of them, the most important, the most sizeable I have ever met. I measured it—"' Auguste dropped the book, but curiosity proved stronger than distaste. '"I love him, I *love* him! I shall marry him. Like Jane Digby and her Sheikh we shall live in our Desert of Beauty for ever."' He closed the book and looked at Egbert, who nodded.

'No wonder he thought of her as his wife. Then when she got back here, she changed. It's odd that Miss Hart, who had suffered in her youth from being treated as an inferior on account of her birth, never gave a thought to treating Pierre in the same way.'

'As Edith said, Hester Hart was not a nice lady.'

'That reminds me,' Egbert said, 'you haven't asked me how I turned up so conveniently last night. Not that I think he'd have killed you. He likes you.'

'How did you?' Auguste put the disquieting thought of Pierre and their relationship aside.

'I went back to the yard to charge Roderick Smythe. You were right, incidentally. He wasn't the clubman, it was Hugh Francis. Anyway, Smythe was sitting there as bold as you like in his cell drinking – he wasn't under arrest and he knew I'd have to charge or release him. He banked on the latter. "Another glass of wine, if you please," he demanded, as cool as you like. And I remembered Edith at dinner spouting from that poem in Hester Hart's handbag. "A jug of wine, a loaf of bread, and Thou beside me singing in the wilderness". Now I don't usually have poetical turns of thought, it must have been your lobster Edith turning my stomach over, but I suddenly thought that fitted our Pierre like a glove, so I thought I'd just check if he was still around at the club. Tatiana told me *you* were, so I strolled down to see you and heard what was going on.'

'It is Edith who solved this crime then?'

'It is.'

'Tonight I shall cook her a soufflé Edith, better than all her beloved Mrs Marshall's recipes put together.'

'We're going on holiday. You won't be near a kitchen.'

Auguste's face fell, then he brightened up. 'I can eat, however.'

Epilogue

Auguste was happy. The breeze out on Eastbourne pier tugged impatiently at his Panama and blew gently at his blazer neck. Edith held on to her new seaside hat, and Tatiana tied her scarf round her boater as though she was in a motorcar. She only lacked the goggles. Egbert took off his lounge suit jacket and allowed his shirt sleeves to enjoy the sunshine.

They had just eaten *crevettes grises* from a stall on the pier, fresh and smelling of the sea. Their holidays had begun. They had travelled here by train.

'Egbert says,' Edith announced happily, 'we are to purchase a motorcar.'

Auguste stared at his friend, who blushed.

'Useful for business,' he muttered.

'Auguste, too, has agreed to purchase a new motorcar,' Tatiana said. 'Will you drive it, Auguste?'

He wanted to shout 'Never', nor could he remember ever agreeing to such a proposal, but Tatiana never lied so he must have. He looked at his wife, dark hair framing the glowing face, he looked at his friends, he looked back to the past and then towards the brave new world of the future.

'Of course I will drive it,' he declared.